Two women—
each fighting a passionate struggle
to hold on to her virtue. . . .

Two stories—
of forbidden love, heartbreaking betrayal,
and undying honor. . . .

One book—
with everything you've come to expect
from "one of the romance genre's
greatest storytellers" . . .

Edith Layton

Now, for the first time in one volume,
all of the desire and intrigue that
Regency England has to offer in these
two wonderful tales . . .

The Duke's Wager
Lord of Dishonor

The Duke's Wager

AND

Lord of Dishonor

Edith Layton

A SIGNET BOOK

SIGNET
Published by the Penguin Group
Penguin Putnam Inc., 375 Hudson Street, New York, New York 10014, U.S.A.
Penguin Books Ltd, 27 Wrights Lane, London W8 5TZ, England
Penguin Books Australia Ltd, Ringwood, Victoria, Australia
Penguin Books Canada Ltd, 10 Alcorn Avenue, Toronto, Ontario, Canada M4V 3B2
Penguin Books (N.Z.) Ltd, 182–190 Wairau Road, Auckland 10, New Zealand

Penguin Books Ltd, Registered Offices: Harmondsworth, Middlesex, England

First published by Signet, an imprint of New American Library,
a division of Penguin Putnam Inc.
The Duke's Wager was originally published in 1983, copyright © Edith Layton, 1983.
Lord of Dishonor was originally published in 1984, copyright © Edith Layton, 1984.

First Printing, August 2000
10 9 8 7 6 5 4 3 2 1

Copyright © Edith Layton, 2000
All rights reserved

For Orson, my constant companion.

1

It was not a fashionable night to be seen in the streets of London. Oh, the moon shone as brightly as ever an autumn moon did, and the air carried the light crisp taste of autumn windfall apples; the freshening breeze carried away the usual stale stenches of the city, and the woodsmoke from many fires added to the clear tang of the night. But then the month of September was never a slave to the fashions of men, so she could be excused for putting on such a show on a night when no other lady of good taste or family would dare to parade the streets of town. But she was obviously only a baggage, so she displayed her charms generously and spread her gifts lavishly and never seemed to mind that no female of repute would savor them this night. No matter, if she was not a female of discretion, why then, neither were any of the other ladies abroad this night.

But that was not to imply that there were no others in the streets. London was no ghost town, bereft of pedestrians and coaches, riders and lackeys, strollers and theatergoers. No, the city was as crowded as ever, the fashionable made up only one facet of its usual throngs. And if the ladies of the town were safely at home, or snugged at several respectable house parties, the gentlemen of their class suffered no such inhibitions. They were free to enjoy the night as they chose.

As were the beggars, warming themselves over scant alley-edge fires, waiting for some more substantial citizens to cross their paths so they could ply their practiced pathetic pleas; as were the sharpers, eyeing the passing crowds for any hint of possible gain; as were the street women, in readiness now that evening had come, to sell their flowers, chestnuts, or bodies at reasonable fair-trade prices. So if the ladies of immaculate breeding were not abroad, it hardly mattered, for the several

1

enjoyments offered this evening were not for them anyway.

Even the Opera, where so many of the select disported themselves on proper evenings, was filling to capacity this evening. For if the finer ladies would not grace their seats, why then, there were an assortment of other members of the gender who would gladly do so. But if these were not ladies who were prime articles on the marriage mart, even the most dispassionate observers would have to admit that they were prime articles of their species. Still, there were few dispassionate observers in their company; it was not, alas, an evening notable for opera lovers, although lovers there were, in great numbers.

The beggars and loiterers and running boys and flower ladies who congregated in front of the Opera did not mind the lack of Society's finest females, rather they knew there would be many young blades with free fingers to toss loose coins to impress their latest conquest. For the street people knew, with their survivor's instincts, that a night such as this, a night of the demi-monde, was far more of a profitable time than a night when a gentleman had to properly escort his lawful wife or dutiful daughters. And they watched as the colorful, blatantly beautiful ladies, peacocked in with their gentlemen.

The street girls would have to be content with waiting in the shadows for the final curtain to fall, so that they could have the chance to accommodate those men of fashion who had not brought their own ladies, and who were either too inept or too luckless to have encountered a friend to invite them to a revel, introduce them to an unattached beauty, or take themselves off with them to a fashionable house of delights. These disappointed blades would be available to invitation for a few moments of less exalted play. The girls were not impressed with the high-flown style of the young women giggling into the Opera house. Some had been in their places at one time, some dreamed of it, all knew that without a masterstroke of luck, these same ladies would be standing at their side in the shadows one day, waiting for the last "Bravo," to compete with them for the stragglers.

Each new carriage that approached was greeted by the assembled crowd, avidly ploying their separate industries, with great anticipation. The war, though far off, was still on, there was a scarcity of the young military men who were so free with their pay, and money was hard to come by. But when the magnificent carriage bearing the insignia of St. John Basil St. Charles, Marquis of Bessacarr drew up to the curb and a large gentleman alighted, sweeping his impassive stare over them, even the hungriest among them did not press any further forward. Here was a knowing one, they thought, and a hard one, who would not need to dazzle his ladybird with careless largesse to strangers. When the flame-haired woman alighted and preened herself for a moment, allowing the crowd to admire her finery and letting their eyes linger on the dazzling necklace which peeped through the open cape, as did the equally dazzling expanse of bosom she exposed to the September breeze, they looked for only one moment and then waited for the next carriage to discharge its passengers. There was money here, but not for them.

"Annabelle!" came the gentleman's amused voice. "Shall I have to rent a stage for you to display both my and nature's gifts? Or would you prefer to accompany me now?" Simpering, she raised her rosy face to his and, taking his arm, allowed herself to be borne off to the theater. "As I once was," thought a drab who peeked out from the side of the wall where she patiently waited. "As I shall be," vowed the young girl who stood beside her.

The Marquis looked neither to the left nor to the right as he escorted his lady up the winding staircase to his private box. Yet he knew exactly how his companion disported herself as she clung to his arm. He knew, without having to watch, how she swung her hips, as no lady he would escort on a more fashionable night would, how she alternately smiled or snubbed the other women she encountered, how she let her eyes promise or deny the young blades who eyed her flamboyant beauty. As no proper young woman would dare, he thought, but then, he smiled to himself, no proper young woman would have earned that necklace she wore in quite the way that Annabelle had. And, he admitted, she had certainly earned it.

Once settled in the ornate box, the Marquis allowed himself to glance over the program of the night's promised delights. But he was not a lover of Opera, and the delights he had promised himself would only come after the performance upon the stage. Annabelle fanned herself and looked out over the audience with great interest, noting old rivals, new contenders, and the vast possibilities of future protectors she might have to beguile should the languid gentleman next to her tire of her. For her, it was both good business and a good diversion to be seen tonight at the theater.

The Marquis, watching Annabelle coolly scrutinizing the murmuring crowd, felt a vast impatience with himself this evening. In truth, it had gone on too long. But, he had to admit, he was growing lazy in the pursuit of his pleasures. It was perhaps simpler to visit those special houses of assignation on a hit or miss basis than it was to fund, feed, and entertain a female such as Annabelle. But it was also more chancy. There was always both the possibility of finding a female who was deft and accomplished, or discovering that one had given up an evening to an unknown who was unacceptable or, at best, marginal. At least Annabelle was a known quantity and, on the whole, reliable.

But there was this necessity of taking her out every so often and showing her off to the town. Or else, she would sulk and whine, and accuse him of being unsatisfied with her services. At first, he remembered—was it only two months ago, then?—he had been well pleased with her. But as the novelty of her talents, and the familiarity of her face and form, had increased, he found himself noticing her personality, her intellect, and her habits—none of which pleased him. For though she could be said to have that most agreeable of traits, "a good heart," it was undeniable that she was ignorant, avaricious, and common. He sighed, if only women could be folded up into a closet until one took them out for the natural pleasure they provided. No, it would not be long until the Marquis of Bessacarr would be hunting a new companion.

He would not find one among his social equals. He would not find one among the dewy misses so dutifully served up at such fashionable places as Almack's, or the diverse watering spas or house parties where the fashionable amused themselves. No, those young women were, firstly, seldom as beautiful as Annabelle, and more importantly, never as accessible. They were there only for a titled gentleman such as himself to choose a wife from. Someone who would dutifully lie down, in a most civilized fashion, upon a duly sanctified and sanitized marriage couch, for the sole purpose of producing another being to carry on his exalted name. They were never, the Marquis thought, even to be considered in the same context as Annabelle. They were not, he thought, with real amusement, even to be precisely considered as "female" in the same sense that she was. Certainly that was not what they, or he, had been brought up to expect. In fact, he often wondered if many of them precisely knew what sort of marital horrors their noble husbands would eventually require of them.

And those other ladies of his class, those who were not quite so newly-sprung, who had already presented their husbands with the required number of descendants and who had been given indirectly to understand that they might discreetly pursue their pleasure where they may, were little better in his eyes. For after all the courting, all the poetic flights, and subtle hand pressures, and interminable weeks of light flirtation and secret messages, and painstaking arrangements for a site acceptable for dalliance, still he inevitably found them disappointing. It stood to reason: They had once been those same demure little debutantes, they had once had the self-same expectations. The infrequent and required usage by their noble husbands had not prepared them for a life of erotic delight. Even the most willful and passionate among them, the Marquis thought, could not hold a candle to Annabelle's practice of the art. She was born to it, he smiled, bred to it and accomplished at it. But still, she was becoming a bore.

As for other women of his class, the ones who had found happiness, who lived in accord with their husbands, who found their enjoyments with them alone and sought no others, why, the Marquis had no experience with them. The life he led was that of a hedonist, as so many of his fellows were. As his was expected to be. He was eight and twenty, wealthy and fashionable, and not at all interested in perpetuating his line at the moment, however much that fact must disappoint the general run of young women available to him this season. They must pass on the torch to their younger sisters, he was not in the market for a wife this season. But looking at Annabelle inflating her already considerably inflated chest so that his spider's net of diamonds could be seen by an acquaintance of hers seated in the orchestra, whose expression of exquisite envy could be read even from this distance, he knew that he was definitely in the market for a new companion.

"Sinjin," she pouted, "it's ever so hot in here, could you procure me an ice, or a sip of something more fortifying?" He eyed her with annoyance, this drinking of hers was no longer the discreet thing she thought it was. All the oil of cloves and mint she ingested could not disguise the ever-present miasma of gin that hung over her. But he rose, and bowed and brushed aside the curtains that enfolded the box. He'd be glad to stretch his legs, and glad for the opportunity to evaluate the other women present tonight, the other women from among whom he'd possibly find her successor. While she, he knew, would certainly be glad of the opportunity to drink deeply from the flask she concealed in her wrap.

He stood in the outer hallway, tall and immaculate in his evening wear, his broad shoulders encased in a close-fitting jacket, his slender waist tapering down to muscular legs, his black hair swept back and cut expertly to accentuate the fine high planes of his face, every visible carefully designed part of him signaling the epitome of the man of wealth and fashion. He stood at the top of his world, by birth, by sex, by fortune and education. And his world was the only world that he cared about.

"Sinjin, by God, it's Sinjin," the rotund, balding young gentleman of fashion to his left cried, dropping his quizzing glass and hurrying over to him. "By God, sir. You thought I was dead, confess it? Did you not?"

"Not dead, James," the Marquis taunted, "only married."

"Ah well," mumbled the shorter man, "and so I was, but you were there, Sinjin, so don't quiz me. But married's not quite the same as dead, sir. I went the round, you dog, I traveled wherever I could where that cur Nappy was not, and then I came back to town. Only arrived last week. Only settled in t'other day. Only been on the town a day or so and hadn't seen you anywhere. Heard that you were cuddled up with a new friend, you dog, and never thought to lay eyes upon you so soon. How good it is to see you, Sinjin, how good it is to be back in town. Museums, Sinjin, cathedrals! Flower exhibitions, by God! None of you chaps ever told me what sort of things to expect when I made the leap! No, no, don't deny it, Sinjin. Only offered me felicitations and gave me a pile of silver and punch bowls that I could never use if I lived to be a Methusalah. Confess it, Sinjin, you never warned me about all the blasted cathedrals I'd have to trek through once I started married life."

"I never married, James," the Marquis said, "so how could I give you the benefit of my advice? And how is Lady Hoyland?"

"Breeding," his companion said briefly. "Quite a good thing."

"So you did not spend precisely all your time in cathedrals, James," the Marquis noted with a little smile.

"Sinjin!" James replied, his eyes wide with shock. "No, not a thing to jest about, my man, the lady is my wife. I can't have you saying such things about the Lady Hoyland, my man."

"Do you wish to call me out, James?" the Marquis asked, his usually fog-gray eyes admitting little sparks of icy light. "It's only that I can't conceive of how the thing could be conceived in a cathedral."

"No, really," James said hastily, looking up at his friend. "Don't jest about such a thing. It's my wife you know, not a joking matter. You know I couldn't call you out, wouldn't want to, but as you are a friend, Sinjin, don't make me a sacrificial victim to whatever sulks you've fallen into."

"Forgive me, James," the Marquis said in an unrepentant tone, bending into an insolent bow, "I had forgotten how pious you married fellows are."

"Well not exactly pious, Sinjin," James confided. "It's just that a wife's one thing, and a woman's another. Actually, I came here tonight to see if I couldn't set up something more befitting to my present station. . . ."

"I understand completely," the Marquis said, remembering suddenly the spring wedding he had attended, with James standing on the receiving line and little Lady Eleanor, her dark plump little person clinging to James's sleeve, shyly acknowledging his towering presence.

"James," he said, a wry smile springing to his lips, "I might have just the thing. Go procure an ice, my boy, a lovely lemon ice, and take it to the . . . companion . . . I have seated in my box. Tell her I am detained. She'll be glad of company, for I shall be a while. And perhaps, James, you'll be glad of the company as well."

"What?" asked James. "That lovely red-headed creature? You wouldn't mind . . . you wouldn't take offense?"

"Not in the least," he replied. "Consider it a belated wedding gift. But I'm afraid you'll have to provide the packaging and the wrapping yourself. And it will not come cheaply."

"Wouldn't expect it to come cheaply," James said eagerly, "but it would be worth it?" he asked in a whisper, like a conspiratorial child.

"I would not suggest it otherwise," the Marquis said airily, as he watched his friend rush off in search of a vendor.

He felt fractionally taller, and freer than he had a moment before, as he strolled off down the corridor, acknowledging old acquaintances and carefully watching the arrival of latecomers.

He had spent the first act of the Opera out in the corridor, reacquainting himself with an old school chum who had the latest bits of gossip to impart, and he had been feeling so free and relaxed that he was a bit surprised when the doors swung open and the promenade of Opera-goers exited for their intermission. This informal parade he knew was by far the most important reason why most of them had come to begin with.

He saw James with Annabelle on his arm as they walked toward him. She looked up at him for a moment as they walked past, and allowed a rueful grin to touch her rouged lips. He remained still, for if she chose, now was the moment that she could create an unpleasant scene. But gin-bold as she was, she was foremost a woman of business, so she merely allowed herself one last regretful look at the Marquis and then turned her attention to her small, plump companion. James, seeing the marquis standing there, took this opportunity to take one of her cool hands in his moist grip and raise it to his lips. St. John said nothing, so they passed by. "Well done," the Marquis thought, noting that the transfer had been made as correctly and formally as any ceremony he had ever witnessed.

Quite a clutch of unattached gentlemen now stood against the walls of the corridors, watching the other Opera-goers stroll by. St. John noticed a few old friends, a few older gentlemen, a few young sparks out to make their mark on the town. He felt relieved to be one of their number again, and pleased himself by watching the women of the demimonde self-consciously flirt past his raised quizzing glass. A slight stir in one group to the corner of the hall brought his attention to the entrance of the Duke of Torquay, his presence signaling the beginnings of muttered gossip. St. John smiled, and saluted the Duke with his quizzing glass.

"Sinjin," the Duke greeted him in his soft hoarse voice, "don't tell me you didn't feel the urge to tell the latest *on dit* about me to your friends the moment you saw me? What, you still stand here just to have a word with me? Do you think I can impart something new and exciting that they haven't yet told you?"

"I don't need to dine out on your exploits, Your Grace," St. John answered, looking coldly at the slight figure beside him.

"No, no, you at least do not," the Duke acknowledged. "You are commonly acknowledged to be my successor, these days, aren't you? When my dissolute ways bring me down to the worms, it will be you who replaces me, will it not, Sinjin?"

The Marquis did not acknowledge the hit by so much as a lift of his shoulders, but still he felt a cold chill at the words.

Jason Edward Thomas, Duke of Torquay, was already, although he had not entered his thirty-fifth year, acknowledged to be the supreme pleasure-seeker of his day. The joke that made the rounds was that if the Duke could find a way to fit it in his bed, he would bed it. The stories told about him and his exploits on the town beggared the imagination, and although the more sensible of listeners discounted half of what they heard, the half they accepted was shocking enough. Still, he was of impeccable birth, title, and position, and many of the gentlemen who listened avidly to stories of his scandalous exploits, would still have gladly handed over the choice of their eligible daughters to him in wedlock, should the elegant widower ever seek marriage again.

And the same young women whose eyes rounded at the abbreviated tales that filtered down to them of his doings, would still have found themselves eager to be wed to him. For his appearance belied all the gossip and scandal that followed him. Of medium height and slender as a boy, his pale gold hair fell softly upon a white brow. His large clear blue eyes and tender mouth seemed more appropriate to a romantic poet than to the sort of man whose name had become synonymous with license. But St. John had seen the Duke at his play. And the Marquis had known some of the women who had known him intimately, and did not doubt most of the stories that he heard. Something deep within the Marquis bridled at being dubbed the Duke's successor, but still he acknowledged the truth of the jest.

"Well then, Duke," he drawled, "it is most fortunate for our audience that we stand here together. It saves them a great deal of effort and eyestrain if we stay here thus, in tandem."

"It does," the hoarse sweet voice acknowledged. "It might, dear Sinjin, save you a great deal of trouble, too, for then I could not make a move you could not emulate immediately," he remarked, glancing up through his long lashes at the tight face next to him.

The Marquis pretended not to have heard, as he felt the unease spread through him, but he was spared any rejoinder as the Duke's head turned.

The wide china eyes flew open and the slight body almost visibly trembled, like a dog at the hunt. "My God!" the Duke breathed in hushed undertones. "Who is she?"

The Marquis looked with relief toward the woman whose presence had stirred his companion so. Yes, he admitted, she was worthy of the attention.

Even at this distance he could see that she was young, almost pitifully so, although many of the other women might have been of an age with her. She wore no rouge, no paint, and so her face looked more vulnerable against the background of this gathering. She was dressed simply and elegantly in a high-waisted blue velvet gown that accentuated her high breasts and slender figure. Her gleaming chestnut hair had been drawn up tightly, and only one long curl brushed against her shoulder. Her eyes were large, wide, and frightened, and a strangely vivid grass-green color which accentuated the clear whiteness of her skin. She was innocent of jewelry, of paint, but it was the innocence in her face that troubled St. John. She could almost pass for a woman of quality. But then, what would she be doing here on this night?

She stood, wide-eyed, her cloak thrown over one arm, as she realized the attention she had drawn to herself by exiting from her box. She turned and spoke in a low voice to the other woman who emerged from behind her, another young woman, but this one all frizzy ginger hair and freckles who wore a plain serviceable dress. A maid? St. John frowned. What the devil would a young woman with a maid be doing here at the Opera on such a night, when the courtesans flirted and vied for new liaisons? Unless she was a shrewd wench who had discovered a new ploy. But the look of fright in her eyes dissuaded him from that flight.

But his former companion, the Duke, had not waited to speculate. With the swift grace he was famous for, he had already achieved her side. She looked up at him in incomprehension. St. John could not hear a word that the Duke spoke so softly into her ear, but he could see the color drain from her already white face. She gripped the other woman by the arm and then almost ran to the top of the long stairs.

For only a moment the Duke stood still, as if bemused, and then he signaled swiftly to his man, who came to his side to listen to the quick, soft instructions and then, nodding, was gone. The Duke strolled back to St. John's side. "Not quite flown," he whispered in that intimate voice. "My man will wait to see her coach, to get her direction. It's a shame that her courage deserted her. She will be quite a success. I think that the stir she caused quite overset her plans. And as to your plans, St. John? I noticed that you have so generously given over your seat to your friend. Would you care to share my box for the duration of the performance?"

"Thank you," St. John bowed, "but I seem to have already achieved my plans for this evening, and so must be off to more profitable sport."

"It will do you no good," the Duke smiled. "I have already set my sights upon her . . . unless you care to vie with me for the honors?"

"I am not quite so exacting in my requirements this evening, Your Grace," St. John retorted. "I'll leave that field open to you. Remember, I am marked to be your successor, not your equal." And, smiling pleasantly with a humor he did not feel, he left.

II

Regina Analise Berryman was in a rage. When she had returned from the Opera, a combination of shame and shock, coupled with the lateness of the hour, had sent her into an unaccustomed state of subdued self-recrimination. She had lain awake for many long hours, until the sheer weight of the night had sent her drifting off into a restless sleep. But when Belinda had drawn back her curtains to admit the shallow morning light, she had awoken to a healthy sense of fury.

She drew the belt on her morning gown and, unable to find her slipper's mate, sent the orphaned partner flying to the wall. "Why," her first words to Belinda were, "did you not tell me *exactly* why last night was not a proper night to attend the Opera?"

Belinda eyed her new mistress warily. This was not at all like the quiet, amiable, green young girl she had been serving for the past weeks.

"Aye, but I told you, miss. I said and I said that it would be more fitting for you to wait for your uncle to return afore you went to the Opera. I did say that, miss, I did."

" 'Aye,' " mimicked the infuriated Miss Berryman, looking like a proper witch, Belinda thought uneasily, with her long gleaming hair tousled and wild, her old emerald green eyes shining like a cat's. "But, Belinda my dear, you did not, repeat *not*, tell me that only . . . courtesans and their protectors would be there, now did you?"

"That's not true at all, miss," Belinda gulped, backing toward the door as Regina rounded upon her. "Why there was ever such a sweet old couple there, miss, and anyway," she said in a rush, "how was I to know who all else would be there? I'm only a poor girl, miss, and never been to the Opera at all, and only heard below

13

stairs that it wasn't the best idea for you to go . . . and I told you so, miss. Indeed I did. And you only said. . . ."

" 'Pooh!' I said," Regina admitted regretfully. "Yes, that's so. I said it wouldn't do any harm and it was a shame to let the tickets go to waste. But why didn't you stop me, Belinda, before I made such a fool of myself?"

"Ah, miss," cried Belinda, seeing and pressing her advantage, "but it isn't my place to stop you. I'm only your maid, miss, and. . . ."

"Only a poor girl," interrupted Regina, deflated. "I know, Belinda. Excuse me."

Regina turned and sank down again upon the bed. She tossed her heavy hair back from her face. Her own fault, she thought miserably, of course. No matter how poor Belinda had influenced her, it was, indeed, still her own fault. She had wanted to go to the Opera. That was undeniable. Only a few weeks in town and she had already made a cake of herself. For when the invitation had come, even though her uncle was away from home and would not return in time for the Opera, she had been determined to attend. She would not sit at home childishly, for lack of an escort. After all, she had reasoned, back at home in the country, when her papa had been alive, they had gone to the local theater as often as possible to see some of the infrequent Shakespearean productions presented by traveling troupes of players. And when Papa could not come with her, there had been no shame in attending with only her governess, Miss Bekins, as her escort.

But, she thought, as usual incurably honest with herself, she *had* wondered if the same manners obtained in the great city of London as did in her little corner of England. She had heard of how glittering and fashionable the theaters were here. Even more, she had thought of all her new dresses, hanging unseen in the closet, and no matter how often she rationalized that she wanted to actually hear a first-rate opera company, that had been the major reason she had so wanted to attend. And who, she thought, furious with herself, would have been mutton-headed enough to take the advice of a little lady's maid on matters of rules of society? Even if there were no one else she knew whose opinion she could have asked, why hadn't she waited for Uncle's return? There would have been other operas, other nights.

Because she belatedly understood, if there had been no harm in her going unaccompanied by a gentleman at home, it had only been because there were few people in the audience who did not know Miss Berryman, the schoolmaster's daughter. And they would no more have thought her fast for attending the theater without her papa than they would have thought her scandalous for attending a lecture without him.

So even if Belinda's eyes had narrowed slyly when she asked if going by herself was "done," and her answer had never been a direct "no" but rather a tangle of "Well, miss, it depends . . ." and "Some ladies do go by themselves, I hear tell . .," she had only half listened. She had not really wanted to be persuaded to stay home. Once she had made up her mind, Belinda had been in ecstacies, thrilled with the chance to see the upper classes at play first hand for the first, and probably last, time. And Regina had caught fire from Belinda's enthusiasms. She had rigged herself out in the first stare of fashion and sailed forth with an eager Belinda in tow, only to discover what she really should have guessed all along: that London was as far in miles as it was in attitudes from her home. And that no one could have guessed that she was only the schoolmaster's daughter from Dorset, gawking at their splendid world; rather they had taken her for a trollop, bent on advancing herself. Regina sighed to herself. She was, she felt, well served for her self-deception and rashness.

She glanced at Belinda, whose hands were twisting under her little white apron, and felt she ought to let the matter drop. As well chastise a cat for stalking a pigeon as to condemn Belinda for seizing her chance for a little excitement, even if it were at her new mistress's expense. My fashionable career, Regina thought glumly, shall go right back where it belongs—between the pages of a book, and in my mind. What a rustic she must take me for, she thought. And, she thought ruefully with a little sad smile that made Belinda's hands steady themselves, what a rustic I am, indeed.

"Never mind, Belinda," Regina said. "It's over, and you shall not bear the blame. We'll forget it. We'll avoid the haunts of the fashionable and we'll rub on together well enough in the future. But," she said, eyeing the laden tray Belinda had set up on a little table near the window and embarrassed that the whole staff likely thought of her as a milkmaid fresh from the country, "could you please tell Cook that although I do come from the country, I do not eat like a yeoman and do not require a breakfast that could easily feed five strong men?"

"Oh yes, miss," Belinda said eagerly. "I do hear that all the young ladies just drink a cup of hot chocolate and have a bit of bread for breakfast."

"I'm not that fashionable," Regina laughed. "An egg or two might be pleasant as well."

"Oh yes indeed, miss." Belinda curtsied, grateful to make an escape. "I'll tell Cook at once."

The Master might have my skin, Belinda worried, as she went down the stairs. But it wasn't my fault, not really. She did want to go. And when would I ever get such a grand chance again to go to the bloody Opera, I'd like to know? So if my fine lady from the country wanted to go, why shouldn't I go with her? I'd never get such a chance again, once he came home, no I wouldn't. Didn't she cause a stir, though? Only think, the Black Duke himself making a proposal to her! Wouldn't I like to have heard what he said to her? Just wouldn't I. So handsome he was, too . . . it's a thing to tell my grandchildren, that is. I know what my answer would have been to him, if he'd asked me, she thought. Did you ever see such eyes on a gentleman, though? Took her clothes right off with them, he did. Now if it had been me. . . . And she entertained herself with thoughts of operas, and dukes, and magnificent offers of finery and jewels, as she took herself off below stairs to regale the others with a highly colored account of the night's events.

But Miss Berryman was not entertaining herself with similar imaginings. She was, instead, sulking in a very unladylike fashion as she sat at the table and sipped her coffee. "What a fool thing to do," she sighed in disgust, "flying off like a true clothhead, decked out like what I thought was a London lady, only to find myself taken for the Queen of the Cyprians."

"Ah well," she sighed, putting down the delicate cup and rising to stare out the window, "I do have a lot to learn in this new life, and I must teach myself not to be so impetuous . . . but . . . it did seem like such an . . . unexceptionable idea. But then, after all, what do I know about the customs that prevail here?"

Regina Analise Berryman had only been a resident of the city which so perplexed her for a scant three weeks. Before that, she had spent the whole of her two decades (except for one brief whirlwind tour of Bournemouth, where an aquaintance of her father lived) in a small house in a small village on the southern edge of the kingdom. Her father had been a schoolmaster at a boys' school of little fame, and less distinction. But he, a large, gentle, and quietly unambitious soul, had been well pleased with his lot in life. True, he might have regretted the fact that few of his students would go on to a life of erudition—most were resident at his school only long enough to receive the rudiments of education. But since they were the sons of merchants, they expected no other fate and indeed chaffed at their lot while they were under his tutelage.

He himself was a younger son in a family of the merchant class. And his perplexed family soon realized his scholarly bent and, more importantly, understood that his nonaggressive ways, his lack of interest in financial dealings, and his incurable honesty ("The day John Berryman tells a lie," his family grieved, "will be the day the King kisses a pig.") made him eminently unsuitable for the freewheeling family business of business. The day he took an unsuitable wife, a girl of no surviving parents and French descent, the two beleaguered families put their heads together and soon were able to ship the changeling son and his portionless wife out to the school where a position had been found for him.

There they lived in undemanding bliss, until the birth
of Regina Analise had put an end to her mother's existence. There John Berryman, with the aid of a governess that the family sent down posthaste, had raised his
daughter in tranquillity and peace. Hearing no terrible
thing from the provinces, the family assumed that no
further evil would befall their strange kinsman and allowed themselves to forget him. Only George Berryman, the schoolmaster's brother, remembered their
existence with any regularity. Indeed, it was his frequent gifts, discreetly made on special occasions, that
supported the odd trio that now resided in the little
house.

And it was an odd trio. John Berryman, having had
very little to do with females until his besotted eye fell
upon his future wife, had no idea of how to raise a
young girl. Thus, the feeding, clothing, and moral training of his young daughter he gladly left to Miss Bekins,
the angular lady of indeterminate years that his family
had engaged for him.

Regina's formal education, he took care of. And this
he found a great pleasure. It could be said that over the
years, she was his only consistently interested student.
And so he filled her head with all the knowledge that
the squirming young future captains of industry rejected. It would have been useless to ask him why he
drilled a young female in the intricacies of Latin, Ger-
man, and French. Or to inquire as to why she required
such a wide knowledge of mathematics, history, and
literature. And it would have been impossible to try
to explain to him that a young woman really only
needed skill with a needle, a pleasant singing voice, a
dab hand with watercolors, and a little talent on the
pianoforte.

Miss Bekins certainly would not have told him so. The
present situation had suited her right down to the ground.
For the family, unknowingly, had hired a serpent to lie
in its bosom. The plain-faced, sensible-looking woman
had been a bluestocking, and a woman of radical opinion. If they had lived with her for a week, they would
have seen it. But they had only interviewed her for an

hour before sending her out on her mission. And John Berryman, in his vague, myopic fashion, had not perceived anything amiss with Miss Bekins in all the years she lived with them.

And so, Regina Analise Berryman had grown to adulthood with very little real idea of what life in her world was actually about. Oh, she could recite history chapter and verse; she could discourse at length on the deterioration of Ancient Rome, she could argue politics with force and intelligence—but she couldn't say why a lady should never sit with her legs crossed, or why a female should blush demurely, or why any woman should consider her husband her lord and master. Or why she required a husband at all. Which would have been suitable if she had grown up to feel as her father did, or look as her governess did. But she had inherited her mother's graceful good looks, along with her father's vivid coloring, as well as some forgotten ancestor's spirit and thirst for adventure.

How she would have fared if fate had decreed that she stay in the gentle countryside of her birth, there is no saying. She had few aquaintances of her same age, none of her class. For in truth, she had no class to which she belonged. She had the manner and grace of a lady, the education of a young gentleman, and the family background of sober, strict bourgeois merchants.

On Regina's eighteenth birthday, Miss Bekins had announced her retirement. With a brief good-bye embrace, Miss Bekins had taken her savings and herself off to Canterbury, there to help a distant cousin set up a school to enlighten the minds of other young females. Two years later, John Berryman paused in the middle of a lecture on the Trojan Wars to cough apologetically and collapse suddenly in easeful death. For several months after her world had collapsed as surely as her father had done, Regina had lived by herself in a torment of indecision. She could volunteer to teach in Miss Bekins' school, but she had no idea of whether the venture had been successful, and whether her arrival in Canterbury would be a genuine help or a further strain on her former governess's finances. She could apply for a position as governess, but she had been given to understand that she had neither the references nor the background to suit the genteel families who required such services. Perhaps, it was gently implied by the local vicar . . . if she set her sights lower, to consider working with a lower class of family.

Her letter requesting the direction of a London family of merchants who would require her services resulted in a sudden, unprecedented visit from her Uncle George, whom she had not seen in the whole of her life. In one brief flurry, overriding all her protestations, such as they were, paid a visit to his brother's grave, and trundled her into a coach back to London. En route to the city, he had firmly informed her that he had never taken the time to marry, but had he done so, she would have been just the daughter he would have chosen, and so that was the only position she had to bother her head about filling.

In the weeks that Regina had lived in her uncle's house, she had received new clothes, her own well-appointed room, and the services of a maid. Not to mention what was to her the bewildering services of a cook, a housekeeper, and two undermaids. She had no way of knowing that her uncle, rather than employing a vast staff of servants, was actually by all contemporary standards simply scraping by. He traveled so frequently that he did not feel the need for a more elaborate staff. Her uncle had taken care of all of her needs in a breath-takingly swift fashion, and then, bowing apologetically, announced that he must depart for yet another business trip.

It was the arrival of a pair of tickets to the Opera, sent by a grateful business acquaintance, that had sent Regina off on her ill-fated excursion. She had no way of knowing that her uncle would have simply let the tickets lie till dust covered them enough to signal the housekeeper to throw them out. She had only been thrilled at the idea of attending the famous London Opera house and, dressing herself in her new finery, she had taken her maid as escort, as her uncle had told her she must whenever she ventured from the house.

The stares, the whispers, the attention she had received at the theater had seemed odd, but not exceptional, at first. But, once seated in the box, the appearance of the other women present had startled her. If this was current London fashion and behavior, she felt sure she would never fit into the scheme of things in her uncle's city. But as the evening progressed and she watched the audience more closely than the stage, she began to get an inkling of the situation from the way certain couples behaved toward each other. Surely, she realized, it cannot be the fashion for a true gentleman to rest his lips upon his companion's throat in public, in a theater! Or for the lady to stroke her escort's hair. Or for a gentleman to ogle a female so openly, or for a lady to smile in pleased pride when being so encountered.

It was only when she left the box at intermission, however, that she had known without doubt what the situation was. The snatches of speculation about her presence that had come to her ears had driven her out, in search of a carriage to return home. But when that elegantly tailored gentleman, the one with the beautiful face of a fallen angel, had seen her and come to her side as naturally as if she were an old acquaintance, and whispered his husky-voiced suggestion into her ear, she felt as if the world had suddenly ended.

For he had stunned her. He had made all the others pale to insignificance and become merely background blur. The first moment she set eyes upon him she had thought he appeared out of a childhood tale of princes and castles. All thoughts of embarrassment and flight had themselves fled as he made his way gracefully through the throng to her side. Those clear azure eyes had sought hers out and had lit with real pleasure, as if he were overjoyed at finding her. His smile had welcomed and warmed her and drawn her answering smile. She could have basked all evening in the glow from that smile. And then, he had, still smiling, bent and sweetly whispered the impossible into her ear. What sort of female had he imagined her? She flushed in shame, just contemplating it. But since it seemed only a courtesan went unaccompanied to the theater on such a night, she could scarcely blame him, in all fairness, for his incredible proposal. In retrospect, his invitation had, surprisingly, secretly disappointed her rather than shocked her.

Belinda's prattle all the way home had assured her of her surmise. The little cat, she had thought with uncharacteristic spite. She knew all the while, and never bothered to inform me of it. What a fool I've been, she mourned. But, she told herself with a little of her old spirit, what difference does it make after all? I shall certainly never encounter such people again, at any rate. Uncle does not traffic with dukes and noblemen, and neither shall I. Who she would be expected to befriend in her uncle's house, she had no idea, for her uncle seemed to have few real friends and no social life at all.

She gazed out the window at the silent morning street of gray houses. Even though this was not, her uncle insisted, a fashionable street, it was firmly middle class and, to her eyes, most pleasant. She noticed a carriage standing still at the curb, its horses at rest, and noted with interest that its sole occupant seemed to be at rest as well. But no other thing on the streets stirred, except for the horses' languid tail-switching.

Ah well, she thought. I shall dress and take Belinda with me to the book shop. I surely will encounter no evil nobleman there. And both cheered and inwardly a little flattened by her rationalizations, she began to dress, forgetting once again that no fashionable woman would have done so alone while her maid lolled, gossiping and unoccupied, below stairs.

When she had drawn her hair back neatly and robed herself in the new elegant green garment that her uncle had insisted was a walking dress, she rang for Belinda and began to descend the stairs. Belinda greeted her breathlessly as she reached the front hall.

"Oh, miss," cried Belinda in a conciliating voice, "you do look ever so elegant, you do indeed!"

Regina did not feel particularly flattered, since Belinda greeted each new dress that she wore in much the same tones. But now, she noticed, Belinda's eyes seemed to sparkle, her freckled face seemed flushed, and she appeared to have an exciting secret. I had no idea, Regina thought, that this was such an extraordinary dress.

"Belinda," she said calmly, "get your bonnet, for I wish to walk to Mr. Hughes's bookshop, and I'm afraid you'll have to accompany me."

"Oh no, miss," Belinda gasped. "You cannot go, miss."

"Why can't I?" Regina bristled. "No one at the shop is likely to have been at the Opera last night. Don't be a goose, get your bonnet."

"Oh no, miss," Belinda repeated stubbornly, and with the swollen breast of one who carries a message of dramatic import, Belinda walked to the window and pointed out. "There, miss, is why you cannot go."

"What the devil are you talking about girl?" Regina blurted, forgetting again that a proper young lady did not speak in her father's accents.

"The Duke's man, miss . . . Sedgly, the Duke's man. That's him to the life, miss. And the coachman, Tom Highet, he's a fellow we all know for his past deeds. He's a big fellow, miss. And up to no good even when he's sleeping, we say."

Regina peered out through the parted curtain. There was a large, evil-looking fellow behind the horses all right, but she couldn't get a glimpse of the man who sat back in the interior of the closed carriage.

"What is any of that to me, Belinda?" she asked in puzzlement.

"Oh, miss," Belinda burbled, her high excitement giving her freckles a splotchy, rashlike look. "It's plain as the nose on your face. We all have been talking about it downstairs. They're waiting for you, miss, they are. You ran away from the Duke last night, and he don't take to that. He sent his man and Tom Highet to abduct you, he did. Just take one step out and they'll truss you like a goose, they will, and deliver you up to the Black Duke."

Regina began laughing. She laughed so hard, she brought tears to her eyes and had to grasp Belinda's shoulder to keep from swaying over. Belinda looked at her in astonishment, which only made her laugh the more. Finally regaining some composure, she asked through little hiccups if she had heard Belinda's words aright, for, she said, "A greater mess of fustian, Belinda, I have never heard. You've been reading too many romances, girl. An evil duke abducting young women in broad daylight on a city street . . . no, not an evil duke . . . a black duke!" She almost sobbed with laughter. "Oh Belinda, you've been dipping into too many romances."

"Oh no, miss," denied Belinda, much affronted. "For I don't even read, miss. Never have. But I know what I know. And it wouldn't be the first time, neither. What of Emily Ketchum then, miss? Eh? What of her, she that worked for the Robins? Abducted she was, and by him. And when her family found her again, she was properly ruined. They had to turn her out. Even if he did give her a sum of money, she couldn't find a respectable job again. And abducted right in the daylight, as you say. And there's tales of others too."

"Emily Ketchum?" asked Regina, sobering.

"Right, miss," nodded Belinda.

"But, even if that's so," Regina said, a little more quietly, "you say she was a servant. Even evil dukes don't abduct . . . proper young women, Belinda."

"Well," said Belinda, choosing her words carefully, "you being from the country and all . . . miss, here in town, there's proper and there's proper, you see. Not saying that you're not proper, miss. But who's your family, after all? Mr. Berryman has money, miss, but not . . . position, you see. He's not an important man, miss. There's no . . . well, miss, you and he aren't of the ton, you see. If a duke was to do you wrong, what would your word be against his? A member of the peerage, miss? No, even your uncle couldn't do much except blacken his name more . . . but it's so black, he wouldn't even notice the more. And where would you be then? You'd best stay here inside the house until your uncle comes home. In time . .," Belinda said, letting the curtain fall back, "he'll forget he saw you, he'll find another game. Maybe your uncle could put a few words in the proper ears, too, to make him lose interest. But until then, you'd better stay in."

"But," protested Regina, torn between a sense of the ridiculous and a growing feeling of trepidation, "what's to prevent him from . . . bursting in here and carrying me off like a Sabine woman?"

"Well, I wouldn't know about them, I never heard of that family," Belinda pondered. "But there's things even he can't do. You can't just burst into someone's house and carry them out, you know, miss." And here she looked at Regina curiously. "Didn't you know that? You might be able to do that in the country, but not here."

Regina assured her that that wasn't the case in the country either and, sighing, removed her gloves. She would stay in. She didn't believe Belinda's warnings implicitly, but after her experience of the night before, she realized that she knew very little of the morals and tendencies of these that dwelt in the city. She felt uneasy enough about the situation to remain in the house, although, she thought, I shall feel like a proper fool if uncle comes home and tells me that it was all a hum.

"Belinda," she ventured, "this is an incredible situation, is it not?"

"It's the way of things, miss," Belinda said knowingly. "It's the way of it."

III

St. John woke to the gentle sloshing sounds of pouring water. He opened his eyes to find himself in his own sun-filled room, his valet moving silently as he prepared his bath. He yawned and stretched and sank back against his pillow. He accepted the drink that his valet handed him and, propped up on one elbow, drank the potion down rapidly. "Hilliard," he asked, gasping, "what was that foul mess?"

"The recipe you gave me, m'lord," his valet answered calmly. "The one His Lordship said was all the thing this month."

"Well, it won't be my thing again," St. John said, rising. "Although it does clear the head, the shock of it isn't worth it."

He bathed and, wrapping himself in the wide towel Hilliard offered, sat by the window and allowed himself to be shaved. It was a sunny, satisfactory morning, he thought as Hilliard labored over him, save for the remembrances of the night before which slowly began to filter back to him. He had not liked the duke's sly presumptions about his reputation. And, he thought, he had not liked awakening alone. With Annabelle safely invested to James, he had gone around later in the evening to a promising young creature at Madame Felice's establishment, but he had found her to be too humorless and too dedicated a handmaiden. She had made him feel as though he were a chore, a difficult project to be gotten through meticulously, with all the proper moves in all the proper places, as though she had memorized the rituals. No, he thought, she was not a candidate for installation in Annabelle's former residence. But, he thought with a small feeling of optimism as he allowed Hilliard to pull on his boots, the search might provide entertainment. And he would continue the search after the business of his day was completed.

"To a turn, Your Lordship," Hilliard commented approvingly as St. John inspected himself in a pier mirror. His boots gleamed, his breeches clung tightly, without a wrinkle, his black coat fitted snugly. "Yes," St. John agreed, and pocketing the several invitations and letters that Hilliard handed him, he strolled down the stairs to breakfast.

It was well after noon when St. John faced the world. He called for his high-wheeled phaeton and the chestnuts, and drove carefully through the streets to his first obligatory call. He had promised himself another look at Melissa Wellsley, the current rage. He had only stood up with her twice at Almack's, but he had approved of her manner and, while he did not fall into raptures about her face and form as many of his contemporaries did, he had to admit that the entire effect she presented was charming. And she was reputed to have an income exceeding that of any other of the young women who had made their bows this season. She was considered the catch of the season, and he felt he owed it to himself to check her again, to see if there was any possibility of her catching his interest.

Once inside the morning room to which he had been ushered, he passed the time in making polite conversation with Lady Wellsley, amusing himself with the effusive way she agreed with his comments, the eagerness she showed to be pleasant to him. But he understood that all the while, she was weighing him, measuring him, estimating what she had heard about his income, his history, and his family ties. Despite half of it, he knew, she would be bound to consider him one of the most eligible partis to grace her drawing room.

As to the income, he thought as she burbled excuses as to her daughter's tardiness (which he knew was because she had been sent to change into something devastating to receive him in), she could find no fault. As to his title, she must find that exemplary, she had only two barons and an earl on the string at the moment. His ancestry, he knew, she would find impeccable. But if she were a wise woman, he felt, she might hesitate about his more recent ancestors, and his own behavior.

His father had been a compulsive gambler, blithely spending both his wife's portion and that which was left of the dwindling estate that he could legally touch, in any fashion that might provide a gamesman's interest. After his wife had died (gossips said that it was from boredom), he had gone on solely for the purpose of spending every last penny he could before the grave overtook him. The rumor was, after the Marquis had himself expired, that the estate was shot to pieces and the new Marquis would come into his estate to find it a paper one, all back debts and penury. But within a few years, when St. John had finally decided to grace Society with his presence, there wasn't a banker in the whole of London who wouldn't have given him unlimited credit. The mystery of how the young man had repaired his fortunes lingered, but fortune it was, so the issue was dropped. The young Marquis had been welcomed to the ton, with open arms.

Other segments of society had welcomed him thusly, too, and if Lady Wellsley chose to be very exacting, she might have had a qualm about this prospective suitor for her daughter's hand. It was well known that St. John was in the petticoat line, that his doings among these graceless females exceeded that which could be called normal in a man of his position. There were tales of mistresses, and wild parties and license. But his behavior in the drawing room was impeccable, even if his behavior in other rooms was wide open to speculation.

But when Melissa entered the room in a froth of pink lace and giggles, and St. John swept a bow and kissed her hand, Lady Wellsley subsided gracefully and took a position far from the pair. "So she approves," St. John thought with amusement, "reputation and all."

As they chatted about the weather and various doings about the town, St. John viewed the girl before him with speculation. She was very attractive, he thought critically, but no, not beautiful. Her black hair was coaxed into enchanting ringlets, her face was lightly dusted with powder to increase the contrast between white complexion and dark hair. Her nose was, he thought, a trifle too snub, her dark eyes a bit too off-center. No, he thought, no beauty, but well enough for her style. Of her figure, he reserved comment. For now, he thought, she was well enough, but a slight plumpness clung to her outline, and he was almost sure that in a few years she would balloon as alarmingly as her so charming mother had. And since he was looking for a female for the long term as a wife, he was not sure that she could fill the bill. But he was willing to reserve judgment. So long as he continued his interest, he knew, Lord and Lady Wellsley would keep her available.

"La, My Lord," she lisped, flushing becomingly, "surely there must have been another lady at the affair who caught your eye as well?"

"But none who caught and kept it," he promised.

He tired quickly of the light banter and, sweeping another bow, he took his leave of the two Wellsley ladies, leaving them to speculate about his attentions as he took himself off into the outer day.

He waved the phaeton away with his groom, and strolled to his club, where he had an excellent lunch. It was when he prepared to leave that he caught sight of James, who was frantically signaling to him from across the room.

"Sinjin," James began when he had beckoned the Marquis to another room, "there is a slight, very slight problem."

"What's this?" Sinjin smiled. "Has marriage impaired your style, James? Did the fair Annabelle find you lacking address, or something else?"

"No, Sinjin, listen," James whispered in a low voice. "It's just that . . . don't fly up, dear boy, but I haven't as yet found . . . suitable quarters for the gal . . . she's still in your digs. I'm sorry," James went on, looking at St. John's clouding face, "but there hasn't been time to transfer her yet. I haven't had time to arrange for my own place yet. I was out of the country for a spell, you know," he apologized, sensing his friend's annoyance, "and, I gave up my other place when I married, y'know, so I wondered if it were possible, if you could. . . ."

"James," said St. John coldly, drawing himself up so that he seemed to dwarf the anxious man at his side, "there are some things that go beyond friendship. I presented you with the female. I will not board her any longer. If you want her, you will have to find your own place for her. I want that house vacated, sir, on the instant, if not sooner. It is," he said noting the red-faced James, "a matter of honor with me."

"Oh certainly," James stammered. "No question about that . . . I was going to see to it. . . ."

"What was it you were going to ask me, old friend?" St. John smiled.

"Ah . . . nothing," James protested. "Just about a piece of gossip, but no matter, I haven't the time now." And he left the marquis standing there, smiling hugely to himself.

The afternoon went by pleasantly for the Marquis. He dropped in on a few friends, he chatted with a few acquaintances, he made plans for the evening. Late in the afternoon, he felt the need for some amusing conversation and so he payed a call on Lady Amelia Burden. She received him in her sitting room, without chaperone, but he knew that in her case, this somewhat daring action would not be misconstrued.

Lady Amelia had attained an age and position in society that enabled her to set rules unto herself. She was not ancient, by any means, in fact she was a few years younger than St. John himself. The fact that she was distant cousin of his would not, in itself, have allowed her the freedom she took in her relationship with him. But her position did. There had never been a hint of gossip about Lady Amelia, and thought St. John looking at her, doubtless there never would be.

She was tall and angular, but on the whole, her face and figure would not have been displeasing to St. John if it were not, he felt, for her one imperfection. It was unfortunate, he mused, as he invariably did when seeing her, that her fine brown eyes should be the seat of the trouble. For Lady Amelia had, since early childhood, been afflicted with a peculiar physical characteristic where one eye was perfect, brown and deep and intelligent, while the other was wont to wander slightly out to the side when she was weary, so that at those times she seemed to be looking out beyond one's left shoulder.

Still her fortune and position and calm, quietly amusing outlook on life had netted her several eligible proposals even in her first season. After all, the jest had run among several highly placed gentlemen: with her charm and fortune, she may look as high or as low as she likes, whenever she likes. And in the dark, they reasoned, one would not notice where she looks. But she had refused them all, and had remained unattached throughout eight seasons, and the Social World, although puzzled, had accepted that she would remain so.

St. John had felt an affinity for her from the first, when the eager little ten-year-old had grasped his hand one day and dragged him away from a stultifying family

gathering to show him her pony and comment with
startling candor on all the assembled relatives. He had
kept in touch with her ever since, standing up with her
at dances, paying courtesy calls that became less courtesy and more friendship as the years went by. If St.
John had ever bothered to think about it, he would have
admitted that she was his one real woman friend. For
the question of dalliance had never arisen in his mind.
He knew that he could never be attracted to a female
with any physical defect, and had, over the years, de-
veloped an easy, sexless amiability with her.

This afternoon, he complimented her on her rosy appearance, and she rang for tea for her visitor. She sat
herself carefully on his left side, so that if her troublesome eye wandered it would not face him, for she had
known for a long time how very much her occasional
peculiarity discomfitted him. She thought he felt it made
her uncomfortable. Although, truth to tell, he was the
only man she had ever known who seemed, no matter
how he tried to conceal it, disturbed by it. But then, he
was the only man whose opinion had ever really mattered to her. Amelia felt that it was only because he
watched her so closely that he noticed, and she was
pleased by both his attention and the sensitivity of his
nature. She admired him the more for his deep concern
for her over what was to others, a triviality.

"Sinjin," she smiled, "I've heard how very particular
your attentions have become with regard to the new
Incomparable. Am I to welcome a new cousin to our
family soon then?"

"Only if you decide to cast off your veil, my dear," St.
John grinned, "and take some fortunate fellow's impre-
cations to heart, for I have no immediate intention of
adding to our illustrious family at the moment."

"On this side of the blanket, you mean, my dear," she
said, relaxing.

"Very wicked, Amelia," St. John laughed. "If only
everyone knew what a dreadful Miss you are."

"Why, you know, Sinjin, and still you put up with my
shocking behavior."

"Ah, but that is because I like to be shocked," he

said. "Now tell me some shocking things, you minx, or I shall think I've paid a call on some very proper young woman, and that would not suit me at all."

They sat and chatted for a half hour or more, till the shadows began to color the room and St. John realized, in the dimming light, how quickly the time had passed. Truly, he thought, she could entertain him, always knowing what sly comment would amuse him, always gauging his mood perfectly, always bringing up the bits of gossip, the little anecdotes that would please him. Ah, he had often thought, if only the Lord had gifted her with a perfect face, he might have been able to make a match of it with her. But as it was, there were still times, even after all these years, when a chance glance at her unguarded face when she was weary brought a little chill to his heart. No, it would not do. It was a pity, he often thought, for in all other aspects she would suit. But he could not bear any physical deficiency in his marchioness. That lady, whoever she might eventually be, should have to be as perfect in the eyes of Society as she would be in his own. And that would have to be absolute perfection. So, although Amelia might only have a slight impairment, to him it would always loom as large as any insurmountable obstacle. Still, he thought, I shall always have her as a friend.

As he rose to leave, she placed a hand tentatively upon his sleeve.

"Sinjin," she said quietly with unaccustomed sobriety, "your sister has asked if I would accompany her down to Fairleigh one of these days. She is having a difficult time with this confinement, and thinks a spell of country air would help her condition. But she implores me to accompany her. She says she will perish from the sulks by herself."

"I would have thought she would have succumbed to them ages ago," St. John laughed. "What is this to be . . . her fifth? She and Gordon seem determined to populate the world by themselves." He laughed, thinking of his silly, vain little sister now fast becoming the most prolific female in the country. "But why the long face, Amelia? If you think you will be bored to tears, simply refuse her, tell her that there is some ball or other you cannot in any conscience miss."

"Ah, but I don't mind. I think I could use a change of scene as well, but she is determined to rusticate at Fairleigh. Her childhood home, she says, comforts her in time of stress."

"And so?" asked St. John.

"But it is your home, Sinjin, and I should not want you to think that I am imposing upon your hospitality without consulting you first."

"Amelia," he laughed, "there is room in that old pile for a dozen of you. Go and rusticate by all means, but be sure to return to me with all your faculties intact, for I do need your wit to ease the way. When shall you be going?" he asked as he went to the door.

"Not for several weeks," she said. "For she does not suffer so that she wishes to miss the Prince's gala next week, or the Castelreighs' party, or the——"

"Dear Mary," the Marquis laughed. "She must certainly be ill, then, for a healthy female surely would contrive some excuse to avoid those crushes."

Raising her hand to his lips, the Marquis took leave of his cousin and sauntered off into the deepening twilight. But Lady Amelia did not immediately turn from the window where she watched him stroll off. Rather she stood quietly, and watched quietly, for many moments after his tall figure had gone out of her sight.

St. John walked for a long time, far longer than was usual for him. He seemed to be strolling aimlessly through the darkening streets. He watched the lamplighters set about their tasks, and only when he was sure that all the fashionable carriages had returned home, only when he was convinced that all the members of his elite fraternity were safely home preparing the evening's pleasures, did he turn his steps and walk with determination. For now he did not want anyone to discover his direction.

He did not mind his contemporaries seeing him entering into low houses of assignation, or houses that contained festivities that loftier members of the Beau Monde

would have been aghast at. He would have braved all
their stares if they had discovered him attending a cock
fight or an exotic exhibition, of the sort that Madame
Felice was famed for. But his destination this evening
was one that he wished no other man of his station to
determine. Quietly and quickly, he melted into the evening's darkness.

IV

The Marquis was in a rage. He stood on the top step of
the house and confronted the little ginger-haired maid.
The air of imperturbability which he so carefully cultivated was gone, his fists were clenched, and in a moment, he felt, he would have to shove the girl aside if he
must, to gain entry to the house.

"I said," he swore through gritted teeth, "that your
master is expecting me. He is always expecting me.
Now move aside, my girl, and let me pass."

"Well, I dunno," the girl said with maddening slow-
ness, assessing the elegant gentleman that stood on the
doorstep as urgently and impatiently as if he were being
buffeted by cruel winds and biting cold, although it was
only a cool, fair night outside. "You're still not saying
what yer business is, or if you come from that handsome
coach out there."

"Devil take it," hissed the Marquis. "It's because of
that coach that you must let me in. Now do you open
the door, or do I do it myself?" he threatened.

This seemed to confirm the girl's worst fears, and she
made as if to close the door on him. As he reached out
one hand to stay her, he caught sight of a grim-faced,
middle-aged woman behind her.

"Mrs. Teas," he called out in relief. "Tell this fool to
give me admittance, at once!"

"Oh, sir!" gasped the older woman, and clutching the
maid by the shoulder, she spun her aside.

"Oh sir," she said, shutting the door behind the Marquis. "Excuse the girl, please do. She's new here, and doesn't know a thing. It won't happen again, I assure you. Belinda, get downstairs. I'll have a talk with you by and by, my girl, I will. Sir," she panted, having quickly escorted the Marquis to a study to the right of the door, "please sit down. Please to wait. The Master's just returned hardly an hour before. But I know he'll want to see you. He's just finishing up his dinner. Please to wait here, sir."

"Tell him not to hurry," St. John said, his temper cooling. "I'll wait here for him," and he took a large leather chair near a neat desk. "But mind you, Mrs. Teas, if the chit's such a fool as I think she is, kindly do not inform her of my name."

"Oh never, sir," gasped Mrs. Teas, red-faced. "That I'd never do, sir," she swore, and she walked quickly from the room.

"Aye," thought St. John savagely, that she had better never do. He sat back in the chair and crossed his elegantly booted legs. Here, in this small dark study, with its innocent looking shelves of books, deep turkey-red carpeting, and flickering lamplight, he was at the same moment both fulfilled and at his most vulnerable. Of all the places on the face of this earth, the marquis thought, this was the one place he must never be discovered.

When he had come down the street and seen, at the last moment, the coach waiting by the curb, with its easily discernible crest, he had known a moment of pure terror. But by then it was too late to retreat. He must brave it out, for if he had turned and left, he would have called more attention to himself. He had kept his face turned from the glow of the lamplight, and raised the doorknocker, hoping that the shadows concealed his face. And thinking that if perhaps the mission of the occupant of that coach was the same as his, there would be sufficient reason for the tale to go no further if he had been recognized. Two men entangled in the same endeavor would not cry attention at each other. But when the maid had refused him admittance, he had known that he could not turn and leave. He had to enter this house, where he had always been welcome, never refused admittance, not for the past nine years and more.

Nine years, the Marquis thought. It had been nine years since he had first entered this room. Since he had been a desperate young man, encumbered with a worthless legacy, bequeathed a mountain of duns' notes, three expensive entailed estates, and no future save that which his name and few hoarded guineas could provide. He could have sold himself on the marriage market, but something within him rebelled at that. He could have tried gaming to restore the estate to what it had been before his father had gamed it away, but he had seen too much of the result of that route in his own house. He had heard, then, through the loose talk among his young friends, that there were certain men of business. . . . Men of trade. Socially unacceptable men who dirtied their hands with commerce but who were amassing large fortunes. And who were always on the lookout for fashionable patrons to cast their lots in with for social advancement, for themselves or for their families. Or for influence, should the need ever arise for that.

The trail he followed had led eventually to this room, to George Berryman, a stolid man from a merchant family, but a man who was reputed to have a touch of gold. He had eyed the young Marquis and, sighing heavily, had asked finally the inevitable question. "And what shall you bring to this enterprise, My Lord?"

"My money, such as there is left of it," the Marquis had answered, "my connections, such as I can utilize, and my influence, such as I will make if this venture succeeds. But, never my name. No never, that I cannot give you."

That, the merchant had understood. Obviously, this was a proud youngster who had got it into his head that it would be social suicide if it were known that he was engaged so deeply in commerce. But he assessed the grave young man and concluded that this was also a bright one, and, by his own standards, an honest one.

And, perhaps this young Noble could, in a circumlocatory way, provide that information, that entree, that access, which he needed in some phases of his business. And so the bargain was struck. St. John Basil St. Charles, Marquis of Bessacarr, whose blood was documented from Norman times forward, became the silent partner of George Berryman, whose blood, though no less rich, was derived from as mixed a pedigree as any mongrel roaming the London streets.

Over the years, St. John had taken a secretive but active part in the business. He had told George Berryman of the plans and maneuvers of the members of Society that he personally knew. Which families were badly dipped, which noble names would discreetly but anxiously be willing to sell off which holdings. Which way the war seemed to be going, the words taken from the top, where George Berryman would never have been able to hear them. All of which gave the pair both the information and access to the goal they wanted. They traded in property mines in the north, holdings in the islands, shipping shares, war supplies.

There were other business dealings whose nature could not bear too close a scrutiny—certain dealings in a certain trade off the Ivory Coast, certain imports from across the not-completely-war-locked channel, business matters best left in the dark where they could grow full and rich, like mushrooms in a damp cellar. But profitable. The pair had profitted. And all that was required now, as always, was trust, and secrecy.

Nine years, St. John thought, which has given me time to regain all that my father had lost, and more than he ever dreamed of.

Enough blunt to restore the estates, to live at the top of fashion, to marry off one small silly little sister in a manner to which she had never become accustomed. Enough money to let me make the world what I choose it to be. More than enough, really. But the prizes were too rich to give up the venture now that the original goal had been reached.

And no one would ever know that the riches had not

dropped into his lap by accident, in the way, St. John felt, a nobleman should acquire his fortune. A fortune acquired as impeccably and easily as his birth and lineage, that was the hallmark of a true gentleman, and he would fight savagely to keep both his fortune and his title impeccable in the eyes of Society.

"Your Lordship," George Berryman said, hurrying in through the door and closing it carefully behind him. "My pardons, please, for the treatment you received at the hands of the maid. She's a new girl, and no one had told her . . . well, your visit was unexpected, My Lord," he continued reproachfully.

"Indeed it was, Mr. Berryman," answered the Marquis as he watched the elder man settle down behind the desk. "But I sent notes and messages, and received no answer. You were to have returned a week ago, and when I did not hear from you, I decided to come and see for myself if there were any problem. You know," the Marquis went on, "that if something . . . should . . . if any evil should befall you, there is no one, I hope, who would have the knowledge that I must be informed."

"No, indeed, but you have made that your stipulation, Your Lordship. At any rate, rest easy, if I should have . . . some evil befall me, there is no way to connect us. I keep no such papers. It would only mean that you would have to find yourself a new partner."

"No," laughed the Marquis, his good humor restored, "you and I are truly wedded, Berryman. If I should be widowed, I should seek out no other partner. I have all that I want now. I continue only because it pleases me to do so now. Now, what of Amerberly's holdings?" he asked imperatively.

"That is what kept me so long," Berryman answered. "He did not want to sell, not really. He equivocated, he hesitated, but in the end, as you predicted, he capitulated."

"Ah!" said St. John, his eyes shining, his languid airs gone, his body alert. "Tell me all, tell me all, I have waited for this. How much?"

The early evening wore on as the two men talked and

pored over their papers. The elder finally handed St. John a bank draft. "There you are, Your Lordship, your full and anonymously donated share. It was a good day's work, for all that it took me two weeks to accomplish it. I must be getting older."

"Old and slyer," laughed St. John, noting the sum on the check with a smile before he put it in his pocket.

"Well then," said St. John, rising and stretching himself. "Well done."

"Your Lordship," said George Berryman in an altered voice, "before you go, there is another matter which I would like to discuss with you."

Something in the elder man's tone made St. John pause. It was not like Berryman to detain him for even a moment after the work of business was done.

"It is a little difficult," the older man admitted, and stared down at his desktop.

What the devil is this about? St. John frowned. For nine years, things have gone on smoothly, does he want a larger share now, for his old age? Which is fast approaching, St. John suddenly noted, seeing as if for the first time the new deep lines in his partner's face, the imperceptible droop to his jowls, the sparse white hair, the pallid complexion. B'God, St. John noticed, he is growing old.

"It is not business, Your Lordship," Berryman went on. "It is in the nature of a personal request."

Now this is new, the Marquis thought, for nothing of this nature has ever been discussed before. When he thought about it, the Marquis remembered that he knew far less of the personal life of his partner than his partner knew of his own. For St. John was Society's darling, and every scandal of his was well documented, while his partner, a bachelor, as he did know, lived his life in quiet seclusion.

Seeing that he had the Marquis's undivided attention, George Berryman went unhappily on. "I have never asked anything of you, in so far as your social influence goes, but now, I am forced to apply to you for a . . . favor."

By God, the Marquis thought, has some lady of fashion caught his eye? Has he a nephew he wants to promote in the Beau Monde? He is in for a disappointment if he expects my help there. But he is too sly an old fox for that.

"Do go on," St. John said calmly, noting the other man's uneasiness.

"Ah, did you happen to notice the carriage out on the street, My Lord?" Berryman said softly.

Suddenly tense, St.John nodded curtly.

"Who would not? It's Torquay's crest, it's hardly anonymous. I was going to ask you about it myself, but it slipped my mind when you gave me the good news about Amerberly. What does he here, Berryman? The same as I? Have you become a bigamist, with two partners?"

"Hardly, sir," Berryman frowned. "He has money enough for both of us, but it is this house that he watches."

"Has he got wind of my involvement?" St. John asked, his lips white.

"No, no," Berryman said. "Nothing at all like that. It is such a foolish thing that I am almost embarrassed to mention it, but I did not think . . . I. . . . Your Lordship, you know I am a man of power, but only in certain circles. And, I finally admit, because I feel it these days, I grow old. Still, here is a situation that neither my worldly wisdom, what there is of it, nor my money can handle. Simply put, then," he said, seeing his youthful partner's impatience, "it is an affair of the heart."

"What?" drawled St. John, much entertained. "Has His Grace taken a fancy to you then, Berryman? I knew his tastes were varied, but really, I am much surprised."

George Berryman only responded with a weak smile. "No, no. But I do not think it a joking matter. It seems that he has taken a violent fancy to a young woman here in my house. If, from what my servants tell me, he is running true to form, he has expectations . . . of abducting her. This, I cannot allow. But who would hear the word of a common merchant against a nobleman?

And he has done nothing, actually, except station his servants to watch the house. No, I cannot say a thing. But, Your Lordship, many years ago you promised me . . . your influence in certain matters. I call upon that influence now, if I may, on the basis of the long years of association we have had. I do not like to do so, but I see no alternative. Could you . . . speak with the Duke . . . perhaps defer his interests? Deflect his fascination with my poor house, put a word in his ear? I would be most grateful."

The words came easily enough to St. John. "Of course, Berryman, I shall do what I can, but for the moment, although I doubt that Torquay himself is sitting in the carriage, could you show me out a back entrance? For it would hardly do for his servants to spy me leaving here. Servants talk."

"And Your Lordship," hesitated Berryman as he showed the Marquis to the back-stair door, "one other thing. . . . As I do grow old, if ever things come to a pass . . . that is to say, may I tell the young woman that she may make application to you for . . . protection?"

"Protection?" answered the Marquis, raising an eyebrow. "I hardly think you mean precisely that . . . not my sort of protection, but," he went on, noting his aged partner's extreme unease, "yes, certainly, as I said, I will do what I can."

Once out again in the clear night, St. John walked a circuitous route to where he could safely call for a hackney cab.

The words were easy enough to say, but he had known even as he said them that there was little he could do for Berryman. How could he make an application to that wickedly smiling Torquay, without Torquay, who was never a fool, oh no, he might be everything else, but not a fool, inquiring as to how, and why, the Marquis was concerning himself with the affairs of a bourgois commoner? "But Sinjin," he could hear the Duke saying in his distinctive whisper, "how came you to hear of my plots against a merchant?" No, he could never give the Duke that hint, that insight into his private affairs, his association with Berryman. The Duke was too quick to pick up a scent for that.

No matter, St. John rationalized as he signaled to the hackney, for it is probably only that new ginger-haired maid that Torquay has spied. It is only a little serving girl he wishes to entertain himself with. And she looks the sort to be well pleased with a moonlight abduction, no matter what her prim master thinks, I know the sort. And, he thought, settling back against the cushions of the coach, "I did say, I would do what I could, and in truth, I can do nothing."

"Regina," said her uncle as he watched the girl pace the length of his study, "please do calm yourself. It isn't so very bad, my dear. So you will stay within the house for a few days longer. Then, I assure you, I have set certain wheels in motion that will put an end to the matter and you will be free again."

"You spoke to the man who came here tonight about it?" Regina asked, shocked.

"I'm sorry," her uncle said, locking away certain papers in his drawer. "But you know I cannot confide business matters to you. I hold many people's confidences, but yes, I did make application to someone whom I believe can ease the situation."

Regina stopped and looked at her uncle, who sat dejectedly at his desk. Oh really, she thought, it is not fair. He tries so hard to make it all up to me, and I am ungrateful and stubborn, and he is such a good old man.

"Uncle," she cried, rushing to his side, "forgive me, you are so weary from traveling all day, and here I besiege you further. I will stay in. I'll read . . . or do needlepoint, or some such thing. I'm well used to my own company. Don't concern yourself so. You look positively ill, are you all right?"

"All right as I can be," he assured her. "It's only that I am no longer young, my dear. There are times when I could wish that I had gotten to know you sooner . . . could have watched you grow. But there was always another bit of business to accomplish. When you are young you think you have all the time in the world."

"You are ill!" cried Regina, her green eyes wide. "I'll call Mrs. Teas, I'll call an apothecary. . . ."

"No, no," he laughed softly. "Don't get into a pet, my dear, it's only that I at last admit that I am old. Many years older than your own father was, Regina. And I must now contemplate the fact of it, now that I have you to consider. Regina," he said, rising and looking at her, noting that what he had considered a soft, pretty child was in reality a glowing young woman. "I will be taking certain other steps to insure your future. At the moment, my sole heir is my nephew, your cousin, Harry. But that is not right. I've made an appointment with my solicitor. I'll change a few things in your favor. No," he said, seeing her about to protest, "there is nothing wrong with a little foresight, my dear. In the meantime, I have some other business . . . yes, eternally business, to clear up in the west. I'll be gone for about a week, and then, after I see my solicitor, perhaps you and I can take ourselves off to some resort spa. I can enjoy the waters, and you can try to bewitch some young men."

He eyed her with worry, for in truth, he did not have any idea of what sort of young men she could consort with. Her birth placed her below the correct people he felt she would be temperamentally suited to, her education placed her above the earnest young men he associated with. But perhaps, he thought hopefully, we might make a match for her with some impoverished younger son, or some young man just out of the military, or even, he dared to think, someone of exceptional family whose empty pockets might make such a match acceptable.

As if she could read his thoughts, she smiled softly at him, and kissed his cheek.

"Dear Uncle," she said, "confess it, isn't business easier to manage than a stray young niece?"

"At any rate," he smiled back, "while I am gone, stay within the house. That matter out there will soon be cleared up. And Regina . . . if, should anything untoward occur to me . . . for I am not a young man . . . that is to say, if I should ever be in a position where I cannot help you should the need arise . . . do not tell any other soul, but you may make application to St. John Basil St. Charles, the Marquis of Bessacar. Simply seek him out and tell him who you are. No, I cannot answer any questions. Just remember that."

"It is graven on my heart," she said, and made a child's sign of crossing her heart and sealing her lips. "I promise you, Uncle." She smiled, kissing her fingertip. "Honor bound."

V

Regina sat huddled in a large chair in the corner of the room as her aunt swept up to Mrs. Teas. It seemed that her vision was blurry, her ears were fogged, her head ached dully. Things had happened too quickly for her naturally resilient personality to have time to assert itself.

One moment she had been sitting in her room, helping Belinda pin up a dress, a dress she was planning to wear to celebrate her uncle's return the next day. And the next moment, this small fierce little woman had entered the house to announce that she had already had word from her solicitors, although how she could have discovered the news so shortly after the terrified servant had delivered it to Regina herself, she would never know.

Aunt Harriet had introduced herself to Regina, and then taken stock of the house that was now hers, or rather her son's. But one look had shown Regina that whatever Cousin Harry had, his mother would control.

Uncle George had fallen as he had entered the inn where he was staying, and by the time the landlord had gotten him decently into bed, he had not had much time left. The only message he managed to whisper to the physician before his ravaged heart had given way as surely as his late brother's had, was one for Regina. "Tell her," he had gasped, "that I'm terribly sorry."

Regina had not gotten to know her uncle very well, so she could not in all honesty be said to be pining for him. Still, the tears she had shed at his graveside were genuine enough. He had looked so very much like her father. His death had so nearly duplicated his brother's. And, selfishly, she knew that the safe harbor to which he had spirited her was now vanished.

Her aunt did not grieve at all. She was a small fury of a woman, and as adept at business as her brother had been. Though, even standing erect with indignation, as she so often did, she only reached to Regina's shoulder, the small wiry body contained all the ambition in the world. All the ambition, Regina had observed, that her poor cousin Harry had not inherited.

Regina could feel some sympathy for Harry, she realized, but very little. In the weeks in which he had moved in to her uncle's house with his mother, she had been aware, through all the confusion, of his apologetic presence. He was a few years older than Regina herself, but he lacked her glowing color. He was a pallid, dark-haired young man. His pantaloons stretched unfashionably across a premature little paunch that bobbled when he coughed, as he so often did, to attract attention. If he would not try, Regina thought, watching him from the corner of her eye, so very hard to be in fashion, perhaps it would not be so noticeable. But the tight-fitting jackets he aspired to only accentuated his perennial slouch and rounded shoulders. And his conversational attempts were poor mumbles, as if he expected to be interrupted at any moment. And, in fairness, she thought, he always was.

"Harry," commanded his mother now, "do say something. I have just told Mrs. Teas that her services will be no longer required. That as we are no longer a household containing only a bachelor and his niece, we require a butler, not a housekeeper. We have enough females here. She has asked for references. Will you take yourself off and compose one?"

"Ah," the unhappy Harry ventured, "but as I did not . . . that is to say, never employed her . . . what should I write, Mama?"

"Whatever seems reasonable," his mother shouted.

"Perhaps," Regina put in, trying to come to Harry's aid, "Mrs. Teas herself can suggest some of the required wording."

"Very good," commended her aunt. "Just so. Go to it, Harry."

When Harry and Mrs. Teas had left, Aunt Harriet sat herself down opposite Regina.

"It's good," she said, shaking her gray curls for emphasis, "that you're coming out of your sulks. I don't mind telling you that when I discovered that I had inherited you as well as this house, I was shocked. George never said a word about your presence, but you might as well know that we were never close. You do know it, so what's said is said. We were both very busy people, and I consider myself no more at fault than he was. But, what's done's done, when all's said. Still, you're a well enough looking girl, though you have more of your mother in you than Berryman, to be sure. But you've a quick mind, and a healthy body, so all's not lost. What do you intend to do with yourself, Niece?"

The abruptness of the question put Regina off balance. In truth, for the past weeks she had been trying to determine the same thing for herself. She was in no better case now than she was when her father had died. She had little money, and less experience with the world. She had never gotten out to see much more of the grand city to which she had been taken. At first, it was because she had lain in hiding from the omnipresent coach which had waited outside. But soon after her uncle's death, it had disappeared as suddenly as it had arrived. But then, her confusion and mourning had confined her to the house. Now a month had passed, and she still had no clear idea of what was to become of herself.

Still, she was never silent for too long, and giving her aunt a long measuring look, she spoke:

"I have a few options, Aunt. I have been considering them. If I could prevail upon you to lend me some passage fare, I could rejoin my governess at the school she has established in Canterbury and establish myself there as a teacher. I could perhaps seek similar employment with some well-placed family here in the city. I would not, Aunt, throw myself upon your charge for too long."

"What about marriage?" snapped her aunt.

"I am dowerless, portionless, and familyless," Regina smiled. "Not quite a catch, Aunt."

"Your looks would take care of that," her aunt spoke. "If any of my girls had had your looks, I would have danced all the way to the bank instead of having to pay off such doweries. There's hope in that line, girl."

"I don't want to marry yet," Regina said calmly.

"Want to wait till you're ruined?" her aunt cried. "For take my word, girl, that'll be your fate if you're not careful. Too good looking to mope about waiting for a prince to snap you up. You won't be able to support yourself too well with a bastard at your knee, Regina. Oh, don't look scandalized, I speak it as I see it. You're a good looking gal. Even Harry, whom I confess I thought never had a tendency toward such things, has been goggling at you."

"Harry?" said Regina with incredulity.

"Yes," her aunt continued. "And I'm glad to see it, too. He hasn't looked at anything but his neckcloth for years. He's been looking at you, though. Here's a proposition, Regina. Take it as I say it, and I'll only say it the once. You can go off to Canterbury, if you wish, I'll advance you the money. But if you go and don't make a go of it, don't come back. I don't want any soiled goods dragging back here. Harry's too soft-hearted and that wouldn't be what I want for him. Or you can try to get a position here in the city, only with your looks, all the positions offered to you will be ones you won't want to take, if you get my meaning. But if you're sensible, you'll hear me out. Harry needs a wife. We've got money enough to make up for your poverty. At least, we already know your family. And you'll bring good blood into the line. And brains. Which, my girl, you well know isn't Harry's strong point. Now I'm not forcing you, or threatening you, but I'm making a good clear business proposition to you. Think about it. But not for too long, I don't want him setting his heart on something he can't get. It'll make it harder for him in future if he does. There's your choices, girl, and fair ones they are, too. Think about it."

And nodding with satisfaction, her aunt walked off to find the cook to terrorize.

"Well," thought Regina angrily, "I do hope the climate in Canterbury suits me, for it looks like I'll be there for some time."

But when Regina announced her decision to her aunt a week later, the week which she had felt would give her time to send the letter to Canterbury announcing her imminent arrival, her aunt had told her not to be so hasty, to let things hang fire for a spell. Then, all at once, Regina realized that Harry had been attempting to woo her. She had not understood what all the desultory, incoherent attempts at conversation had been, but when on the heels of her aunt's startling decision to allow her to stay for a while longer, Harry proffered an invitation to the theater to her, she had understood.

She had not had the heart to turn down his shyly muttered invitation, and so, on this fine frosty evening, she found herself dressing in one of the lovely gowns her uncle had purchased for her.

"No mourning clothes," her aunt had warned her in the beginning, "for I don't believe in them. George himself wouldn't have expected it, and a fine sight I'll be in all my bright colors, when my own niece is dressed like a crow."

It will be only the one evening, Regina thought, guiltily, and at least he won't feel like such a complete failure, and oh, I do want to get out of this house for a spell.

Belinda fussed over her hair for what seemed like hours, patting in little curls, brushing out the long cascading curl that swept over one shoulder. The little maid wore a small, secretive smile.

"Belinda," Regina laughed, "Cousin Harry is not the Prince Regent. Why do you go to all this extraordinary effort?"

"Because, miss," Belinda grinned, "who's to say? It might be an extraordinary evening."

"I'm off to Canterbury within the week, Belinda," Regina said. "As well you know it, for you will have to get a new position when I leave."

"That's as may be," Belinda grinned.

"Well leave off," Regina said, rising, "for I'm all finished, and now I'll have to wait an hour for Harry to get his neckcloth right and my aunt to have her hair papers taken out."

Belinda, smiling largely, tittered out of the room. Regina stared after her with deep distrust. She had never felt an affinity with the girl, and this new behavior she was showing was unsettling. As the moments passed, Regina sat quietly, thinking about her forthcoming trip, hoping that she was suited for the new life she was going to attempt to make for herself. While the tuition of small girls might not seem very exciting, she thought, there might be compensations.

Belinda poked her head in the door.

"Oh miss," she smiled, "there's someone to see you, and I've taken the liberty of showing him to the study."

"To see me?" Regina asked, and seeing Belinda's affirmative nod, realized that it might be another of her uncle's business aquaintances. Several of them had paid courtesy calls to her that first week. And since she could not think of another living soul who would seek her out here, Regina went down the stairs reasoning that it was some aquaintance of her uncle's who perhaps had been out of town when the tragedy had occurred. Only, she hesitated at the door to the study, what will he think of me not wearing black? And she gazed down at the sweeping green gown that she wore.

Ah well, she thought, as Aunt says, what is done, is done and said. And with Belinda hovering behind her, she entered the study.

It was dimly lit, and in the first moment her eyes had to accustom themselves to the shadowy light thrown by the sole burning lamp. She could hear Belinda giggle as she closed the door behind her. What is the matter with the girl, she thought with annoyance, leaving me alone here with a guest?

But a moment later, when she could see who stood

before her, smiling beatifically at her, she could only draw in her breath with a gasp.

She recognized him instantly, for he had never been too far from her thoughts, and acknowledging the recognition, he bowed. He looked, she thought inconsequentially, as disturbingly beautiful as he had that night at the Opera.

His pale hair reflected the dim glow of the lamp, his large innocent blue eyes smiled at her. The nose, she thought, is too long and thin and straight for a cherub, the face too lean, the mouth too curling. But there is such an air of disarming innocence. He wore dark evening dress, and she could see that the tapered coat that covered the slight frame did not conceal the long muscles of his shoulders, nor did the close-fitting breeches obscure the tight strength of his legs. When he spoke, it was in the same hoarsely sweet voice that had haunted her dreams all these past weeks.

"I see," he said softly, "that age has not withered you. I'm sorry I couldn't come sooner."

Her back stiffened, "But custom will stale me, sir. I take leave to tell you to get out."

He looked at her with great interest. "Wit too? I am most fortunate. But I shall not 'get out,' Regina, at least not yet, when it has taken me so very long to get in."

"How?" she began, but he cut her off with a wave of one long pale hand. "Very simple stuff, Regina," he said caressingly. "Nothing to even gloat about. A few coins, a few kisses on the right lips, and any door will open to you."

She shook her head, sending the curl of hair tossing back against her shoulder. "Why have you gone to all this trouble, sir? Following me, watching the house, and now, coming here? I made it quite clear the last time we met, when you insulted me, that I want nothing to do with you."

"It was no trouble at all, and not at all an insult," he said, smiling with some inner joy. "And what you want, Regina, has very little to do with it. I saw you, and lost my poor heart. I was enraptured," he said, placing one hand over his breast. "Is that what you want to hear? No matter. It's true. You are very lovely. And being inaccessible made you even lovelier, if possible. I offer you that much-used organ, Regina. Be mine," he crooned.

"Well, you certainly are mad." Regina smiled with relief, thinking it was only that he was a little deranged, or a buffoon. "But now that you have made your remarkable offer, I tell you that I am untouched by it, and want nothing to do with you. Now sir," she went on, disturbed by the ceaseless smile, "I'm sure that there are many women who would be most honored by your confession. Unfortunately," she shrugged, "I am not one of them. You find before you a female most singularly untouched by gentler emotions. So pray take yourself elsewhere, before I have to call my cousin for assistance in convincing you of my sincerity."

"Harry?" purred the Duke. "Oh hardly Harry. Can you imagine him laying hands upon a duke of the realm? Really, Regina, you are not giving me any credit at all, are you?" She noticed that now he had stopped smiling and was looking at her steadily. "It's very simple, my dear. Very unfair, if you will, but nonetheless, simple. I am not a good man. I am at the present, as a matter of record, rejoicing in one of the most evil reputations in all of England. But don't pity me, Regina, for I swear it is well deserved. But I am very wealthy, and I am a duke, a duke of all things. And you are a commoner. Moreover, much to my joy, you are a commoner with no connections at all. No resources. No protector. You are my natural meat, Regina. My natural prey. I want you. Not, perhaps, in a spiritual fashion, rather in a very mortal fashion. For I, too, am a creature most singularly untouched by the gentler emotions. It is not gentle emotions that I spoke of, though. But I do want you, and what I want, I eventually have. Do you understand? You will profit by the experience, I think. You most certainly will be much richer for it. So be a good, sensible girl, and come along with me now. My carriage," he said, sweeping a bow, "awaits."

"You are mad," she gasped, her eyes widening, "I am not a broom, or a tiepin, or . . . a snuffbox . . . a thing that you can see in a shop window and want, and take. I am not an object for your pleasure," she went on. "I am a living, breathing person. No one can just take me."

"You're making it all very difficult, but exhilarating," he said. "And you know very little. I can most certainly take you, Regina, any time I choose, even right here."

She backed against the door.

"But I think I won't," he mused, "because I do like leisure and comfort. And if you were a tiepin or a snuffbox, I wouldn't want you quite so much. And the fact that you insist on being recognized as a thinking person, with certain rights, makes you all the most stimulating," he said, now smiling radiantly.

"You are like some creature out of a bad dream," Regina cried. "For all that I speak sense to you, you smile and smile, and continue as if I had said nothing. You seem to be untouched by reality. This is my uncle . . . my aunt's house. I have a staff of servants here, my cousin and aunt are at this very moment waiting for me. Soon they will look for me. And you stand here and smile and tell me that you want me, that I am to come with you . . . surely you are playing some elaborate joke. . . ."

"You think," he said, considering, his head tilted to one side, "that the houseful of servants and aunts and cousins make a large difference?"

She heard her aunt's strident voice in the hall, and shored up by the shrill sounds, held her head high. "Yes, and now, Your Grace, if you would leave. . . ."

He had heard the sounds as well, and seemed to be listening closely to the progress of the noises.

"Yes," he said, and smiled again. He walked close to her, so close that she could scent the faint aroma of Bay rum and wine and tobacco on his person. The large wide blue eyes, now unsmiling, looked down into hers, and with a quick grace, he reached and drew her to him. His lips gently, she thought with surprise, very tenderly covered hers.

In that first instant, her shock gave way to surprise at the tenderness, at the small thrill that involuntarily raced through herself at the touch of those warm soft gentle lips upon hers. He held her as gently as she had ever been held, although her confused mind remembered that she had never been thus held. Still, he pressed his body to hers, and she felt him communicate an urgency of desire to her. In that first moment, she swayed against him, responding to the startling effect his presence had upon her, but before she could recover herself, indeed at the very moment she felt her resolve returning and her body tensed to push him away, instead, he cast her roughly away from him and said in a loud harsh voice, "No good, Regina, no good, I will not take you back."

She turned, startled, to see her aunt framed in the now open door, looking at her aghast, and her cousin, staring at her with shock.

"I'm terribly sorry," said the Duke, sweeping a bow to her aunt, "to discompose you good people. Allow me to introduce myself. Jason Thomas, Duke of Torquay," he went on, seeming very cold and contained. "Forgive me for this unseemly intrusion. But Regina had sent me a note of urgent import, and I came here posthaste. But," he said, his blue eyes cold and narrowed, "I found only that I was to receive the same message I have received before. I do apologize for entering your house unannounced, but she had said it was a matter of some secrecy. I beg your pardon, and will take leave of you now."

He walked to the door and hesitated for a moment, looking down into Regina's dazed eyes. "I'm sorry," he said in a clearly carrying stage whisper, "but it is over, Regina. I will not take you back. Your cousin looks like a good enough chap. Take care not to damage your future any further, my girl. For I will not acknowledge the child."

And with one more courtly bow and a set cold expression, he left.

She packed her things quietly but quickly, as her aunt insisted. She tried to shut out the sounds of abuse from her aunt, but still some of the words drifted through. ". . . Butter wouldn't melt in your mouth . . . sweet and quiet . . . battening on our largesse . . . throwing

out lures to my son, and with a bastard already well on
its way. . . ." She had to carry her own traveling case
to the door. Belinda was nowhere to be seen. Regina
felt she had already gone, counting the coins she had
earned.

She wore a cloak, and was glad of the hood which
concealed her face, for she did not want her aunt to see
her tears as she said again, yet again, "I know you will
never believe me, but it was not so. It is not so." Harry
only stood and stared at her as though she were from
some foreign land.

When the door slammed shut behind her, she lifted
the case and descended the steps. At the bottom of
them, when she reached the street, she felt someone
take the grip from her frozen fingers, felt a hand propel
her toward the street, and was roughly pushed into the
carriage. She sank back against the cushions and saw
him sitting across from her, smiling, smiling happily in
the darkened coach.

"You see, Regina," he said in that curiously confiden-
tial whisper that she had shivered in remembrance of,
"you see how very simple it was?"

VI

"I do not understand, I cannot understand," she said
slowly, addressing him, looking toward the dim blur of
his face in the shadowy interior of the carriage. They
traveled unhurriedly on through the streets of town,
the well-sprung coach swaying only slightly, and she
had gotten a little time to collect her wits; so she went
on in a low voice, almost reflectively, "You know, there
are times, usually times of stress, when one is haunted
by bad dreams."

"My governess was of the opinion that they were
brought on by a bad conscience, or a surfeit of sweets

ingested before bedtime," he said conversationally, relaxing against the plump cushions.

"No," she shook her head, "no, that is not what I'm trying to say. In these troubled dreams, there is often a figure . . . or an object, something that would be quite benign, actually harmless in a waking state. But in these dreams, this object is invested with all sorts of sinister, dreadful terror. One does not know what sort of harm it betokens, but one knows it would be ruinous to oneself, and so throughout the dream, one runs from it. But, even in crowds of people, even alone in a locked room, somehow, by the magic of dreams, it comes through, it confronts . . . you can never escape it."

"An object?" he said with amusement.

"Anything, I suppose it is different for each dreamer . . . anything from a table to an owl to a mouse, but the terror comes from the fact that you know it is malevolent, and you do not understand why it constantly pursues you, or what harm it means, and why you cannot escape it."

"But I am neither a table nor a mouse, Regina, and I mean you no harm. But yes, your analogy holds in one respect, you cannot escape me," he mused in a gentle voice.

"And if," she went on, lost in her train of thought, "you have not already been fortunate enough to waken, shivering in terror at your close call with danger, and if you go on dreaming, there are times when you turn and face the pursuer. But no matter what you do, it is unswervable. If you hack at it, the pieces rise to chase you; if you set it afire, it follows you in flames, it is indestructable, it is relentless. But it all is only a dream; through it all, some part of you knows that it is only a dream, for no living creature could be that deficient of reason, that implacable. A living creature could be reasoned with," she said, staring hard at him.

"Why, what interesting dreams you have, Regina. You must tell me more about them some time," he yawned.

"Why?" she asked, fighting back the tears, for somehow she knew that tears would be her undoing, that tears would disable her.

"Why?" he smiled again. "Perhaps eventually even constant lovemaking becomes fatiguing. We must talk at some time."

"You know what I have asked," she said, sitting up as straight as she could in the shifting vehicle. "Why have you done all this? What joy is there in this? You do not even know me. You cannot care for me."

"What a strange child you are," he laughed, and rising gracefully, he swung himself over to sit beside her. He settled back again, his pale head resting against the squabs, took one of her cold hands in his, and idly traced a pattern on the palm of it with one long finger.

"Of course," he said soothingly, in his normal clandestine whisper, "I do not care for you. Why should I? I care for very few people, Regina. In point of fact, I care for none. But the joy in it? Ah, then, there's a different story. I don't care to repeat myself, but you do undervalue your attractions. You are very lovely. Very new. Very desirable. I wanted you when I saw you. So I set out to get you. There is joy in getting what you desire, Regina. And as for other joys . . . you will come to understand them, too. I shall see to that."

"No," she cried, trying to snatch her hand away, but he only held it the tighter, in a surprisingly strong grip.

"No," she continued, but more quietly, trying to keep her voice even. "I will not find joy with you, Your Grace. There is no joy for a prisoner, for an object, for a creature that is fashioned to serve someone else's desires. It was not for this that I was born, and educated, and live."

"How well you speak," he commented, placing a light congratulatory kiss upon her wrist. "It will be such a diversion, after all these years of hearing nothing but giggles and sighs and ladylike sobs of mournful protest. You speak almost as well as a man. It will be a novelty to make love to a woman who seems to have a man's mind. Perhaps it will be the best of all possible things. But as for your protests, Regina, I hesitate to contradict such an enlightened mind, but you do not know of what you speak in that case. You are ignorant of all the things that I am master of. You are, since you do seem to enjoy analogous reasonings, rather like a newly hatched chick who asks the hawk what possible joy he finds in soaring. You will understand," he said, moving quietly close to her.

She could feel the warm dry heat that seemed to emanate from him and, forcing herself to look directly at him, not to shrink back, as she felt he expected her to, she said, "But there are creatures who were not born to fly, who were never intended to do so."

"Oh, but you forget our tender parting kiss that your aunt interrupted, Regina, I think you, at least, were intended to soar," he chuckled.

"Can't you understand," she cried, raising her voice for the first time, "that this is so wrong, so ridiculous for me? I do not want to be your mistress, or your diversion, or your desire, or anything to you. I only want to be let alone. I want to live my own life."

"And a good life it will be," he said, reaching out to smooth back a lock of her hair. "Why you shall have fine clothes, and a lovely place to live, and jewels, yes especially emeralds to go with your eyes, and congenial company. And when it ends, a tidy income to see you on to whatever your own desires will be."

"None of which I want," she raged, brushing his hand away. "If I cared for you, still I would not want those things. But I will not be forced into a life of servitude, a life which is supported by selling myself. I would sooner cut off an arm or a limb to sell, than sell my entire self for what you consider luxuries."

He looked at her with a growing puzzlement, his wide blue eyes suddenly deeper, a curious expression in them.

"I did not expect any of this," he said looking into her face closely, "when I planned this. You speak to me as if we were equals. Where are your womanly graces, Regina? Why do you not cry, or threaten, or rage, or bargain with me? Why do you not say, 'Not emeralds, sir, if you please, diamonds.' Or, 'Oh pity, sir,' or, 'Think of me poor mum, sir, who'll support her while I'm gone?' or even, 'What of my reputation, Your Grace,

however shall I marry now?' But no, you don't say a
word that I expect."

For a moment, Regina was taken aback. For it was
true. Why hadn't she struggled or screeched, she wondered with sudden shock? She had entered the coach as
timidly as a mouse and had sat and prosed on to him as
though they were on their way to an afternoon tea.
Perhaps it was because she knew herself guilty for
attending the Opera that night in the first place, and
could not find it in her heart to blame him for his
original wrong conclusion about her. But he had done a
dreadful, immoral unthinkable thing and she should be
roundly denouncing him and shrilling at him now. But
perhaps she hadn't because after all those conflicting
dreams of him, she thought of him as someone she could
sit and talk and reason with as though she had known
him forever. But that was foolish, for nothing he had
done since that first meeting had given her an ounce of
reason to trust him. Before she could order her whirling
thoughts, he moved closer and all thoughts vanished as
she realized how very near he was to her in the darkened coach.

"Why," he laughed, "here we are, in the midst of a
daring infamously vile abduction, and you sit there and
discourse at me, you reason and explain as if we were in
a schoolroom. Has it not occurred to you that you are in
the fell company of a vile seducer, a man without conscience, a man who has spent the better part of his busy
day daydreaming about the indignities he will soon visit
upon your person? No, you simply sit there and discuss
the situation with me, as if we were kindred spirits. As
if we were old companions met to thrash out philosophi-
cal questions about good and evil. Oh you are a delight!"
he crowed, and reached out for her.

But she put out two hands and held him off, saying
quickly, "But perhaps we *are* kindred spirits. For I was
not raised to have any more feminine graces than you
were."

He sat back and looked at her.

She pressed what she hoped was her advantage. "Only
think," she pleaded, "I may be just a commoner, of

mixed birth and shadowy antecedents, but I was not educated as were the other women of your world. I do not know their guiles or ambitions. I have been reared with different expectations. I was raised to think of myself always with honor, with dignity. Only for one moment put yourself in my position. Would you sell all your principles for a jewel? For a comfortable set of rooms? For a sum of money? Your Grace, only answer me one question please, only one, and then I will . . . then I can speak no more. You have been trained to give. You have been used to taking. But could you ever . . . sell yourself? And if you could not, can you try to understand why I cannot?"

She felt him almost physically recoil at her words. Then he began to laugh. A different laugh than that which she had heard before. A rich, full laugh. When the laughter subsided, he straightened and seemed to stare off into space. Then he turned again to her.

"Well done, oh well done, Regina," he breathed, a new and excited look on his face. "You have somehow managed to awaken the one last little remnant of that forgotten childhood quality in me—Honor. I did not think that any of it remained. And a certain sporting instinct. No, I should not say gallantry, I'm sure I never had that, but a certain sporting instinct, yes. You are an original. That face, that lovely hair," he mused, "the clean sweet scent of you . . . I do still want you very much, Regina. Perhaps now more than ever. It's pity you weren't born a titled lady. I swear I'd even propose on the spot if you were. But," he said half to himself, "delayed pleasure is often the best. Yes," he seemed to decide suddenly, "yes, it will be most amusing. Regina," he breathed, "I shall make a bargain with you. But one I am sure of winning. Still, it is a sporting gesture."

"A bargain?" she whispered, fearful of another of his swings of mood, yet hopeful for the first time.

"Yes, a bargain," he smiled, the same smile of inner satisfaction that she so frequently noted on his face. "I shall let you go. Go free, and completely on your own. I shall set you down in the midst of town alone. Completely free, as you asked. You have certain handicaps. No home to return to. No finances. You see, I did my research well. No family. Quite a dreadful situation for a young woman to find herself in, isn't it? But still, you have certain advantages as well. You have beauty and wit and a quick mind. But your greatest handicap will be that you are overburdened with a sense of honor. You will not sell yourself, you say. At least not to me."

As she began to speak, he silenced her with a wave of his hand. "Yes, I accept that you will not sell yourself to any other. After all, I have some pride in my external appearance. After all, there are some things that both my mistresses and my mirror do tell me. I am not yet aged. Or fat, or gouty. And although I cannot say why, I am yet unafflicted with the pox. Though not from want of opportunity. Has that thought been troubling you? Let me reassure you, this poor croaking voice of mine is a family characteristic, no foul disease yet taints my body. I shall not infect you with my embrace. Which is more, little innocent, than can be said for most of the men in my position these days. As for what foul breath taints my mind? That, no doctor could diagnose. I have gone beyond libertine, yet not—although that is open to argument—completely degenerate. At least," he laughed ruefully, "I have not yet lusted after exotic animals, or my fellow man, or formed a passion for any breastless children. You do not understand completely? All to the better. At least I know that you do not find me loathsome . . . physically, that much I do know, whatever you do think of my poor warped mentality.

"So. I shall set you free and you shall be as a little green-eyed fox in the forests of London. I shall keep my hounds on your traces. I shall know every moment of how you fare. Wealth has given me access to Argus eyes. Here, in the center of town, I shall loose you. What a fine game!"

"I may leave now?" she asked quietly. He raised himself and went to the window of the coach to signal to an unseen outrider and whisper some instructions. Settling back again, he went on, with laughter in his voice, his face showing bliss.

"Oh yes," he said, "but . . . oh, come now, don't look so crestfallen, you knew that there would be a 'but,' didn't you? But then, you must find a proper place for yourself. A safe harbor. A moral," he emphasized, "and safe harbor. If I find that within a certain period of time you have done so, I shall wish you joy, and keep only these tender moments safely locked away in my memory. But if you have not, I shall come for you again. And this time, Regina, you may play Sherharazade with a thousand tales of morality and honor and truth, it will not avail you. You will have failed the test. You will be mine to do with as I wish."

"How long a time?" she asked.

"Oh ho," he grinned. "Since I am the rulemaker, the inventor of the game, and the scorekeeper, that is my concern. Your concern is to prove to me that we are indeed equals. Or rather, since you have attacked me on the subject, that you are superior to me, if not in birth, then in that elusive thing—Honor. That you can forge a decent place for yourself in this world without using all those 'feminine' graces that you claim to be unaware of. That you can, homeless, friendless, moneyless, keep yourself from starvation with 'honor.' Give me a living definition of the word, Regina. For I swear, I have never seen it in a creature as lovely as yourself. It is a bargain? The game is to go on?" he asked.

She nodded, and they rode in silence for a small space of time. Then the carriage slowly came to a halt.

"Good," he said, looking out the window. "Not a back slum, not a place filled with terrors, simply the heart of town. You may go, Regina, and begin the game. But first," he added, as she rose to go to the door, "we must seal the bargain."

He pulled her down to his side, with the unusual strength she had noted before, and raising himself so that he looked down into her bewildered eyes, he spoke so softly, she had to strain to hear him.

"All bargains should be sealed with a kiss, Regina, haven't you heard of that cliché?"

He brought his lips down to her again, and though she tried to remain passive, she again felt the curious

response that came involuntarily to her. When he raised
his head, he smiled so tenderly that she felt confused
again. "Ah, how I despair of letting you go so soon,
even if it will only be for a little while," he sighed.

"But still, a bargain is struck, and the game is begun,
little fox. When I return, there will be time enough for
both of us. And I have the uneasy feeling that you will
take up a great deal of my time in the future. Still," he
said, letting her go, "the game is on . . . go then,
Regina." And he swung open the carriage door and
stepped out.

He handed her down, and she paused on the deserted
street and looked at him.

"Do go, go," he said kindly, "or I shall change my
mind. But remember," he called after her retreating
back, "I shall be watching. Make it a fair game. A good
game."

The Duke sat lost in thought as the carriage conveyed
him home. He had already given certain instructions to
the outrider, and he knew that there were other plans
to be made and arranged for when he reached his house.
Many diverse plans and counterplans. But for now he
sat back, the usually pleasantly amused face set in unfamiliar harsh lines. He was remembering, and he did
not care to do that.

The evening had not turned out the way he had planned
it. That was a novelty. For many years now, he had not
been surprised by the results of any of his machinations.
He had a quick mind, and was a good judge of character, and seldom found himself engaged in anything that
he had not prefigured in his mind. This evening, even
now, he had thought he was to have begun the girl's
education. Even now, he sighed, he had supposed that
he would have been slowly stripping off her gown, slowly
preparing her for the hours that he had reserved for her
company in his arms. But somehow, she had turned him
around, she had made him doubt himself, she had convinced him momentarily of her sincerity, she had somehow engineered the idea of the incredible game he had
invented.

He had not wanted to force her. He had never had to force any woman. The thought appalled him. He had always chosen women for both their beauty and their availability. There was, of course, always that initial coy show of reluctance; he expected it. It was all part of the game. But every initial protest he had ever encountered had always resulted in speedy, joyful participation. But she had gazed at him with those incredibly innocent eyes and spoken in that well-bred careful little voice and he had found that, amazingly, he wanted her good opinion. And though he would have sworn she was no better than any other female he had ever desired, he had hesitated to force the issue. How could he have believed her, he wondered, a chance-met female nonentity who had gone on the prowl for a protector at the Opera? But she had refused him. That was irrevocable fact.

"I am still in control, though," he brooded. "And the game will be a brief one. And the ending will make it all worthwhile," he reassured himself. "It will be great sport," he tried to tell himself. But still he was uneasy. Had she bested him? Was he still in control?

He did not care for uncertainty. He had planned his life to avoid it at all costs. He was not a good gambler. He lived a life free of risks. Or at least any of the risks that he cared about. His body, his reputation, were not things he especially valued in any sense. His inner person was the only untouchable thing he cared for. And he had made sure that that small unexamined part of himself was never threatened in any of the ways he threatened his person.

It had always been so. Even as a boy, when he scaled the tallest trees, took up any outrageous dares that the other boys flung at him, he never worried about the possibility of physical harm. And having no trepidation, and a naturally agile body, he had never come to harm. He had been forced to prove his physical superiority, for even then, his delicate, almost pretty face had marked him as prey to older boys. But once having confronted him, no other boy had ever dared him again. The slight frame concealed a wiry, hard body, and when he fought, he fought full out, with no fear of damage or even death. Even the much older and stronger of his peers quickly learned that he was in earnest when he threatened them. He was never bullied or taunted about his appearance more than once.

He had also learned early on how to conceal his heart. How to conceal it so well that he soon forgot about its existence altogether. His father, a nobleman many years older than his wife, had been a settled bachelor when the young girl whose beauty captivated him entered upon his life. After the birth of his first and only child, his wife had informed him that conception of another child would surely take her life. Confused and torn between desire and suspicion, the elderly Duke had taken refuge in his estates till a lingering disease forced him into seclusion. He had not even lived to see his son's fifth birthday.

But his youthful wife had no use for seclusion. She dreaded even one waking moment solely in her own company. She was as beautiful a woman as her son was as a boy. Pale and fair-haired, she too had an air of deceptive fragility. But her many lovers soon learned that she had an indefatigible strength. And a bottomless void to fill with compliments, and attentions and flattery. Even when she tiptoed into the nursery on rare occassions to see how her son was growing, she would whisper to him, "Jason, love. Do you like Mama's gown? Is her hair pretty?" And no comment of his that did not center upon her was attended to.

When the young Duke was let out of lessons early one afternoon in his tenth year, he had run away from his protesting governess and raced unthinking into his mama's gilded rooms to tell her of his progress in his studies. Paused in the doorway, he had seen for the first time how very much she required personal attention, and also how exactly a man and a woman could find uses for each other. The governess had held his head for an hour until he could retch no more. But he never mentioned the matter to his lovely mama again, and she had never asked him if he thought she was pretty in the head groom's arms, or if he had admired the paleness of her face against the head groom's dark groin. She had avoided him after that. And he had been sent willingly away to school.

She avoided him further, in his sixteenth year, when he had begun to show the promise of a radiant manhood even more spectacular than her blooming womanhood had been, when she discovered that the rash that had plagued her for years was, in fact, the French pox. Then she had taken herself off to foreign quacks, and spas and resorts, forcing herself to drink the foul concoctions, be immersed in evil-smelling baths, and have strange scented unguents rubbed into her skin, to alleviate the spread of the disease. In her son's eighteenth year she had dosed herself, and had drunk one bottle of laudanum and was halfway through the second when the sleep she sought had finally mercifully come.

The young Duke of Torquay had learned, from an early age onward, the uses of strength, the necessity for keeping one's own counsel, the importance of lacking affections, the frivolous nature of beautiful women, and the importance of living a life that held no surprises. There was only one lesson more that he felt the need of learning.

In his nineteenth year, when he took himself and his assorted servants off on a grand tour, he had made certain inquiries. One soft June night, in Paris, he had found himself in the ornately gilded, perfumed boudoir of a famous courtesan. She was not the first he had visited, nor was she, even then, nearly the first woman he had known. His astonishingly good looks and pleasing manners had already given him entree into many such rooms, redolent of perfumes, rooms so reminiscent of his departed Mama's. And rooms that even his Mama wouldn't have dared to enter.

The woman had proven her worth, proven the reliability of her growing reputation, and an hour later, when she had turned to look up into the sweet face of the boy who lay propped up on one elbow, toying with a strand of her dampened hair, she had cooed, "You are satisfied, *mon Brave?* It was all you expected?" And had been shocked when he had merely smiled and, in that hoarse voice that had intrigued her so, had replied in his perfect French, "No, *ma cherie*, no, not at all."

"But this I cannot understand," she had cried, shocked. "Where have I failed? Where have I offended?" He had merely laughed and shaken his head.

"No, you misunderstand," he had said, staring at her intently. "What you do, you do very well. There may well be none better. But that is not what I came for."

"Well," she had said, much affronted, "if your taste runs to young boys, you have certainly come to the wrong place."

"No," he had laughed, "it is not that. Listen *cherie*, I came for something else, something very simple, that you have not given me. I have a small proposition to make to you," he had begun.

"No, no, no," she had cried violently. "If it is pain you want, you must go elsewhere."

"Listen," he had said seriously, "this is my request. You are famous for what you do, and, as I said, you do it very well indeed. But be honest, my little French *amie*," (and here she smiled, for this little cockerel, with his spare white body, to call her lavish configurations "little" was very amusing, but pleasant), "all that you have done tonight, you have done for me. And it was well done. But, to be honest, *cherie*, I have done nothing for you but enrich your purse and continue your fame. You did all the work, my friend, I have only responded to your excellence. And that is what I have always done. And, with your clients, my dear, what you have always done. Tonight, however, I seek more. I want you to show me, to tell me, to instruct me, as to what I can do for you. How I can make those little sighs and groans reality, how I can please you."

She had stared at him in incomprehension.

"Try to think," he had said, a half smile playing about his lips, "of what you like your own lover to do for you . . . your pander, or your lady friend, I do not care to know. But only think of your own pleasure, and instruct me in the mysteries of your own body. That is what I require. I will pay well for this knowledge. And if you are a good teacher, I will learn quickly."

The novelty of his request caught her interest, it was the first time—and she had long past forgotten all her first times—she had been offered such a challenge. And he was good looking enough, she thought, to make such a venture amusing.

At first, it had been a novelty for her, almost embarrassed as she patiently instructed him. When she finally showed him, almost as if he were a physician, where the ultimate seat of all her pleasures resided, she had felt a little foolish. But he had been such an eager, pleasant child about it. He had eventually laughed. "After all that, this? This little hidden part? This valiant little imitation is the answer?" And she had, as the long night went on, showed him all, all she knew, till near dawn, exhausted, she understood that there was nothing left to explain to him. He knew her body and her responses now almost better than she did.

Resting her head against his chest, she had whispered, "You have certainly learned quickly. But why did you wish to learn such things?"

"Because," he had said, planting a kiss upon her dampened brow, "I did not know. Because, it is only good tactics to know your enemies' weaknesses, and because," and here he whispered so low that she was never quite sure that she had heard him correctly, "because such knowledge is power."

She had bade him farewell in the morning, and because he had given her a night that she was not to forget for many years, she had implored him, "Only seek out clean girls, *mon Brave*, do not infect yourself, take care of yourself." And he had answered quietly, "I always take care of myself, I lead a charmed life."

Armed with all his various knowledges, he had gone on to lead a daring life. He had gone from excess to excess, and had never swerved from whatever course his talents led him surely to. He had never cared for any opinion but his own. Except perhaps, for the once, on the one occasion of the short-lived marriage he had undertaken. When he had achieved the age of twenty-seven, he had for the first time acted the way a gentleman of title and possessions was expected to. As he had decided that it would be well to ensure the succession, and provide an heir to the fortunes he enjoyed, he had offered for the leading debutante of the season.

She was a pretty enough little thing, he had felt, a bit giddy and light of mind, but during the two times he had conversed and danced with her, her airy little laugh and fine-boned face had pleased him. And her fortune and birth were of the highest available that season.

He had quickly discovered, during the brief months they had together, that there was no commonality of interests between them at all. If her perception was not nearly so lively as her flighty demeanor had led him to expect it might be, he had at least held out some hope that there might eventually be some common ground that they might find so that the union might not be as unendurable as he was fast finding it to be. But all his arts could not move her to a natural, easy communication with him. She seemed, instead, to fear him, avoid him, and merely endure his company.

With all his wide experience, he still could find no way to wrest any real pleasure from the rigid little body she so dutifully presented him with each night. Nor could he, despite his unusual spell of fidelity and concentration, bring her to any enjoyment of the art he had mastered so long ago.

The last night he had tried, he had slipped into her bedroom as usual, after she had dismissed her servants, and quietly approached the wide bed where she lay, wreathed in white lace. As he had gently drawn the covers back, she had, for the first time, smiled as she greeted him. He had responded to that one gesture of friendship with ardor, but she had pushed him away and pouted. "Jason, my dear, that isn't really necessary any longer."

He had drawn away and asked, with a teasing note in his voice, "Why, have you found another diversion for these hours?"

"No," she laughed with genuine joy, "but we really don't have to . . . do that dreadful business any longer. I am with child already, you see." He stood back from her. "Dreadful?" he had asked with genuine surprise.

"Well," she had smiled, "but not when I understood that you must if you were to have an heir, then I could see that the thing was inevitable. But now that you have accomplished it, what would be the sense of it? I'm not one of your fancy pieces, Jason. There's no pleasure in such degrading things for me. Oh yes, I do know about all those . . . females, and I do understand why you must seek them out . . . now, more than ever, I suppose I do understand. But pray understand that I do not mind, so long as you are circumspect about it. And you needn't bother with me now that you are to have the heir you desired."

He stood looking at her for a long moment, and then with that strange half smile he so often wore, the one which frightened her so, he had said, "Needn't bother with you, my dear?" and had come closer to her. She shrieked and drew up her covers. "Jason!" she had gasped, "you forget, I am your wife! I am to bear your child. Do not attempt that vile business again! It has served its purpose. I am not to be disturbed in my mind, if the child is to be born aright!"

He had not disturbed her again. He had turned and left. He returned to her only when the child, a frail little girl that bore the stamp of her own face, had been born. He had stayed with her all during the time the child-bed fever had raged, and when it had taken her insubstantial body completely, he had stayed for her interment. Then, leaving the sickly child in the care of excellent wetnurses and staff, he had left again. And gone on to live his life as he had begun to live it before the mad notion of marriage had ever crossed his mind. He had gone on to excess, and the pursuit of self-satisfaction, and never again had cared for any other being's opinion but his own. And this philosophy, he felt, in its own way, had given him whatever happiness he felt he had the right to expect in the world he had made.

But this night, as he rode back to his house, he was disturbed. He had set out to accomplish one thing, he had begun another. He had named the game, but he had not really wanted to play it. He found himself, as he had said, now both scorekeeper and judge, inventor of the rules and keeper of the tally. But still, he had not planned it.

He'd been so sure that he was right. That the wayward chit with the glorious face and seductive eyes, newly on the town with no title, or family, or bonds, would have leaped at the chance to be his newest paramour. He had sworn he had seen the desire in her first glance at him. And he had been certain of it in her rush of response to that first kiss. That is what had armed him to go on to the lengths he had. She should have come to him willingly, with laughter at his daring and anticipation of her adventure with him. Perhaps it was just some new game she played to pique his interest and raise her fee. He would welcome a new game. He was, in truth, very weary of the old ones. But possibly, just possibly, she was in earnest. She had cast that stranger, doubt, into his mind. And so he had gambled.

He had acted impetuously. He did not like to gamble, for in gambling there was always the possibility of losing. He would not lose. He could not, he thought fiercely, lose. This, then, was the final honor left, the final one he admitted to. He would not lose.

VII

St. John Basil St. Charles relaxed against the cushions of his carriage and felt at peace, for once, with his world. The hour was late, the wind outside was wickedly cutting, but here, snugged in his well-sprung conveyance, he was at ease, comforted, drained of tensions and desires. He was sated with wine, with food, with pleasure, and only awaited his bed.

Maria Dunstable, a passable dancer, late of the Opera, had been, he reflected, a very good choice. She had made herself at home almost at once in Annabelle's old quarters, making quick work of stowing her clothes, displaying her various mementos, permeating the rooms with her own individual blend of perfumes. She was quick-witted, adaptable, and still young enough to be amusing, while experienced enough to be adept. They had not yet reached the point in their relationship where she wheedled for more liberties or felt secure enough to run up more expenses. How long she would last in her new situation, St. John felt, depended entirely upon her own actions; for the moment, he was well pleased.

He allowed himself the luxury of a most undignified gaping yawn and a long stretch of his limbs; still, he thought, it would be good to sleep now in his own, undemanding bed. The gray light outside the carriage showed that another cold dawn was fast approaching. St. John alighted from his carriage and walked slowly to his front door, pausing for a moment to scent the air. Snow, he thought, was soon in coming. For a moment, he thought he saw a small shadow detach itself from the darkness near the alleyway leading to the back of his home, but then he shrugged and paid it no further attention. On such a chill night, there would be little likelihood of footpads, and certainly none who would dare frequent this fashionable street.

A drowsy footman opened the door for him, but no sooner had he flung off his cape when he was surprised to see his man, Hilliard, enter the hallway, dressed as if it were broad daylight, and waiting for him.

"Surely you have mistaken the hour, Hilliard," St. John drawled. "It lacks five in the morning, not five in the afternoon."

"I understand, My Lord," Hilliard replied. "But there was a message for you, My Lord, that I felt might not wait until a retarded hour."

St. John gave him a quick sharp look. Hilliard was no fool; only a matter of importance would receive such unusual treatment.

"What is it, then?" he asked, suddenly feeling the languor dissipating and an uneasy feeling of alarm coming over him.

"A young person came here this evening, sir," Hilliard said impassively, "who looked quite the lady. However, she would neither give her name nor state her business.

She would only give me a message she said was to be hand-delivered only to Your Lordship. And she asked if she might wait for your arrival, even though I explained that it might well be late, or even this day when you finally arrived. Nonetheless, she was adamant, and insisted upon waiting."

St. John put out his hand to receive the small slip of paper Hilliard offered. He scanned it quickly, and it made him draw in his breath in a short gasp. For the message contained only two words scrawled upon it. It read only "George Berryman."

St. John stiffened. He shot a quick look at Hilliard. How much did the man know of his private affairs, how much did he surmise, to understand that these two simple words would indeed be of paramount interest to him? For George Berryman, St. John knew, was dead. Dead and buried these many weeks. Mrs. Teas had given him the hurried news when he last had visited the house, and he had bowed and, stating his condolences, had slipped away, as he had always intended to, never to return. That phase of his life, although entertaining, profitable, and much relished, was over with now. Over with the instant that George Berryman had drawn his last breath. But now, who wished to revive the matter?

Was it an attempt at blackmail? Or was there some unfinished business about which George Berryman himself had given directions that the Marquis of Bessacar should be sought out after his death? That would be unforgivable, and dangerous to his standing. St. John stood still, his eyes still bent upon the little note in his hand. He brought his hand to a fist over it, and then inquired, with deceptive calm, "And where is the young person now, Hilliard?" For he thought, it was not without the realm of possibility that Hilliard had some notion as to what his actions these past years were, they had lived in such close proximity. But still, he trusted the servant, and had known him for too many years to think that this was a ploy on the man's part.

"She waits outside, My Lord," Hilliard answered, and seeing the swift surprise in his master's eyes, continued, "As she had neither a maid nor a companion with her, and as I did not recognize her, I thought it best that I not allow her entry into your home, My Lord. And since she insisted upon waiting, I gave her leave to wait in the alleyway. If she is still there, she will have been waiting for some several hours, sir. Shall I fetch her? Or do you wish to let the matter pass? I did not presume to attempt to foresee your answer."

The Marquis relaxed. No, Hilliard was not part of this. He was too shrewd to wade into the murky waters of blackmail. This woman was obviously no confederate of his. He had signaled that to the Marquis by not allowing her inside the house. And he certainly would not have forced a confederate of his to wait in the street for all those hours on such a bitter night. By his decision to allow the creature to stand in the cold night, he had both signaled his innocence of the affair to his master and washed his hands of the situation, even though he had certainly known of its importance to the Marquis.

"I am intrigued, Hilliard, at the mysterious aspects of the affair," St. John said, pretending to stifle a small yawn. "So disregard the lateness of the hour. Lay a fire in the study and permit the woman to enter."

St. John was comfortably ensconced in a chair by the fire, a dressing gown drawn over his clothes, a brandy in his hand, when Hilliard announced the young woman. "The person to see you, My Lord," Hilliard sniffed, doing the best that he could at an introduction and having no name to go by.

St. John heard his man very well, and heard the door quietly close, and by the rustle of a dress, knew that the woman was within the room, but he played for time and ascendancy in the matter by continuing to stare into the fire for several moments, his back to visitor. When he felt that enough moments had ticked by, he said, without bothering to turn his head, "State your business, please. The hour is late, and I have only admitted you because your note was so cryptic. Begin, and tell me all that you would not tell my man."

A slight pause followed, and then he heard a soft, well-bred voice say, in a hesitant tone, "I am sorry to disturb you at this hour. But indeed, I did come earlier,

but you were not yet arrived home. I .... I do not
know you, Your Grace, and neither do I understand
why I was told to seek you out . . . but my late uncle,
George Berryman, told me shortly before his death that
if I should ever need . . . advice, you would stand as
my . . . advisor."

At the word "uncle," St. John turned around quickly,
with a frown, to finally see who this visitor was. She
stood partially in the shadows, but what he could see
took his breath away for the second time that night. He
gestured to her impatiently. "Come close to the fire," he
commanded. She moved forward slowly.

It was strange, he thought, that he should recognize
her almost at once, although he had only seen her the
once, and so fleetingly. Although she was no longer
dressed with the elegant care that she had been that
night at the Opera, indeed, she seemed almost somber
in the dark cape she clutched to herself, her worn traveling case standing by her side, there was no mistaking
the high cheekbones, the small tilted nose, the dazzlingly
white skin, and most of all, the luminous dazzling green
eyes.

He rose and quickly ushered her to a chair near the
fire. Her hand, he noted, was cold as a dead woman's.
He poured her a glass of brandy and told her to drink it
quickly, standing over her as she did so.

"George Berryman, your uncle?" he breathed, watching her closely as she coughed against the unusual taste
of the drink. "Drink it, drink it," he commanded. "You're
chill as stone."

"I would not have had you wait outside on such a
night if I had but known, but my staff has explicit
instructions, and you refused to give your name."

"I understand," she said quietly, still sitting upright.
"You need not concern yourself. My actions were . . .
unusual. But if I might explain, you will see that I had
no other course open to me."

He drew a chair up beside her, and watched her,
fascinated by those expressive green eyes, and well
caught by the implicit drama of the situation. George
Berryman's niece? He could hardly credit it. She was a

magnificently lovely creature, with the airs and manner of a lady of Society. He felt a familiar racing of his pulses. "Take your time," he said in a comforting tone, "and tell me what the matter is about."

She hesitated once again, and then looked into the gray eyes opposite her. He was a formidable looking man, she thought, and faintly familiar looking as well, with his high Indian cheekbones, those changeable, heavily lashed gray eyes, and the perfectly sculptured, almost classical mouth. But when the mouth tightened, and the eyes turned to a cold steel hue, she felt he might be very intimidating. Still, there was a naggingly familiar cast to his features . . . although, she felt, she surely would have remembered such a fine looking man if she had seen him before. But she had expected him to be older, at least her uncle's age. She was chilled through her entire body. How many hours had she waited in the dark and wind-filled alley, shifting from foot to foot to keep her blood moving? But she had not known where else she could have gone. After she had stumbled away from the Duke, she had wandered the streets for a time, until the frightening moments when a group of young fashionably dressed men had accosted her, demanding her price, her rate schedule. She had fled them, and finding herself alone, had been forced to decide upon a course of action, any course of action.

She did not doubt that the Duke was serious at whatever strange game he had begun. He frightened her with his implacable surety, his nightmare power, and his mad conviction that this was a fair "game." She had no home to return to, no funds to see her through to Canterbury, not even enough funds or knowledge to secure a respectable lodging for the night. She was, as the Duke had said, singularly weaponless in this great city. But then, she had remembered what her uncle had said, she had remembered the name of the Marquis of Bessacar, and as much as she had hated to force herself upon the goodwill of a stranger, still she had reasoned, her uncle would not have directed her so without a good reason.

Taking all her courage, she had inquired as to his

whereabouts from street vendors she had seen, and while some had chased her away with lewd comments about her state, for she had quickly realized that without an escort she was as much as advertising herself upon the streets at this hour, finally a flower vendor had taken pity upon her and given her the direction of his house. After she had delivered her message to his man, she had no choice but to hastily scribble her uncle's name upon the paper and wait for his return.

Now, with the unfamiliar liquor warming her veins and giving her false courage, and the fire comfortably thawing her, she drew in a breath and began to explain the situation to the handsome, concerned gentleman who sat quietly, giving her his undivided attention.

He interrupted her story only the once, when she first mentioned the Duke. "Torquay!" he breathed, and then, when she paused, he said quickly, "Go on, go on."

When she had finished the tale, which was, she realized herself, almost fantastical in its brief telling, she sat back at last and closed her eyes wearily. Would he believe her? Indeed, she scarcely believed it herself. Somehow, the lateness of the hour, her own weariness, and the otherworldly quality of her situation made her for the first time feel volitionless, without concern, at last, for her own fate.

He sat silently for a few moments. Then he looked at the exhausted but still lovely face before him.

"Does anyone know of your whereabouts now?" he asked.

"No one," she answered quietly, "for I never heard your name at all except from my uncle's lips."

"Mrs. Teas never mentioned me?" he persisted.

"Never," she said softly. "And my aunt dismissed her soon after my uncle's death."

"This game of the Duke's," he asked slowly, "do I understand that he expects you to find a suitable place for yourself, alone and unaided, or he will claim you?"

"I can scarcely blame you," she said, opening her brilliant eyes, "for doubting that part of my tale, for I myself cannot credit it . . . it seems so melodramatic, so much of a. . . ." She fumbled for words, but he leaned forward and clasped her chill hand in his two warm ones.

"No, no," he smiled. "Though it may surprise you, I assure you, it does not seem at all fanciful to me. You see, I know Torquay. . . . No," he said comfortingly, as she gave a sudden start, "not precisely as a friend. I do not approve of his activities, although, I know them well. He is a man without scruple, a man who lives only for his own pleasures, a man . . . whose name is by-word for license. And a man with an eye for beauty—and my dear, it is only natural that he should have been drawn to your loveliness."

She withdrew her hands from his and sat up straight. "I go too fast," he mused to himself, and standing, went on, "Have you no other living relatives, then?"

"None that I know. None that I can apply to. Father and I lived a quiet life. The life of a schoolmaster's family . . . but no, you are not to think that I require . . . you to settle my future for me . . . no. You see, I still do not understand why Uncle gave me your name, and why he felt I should apply to you. But I only do so as a temporary measure. I need . . . a place to retreat to . . . only for a few days. For, you see, as I explained, my governess has a school that she now runs, and I feel sure that she will welcome me, but I cannot see how I may reach her. If I could but . . . borrow, only borrow, some funds from you. Only the fare to Canterbury. Once there, I could secure a position at the school, and repay you. I seek no charity. Only a loan," she insisted, color flooding her face in embarrassment.

"Let us have no talk of obligation," he said in a warm voice. "You did right to seek me out. Your uncle . . . was in the position to do me a great favor many years ago, when I was only a boy. I did tell him that I would be glad to reciprocate at any time. Any favor that I do for you, I consider in payment to that debt I owe to your uncle, Miss . . . Berryman?"

"It is Regina Analise Berryman, Your Grace," she said. "Only I do not wish to presume upon you for more than . . . a loan."

"Nonsense," he said heartily, in the most avuncular

fashion he was capable of. "I owe your late uncle a deal more than that." He turned and was lost in thought for a moment. And then he turned back to her.

"And I would very much like to thwart the plans of my good friend Torquay, for my own reasons. See here, Miss Berryman. . . . Ah, that is so stiffly formal, may I call you Regina, as I am sure your uncle would have given me leave to?"

"Of course," she said.

"Very well then, Regina. Now I have a very good idea. London is not a good place for you at present. Torquay is right, he does have eyes and ears everywhere. And for you to bound off to the wilds of Canterbury with only a hope of finding your governess well established and able to help you, is folly. I am sure that is one of the first places Torquay will seek you if he cannot find you in London. And if you haven't secured a position for yourself. . . ." He let the sentence hang. "But, if you follow my directions, we can establish you well enough to confound Torquay and ensure your own happiness in future."

She looked at him with hope.

"Come with me, Regina, now," he said. "We will ride to one of my estates, Fairleigh. You will have, I'm afraid, to travel with me in a closed carriage, but simply by being here this night I'm afraid we have already overstepped the proprieties. No matter, no one but you and I will know of it. And Hilliard, but I have his discretion. Once at my home, you can compose yourself. You can send a message to your governess and wait, in security, for her reply. If she cannot accommodate you, I have, I assure you, sufficient influence to procure you another position."

"But no," she quickly said, sitting up suddenly. "Indeed, I cannot . . . just cast myself upon your goodwill. It is not even a question of proprieties, My Lord. I did not come here for your absolute protection. I cannot expect you to accept full responsibility for my present position. No, no, I am sure that is not what my uncle desired, and neither is it what I expected."

"Regina," smiled the Marquis, taking one of her cold

hands, "allow me, please, to determine the extent of my debt to your uncle. And also, you must allow me to pursue the course to which my own sense of honor surely leads me, or would you also redefine my own code?"

She looked at the handsome, gently smiling face so near to her own, and felt the lateness of the hour and the effects of her long wait in the cold. In all conscience, she was wary of allowing a stranger to take the matter of her future out of her own hands, and yet, what other course was open to her? And as he said, it was not as if he were a complete stranger, and he had his own private score to settle with the author of her difficulties. Still, she felt she should at least offer up some further demurrers to this elegant benefactor.

"But," she added, "surely if the Duke discovers that I have gone with you, he will account it as a failure on my part. He was specific, in that I was to establish myself . . . without resorting to . . . 'Feminine wiles.' " She lowered her eyes.

"I assure you, Regina," St. John smiled, "that I do not put myself out so for any other female, no matter how distraught or lovely. No, I do this for your uncle. It is a debt of honor. Now, rest awhile, while I prepare for the journey. It would be well for us to leave before full light so that we will be unmarked."

She smiled in assent, and when he left the room, rested her head back against the chair, feeling oddly content, and secure, as she had not for a long time.

The Marquis of Bessacarr confounded his household by rousing them at an ungodly hour before dawn and ordering his traveling carriage prepared.

And before the first weak struggles of the sun to pierce the leaden morning skies had begun, he, accompanied by a caped and hooded figure, entered the vehicle which had, uncharacteristically, been drawn up to the back entrance. No one was there to see the strange departure except for Hilliard, who oversaw the procedure with customary aplomb, no one, that is, except for Hilliard and the barely discernible figure of a small street

boy, who stood seemingly engrossed in his task of
sorting through the curbside litter. And who left, at a
dead run, as soon as the carriage had turned the corner.

It was high afternoon when the dusty coach finally
turned into the long drive at Fairleigh. A few snow-
flakes were filtering down from the now solidly leaden
skies. St. John sat back and smiled as he gazed at his
companion. At his insistence, she now slept quietly in
the other corner of the carriage, a warm blanket tightly
secured around her. Lovely, he thought, even with those
remarkable eyes now shuttered. The thick rich chestnut
hair had spilled out a little from its tight confines and
traced an alluring shadow about her cheek. Yes, he
thought, all would go well.

She had surprised him on this journey. She was not of
his class, or of the Quality, that he knew just from a
quick précis on her antecedents. She arose from a family of merchants, from an admixture of the stolid
bourgoisie. She had even hinted of having had great-
grandparents who were such exotics as Armenians—or
was it Arabians?—and one branch of heritage that was
certainly of the Jewish merchant class. But, he thought,
she was like a swan arising from a barnyard nest. For
her face and figure clearly bore the evidence of the
fine-boned grace so desirable in his own class. She had,
before he had advised her to sleep, attempted to entertain him as they rode the long, tedious miles. Despite
her fatigue she had been in turn amusing, informed, and
gracious as she had sketched her history with candor
and charm. And her conversation was filled with wit,
and intelligence and thought, which, he chuckled, was
certainly not expected, particularly in young females of
his own class. She was an original. She seemed to think,
he mused, that it was proper, even desirable, for a
female to have the ease of conversation and scope of
knowledge that a man might wish to possess. She had
evidently been reared in a most peculiar fashion, by
that bluestocking of a governess whose protection she
so relied upon. But her beauty banished all thought of
straight-lacedness from his mind.

But, he warned himself, any attempt at physical close-
ness or gallantry on his part seemed to put her off, and
caused her to withdraw. Ah well, he sighed, surely that
was a barrier he could overcome. In those first moments, in his study, he had thought wildly of his options. Nothing could have been more fortuitous than her
arriving on his doorstep. It presented a perfect opportunity of settling the score with Torquay. What better
revenge than to steal her right out from under his nose?

But, he had cursed under his breath, there was Maria
Dunstable, newly ensconced in Annabelle's old quarters.
And there was not sufficient time to give her her congé
and vacate the premises. Neither was there time to
secure new apartments for his latest find. No, not safely, not with Torquay sniffing about. Then the thought
had come to him that Fairleigh would do well for all his
purposes. All the fashionable of his acquaintance would
be in town for the height of the season. The countryside
would be deserted. The old mansion would be empty
save for a skeleton staff of servants. There he could
board Miss Berryman. There he could woo her. There
he could win her away from the mad idea of incarcerat-
ing herself amid a pack of brats in the countryside.
There he could win her heart. There, eventually, he
knew, he could bed her. And then, he could return with
her, in triumph, to town, to flaunt his prize beneath
Torquay's envious and defeated eyes. And she would,
he thought, watching the quiet rise and fall of her breast,
probably last longer with him than any of the other
mistresses he had supported. He actually liked her. She
was innocent, as well, that he would swear to. It added
an extra fillip to the game. Yes, he smiled, Torquay, it
is an excellent game.

It was only when the carriage drew up to the front
entrance of the imposing brick manor that he gently
touched her hand, to rouse her. She woke instantly and
stared about her, as if she did not recall her surroundings. But once her eyes alit upon his face, she smiled.
"Are we arrived?" she asked, in a voice thick with
sleep. He restrained himself from bestowing the kiss

upon her flushed face that he felt himself yearning toward.

"Yes," he smiled. "We are here, you are safe."

But a moment later his eyes widened in shock as he saw the door swing open, and recognized Amelia Burden's tall form in the doorway, a pleased and quizzical expression upon her face. "Damn," he groaned to himself, for he had forgotten her plans to rusticate here at Fairleigh with his breeding sister. Forgotten, that is, that they would actually carry out the unusual plan at the very height of the social season. He hesitated; it was too late to whip up the horses and make for another destination. Too late to turn away without an explanation. He turned to Regina.

"My dear," he said, forcing his voice to remain calm, "leave everything to me. If I say a few things that . . . stray a bit from the truth, remember that I wish to keep your presence here a secret from Torquay. Servants do gossip. So bear with me, and only concur with me, and all will be well."

She nodded fearfully, and springing down lightly from the carriage, he offered her his hand. "I shall carry it off," he vowed. "And it might even add to the piquance of the situation to carry it off this way."

"Ah, Amelia." He bowed as he came abreast of her. "Allow me to present the daughter of a dear friend, who must, for the moment, remain a trifle 'incognito,' so I must call her 'Lady Berry.' All will be made clear to you in time, I promise. Unfortunately, her abigail took ill upon the road, so I must prevail upon you to procure her another. Lady Berry, may I present an old and dear friend, Lady Burden? I am sure you two will find much in common."

"Lady Berry," acknowledged Amelia, giving St. John a curious look. "Pray come in, it is freezing outside. You have arrived at a fortunate hour, we were just about to sit down to luncheon."

"Oh, please," Regina answered, with an odd look in her sleep-misted eyes, "no, no formality, please, you must call me only 'Regina.' "

VIII

Regina was unusually silent through most of breakfast. She sat quietly at the table, sipping at her coffee and watching the morning rituals of Fairleigh revolve about her. St. John, as he had insisted that she call him, sat at the head of the table, lightly fencing verbally with Lady Burden. His sister, Lady Mary, seemed to be devoting most of her time to consuming the enormous amount of delicacies upon her plate. "I'm eating for two, you know," she had simpered, and then proceeded to turn her entire attention to the task before her. What seemed to Regina's dazzled eyes to be a battalion of servants, silently glided in and out of the room, bearing in, and then away, platters of ham, kidneys, lamb cutlets, eggs, toasts, and muffins, and pots of coffee and chocolate.

Even in her extreme fatigue the day before, she had not failed to be impressed by the gracious opulence of the house to which the Marquis had brought her. He had explained her exhaustion lightly, and she had been, after only a brief introduction to his constantly smiling sister and her quizzical companion Lady Burden, immediately shown to a comfortable and lavishly furnished room. A tray had been brought to her by a quiet servant girl, and before she had had time to feel regrets or faint alarms about her surroundings, she had been assisted in disrobing and, soon after, fallen deeply asleep.

But this morning, she felt all the reactions to her new situation that she had not had the presence of mind to experience the day before. The household seemed to run on smooth, silent wheels. No one of the servants that she had encountered engaged her in the sort of conversations that the staff of her uncle's house had done. They all, from the parlormaid to the housekeeper, merely seemed to accept her and treat her with a deference that she did not know quite how to handle. Therefore, she had assumed a protective air of calm acceptance which, she was not to know, only served to verify in their minds the fact that however unorthodox her arrival had been, surely she was quite the Lady of Quality.

But she longed to speak to the Marquis alone, if only for a few moments, to discover how quickly he could dispatch the message she had written, immediately upon wakening, to her dear Miss Bekins. The sooner, she felt, that she was out of this house, no matter how comfortable it was, the sooner she could resume her own identity, the happier she would be. For it was not in her nature to act out a part, and the part she was forced into at present, inhibited her every movement.

She glanced over to Lady Burden. She had been listening to the conversation, and much admired the older woman's quiet wry humor, and would dearly have liked to have spoken to her without the stiff affect she now assumed. Lady Burden, she thought, had great presence and an air of deep and abiding calm. Regina sighed a little more deeply than she would have wished to.

"But my dear Regina," Lady Burden said quickly, "we have been neglecting you. . . ." She hesitated, for after all, she wondered, what was a safe subject to bring up? St. John had told her some mare's nest of a tale last night, which his sister had swallowed whole. But Mary was an avid reader of popular romances, and hadn't two wits to rub together in the whole of her dear little frivolous head, Amelia knew, so that any tale St. John had spun, from the most gothic to the most outrageous, would have served to satisfy Mary's never too powerful powers of comprehension.

But really, Amelia had thought, St. John had done it almost too brown. Lady Berry (a name that Amelia, who knew most of the important names of her contemporaries, had never yet encountered) was supposedly a young girl fleeing from a wicked cousin, who was trustee to her fortune, and who was attempting to marry her off to a spotty and dissolute young man before she reached her majority? Her birthday, St. John had explained, which was to be an occasion that would occur within a few months, would free her from her trustee's clutches. St. John, an old friend of her deceased father, he had explained, was only accommodating Lady Berry until he could contact her maternal uncle, who would then succor her until her natal day dawned.

Really, Amelia thought, only years of training had kept her from giggling right to his face. In the first place, the child would certainly not turn twenty-one till at least another winter and summer had come and gone, and in the second, she had ceased to believe in wicked trustees and evil stepmothers the moment she had abandoned her nurses' knee. What sort of a coil has St. John gotten into now, she wondered. And the poor lovely child, it is obvious that she is a lady, if not the "Lady Berry" St. John has dubbed her, and also very apparent that she is deeply unhappy—with both this masquerade and whatever else has actually happened to her.

"No, no, really," Regina said hastily. "It is only that I regret my appetite is not equal to the variety of good things that I see before me. You know, the feeling that you had as a child when there wasn't room for one more morsel, and then the most delicious desert was brought out?" She laughed.

"But my dear," Mary quickly put in, "we haven't any dessert at all this morning. Is it what you've been accustomed to?" she asked hopefully. "For indeed, I haven't heard of it before. But you can, I'm sure, make do with some sweet rolls and jellies. If you wish a dessert, however, I'm sure we can have one for you tomorrow."

"No, dear little dunderhead," St. John laughed. "That isn't what Regina meant at all."

"Well," said Mary, carefully wiping up the last traces of her creamed cutlets with a small piece of bread and popping it into her mouth, "I'm sure it might be a good idea at that. At any rate," she sighed, smiling what she hoped was the proper maternal smile and delicately patting her burgeoning belly, "I must ask you all to excuse me now, for the doctor said I must have my rest after meals." And, pushing away her chair, she rose as majestically as she could and left the room, listing slightly from side to side as she did so.

St. John laughed as she retreated. "My sister is a dear little widgeon, Regina, you must learn to take her exactly as she comes to you."

Regina wasn't sure as to whether she would allow herself the impudence of the smile that had been hovering near her lips, or whether she should rise to the defense of the Marquis's sister. Again, she felt wretched, not knowing exactly what her position here was to be.

"And now," began St. John, rising, "I do have business to attend to today. I'm sure you can find something to do today, Regina, until I return."

"But," Regina cried, rising even as he did, "if I might, that is to say, do you have a few moments, My Lo— Sinjin? There are a few things that I fear cannot wait until you return."

Amelia busied herself by peering down, with great interest, into the dregs of her chocolate. St. John glanced at Amelia quickly, frowned, and then said lightly,

"To be sure. Come into the study, Regina, and I'll see what sort of problems you feel have arisen."

Regina, looking helplessly back at Amelia, swiftly followed St. John's exit. Once seated opposite him in the luxuriously appointed study, she began at once, stammering,

"Your Grace, I simply cannot, cannot do it. I don't know what sort of story you've told Lady Burden and your sister, but I, I am no good at dissembling at all. And I haven't the faintest idea of how to go about as 'Lady Berry,' a young woman of fashion. And as I am to spend time with Lady Burden, please, can there not be a way that you can take her into your confidence? Else, I am sure it would be to both our advantages if you would just . . . send me off to Canterbury on the instant. I know, I just know that I will make a cake of myself. I am not fashioned to be an actress. Oh, and yes, here is the letter to be posted to Miss Bekins." Withdrawing it from her skirts, she went on hurriedly, "Still, if it is a choice between acting a part until I have her answer and going immediately perhaps it would be better not to post it at all, but rather to post me—with haste." And she laughed shakily.

He stared at her for a moment. In the early winter light that shone weakly through windows, she looked very young, very dewy, very vulnerable. Her pallor suits her, he thought, but then anything would. Yes, he sighed, looking into the candid widened green eyes, she would make a blunder. Amelia is too sharp for her. Some compromise with the truth must be made.

"Very well," he said, smiling, "I will speak to Amelia, but we needn't bother with altering one detail of the story with my sister, I assure you. She delights in the tale I have told her, and pays so little mind to reality in any case that it would only confuse her to be told aught else at this point. But Regina, I cannot tell *all*, for my own reasons—you must trust me—to Amelia. Please bear with the few, very few discrepancies I must include in your story. All right?"

She nodded. He took the letter from her outstretched hand, tapped it a few times on his own hand, and then rose and went to the door. He found Amelia pretending to be engrossed in a rapidly cooling muffin.

"Come girl," he laughed. "You have no more interest in consuming that than you have in partaking of plum pudding, at the moment. Come with me, and all your curiosity will be satisfied."

Once inside the study, St. John stood with his back to the nicely crackling fire and began to tell Amelia the true story of Regina's appearance.

"Only remember," he prefaced, "that I take you into our confidence at Regina's insistence. She will be here for a spell, and I believe wishes to be friends with you, only not on a note of deception. But we both trust your unswerving honesty, my dear; it is most important."

Amelia, too interested to take offense at St. John's tone, readily agreed to absolute secrecy. St. John went on with the story, but, Regina noted sadly, although he told mostly the bare facts of the matter, still he left her exact name and patrimony a secret. He would only say that while she was not "Lady Berry," he could not divulge her true name or circumstances. Only that he

did indeed owe her family a debt. He also said nothing
of her attempt to gain a position teaching with Miss
Bekins, rather only that she must remain in hiding from
Torquay until "a certain family member" of hers could
be located. Ah well, Regina thought, that much at least,
I can keep my lips closed about, although why he found
it necessary to dissemble about her family and plans for
the future, she could not fathom. Still, she thought, half
a loaf is indeed better than none.

"How enthralling!" Amelia said, her face animated.
"In hiding from Jason! Delightful!"

"You, you know him?" Regina asked, aghast.

"Indeed, who does not?" Amelia answered. "And although, yes, I agree that he is most probably totally
evil, and not at all the sort of fellow you should consort
with, forgive me, Regina, but I do hold a warm spot in
my heart for him."

"Wicked wench," St. John laughed. "Only you would
say that, you know. Is there anyone you despise at all
on the face of the earth?"

"Oh a great many, Sinjin, really, but not Jason, for
you see, he is the only man of my acquaintance to have
ever made a totally, neither financially nor matrimonially
induced, but gratuitous, indecent proposition to me. It
was wonderful for my vanity, although I do feel he
offered just to cheer me up. He does have excellent
taste in females, really."

St. John flushed. "Really, Amelia, I hardly know
whether to credit you or not. If it would cheer you, I
should have offered you just such an opportunity myself."

"Ah, but I should know for a certainty that you were
offering out of goodwill alone, Sinjin, whereas Jason did
it so beautifully that I shall never be sure of what his
intentions really were."

St. John bowed with a cynical smile.

"Amelia, my dear, I leave you to care for our little
fugitive, my only fears being that you will corrupt her
more completely than ever the Black Duke could."

"Never mind, Regina," Amelia smiled. "For I am
really a paragon of good taste, and for all my wicked
tongue, I blush to say that I have never overstepped

the bounds of propriety, no matter how much I may have longed to. Now that I am included in your confidence, I propose to entertain you without a shadow of hesitation. For Mary really does not need me at all, and I confess that until you arrived I was very angry with myself for consenting to accompany her here. It appears that all she requires is a stack of dreadful novels, a handy paper of sweets, and a large bed to doze in, without interruption from either her devoted husband or her assorted offspring. But with you here, we shall have a good time while Sinjin attempts to contact your relative. In fact, this very afternoon I shall take you on some calls to acquaint you with the local gentry."

"Is that wise?" Regina asked fearfully, her eyes involuntarily going to St. John's tall person lounging negligently by the fireplace.

"Of course," he reassured her. "After all, he does not know your direction, and even if he did discover it, even Torquay has the taste not to snatch you from Amelia's keeping. No, he will not presume to steal you away from here. Even he knows that a gentleman does not poach upon another gentleman's property."

Amelia shot him a curious look, but then, gathering herself and composing her features, she extended her hand to Regina.

"Come, Regina, let us leave this tiresome gentleman to his business for now. You must change clothes and accompany me, and I assure you, with the business I am about this afternoon, I shall be very grateful for your company."

St. John watched them leave, a calculating look coming into his eyes. Yes, he thought, it can be done, even under these circumstances. He stood lost in thought for a few moments, and then turned to leave the room. He paused only for a moment while, almost as an afterthought, he carefully fed the letter he was holding to the merrily crackling flames in the fireplace.

The days spun by so pleasantly that Regina had hardly the time or the inclination to wonder why her dear Miss Bekins was so tardy in answering her letter. Amelia was the most delightful of companions. She was witty and well informed, and while she was kindness itself in all her dealings with Regina, and all other members of the household, her tongue was never stinting in her candid, sometimes too perceptive comments about other members of the society in which she moved. She had been at first amazed, then genuinely delighted at the scope of Regina's knowledge which she had gleaned from books, but appalled at the depth of her lack of experience in society. She had quickly designated herself both friend and tutor to the younger girl. And Regina felt a real warmth and affection for her poised and immaculate new friend.

She still held the Marquis in great awe. And try as she might, she could not bring herself to act naturally in his presence. His cool good looks intimidated her, his amused and benignly tolerant attitude toward her made her feel like a veritable bumpkin, and his unexpected friendship still puzzled her. Yet she enjoyed their frequent *tête-à-têtes*, their customary strolls about the grounds when the weather was clement, and their quietly stimulating evenings, when the three would sit downstairs and play cards, or chess, or group around the piano and sing. Lady Mary, Regina soon found, partook of none of these activities, contenting herself with infrequent visits downstairs when any of the local gentry came to call, preferring to spend most of her time luxuriating in her increasingly evident state, at ease in her rooms, surrounded by sweet meats and novels.

In all, Regina would have been pleased with her sojourn at Fairleigh if it weren't for three nagging details that assailed her nightly, when at last she was alone in her room. The first was, of course, her governess's lack of response to her letter; the second was her never repressed sense of obligation toward the Marquis for his solicitousness and his protection; and the third was the observation that she had first doubted, and then later become more and more convinced of. For now she was sure of it—each time St. John came close to her, each time he allowed his lips to brush her hair whilst he whispered some strategy in cards at her, each time he asked her to accompany him for a short walk, she could feel Lady Amelia's reaction.

She had quickly noted her new friend's eyes constantly, if surreptitiously, tracked his movements in whatever room they were in. She could sense the way her companion's spirits would rise when he joined them, she could almost feel, with the ends of her skin, how Amelia's interest rose and fell according to his entrances and exits. No, she no longer had any doubt about Lady Burden's true feelings, nor, sadly enough, about St. John's lack of either interest in or understanding of them. But she liked her new friend too dearly to ever indicate that she had discovered what, she was sure, was supposedly a secret known only to Amelia's own heart.

For herself, no matter how solicitous or handsome the Marquis appeared to her admittedly inexperienced eye, she still felt a certain constraint with him, a lingering shyness in her manner. Although they talked together long into the nights, and played cards, and took long walks out about the grounds, she still considered him somewhat withdrawn; that formidable dignity she had at first noted in his manner was still there.

This evening, they sat in the downstairs study, Regina's favorite room, and played cards. Regina was a wretched player—St. John always laughed and told her she would never win until she learned to cover her delight when she was dealt a fair hand—so tonight, she watched as Amelia and St. John matched wits at the game.

"I shall never understand," Regina sighed as the game came to an end.

"What shall you never understand, my dear?" St. John laughed, as he folded up his hand and signaled Amelia's victory. "What possible subject do you find beyond your comprehension?"

"Your friends," Regina blurted, then, coloring, tried to amend her rash statement. "That is to say, the manners prevailing among them, that is. . . ."

"What Regina is struggling with," Amelia put in with

amusement, "is the shock of her meeting the Three Graces this morning."

St. John threw back his head and laughed, with genuine amusement. "Did she meet them today? Oh, that is a scene I would have given a pretty penny to see. Our resident bluestocking coming up against the Squire's fair litter."

Regina blushed at the laughter the other two gave way to. It was true, however, that the morning had brought about her introduction to the three daughters of the local squire. They were pretty enough, in their fashion, she supposed, to have been given the nickname in the locality of "the Three Graces." But the hours that she had spent in their company had been totally unnerving for her, it was as if she had been forced to spend the morning in the company of Hottentots, so complete was the lack of understanding between them.

The oldest of the girls was engaged to a minor baronet, much to her family's glee; the middle girl was due to be presented this season, when an attack of measles in the household had curtailed her plans; and the youngest was looking forward to her own season in a year's time. They had arrived, in a veritable snowstorm of ribboned bonnets and lace and what Amelia had dubbed "fashionable folderols," by pony cart, accompanied by their silent, timid governess.

And, after being introduced to Regina, they had proceeded to fill the morning with an avalanche of small talk. They could, to Regina's dumbstruck discovery, talk for hours on end about bonnets, skirt lengths, and slippers. They did, to Regina's slow and vaguely horrified comprehension, sweetly and thoroughly demolish the reputation and pretensions of every female of their aquaintance, up to and including each other's. For Miss Betty was heard to softly mention that her sister's affianced was so delighted with the wedding arrangements that she vowed he had put on two stone just from sheer happiness. Miss Lottie had countered sweetly that Miss Betty was so overjoyed herself at the thought of the forthcoming event, that she had broken out in spots in anticipation of her sister's forthcoming nuptuals. And while Miss Betty's graceful hands hastily fluttered up to her face to verify her smooth complexion, Miss Kitty had silenced both her sisters by observing, with a charming lisp, that she had indeed noticed how haggard both her elders had become with the excitement of having measles in the household. "I vow," she had sweetly said, "that they both have lotht their lookth over the thircumthtanthes."

For Regina, the morning had been both educational and frightening. It accentuated the gap between herself and these young creatures of fashion. For while Amelia seemed quite able to keep up her end of the conversation, Regina had sat close-mouthed, unable to think of a blighting comment on one of their acquaintances, or a trenchant observation about the new fashions, either of which, she was sure, was the only acceptable contribution she could have made to the conversation. She had no way of knowing that her glowing good looks struck a terrible animosity in the hearts of the Three Graces, mitigated only by their desire to learn more about this mysterious visitor to Fairleigh. Already the most bizarre rumors as to her identity had begun to circulate in the vicinity. She had been guessed to be everything from an émigré countess from across the channel, to being that wicked St. John's new mistress.

When the three young ladies had become aware of the time that had passed, fruitlessly, for their twofold ambitions of discovering more about Lady Berry, or catching a glimpse of the headily handsome and eligible Master of the Household, they had taken their leave. But not before accomplishing the purported main reason for their visit.

"Now that all ith well in our houth," Miss Kitty had announced, "you mutht come to the ball that Father ith giving. It is thuppothed to mend our hearth for our abthenth from town thith theathon. And jutht everyone will be there. Even my thiththerth beau."

"You absolutely must come," the other two had insisted.

"Even though it may seem provincial to you," Miss

Betty had said to Regina, "it shall be quite the affair of the year for us."

St. John sat laughing at Amelia's wicked descriptions of the visit and her uncanny imitation of Miss Kitty's affected lisp, but his face became immobile when she mentioned the invitation to the ball.

"So you see, Sinjin," Amelia went on blithely, "we are to have a chance to show Regina some real country sport, after all, for I am sure she has never seen the likes of the ball that Squire Hadley is going to give."

"I have never attended a ball," Regina said hastily, noting St. John's suddenly cold demeanor, "for . . . there were not many of them in our locality," she finished lamely. "And I do think it would be wiser if I did not go, after all, Amelia."

"Regina is right," St. John said coldly, cutting across Amelia's protestations. "She would feel out of place there, and it would be better if she did not attend."

"Stuff!" cried Amelia beligerantly. "Sinjin, surely you and I could make her feel at ease, and it would be an opportunity she should not miss."

"Oh no," Regina said hastily. "For one thing, I haven't a ball gown, and for another . . . I don't wish to shock you, Amelia, but I cannot dance. Not one step. I," she went on, noting the horrified look on Amelia's face, "well, that is to say, neither my governess nor my father seemed to ever think that was important."

"Sinjin," Amelia protested, "surely you can practice with Regina. Within a day, I'm sure you can teach her enough to account herself creditably at the ball. And I can surely lend her a ball gown."

"No," St. John said with a guarded look upon his face. "Not that it wouldn't be a pleasure, Regina, but you seem to forget that Regina is, in effect, in hiding here. It would not do for her to attend a large ball. Surely her presence would be remarked upon, and just as surely, it would bring Torquay down upon us."

"But Sinjin," Amelia went on, puzzled, "you yourself said that even he would not 'dare to poach upon another gentleman's property.' "

"No," he said with suppressed anger, "but let it be,

Amelia. There is no reason to stir up the calm we have found here. There is no reason why some paltry local ball should precipitate events that might be disturbing to Regina. At any rate, she will soon be gone from here," he concluded mysteriously.

Amelia let the subject drop, but it was clear that she was displeased with the turn of events, and shortly after, suppressing what were surely huge mock yawns, she took herself off to bed.

Regina rose to follow, but St. John stayed her with a light touch upon her arm. He stood before her, an unreadable expression in his smoky eyes, and said finally, flicking back a stray wisp of her hair with his forefinger, "Understand, Regina, that I do what is best for you."

"About the ball? Oh, but that makes no difference to me at all, surely you must know that," Regina protested, a little nervous at the Marquis's closer proximity and closer scrutiny. "But what you said later . . . is it true? Have you received any answer to my letter? Is there any word from Miss Bekins? For although it has been pleasant here, I confess I yearn to be on my way to my new position . . . before I become too unused to working, before I begin to actually think myself 'Lady Berry.' "

He smiled. This was a theme she constantly enlarged upon in his presence, her desire to be "her own woman," to be less beholden to him and his "charity," as she termed it. He looked down at her, and again was drawn to the clear green eyes, again felt the desire to kiss that small indentation to the left of her lips, again controlled himself against the impulse to hold her to himself and run his hands along the surprisingly ample curves that shaped the slender body. But as he took a step nearer, he could feel her corresponding retreat.

"Not exactly," he sighed. "But soon, very soon, I have the feeling, Regina, you will be away from here, you will be safe and taken care of, and so pleased with your new life, that you will not regret in the least the lack of your attendance at some trumpery local ball."

She looked at him in some doubt, for how could he be so sure of something she had not a hint of happening?

"Do you mean," she asked quietly, "that you have some idea of a different position suitable for me if I do not hear from Miss Bekins?"

"Yes," he said, his gray eyes darkening. "Oh yes, a much more suitable position . . . and soon, I think."

"Then I am again very grateful to you, Sinjin," she said, and aware again of the strange new tension in his position, she sketched a curtsy and withdrew.

"Soon," he said to the empty room. "Yes, very soon."

For the time was ripening, he thought. He sat back in a chair and studied the fire. Soon, he would achieve a twofold aim. He would have her under his very real protection, and have Torquay in an unenviable position.

Torquay. He let his thoughts stray to the irritating subject. How very often that hoarse sweet voice had mocked him. How very often he had recoiled when he had heard their names coupled. It was true that he pursued much the same game as the Duke, but something in him rebelled at being dubbed the successor to the title of most debauched nobleman in town. And yet, the time he had gone around to Madame Sylvestre's establishment when he was in his cups and had found Torquay there, in a gilded doorway, with a bright-eyed, salaciously smiling slender young female at his right side and an overblown garishly painted ageing trollop snuggled protectively on his left side—the Duke's flushed face and glittering eye left no doubt as to his plans for the evening's entertainment, and when St. John had allowed a faint deogatory smirk to touch his lips, Torquay had turned and whispered in that obscenely honeyed voice, "What? Distaste, Sinjin? But wait a few years, my dear boy, and you will find yourself pursuing the same sport. Unless you care to join me now? I'm sure Aggie," and here he hugged the old bawd, "has room in her heart for both of us."

And St. John thought of his involuntary shudder as he turned away without a word.

He thought of the many times he had professed interest in a new female only to find that days later, she had become the property of the Duke. He remembered how often Torquay had sidled up to him when he was at the height of enjoyment at some of the more disreputable parties and had stripped him of all pleasure by a well-placed word, by an accented innuendo. He winced at the way the Duke, almost intuitively, always knew just how to disconcert him at any occasion. He thought of the immense fortune the Duke controlled and could not seem to dissipate. In all, he thought, if he were to be honest, he both envied and feared the man. Envied his possessions and the skill with which he led his dissolute life. For with all his excesses, he still had entree into all but the most conservative of fashionable circles. But he feared the reputation the Duke held, and the slow, sure way it was beginning to settle upon his own shoulders.

Damn the man, St. John thought. And I shall. For this is one time he has made a wager he shall lose. And I shall win.

IX

The clouds were scudding by overhead, but with no real mean intent, so Regina, having dressed warmly, ventured to take a long walk alone across the wide and various grounds of Fairleigh. She had felt an overwhelming need to be by herself, to walk until her feet numbed, to think, and to finally plan again her own future.

For no, it would not do, she thought, shaking her head as the skirts of her long coat brushed against the long grasses on the meadow track she paced, for her to let herself drift any longer. Things were becoming uncomfortable at the house, and there was a great deal to think about. Amelia was still angry this morning at St. John's command that Regina was not to attend the ball, and that there was to be no further discussion of the idea. Amelia had tried to cajole Regina into reasoning with the Marquis and impressing upon him what a snub it would be to the Squire if she did not attend, and further, that her noncompliance with the invitation would

surely spike more gossip about the mysterious lady at
Fairleigh than ever her attendance would. But Regina had
remained adamant. After all, she reasoned, she was here
only on St. John's charity, which was a thing that Amelia
did not know, and it would not do for her to impose.

But impose she had, she sighed, for here she had
already caused a breach between Lady Amelia and the
Marquis. This morning, at breakfast, they had hardly
spoken to each other, and the conversation, such as it
was, was carried solely by Lady Mary's meanderings
about "breakfasts she had known."

And then there was St. John's veiled comments about
her own future. Could it be that he had discovered that
Miss Bekins was indeed in bad financial straits and
could not employ her? Was he even now disturbing
himself as to what sort of position he could find her in
its place? And honestly, she mused, his attitude lately,
his increasingly familiar attitude, the easy endearments
that slipped from his lips, the unavoidable admiring
glances she had intercepted, these might all be part of
the affect of any eligible nobleman, but they disturbed
her and made her feel unsure of herself. For while she
liked him well enough, and trusted him completely, she
knew very well that there was no point in entertaining
any warmer thoughts about his intentions. For when all
was said and done . . . he was a titled nobleman of
great wealth. She was an impecunious commoner, with
no standing in any social world that she had yet encountered. And he was beloved to Amelia. While she was, in
truth, only an imposter, landed on him by her uncle.
No, she insisted to herself, it was time she moved on.
But to where?

She was brooding on possibilities she might consider,
ways in which she could win free without insulting his
honor or hospitality, when she became aware of the fact
that she was no longer alone in the wintry meadow. She
looked up from the path she had been staring down at
as she walked and saw a figure ahead of her, leaning
negligently against a half fallen stile.

Oddly enough, her first thought was not one of fear,
or horror, or panic, but rather one of amused annoy-

ance. Must he always, the thought came unbidden, be capable of such dramatic appearances? For as if the frozen day itself were in league with him, at the moment she discovered him, a weak ray of sunshine broke through and illuminated him, in all his casual splendor, making an unlikely halo around the fair wind-touseled hair.

He leaned back, at ease, clad in dun-colored skin-tight buckskins, a scarf knotted carelessly about his neck, his dark gold coat accenting the fair complexion, his mobile lips drawn back to reveal even white teeth, and his lucent blue eyes now lit with real enjoyment.

"What?" he said in his distinctive whisper, "the maiden spies the dragon and she does not give a piercing shriek? Or take to her heels? Or swoon, with considerable grace, to the floor? Come, Regina, you disappoint me. Rather than losing your head with terror, you are looking absurdly put out. Petulant, I might say. But the look suits you. As indeed, what does not? You have grown, if possible, even fairer, here in the wilds of the countryside. The winds have not been unkind to you. Your nose does not show a red tip, your eyes do not water—what an extraordinary beauty it is that even the cold enhances. This inclement weather has only brought a rosy glow to your alabaster cheek, only shined your eyes till they sparkle like the sea on a turbulent day."

She walked up to him, after that first moment of surprise, and said, almost before she was aware of it herself, "Can you not speak straight out? Must everything be couched in that sinister poetry you affect?"

He seemed, for one second, taken aback, and then he let out a genuine laugh, oddly pure in contrast to his hoarse voice. His eyes lit up to the shade of a summer's day.

"Oh, you are not afraid of me any more! Here's a new turn. You are so cosseted, so protected, so sure of yourself, that at last you are no longer afraid of me." His eyes grew grave and he added, "But you should be, Regina, indeed you should be."

She recognized that what he had said was true; no, she did not fear him here, and now. It was as if she had in some small, hidden part of herself been waiting for him to reappear. The thought of him had so often alternately both chilled and warmed her during the nights when she could not sleep, turning her stomach to ice but also changing her heartbeats to drumbeats. Somewhere here, in the reality of the dappled light of a cold country day, in a meadow, so close to her friends and protectors, she no longer feared him at all. Rather, she looked forward to their encounter.

"No, you are right. I don't fear you here. For what can you do to me here?"

He laughed luxuriously.

"Oh my dear," he said, "countless things, I assure you. I could signal to my henchman, who might be hiding in the brush, and toss you into my carriage, which might be secreted down the lane. For I have no honor, or very little, and I do not care for Sinjin's opinion at all, and whatever Sinjin might say about me would quickly be discounted in the circles we two are best known in. Or," he went on, after a quick glance under his long lashes at her face, "I might become impatient and toss you to the ground right here, and have my way with you. Only, you are right, it would be very cold, and very uncomfortable, and not at all in my usual style or the way I plan to end the matter. Still, no one would be concerned with your fate at all, 'Lady Berry,' once it became known that 'Lady Berry' is not quite the titled lady it has been hinted she is. In fact," he mused, "yours is a very false position, and it has given you a false sense of security. For I'm sure even Lady Burden and His Lordship's sister would be most put out if they discovered they had been entertaining a fraud—a common chit thrown out of her own family home for her indiscrete carryings-on with a hardened rake. Oh, I would weather it, it would be only, after all, another black mark on a long list. And Sinjin would be winked at, as he and I are cut from the same cloth. But the ladies . . . ah, I think they would be devastated, betrayed, and uncommonly angry at the little cheat they had taken to their bosoms. For they would not be angry at Sinjin, love, his sister dotes upon him, and

Amelia, well . . . she is not as unaffected by His Lordship as she would like to be thought to be. No, the onus would all be upon you, my love." And, seeing her arrested expression, he went on, "No, it is a cruel world, Regina, you ought to have thought of that yourself. You ought not to have been cozened into a false sense of security."

She stood silent, watching the sun play upon his hair.

"Yet, in a sense," he said softly, "but only in a sense, you are right. Here, and now, you have no real reason to be afraid of me. I did, after all, make a pact with you, and the game is not yet played out, although it draws to a close. But here, and now, yes, you are safe. But as for tomorrow?" He shrugged, and an ugly expression crossed his face. "And tomorrow might come very quickly, love. For although I know you are not yet Sinjin's mistress, he is, after all, living too close to his sister and her good friend at the moment. I wonder at how soon you two plan on consummating the event? You will not, you know."

But at this point a sense of such outrage gripped Regina that she scarcely saw the harsh look that had flitted across the usually pleasant face before her. A sense of outrage at her present situation, a sense of fury at the suggestions he was making, a sense of the preposterousness of the present confrontation. That this seemingly angelic man lounging against the stile before her should have forced her into the straits she found herself in, magnified by the humane and polite treatment she had received these past weeks, overwhelmed her sense of proportion. She spoke in fury, she railed against him:

"No! No, all you say is dirtied by your own false perceptions of the world around you. You are to be pitied, My Lord Duke, in that you see your world through eyes that cannot discern good from bad, through a philosophy that has nothing to do with the way real people live their real lives. You are like a man mad for a taste of wine. He does not see the scenery around him, he does not see the people going about their lives, he sees only opportunities to drink, his eye picks out only those places, those establishments, those people, who can provide him with his need. You do not see with any clarity at all, you are so drunk with the need for debauching, for degradation of yourself and others."

"No," she went on, shaking her head, "I do not think Lady Burden would despise me. No, I know Lady Mary would not. And I don't think Sinjin would allow you to merely . . . come along and destroy my life. I know he would not. He and I . . . we have no plans for any such arrangement that you speak of. I applied to him for help because my late uncle instructed me to, should I ever need help. And with no self-serving thought, he has assisted me. You are certainly mad. And no," she said, holding up her head, "no, I do not fear you so much as I pity you from the bottom of my heart."

"You may well be right to," he mused, watching her closely, "I do not argue that. But it is 'Sinjin' now, is it? Ah well, he is more clever than I thought. So George Berryman was incautious enough to mention the great Marquis to you——"

"You knew my uncle?" Regina gasped.

"Yes, of course," smiled the Duke. "Who among us who ventured into business did not? Only I did not deal exclusively with him, as some others did. An honest man, your uncle, according to his lights, that is, for whoever deals overmuch in business cannot afford to be too honest. As your father soon found out. Ah yes, I know all about you, Regina Analise. I do not wager on dark horses. I make it my business to know all the odds in whatever game I choose to play."

"Why, for once, without dissimulation, why? Will you tell me why you choose to play this particular game?" Regina demanded, still raging at the slight figure before her. Seeing his closed expression, she softened her voice and almost pleaded with him, "Since there is so much that you know about me, can you tell me something about yourself? Some true thing?" she asked, watching him, realizing that she knew nothing of the actual man that hid beneath the blandly smiling, smooth exterior he presented.

"Some true thing?" He laughed. "Oh my dear, there is no true thing about me at all. But come, sit here beside me and I will tell you all you wish to know about me. There has never breathed a man who would not be pleased to tell all about himself, ad nauseum, to a young and beautiful woman who looks at him as you now look at me. Come and sit with me, Regina love, and I will tell you stories about myself, Oh I will sing you songs of me till darkness falls, and beyond, if that is what you wish. We will talk as old friends, or as new friends, for however long you like. But remember, I am most certainly mad. And placating me, and talking with me, and trying to understand me, will not alter that. I will still keep you to our game. I will still oversee you to make sure you keep to all the rules. But yes," and he grinned, the expression, the sunlight, the wind-touseled hair making him seem suddenly younger, less threatening, more human than she had ever envisioned him.

She knew then as he waited, smiling, for her answer to his outstretched hand, that she could not turn and walk away from him, as every instinct cautioned her to. She could not, as a proper lady should, run trembling back to the warm security of Fairleigh. She must, she felt, confront him. Meet with him, so that she could reason with him, perhaps even appeal to him. Perhaps she could beguile him into betrayal of his true motives. For she could still not accept that he did all he did out of sheer perverse amusement. Certainly she could, she thought, know him. And all that she had been raised to believe told her that no creature she could know, could still remain an enemy to her. It was against all the sweet logic that Miss Bekins and her father had inculcated her with. Yes, she decided, she would speak with him.

She accepted his assistance, and perched herself up upon the stile beside him. And with the chill wind whipping around them, they talked.

Afterward, she could never reconstruct the conversation of that strange afternoon. They had stayed, talking, no she ammended, gossiping like two old cronies, while the sun sank slowly over the horizon. She had asked him questions, he had answered with wit and style. But although he spoke of himself, she could not learn anything about his motivations. He told her about his education, his travels. He regaled her with stories about the society he traveled in, till tears stood in her eyes and she gasped with laughter. He entertained her with anecdotes, he charmed her with rumors, he quoted poetry, and when she capped his verse with the next line, he capped her quotation once again. He showed her a glittering treasurehouse of a mind, but he showed her not one glimpse of the shadows within.

Every so often the oddity of the situation, the strangeness of their meeting was borne in upon her, and almost as if he could read her mind, he would lure her away from her thoughts with whimsy or humor. Ah, she thought, recovering from a wave of laughter he had submerged her in, how likeable he is! But then, suddenly, as if a cloud had passed over his mind as it had over the weakening sun, he spoke slowly to her, "You see then, Regina, that it will not be so terrible, after all, your fate to be with me."

She opened her eyes as if awakening from a dream, and looked at him. "No," she said, "this is so absurd, Your Grace, indeed you know it is. For we have spent the afternoon like friends. We have shared our thoughts, you cannot still be . . . serious about this ridiculous wager."

"Oh, but I am," he said seriously. "You see, you do not know me after all. How well you look in sunlight, Regina. Not many of my female acquaintances could say the same, but it suits you well, almost as well as candlelight. No," he said, taking his hand and turning her chin up, "perhaps even more than candlelight."

She pulled herself away from him and, trying to keep up a light note, said, "But it suits you too."

"Only because this afternoon is aware of the signal honor I have given it. I do not go abroad too much by day, see how the sun has tried so valiantly to flatter me, to convince me of its good offices? If it were better aquainted with me, if it knew it had my favor constantly, it would turn and slink behind a cloud. It is only those we hope to win that we put ourselves out for; those we have already added to our list of conquests, we can afford to ignore. When favor is won, it is foolish to go on courting, is it not? But shine as it will, it knows full well that this is not my time of day, I still prefer to be burnt by its sister moon, and bask in her cold silvery rays for my health's sake."

"Yes, surely," Regina said, "once we have won a friend, we do not go on 'courting' his friendship, because we know ourselves secure in it. Still, once we have a friend, we do not ignore him, rather we are at ease. There is comfort in not having always to be on one's best behavior."

"What lovely friends you must have, my dear," he said. "Perhaps if I too were poor and defenseless, and beautiful, I would have such friends. But then, I have found that it is very easy to befriend someone who has less than I. Someone who looks to me for favors. They are so easy to please. They are so willing to accommodate. They are so eager for friendship."

She recoiled from him. "No," she denied, "that is not friendship, that is patronage."

"Ah," he said, "you've put your little white finger on it. For I have found that when a man has wealth, influence, and position, he is hard put to tell the difference between friendship and patronage." He spread his hands in a gesture of dismay. "How is a man to know what is asked in friendship, and what is requested as patronage?"

"Friendship," Regina said, feeling foolishly like a governess explaining a moral lesson to a stubborn small charge, "is freely given, without expectation of recompense, of anything—except for the hopes of a return friendship."

"Then I think," he smiled, "that on the whole I prefer patronage. At least I can well afford that. It costs me really very little, whereas any freely given trust and concern would well bankrupt the little resources I have of those remarkable feelings. That could well cost me more than I care to lose. Don't look so outraged, my love, you will find that there are a great many men like me in this world. A great many who prefer those sorts of well-defined relationships, such as employer and employee, debtor and benefactor, king and subject. For example, my lovely little headmistress, do you honestly think Sinjin offers you free use of his house, his resources, and, I am sure, his heart out of friendship?"

"No," she admitted, for even she could not claim to be the Marquis's friend. "But," she said, "he offers me comforts—not out of patronage, either, rather out of a debt of honor to my family."

"Oh, Regina," sighed the Duke, his face strangely gentle in the fading light, "you are such fool."

"You know," he said, more briskly, "that I will eventually hurt you, perhaps only a little physically, but I certainly will hurt your pride, your sense of decency, your image of yourself. I will show you a Regina Analise that you never dreamed existed. I, likely, by the time I am done, will have you despising yourself, as much as, or more than you will come to despise me. For I will show you what a traitorous body you are locked into. I will pit the demands of that body against all the high reasonings of that well-furnished mind. And I will win. But with all that I will do," he went on, ignoring the horror that had come into her eyes, "I will not break your heart. No. Never that. For I will never ask you for that. That I will leave to your own self. But you are too generous with that poor organ, Regina. You are almost promiscuous with it. And never doubt, it will be broken. For you will give it where you should not. Take care with it, Regina. I will have you, no matter what. But I should rather have you intact, in all ways. I should prefer it. But you are such a little fool."

She stood and shook out her skirts, tears welling in her eyes. She did not understand him. She had spent the whole of the afternoon with him, she had thought she had come to some easy ground of acquaintance with him, and now that evening had almost fallen, the slight, elegant man beside her was as much of a stranger, as much of a threat, as ever. She would not speak; she only turned to return to the house.

He stayed her with one arm; the strength of it held her still, she neither struggled after his first touch, nor moved a pace to escape. He pulled her to him so that they stood close enough to be mistaken for one figure in the empty meadow. She felt the warmth and strength of him held in check, and irrationally, was content to stand there for those moments, so close as to almost touch, so far as to only stare into each other's eyes. What she saw flaring in his, and what she suddenly did not wish him to discover in hers, forced her to drop her gaze to her shoetops. Only then he stirred, and recollected himself, and released her, only holding her lightly with a touch upon her hand.

"I will see you at the Squire's ball," he said, looking down into her lowered eyes.

"No," she said, "I shall not go."

"Oh, don't be foolish," he said. "Once again, we will meet on neutral ground there. Even I do not seduce women at a country squire's ball. Especially not when mine host, the Squire himself, has plans for me becoming his son-in-law. You must come to see at least how many 'friends' I do have. How well received I am in society."

"The Marquis has said that I must not," she said, childishly even to her own ears.

"Why not?" he asked.

"So that you would not discover me," she answered.

"Ah, but I have, so now you may come."

"I cannot dance," she said, despising herself for her weak answer. "I have not the right gowns."

"All that is nothing," he laughed. "Surely you have more spirit that that, Regina. You will not cower beneath the bed, while I caper at the ball?"

"No," she cried, her eyes flashing. "No, I shall be there. But I swear, it is the last you will see of me. For after that, I will be gone. Gone on to decide my own future. As you stipulated. And then you can find some other poor creature to torment for your pleasure. But not me, I swear it." And she tore herself from him and ran back to the comforting lights that began to appear in the windows of house beyond them. She felt anger at herself for her undignified haste to be away from him, and for her complete capitulation in the matter of the ball. Surely he must be laughing now, she thought disgustedly, at the success at which he had manipulated her response."

But the Duke of Torquay, leaning back against the stile where she had left him, was not laughing. The look in his wide blue eyes was rather the look of a dreamer, but his tightly clenched fists surely did not signify a pleasant dream.

"But where have you been?" Amelia greeted her. "Sinjin and I were becoming worried. We thought you were in your room, but as the darkness came we. . . ."

"We almost organized a search," Sinjin said, coming toward her and taking her hands in his. "But you're frozen! What were you doing out so late?" he demanded, almost in the tones of an angry father, Regina thought.

"I was talking with the Duke of Torquay," Regina said, with a shadow of a smile.

When they had bundled her off to the study and bade Lady Mary to take dinner without them, both Amelia and St. John turned their full attention to Regina. She sat huddled in a large chair by the fire, fortified by St. John's perennial cure for the chill, a glass of brandy, feeling very much like a truant schoolgirl. Amelia's face showed worry and concern, but St. John, standing by the fire, seemed to her to be gripped by some inner tension, so abrupt and cold was his manner.

"No," she explained again, "no, I did not think to run back to you. Because," she said, appealing to St. John's grim countenance, "I thought, I really thought, that if I could speak with him . . . reason with him, I could solve the whole of it."

"And did you?" St. John asked coldly.

"No," she sighed sadly. "For all we talked, for all I said, for all he heard . . . he is unchanged. I cannot understand". . . . She trailed off.

"Of course you cannot, that is the whole point. You have no experience with such a creature," St. John said. "And you were a fool to try to reason with him."

"That is much the same as he said," Regina murmured softly.

Amelia spoke. "And how did you leave it with him, Regina? Did he threaten you? Did he make any . . . advances?"

"We only spoke. And he said that he was looking forward to seeing me at the ball. When I told him I was not going, he taunted me for my cowardice. I'm afraid I lost my temper. I told him that I was not afraid, that I was going."

St. John made a muffled exclamation and Regina said hurriedly, "But you needn't worry about that. For I have thought the whole thing out, and I, of course, shall not go. For I shall not be here at all. It is time, it is past time," she said imploringly to St. John, "that I was gone from here. I have already stayed too long. This flight of mine has gone on too long."

"Yes," St. John agreed.

"Sinjin!" cried Amelia in shock. "How can you say so? How can you countenance Regina's leaving us when you have not yet heard from her relatives? It would be like casting her to the wolves."

"I said nothing about her leaving," he said. "She shall stay, and stay with the full accordance of all of us. But she shall no longer hide. No more futile flight. You will come with us, Regina, to the Squire's ball. You will come in full sight of Torquay, and he will be made to see that he cannot frighten you. And that he cannot have you."

But seeing Amelia's quick look toward him, he smiled. "Have you, that is to say, in any construction of the word."

"I don't want to go," Regina said stubbornly. "I don't desire to go. I don't wish to go. I only want to leave here."

"You are understandably overwrought," St. John said. "There is only one thing. For other reasons," he explained to Amelia, not looking at her, "it would be better if she remains . . . incognito. If she remains silent as to her visit here."

Amelia gave him a long look and rose from her chair.

"Of course," she said stiffly. "But now, perhaps these dramatics have taken away your appetites, but I assure you, they have only whetted mine. I will join Mary at dinner."

St. John stood looking into the outer distance until Regina said quietly, "I really do not want to go to this affair, you know. And I really don't understand why you insist on my staying here. And I don't understand why I am still to play the role of 'Lady Berry.'"

St. John came over to her and raised her from her chair.

"I know you do not, little one," he said caressingly, his expression softening. "But do you not trust me now? Did your uncle not give you to my care? Do you doubt me now? Have I ever done any wrong toward you?"

"No, to all those ungrateful things," Regina said, feeling ill at ease in his light grasp. "But I grow weary of this all, I am not fashioned for such . . . as Amelia put it, 'dramatics.'"

"No," he said, "you are not. And you will not have to continue in them for much longer. There is a new development, Regina. But no, now is not the time to speak of it." He traced a light caress on her cheek with his hand, and sighed. "No, not now. Now we must have dinner. Now we must make friends again. Now you must trust me. Do you, Regina?" he asked, looking deep into her puzzled eyes.

"Of course," she said. "I would not be here otherwise. It is as if you were . . . family to me now."

"But not father, I hope," he laughed, "nor brother. Preferably something at the same time much closer, and much farther." And with a laugh, he offered her his arm, and said, with mock solemnity, "To dinner then, Lady Berry."

X

"Make a curtsy to your father now, My Lady, and greet him warmly, for he has come a long way just to see you," the governess commanded, and obediently the little sallow girl dipped and swayed, and executed a neat little mockery of a curtsy. Only there is no mockery in her eyes, her father thought, with a curiously unreasonable pang of discomfort somewhere in the region of his chest as he gravely regarded those clear blue eyes, so uncannily like his, yet so completely alien to his. For they gazed at him bereft of expression, vacant and cold.

Not an auspicious meeting, he thought wryly, wondering again whatever had possessed him, why in the world he had obeyed that vagrant impulse, as unnatural and beguiling as a breath of spring air in his December room; that maddening impulse to be quit of the Squire's vast company. And to quit that admittedly deadening company for a return to his ancestral home, for a return, as it were, to the scene of his capital crime in begetting this unloved, and unlovingly begotten child. Age, he reasoned sardonically, encroaching age, it must have been. Only that would account for this absurd urge to finally see what I have left this earth heir to, to see what I have given my name and fortune to. And, he admitted, a not unreasonable urge to free himself from the saccharine entanglements the Squire's unlovely daughters seemed to be inviting him to.

The ball being a fortnight away, the Squire and his dependents had regretfully let him go from their guest quarters, blaming the pre-gala commotion in the household for his unexpected departure and promising themselves a dead set at him the night of the ball.

"Oh, the carpenters make such a racket, I do apologize, Your Grace," the Squire's wife had lamented. "But, indeed, we must have lovely lacy indoor trellises around the ballroom to bedeck with lovely blossoms for the illusion of spring, you know?"

"The housemaids' deuced commotion, all that bustling about, and scraping and polishing, can't blame you for quitting us, sets a fellow's teeth on edge, all that smell of beeswax and soap. But you know how women are about such folderol," the Squire had commiserated heartily.

But they had been more than anxious about his departure, even though he had assured them of his return the weekend of the ball. They had been desolate at his leaving.

Amazing, he had thought, as the Three Graces waved him farewell with real tears in their eyes, amazing how acceptable I still manage to be. Not in the highest circles, of course, but then the Squire's household is far from those exalted reaches. But still, he had wondered in real bafflement, they have heard all the tales of my adventures in that demimonde which is as unreal to them as their little lives are to me, and yet, they positively yearn for me to bestow my tainted name upon one of them. "Come away from the Dungheap for a moment, My Lord Duke," they call, "and join us in wedded bliss. But be sure to bring your fortune with you, and wipe your feet please, before you walk us down the aisle." A great deal more than my feet must be wiped clean, my dears, he had countered to the silent enticements, a great deal more; my entire past, I do believe, my dears.

And here, he thought with heavy irony, is the object I rode all the heavy miles for, spurred by that unreasonable whim. Here is a little squashed and sallow girl child, who, by the look of her, has never entertained a fancy, much less a whim. She has much the look of her mother, poor thing, the Duke thought, too much the look of her mother. But then he had seen the eyes, and noted that her complexion was as white as his, and even though black curls trembled about her forehead and the nose had the same foolish tendency to point upward as her mother's had, still there was none of the light or inconsequential in her aspect or her demeanor. No, he thought, allowing his lips to curl in their first true smile since he had arrived. The poor lady never played me false. If she found no comfort in my embrace, she sought no other's either. I cured her of that tendency, if indeed she ever possessed such a tendency. She died as chaste in spirit as she was born. But see what we created, that pure lady and her impure wedded husband. A creature neither foul nor fair, but leached of all life.

The Duke of Torquay stood in his library, which he had not visited for six years, or rather his father's library, for so he still regarded it, as all he had done with the room since he had inherited it was to have it cleaned thoroughly and furnished in shades of maroon and gold to take the curse of his father's gray scholarship from it. He gazed down upon his only begotten child. She stood, small and patient as a marionette, expressionless, before him, dressed properly and expensively in a little blue dress chosen to accentuate her eyes, her feet in small blue slippers, her black hair falling to her shoulders. The Duke, dressed in riding clothes of various shades of brown, stood before her, his fair hair touseled, his face wearing a mannerly smile. We make a delightful picture, he thought with amusement, quite an admirable still life.

"I don't expect transports of delight, my child," he said in his low hoarse tones. "After all, you have only my word for it that I am your father, and the word, in any case, is meaningless to you, as we have never met. But I bear gifts, you see, to ensure a warm welcome here. Allow me to present you with a token. One which the shop girl assured me would be the envy of all your acquaintances."

He made a protracted show of unwrapping the parcel on his desk, and finally, after what seemed like a mighty struggle with the tissue within, shrugged and beckoned her to his side.

"See what a weak fellow I am." He smiled. "I cannot seem to unearth the thing. But you are all of . . . six, is it?" She only nodded gravely in return. "Ah then, and a fine strapping big girl, perhaps you can take it out for me."

She reached into the box and, without fuss, peeled the tissue away from the gift. It was a large doll, an expensive, overly dressed French doll, all bubbling lace and sleek satin with a porcelain head, with pouting lips and high color and long lashes that opened and closed over eyes almost as blue as her own. She gazed at it seriously, and then handed it to the Duke.

"Here you are, sir," she said quietly.

"But it is for you, child," he protested.

"Oh," she said quietly. "Then thank you, sir," and she held the doll at her side at a distance like an alien thing and looked at him again, waiting for him to speak.

"Well then," he said with false heartiness, thinking mockingly that he sounded like one of those fatuous avuncular uncles he had known as a child, or like an overeager child molester he had once seen trying to entice slum brats playing near the square until a zealous merchant had seen him and chased him howling down the street. "And what pastime did my sudden arrival call you from today? What had you been doing before I came and summoned you?"

"Lessons, sir," she replied gravely. "Drawing."

"And were you enjoying yourself?" he asked.

"Yes, sir," she answered.

"Well, then," he said, "I don't want to disrupt your schedule overmuch. You may return and we will see each other later. At dinner, then?"

"Yes, sir," she replied, and executing her perfect curtsy, she turned stiffly and left.

"Miss Barrow," he called, and the retreating governess turned and reentered the library. "Miss Barrow," he said sweetly to the spare, gray woman, "is she always like this, then?"

"Like what, Your Grace?" the woman answered, puzzled.

"So very polite, so very proper. I realize, naturally, that she doesn't know me from Adam, but does she never show any animation?"

"Your Grace," the governess answered, unsure of his tone, "it is not that she does not know you. She has been trained to be a lady. She has been taught that which is right and fitting in one of her station in life. Do you find that extraordinary?" she asked with a hint of steel in her voice.

Ah, then she has heard of me, the Duke thought, amused. "No, Miss Barrow, I quite understand. It is only that when I was her age, I was more inclined to childish pursuits."

"She is to be a lady, Your Grace," Miss Barrow replied. "She has to put such things behind her."

I should like to light a fire behind her, the Duke thought, and you as well. "Thank you, Miss Barrow," he said, dismissing her. He turned and sat in the great maroon chair that had been his father's. The sunlight glinted in the long windows, and although the maroon carpets absorbed much of it, the gold shone, the gold spun in the air in the little dust flecks that arose as he sank into the chair. The gold glowed from the draperies and echoed round his flaxen hair, and yet it seemed to him that the room was yet gray, his gray father's gray room. And why should I care that the world is determined to bring her up as a replica of her mother? It is, after all, only a case of one artificial flower reproducing another, he reflected. Would it be better for her to be a replica of her father, he thought, scornfully? And why did I even venture here to begin with? She has lived six long years in comfort without me, and doubtless will survive sixty more very nicely in the same fashion. Why should I care here and now, when I did not then? What has addled my wits and brought about this uncharacteristic fever of fatherhood? He lay his sunset-gilded head back upon the chair and closed his eyes, extinguishing their blue flame. Premature senility, he sighed, or an excess of boredom, or enforced celibacy, too much Squire and too many hopeful daughters have driven me to this charade of concern. But not boredom, he thought, opening his eyes again. No, this new game I have embarked upon is everything but boring. And she, and all my subsequent machinations since that damned night at the Opera, every plotted moment up to this unplotted one, have been because of her. And the game grows beyond my control. And that disturbs me more than anything has since I was that poor sadly squashed child's age. And that which disturbs me the most is myself. For I feel the stirrings of something very much like humanity within, and we can't have that, can we, My Lord Black Duke? We can't tolerate that at all. For I think, he sighed to himself, that it will result in a kind of death, one crack in that frozen void and, like a rushing spring thaw, I will be washed away in those unleashed torrents. It does no good to undam that which has been safely secured for so long. And for what, he laughed, for one poor, untried, untitled, unworldly female who has too many scruples, and a head full of bookish morality, and who, moreover, has not had enough temptation put in her way of becoming a saint? Oh no, Miss Berryman, he thought merrily, you of the exquisite face, form, and morals, you do not qualify as yet for a mantle of sainthood. All saints must be tempted to the limit, and I have not yet begun. Not nearly, he anticipated, brightening. And, feeling much better, the Duke of Torquay rose and stretched and went out into the chill air to find a proud mount to carry him on a nostalgic tour around his broad acres.

The day telescoped to three, and with each advancing hour he found himself becoming more unsettled. He was not used to spending so much time in his own company. In town, each night would provide its own diversions, and he could always ensure that there was at least some entertainment or some other human being he could converse or have some sort of concourse with. But here in the country, he found himself quite alone. He could not bring himself to open one of his father's books, as if the very dust motes would release visions of his youth, his father, his mother. And when he rode out to visit with his neighbors to reacquaint himself with them, he noted their wary attitudes. Those with comely wives or young daughters either hid them away or displayed them to him like pearls on a jewelers' cushion. On the whole, he preferred those men who secreted their daughters, but their attitudes were ones of uneasy deference. So he rode, and wandered, and watched his own daughter. And though he longed to be away, to return to the only life he knew, to take up the game again, perversely, he could not leave. At least until he had made some provision for his own daughter. For she unsettled him the most.

The little Lady Lucinda could not be said to be unacquainted with him now, and yet she was as still and stilted with him as ever. But, he noted, she was much the same with all those who came within her sphere. She showed no real emotion with her governess, with the servants, or even with other young children, those of his tenants that he pointed out to her when he took her riding with him in the afternoons. She was as cold and uninvolved with them all as she was with him. Only with animals, with her pony, with the stable dogs and kitchen cat, did she allow herself to smile, even, on occasions when she thought no one noticed, to laugh. And it was only on those rare occasions, that he saw, unclouded, his clear paternity in her unguarded face. On the third night then, since time was drawing close for him, and the ball he anticipated with such mixed emotions was only a little more than a week away in time, he sat at his desk and carefully composed a provocative letter. This done, he sat back with a rare real smile upon his face. If she still lives, this will provoke her enough to return, he thought, even if she is on her death bed. And, summoning a footman, he made arrangements for his note's immediate delivery.

It is only a small thing, he chided himself, and on balance with my sins, will perhaps only extinguish a very small flame when I am consigned to my eventual eternal torment, but it might make a great difference to the child, and I owe her that much at least. Owe? he thought quizzically. There I am speaking like a Miss Berryman again. But looking around the sumptuously furnished room, picturing in his mind's eye his rolling lawns and wooded parklands, his marble halls, even his daughter's exquisitely furnished rooms, the word *owe* did seem a little foolish. She has everything already, he thought, but perhaps, in deference to the absent Miss Berryman, there is, yes, one thing else that I owe her, and since I surely cannot provide it personally, I shall

have another supply it. Thus I pay one debt. One moral
debt, though, Miss Berryman, does not make a habit, I
warn you."

She arrived exactly two days later, and, staring at
her, he could not believe so many years had passed.

"You needn't goggle, My Lord," she remarked acidly,
taking off her gloves. "No, I am not risen from my
grave."

"Not from your grave, my dear Pickett, but rather
from a night's sleep, for I swear you have not changed a
hair."

"I have changed several thousand, Your Grace, unless your advanced age has clouded your vision, for as
you can plainly see, they are all quite snow-capped now,
and when last we met, they were the hue of a raven's
wing."

"And this," he crowed with delight, "from the lady
who would knock me silly for only a little fib. Why
Pickett, my eternal love, you were gray as a goose
when I last saw you. And why the 'Your Grace,' when I
swear the only title you ever acknowledged me by was
'rogue' or 'devil' or 'wretch.'"

"Not so," said the small wiry woman, lowering her
strident voice. "For once I was wont to call you 'Jason,'
before you reached your majority, My Lord."

"Oh come," he said, taking her hand and leading her
into the room. 'Your Grace' and 'My Lord' are uneasy
on your lips. Call me 'wretch,' then, or 'rogue,' though
I'd prefer 'Jason,' but do not bury me and our past
under such a heap of civility. I am glad you have come
back, Pickett, I truly am. You bring back my youth."

"I should not think you would wish it brought back,"
she said, her bright gray eyes searching his face. "Or
anyone who brought it back to you."

"No," he said soberly, "not my youth, then, but you,
certainly, for we shared the one endurable part of it,
didn't we? You were more than governess, Pickett, you
were my one friend."

She stood and stared at him for a moment and what
she saw displeased her, for she pursed her lips and then
shook her head.

"And still am your friend, but where is this 'squashed child' you wrote of? For nothing except the visions of a sadly flattened little person would have dragged me from my hearth in my richly deserved retirement. No, that is not true either. The world is filled with flattened children. Your unfortunate daughter alone accounts for my presence, Jason. Although I think that now, as then, you tend to exaggerate. Still, I am here, as you see. But I warn you, only to observe. I promise nothing else, as yet. Where is the child?"

"You shall see her at dinner. Which you shall have, my love, as soon as you freshen up. It must have been a weary journey. But it is a miracle how you have not changed," he commented as he led her up the long staircase to her room. But then he noted that although the years had not seemed to touch her at first glance, her carriage being just as erect, her homely, wise little face just as shrewd, her voice just as distinct and piercing as his childhood memories had enshrined them, yet she walked a little more slowly, a few more wrinkles sat upon her forehead, and her movements were a little more stiff. And yet, he thought, when last she saw me, my only sin was selfishness, my only crime, a child's thoughtlessness, my only lack, a conscience.

"I suppose, basically," she said, "no one of us really changes. Have you, Jason?"

"No," he said lightly. "No, basically, I haven't."

"Rest easy," Lady Burden caroled from the threshold, sweeping off her cloak and handing it to her maid. "For the foul beast has left his lair."

"Shh!" St. John hissed irritably. "For I'm about to put the poor girl in my debt for, I'd estimate, at least ninety-seven years. Your bid, Lady Berry, but have a care, for you owe me a king's ranson already."

"No," Regina laughed, putting her cards face up on the table, "I know when I'm beaten. But what 'beast,' Amelia? And why do you look so jubilant?"

"Bidding with such cards in your hand, Regina? Oh, you'll never make a Captain Sharp with this sort of play. I thought I'd taught you better. Well," Lady Burden said, plumping herself inelegantly down on a couch, "I've just come from a spirited visit to the Squire's, and lo! it's a house filled with lamentation. It seems all the chaos there, owing to their preparation for the ball, quite chased their honored guest away. Torquay just up and left them in the lurch, giving them some sort of nonsense about looking in on his daughter at Grace Hall. Which is a rare bouncer, if ever I heard one, for everyone knows he hasn't clapped an eye on his offspring since she appeared in the world. And Grace Hall has seen nothing but his heels since that day. He promised to be back for the ball, but much faith they have in his promise, and they are exceedingly distraught at his escape."

"Why should they be lamenting his departure?" Regina wondered, for she thought all polite society reacted as St. John did when he heard the Duke's name, with a slight moue of distaste.

"Why? Heavens, girl," Amelia laughed. "What sort of ball will it be with just a trumpery Marquis and a lady or two in attendance? A proper duke got away. Or rather an improper one, but still, he got clean away."

"I should think," St. John said, rising and walking the length of the table in the card room, "that they would be relieved for their daughters' sake."

"Oh come, come, Sinjin," Amelia gurgled, "not everyone is as circumspect as you are. Why the Squire quite fancied having a noble son-in-law for himself, to say nothing of his wife's being quite giddy from such a close encounter with such a sizeable fortune. Even the maids are sighing, for he has such a heavenly countenance, my dear."

"To hide a satanic heart," St. John muttered.

"Why, you sound quite priggish, my dear," Amelia countered, gaily, but keeping her eyes steadily on the Marquis's pacing figure.

"Can you have forgotten," St. John said earnestly, "what Torquay's machinations have caused Regina? Can you possibly have simply obliterated her flight from your mind? You seem to stand Torquay's defender. Why don't you just drop him a note and tell him to come around and pick Regina up this evening? You might pack for her while you are at it."

Lady Amelia flushed and sat quietly for a moment. Then she rose and straightened her skirt. "No," she said thoughtfully, "I had not forgotten. And I do know his reputation. But you do not have to suggest that I am acting as his pander either, Sinjun."

"Amelia!" St. John wheeled angrily upon her. "You go too far."

"No," Amelia said quietly, "I don't think so. You have said that Jason has designs upon Regina. I don't find that unusual, for Regina is an unusually lovely girl, who, as you have said, at the moment does not enjoy the protection of her family. I make no doubt that Jason is unscrupulous. But he is not, Sinjun, some unearthly demon from hell. He is, after all, only a spoiled, decadent Englishman, and Nobleman at that. He is not some muttering madman. He is still accepted in a wide circle of our acquaintance, and as yet, he has only badly frightened Regina with words. Or so you have told me. And as far as having a 'Satanic heart' goes, Sinjun, I am a full-grown woman, and although his reputation is bad, I know of gentlemen with much the same proclivities as his. You may detest him for your own reasons, but do not turn upon me as though I were some sort of heartless monster because I choose to make light of the situation, Sinjun. I swear I deserve better than that from you."

St. John moved swiftly to her, and grasped her hands in his. He looked steadily at her, and she could not tell, for once, whether he was as usual staring fixedly at the bridge of her nose, or at last, looking deep into her poor besotted eyes.

"Amelia, forgive me. I did not mean it as it sounded. It is only that I detest the man, and it seems, cannot take anything about him in a light vein."

Regina sat at the card table and watched them. Somehow, she thought, the two of them, standing so closely together, seemed rightfully matched. Both tall and straight, gifted and landed and fortuned, they seemed a true pair. Not for the first time, she thought herself an uncomfortable intruder in their own special world.

"Why do you detest him so, Sinjun?" Amelia asked. "You are no prude, my dear. Many times I have heard you laugh at adventurers far more lost to reason than he is."

His eyes wavered and he released her hands. He strode back and seemed to stare at the leaded panes of the frosted windows.

"It is only that I know what sort of fellow he really is, and it irks me to see him go scot-free, when a fellow of lesser rank would be rotting in Newgate for the same crimes."

It sounded weak enough, even to his own ears. Worse, he thought with chagrin, it sounded unlike him. Sanctimonious, priggish, even puritanical. Amelia, who had her ear to the social ground, had picked up the false note immediately, he realized. She looked puzzled. As well she might be, he thought viciously, for he was as well. The whole situation was damnable. There sat that lovely girl. All white and soft and compliant. All rounded and swelling, naive and ripe for him, and they were just friends. For these past weeks, he had had to play at being some stupid mythical fellow. Brotherly, fatherlike, everything but loverlike. She was homeless and friendless, she liked and respected him. How easily he could have moved her that one necessary step further into his life, had he been able. With little whispers, soft breaths, slight embraces, light kisses, and lighter promises, she could have been his by now; in gratitude, in pleasure, in love. But he had been thwarted, chaperoned and hedged in by circumstance. Forced to be natural and easy with Amelia, distantly friendly with Regina, and wary, always, of Torquay. Torquay, again Torquay. Small wonder he detested the man.

How easily Torquay could carry off a female, how simple he made the process. He had only to widen his china eyes and stare at some female of the demimonde and she was his. He had only to slightly court some light lady of Society and she closed her doors to all others. And, what was maddening, the stench of his reputation only seemed to enhance his desirability. And always, always, where he encountered St. John, there would be those light words, that little aside, that know-ing smile, as if to say, "See, this is how it is with me. With you as well. You are no better, only, dear boy, far less successful." He seemed to amuse himself at St. John's expense, that was intolerable. And now, in this damnable affair with Regina, he saw himself in the role he played through her eyes: earnest, prim, and dull. While the absent Duke, by comparison, was all fire, all impulse. He did not want Amelia feeding any subterra-nean illusions Regina might have about Torquay. He did not want to lose her to Torquay, as he had lost others. Not this time. Not this woman. It was not fair. She had fallen, as if by fate, into his hands. And there he would see she would stay.

"At any rate," he managed to smile, "it's not impor-tant now, is it? If he is gone, then Regina's road will be all the clearer, and her freedom achieved sooner, as well. Come, let's forget the fellow, we all make too much of him. Let's play at cards, and be friends again."

"Very well," Amelia laughed, but the laughter was brittle.

"You must teach me better, Sinjun," Regina said sadly, "before I owe you my very soul."

I will own that, and more, St. John promised her with a quick look, and soon, sooner now than I thought.

And Lady Amelia forced herself to look down quickly at her cards, and commanded her hands not to shake.

And Regina, looking up into his warm gray eyes smiling at her, thought only of how fortunate she was in her friends, and how undeserving she was of their concern.

XI

"I vow," the Duke said, smiling down at the company from his observation post at the head of the table, "I do not know how any of you good ladies can manage to keep your eyes open during the day, after a succession of riotous evenings such as this."

"Unkind, Jason," Miss Pickett commented sharply as she spooned her soup, not missing a drop in the delicate rhythm she had established to clear the bowl.

Miss Barrow stiffened at the familiar tone the other lady had used, and straightened herself further in her chair. Little Lady Lucinda seemed unaware of the adults at the table, and merely edged a carrot in her bowl closer to a navy bean and appeared to admire her artwork.

They sat formally at the long damasked table, with footmen poised behind their chairs, alert to the immediate remove of each successfully accomplished course, and they sat for the most part silently, as they had for five successive evenings. Occasionally the Duke and Miss Pickett would rouse enough to involve themselves in what Miss Barrow regarded as highly improper banter, with Miss Pickett, she felt, too often forgetting her position, and His Grace never remembering his. But, she felt strongly, she did not wonder at his careless attitude toward his rank, and not even at half the tales she had heard of him, if that farouche, indelicate female opposite her had indeed been in sole charge of his early upbringing. For her part, she was determined to show by her impassive, but tangible disapproval, that his daughter's governess, at least, would spare this child such a slipshod education.

She had seen not only a slight, almost imperceptible although definite, to her hawklike vision, change in her charge's demeanor since the Duke's arrival. But a definite change, and not for the better, since Miss Pickett's appearance. That woman insisted on trying to draw Lady Lucinda into conversation at the most inappropriate times, with the most inappropriate questions. At an art lesson yesterday, for example, Miss Pickett had carelessly ambled, yes ambled, into the nursery and asked Lady Lucinda why she only put one blossom on her watercolor of a tree. And the child had answered, rightfully and dutifully, laying aside her brush, that it was to give the tree a proper modest balance with the rest of the landscape, and to avoid a vulgar blotch of colors. "Oh I don't know," Miss Pickett had replied. "My favorite trees in spring are those that are the most vulgar, the most positively garish in their display of color, aren't yours?" And when the child had tentatively, at first, and then with Miss Pickett's approval begun eagerly to overlay the tree with great conflicting stabs of color, horrendous blobs of color, Miss Pickett had almost cried out with delight, and Miss Lucinda, emboldened by the creature, forgot herself so much as to dissolve into giggles, all the while darting little sly looks at her outraged governess.

And that, coupled with the incident at the reading lesson, the contretemps on the nature walk, and the common display at the pianoforte, had put Miss Barrow on guard, and made each successive evening at the great dinner table more uncomfortable. And why she and her charge should be summoned to the dinner table with His Grace and that creature every night, instead of dining modestly in the nursery as usual, was a puzzlement. Miss Barrow glowered down at her rack of lamb with such force, that had it been a sensible thing, it would have cringed. She would wait them out. The Duke could not content himself with pastoral pleasures for long, she felt, and whatever freak of temper had sent him posting back to Grace Hall to disrupt his daughter's life would soon pass. She was only grateful that this shocking ex-governess was the only company he had summoned, and that he had not filled the Hall with the even more disreputable of his fell companions.

"Why don't you eat your potatoes, child?" Miss Pickett now asked, noting how Lady Lucinda was poking each parslied marble-shaped little orb into a corner of her plate.

"I don't care for them," Lady Lucinda replied carefully, and then with a glance at her governess, "at least not tonight, thank you m'am."

"I should think you'd prefer some nice fluffy potatoes," Miss Pickett decided, and was about to signal to a footman when Lady Lucinda hastily said, "Oh no, m'am, I'm not allowed them."

"Reasons of health?" Miss Pickett frowned.

"Reasons of manners, Miss Pickett," Miss Barrow stated ominously. "M'lady was prone to dauble in them. She would—and here all lectures were to no avail—continually play with them at table, making quite a revolting mess of her plate, so she has been forbidden them till she can make a more reasonable effort at the table."

"Play with them?" Miss Pickett smiled. "Why what on earth did you do with them, My Lady? Shy them at the butler? Lob them at the chandelier?" And Lady Lucinda gave a little gulping, half concealed giggle, but no further answer. "Well," continued Miss Pickett in ringing tones, "I can distinctly remember being more circumspect myself. I was fond of sculpting mountains in them, and your father, I recall, had a decided partiality for creating opposing continental armies, with a river of gravy separating the warring factions."

"Castles," Lady Lucinda replied unexpectedly, "and sometimes mountains, too."

"I do not find this amusing," Miss Barrow said dangerously. "I do not find the improper manners of a child a source of amusement, or a proper topic of discussion before her."

"But she is a child, Miss Barrow," her antagonist said unrelentingly, "and should on some small occasions be allowed to remember it."

"Your Grace," Miss Barrow said, quivering, half rising from her chair in affront, and appealing to the only voice of authority in the room. "I do not find this discussion proper in front of your daughter."

"I am seldom," the Duke smiled smoothly, putting down his fork, "called upon to arbitrate in matters of vegetables. But now that it is called to mind, I recall that yes, I did prefer those that were soft and smooth and rounded. But then," he added thoughtfully, "it is, of course, to be remembered that I would prefer any objects so pleasantly defined, even now."

"Your Grace!" Miss Barrow rose majestically. "I do not have to to tolerate such topics of conversation and such vulgar innuendo."

"Of course you do not," he answered in bored tones.

"And you will do nothing to stop it?"

"No, nothing," the Duke answered, casting the outraged governess a level blue look.

"Then I shall have to leave."

"You must do as you see fit," he replied.

"I mean, of course," Miss Barrow announced, casting her last spear, "to leave your employ."

"That," the Duke said softly, his daughter's widened eyes upon him, "is what I assumed you meant."

"And now?" Miss Pickett said, her voice disturbing the quiet in the emptied room.

"And now," the Duke replied, carefully inspecting an apple that had been left in the bowl upon the table, "I am bereft of a governess for my poor child, and all due to your vicious tongue, Pickett." He shook his head slowly and regretfully. Miss Barrow had left with a gasp, Lady Lucinda had been sent to bed after a sweet and calm chat with Miss Pickett, and the Duke had waved away the footmen after they had cleared the remnants of the uneaten meal. The fire crackled quietly in the fireplace, and the candles guttered in their silver sockets.

"That you, of all people, should bring me to this, Pickett," the Duke sighed.

"Of course, it was wonderful how you engineered it, Jason," Miss Pickett said slowly. "And quite like the boy I knew. You knew, of course, what the sight of the stick that prig Barrow was converting that poor child into would do to me, and you knew my reckless tongue.

And, of course, you knew to a nicety, what her reaction would be, as you always seem to know what people's reactions will be."

"I am a knowing one," the Duke answered somberly, carving a small round disk from the apple. "Although 'nicety' is seldom a term applied to me."

"Of course, you did know how to entrap me, but wouldn't it have been simpler to simply dismiss her and ask me?"

"But simpler may not have been as effective, and there was the merest possibility that you might have refused," he replied reasonably.

"I would have," she said sadly. "I am too old, Jason."

"You, too old?" he said, his eyes widening. "Oh never, Pickett, you never were, you never will be."

And he remembered all the years before he had been sent away for his education, all the years when her vigilance had protected him, those early years when she would plan walks and tours and rambles, to keep him from the house when his mother was entertaining her "guests," her "gentlemen callers." All the years of her unceasing efforts in his behalf, her attempts to turn a slight, almost too beautiful and sensitive boy child into a responsible sturdy man. How she had introduced him to the groom, and the stablemen, and the boys who worked about the house, so that he could learn the art of fisti- cuffs, so that he could learn the world of men. Of how she had toughened herself, had cultivated her astrin- gent personality. She had hidden her concern for his bruises, both physical and mental, so that she would not smother him, cosset him, soften him, and all so that he could grow strong enough to face the realities she had so successfully hidden from him until that day he had escaped her notice and burst in upon his mother at her sport. "You too old Pickett?" he laughed. "When there is a need for you?"

"Too devious though, Jason," she sighed. "Oh I'll do it, of course, I'll raise her as best I'm able, but you did not used to be so devious."

"But it comes so naturally, I must have always been so, my dear, it just escaped your doting eye."

"Not quite so devious," she insisted, and then looking at him there, his legs stretched out, the apple and the knife held in his careful white fingers, his attention carefully focused on them, she blurted, "And all those other tales I have heard. Yes, I took care to try to hear about your exploits. Those tales, are they true?"

He did not look up from the apple, but only drawled in his fogged whisper, "Now which tales could you be referring to? There are so many. And rumor adds long tails to short ones. Ah well, for reasons of propriety, I cannot possibly go into them all. As well as for reasons of time, for although the night is yet young, it might take us till tomorrow to be done with them all. Suffice it then to say, yes, half of them, whatever ones you heard, are quite true."

"Half of them is too much, Jason," she said sternly.

"Send me early to bed, will you?" he smiled, looking at her now with that sweet smile that first won her when she had seen him all those years ago. There was such a melting power in that smile then, she thought, and even more now, no wonder he can go his way unchecked.

"Too much, Jason," she sorrowed. "I did not point you that direction."

"The bitch whelps true, Pickett," he said with a fleeting expression almost like a snarl. "I am my mother's child."

"And you court her end?" Pickett's voice rang out.

"Oh let be, my love. I live my life, I am well content, I harm no one but myself." He rose and walked the length of the table, stopping only to inspect the centerpiece with unseeing eyes. The silence grew in the room, and he absently shaped the candlewax with a stroking finger. "At least as yet," he whispered absently. "At least I think I have harmed no one else as yet. No, all were willing, all are willing to lead the merry Duke a merry dance for a pretty price. And if I prefer the dance, Pickett, what of it? I have been a wallflower. I have had connubial bliss. I am not suited to it, let me to my pleasures."

"And are they pleasures, Jason?" she asked, unrelenting.

"You put me to the blush, my love. At least I find them so. And others have assured me of it. At least," he qualified again, "as yet, they have."

"But not all?" she persisted. "Is there another person you are involved with now? You sound not as sure as a merry Duke should be. And this sudden visit to Grace Hall, this sudden concern for the child, is there a reason?"

For a moment in the dimness of the room, the years fled away for both of them, the old, anxious woman perched upon her chair watching the slim, fair impeccable man. For a moment, he hesitated, as if to talk again, without artifice, without concealment, to another being. But then a log cracked in the fire and the moment passed. He straightened.

"Another person?" he said quizzically. "Oh how full of tact you are my quaint Pickett. 'Another person,' so all the tales have reached you after all? But you hope that the 'person' is a female one, and a pure, honest, well-bred one at that, for somewhere in that reasonable breast lurks the unreasonable belief that your nursling will be saved by the love of a good woman."

She knew the moment had passed, and so she retorted, "Nonsense, arrant nonsense, Jason. The love of a good woman would roll off your back like water off a duck's. I make no doubt you've enjoyed the love of a good many women and some of them good women at that, but that would not change you in the least."

"So glad," he bowed, "to see you have not lost your senses, or have been spending your retirement wallowing through reams of bad romances."

"But," she said succinctly as she rose to leave, "the love *for* a good woman . . . ah that, my lad, would make all the difference in the world."

"As ever," he said half to her retreating back, half to the candle he had sculpted, "you have an acid tongue, and a way with words, my dear, a remarkable way with words."

*   *   *

The moonlight drenched the room, and he lay there, on the great bed, silently. As well try to sleep in the glare of noon, he thought, but he did not rise to drape the windows, for he could never bear to sleep in pitch dark, never bear to lock out the moonlight. There will be dark enough in the tomb, he thought, no need to simulate it now. But he could not sleep, and blamed the moonlight, until he realized that while every muscle in his body yearned for sleep, no part of his brain would have any part of it. So he lay there, wide-eyed, seeing the shapes of the room, the edges of the great canopy, above him, much, he thought as it must have looked to his parents the night he was conceived, and to his grandfather the night his father was conceived. And doubtless, he thought wryly, so had his late wife studied the canopy intently the night that poor little wretch was conceived, in fact he remembered her unblinking gaze quite well.

He had dismissed his valet early, and the only concession he had made to sleep was in having had his boots removed, for he lay there on the coverlet, fully clothed. It was as if he awaited his departure in the morning with such eagerness that he did not even wish to bother with the convention of undressing, preparing for sleep, rising and re-dressing, as if all of that was just an unnecessary delaying tactic. Not for the first time he wished he could be at a place just by the wishing of it, without the bother of everyday mechanics to convey him. This visit to my childhood, he thought wearily, has made me as a child again, with a child's fancies.

While his body lay tense, yet inert, his mind ranged far. At least the child has Pickett now, he thought, and Pickett has another crusade to enliven her. Not the sheltering of a boy from a licentious mama, but the sheltering of a girl from a profligate papa. What cycles dear Pickett has seen, he thought, laughing lightly in the semidark. And so I have resolved all here, he thought, knowing that he had done very little, knowing once again that he had again only arranged things to his own comfort.

Comfort, he thought lazily, ah that would be a good

thing. The thing of it is that I am unused to celibacy. In fact, I cannot sleep without my strange comforts. It is that, of course, and the damned moonlight that keeps me lying here, stark staring awake while the rest of the household snores the roofbeams off. Some round, light, laughing thing here in my bed with me would ensure eventual sleep. But no, I am the model papa, as stern and pure and self-denying as a picture upon the wall, and thank God I will be off in the morning and about my pleasures once again.

And when he thought of his present pleasures, and when the image of that pale, green-eyed face swung before him, and the image of that white neck, and the breath that caused the high breasts to rise and fall, and the remembrance of that light step, and the recollection of that breathless little nervous laugh she gave when he shocked her, came, he rose from the bed and roamed the room thinking that such thoughts did not serve him well when he lay sleepless in an empty sacrificial thankless bed. But not empty for long, he thought, for I will have her, and that is becoming more important to me with every empty night I spend. For somehow she had killed his desire for others. And, confused, he accepted his continence and, uncharacteristically, refused to analyze it. Unable to change it, he had decided it was a clever and conscience decision on his part. He applauded his decision not to settle for substitutes at this stage, deeming it rather like a man refusing to gorge on sweets before a gourmet dinner. He had no desire to take the edge off his appetite, he reasoned.

Ah those appetites, he thought, holding his head in his hands as he sat on the edge of the bed. Appetites for shapes and textures of pleasures that seemed both never-ending in their sequences and curiously less satisfying with each encounter. But there was this aura about her, he insisted to himself, that did not seem only to spring from his habit of embuing each new one with imagined attributes to whet his tastes. There was that in her which he would not have made up, that which he would not, left on his own, have imagined. That curious moral rectitude, that gallant and naive assumption that there was such a thing in her world as honor, as fair play. What had she said that curious night in the coach, she would not sell herself, would he?

What a shock that had been. It was as unexpected to him as roaming through a pleasant field of flowers and gathering one with a wasp inside. It's true he had gone too far. He knew that, but each time in the past when he had thought he'd gone too far, even he himself had thought so, Society had only clucked and shrugged and looked the other way. And what was the difference, he had thought, between this abduction and that other? That giggling little serving girl that he had accosted in the hall at a friend's house that cold winter's night. That . . . Emily, yes, Emily Ketchum, had been her name. The one with the provocative birthmark near her delightful lips. "Come live with me and be my love," he had breathed in her ear, half flown with good wine, as she had helped him on with his cloak. And she had simpered and a calculating look had come into her eye and she lain her little hands on his chest and pouted, "But how? Your Grace, oh the mistress would skin me, and my mother, oh she'd tan me if I up and went off with you." "Shall I abduct you then, my heart?" he had suggested, tasting her earlobe and liking the flavor. "Oh yes, sir!" she had assented quickly. And he had laughed, and laughingly brought the coach to the back door, and stifled with laughter, doubled with laughter, carried her giggling, wrapped in his cloak, out into the night. And she had fared well when he grew tired of her, in comfortable keeping even now to an acquaintance of his.

So why had this been different? She'd had no real prospects, no connections, no family. She was of common birth, with only that mushroom of an aunt and that simpleton cousin. He had expected her to turn to him, there in the coach, eyes sparkling, and accept his terms with pleasure. What better could she have done with herself? Why had she gone, so desirable, available, and unchaperoned to that blasted Opera, if she had not been looking for such an accommodation? And if she had lost courage then, had he not made it that much easier for her? She had responded to his kisses, he knew. She must know of his fortune, where was the impediment? What woman had he known in the last decade who would not settle for money and pleasure? But no, she had turned on him. She had repulsed him and had given him a stern little lecture on morality instead. Almost as if she were Pickett, transformed, young and lovely.

She disturbed him. She fit no pattern. He had not meant to speak to her again until the game was up, but had gone to meet her there then, in that freezing meadow, out of a desire to understand where the impediment lay. And she had been a delight. They had talked the afternoon away. There were times in that strange, cold afternoon when he had forgotten he was conversing with a woman, so far did her interests range, so quick was her clever tongue. And so each time, when he had refocused upon her appearance, her loveliness had come to him with breath-catching shock. And still she had prosed on about honor, and friendship, and morality, as if she were some sort of odd, seductive little deacon. Yet he swore her eyes had hinted at less pious delights. And almost she had him convinced of that impossible innocence when she had risen to go back. Back to St. John, and his protection. And what sort of innocence would lie undisturbed in St. John's house, in his very bed? Did she believe he would continue his exemplary behavior once beyond his sister's and Lady Burden's watchful eyes? That, indeed, would be innocence to boggle the mind.

He did not know why he disliked the Marquis with such violence. It was, after all, rare for him to dislike anyone with like intensity, for to dislike someone was to indulge in some form of passion, and he had thought that he had used up his passion in mere passion long since.

Perhaps it was because that strong, tall, socially impeccable young man nightly wallowed in his same sewer, and daily walked the road of righteousness, raising his eyebrows in distaste at tales of the Black Duke's misadventures. Perhaps, he admitted, it was that in St. John's eyes he saw reflected his own past, and his own sure future. Or perhaps, he thought, with the clarity that only solitary, exhausted late-night thought delivers, it was that St. John so often, as if by reason of some malevolent fate, had seen him at his worst, had seen him in situations that he himself shrank from remembering in the cold daylight.

That night, for example, that he only allowed himself to remember on nights such as these. The night when he had gone around to Madame Sylvestre's select establishment for an evening's diversion, and had discovered what his world's estimate of himself was. In recent years he did not care to patronize such establishments. He much preferred to have some light creature in his own keeping, some female who would, at least, pretend to look up at him with some semblance of recognition and delight when he opened the door. But at that time, for some reason he could not remember even now, he was by way of being a frequent customer there.

He had been greeted graciously and, taking his cloak, they had led him to a gilded room. Entering, he had found a lovely young woman within. She had taken his coat and prattled softly, laughed deliciously, and given him glimpses of the delights that lay in store for him. She had looked to be exquisite, a prime, healthy young creature, and after a few embraces he had been sure of a pleasant evening. But first he had had to order and partake of a quantity of wine, a thing he often had to do in such arrangements, to deaden a certain relentlessly critical portion of his mind, to free another segment of his brain to unhesitatingly appreciate such a treat.

But some time during the preliminary tangle, in the wine-soaked explorations and preparations, the door had opened and another female had come in. He had been, in that moment, amused at the proprietress's estimate of his needs. But then, even though fully fogged with wine, the appearance of the second female had stopped the play and he drew back with difficulty and gaped. She was not the sort of woman one expected to find at an establishment such as Madame Sylvestre's. She looked like Covent Garden gutter ware. Ageing, overblown, overpainted, not overly clean, with impossibly hennaed hair, she simpered and began to remover her tawdry finery.

"C'mon lovey," she had cajoled, reaching for him and revealing a gap-toothed smile. "It'll be lovely, it will. The two of us for the one of you. There's a lot I know."

At first, he had been amused, and for one mad moment had wondered at how it might be, a night of textures, an opportunity to explore textures and differences and shapes. But then, even in his castaway state, he had recoiled.

"Awww Aggie," the younger woman had laughed. "You've gone and lost your golden guinea. I told you to wait a bit, but you rushed in too soon. You see," she explained anxiously, unsure of his reaction as he sat staring, "Lord Barrymore, he's outside, and he payed Madame a sum, and he brought Aggie here and promised her even more to entertain you. He's wagered a sum, he said, with another gentleman. He wagered that you'd throw no female creature out of your bed, so long as she's willing. Ah, but look you, Aggie, he wants no part of you."

Nervously, the older woman backed away, holding her wrapper closed around her ample breasts. "You're not mad at poor old Aggie, now are you, sir?" she cringed, whining. "I only did it cause they told me as to how you'd like it. I'd like it fine," she said encouragingly. "And they all said as how you'd think it a rare jest and go along."

Of course, it has come to this, he remembered thinking as he rose to pour himself more wine with a shaking hand. It is, after all, only a natural progression. And in some strange fashion, he'd felt a small satisfaction at his own aghast reaction. Why should they not think it, haven't you worked diligently toward this? They believe there is nothing you are not capable of. Even attempting a poxy Billingsgate whore. And what shall you do now? What a comedy it would be for the blackest of them all to go raging out of here crying his discretion, his taste, his honor. All, everything, except this, then? You dare ask them to believe that? Then let them believe what they will, he swore, for no matter what the protest, they will.

"No Aggie," he had finally said when he could control his voice. "No, I'm not angry. And you shall have your golden guinea, for you may tell Lord Barrymore anything you like. But," he said smiling, holding up his hands in mock horror, "there's an extra coin in it for both of you if you swear not to tell a soul that I have imbibed so much this night that I truly fear I cannot please either one of you and am best off retiring like a monk to my own cell."

And after fending off their concerned attempts to reassure him as to his capabilities, he gave them both some silver and led them to the door, an arm about each of them. And then, there in the doorway he saw St. John, the lofty Marquis of Bessacarr, regarding him with loathing. And in the throes of his own strange exultant humiliation, his own soul wincing, he had whispered fiercely to the Marquis, "What? Distaste, Sinjun? But wait a few years, my dear boy, and you will find yourself pursuing the same sport. Unless you care to join me now? I'm sure Aggie has room in her heart for both of us."

And later, standing alone, his hands stretched out stiffly against the table to forbid them from trembling, and staring down at the bottle of wine he scarcely believed that he had drunk, so sober was he now, he had thought, yes soon, at this rate it would not be long. Soon there will undoubtedly come the day when I will no longer care. And all will be lost in the endless search for textures and pleasures.

All what? What was there left to lose, he thought now in fury. What was that last vestige he feared losing? That remnant he guarded as jealously as that green-eyed wench protected her virginity? Her favorite word, Honor?

Honor, he thought wearily, as dawn bleached the sky, no matter, soon she will come to me, on my terms, and without honor, and I will take her without honor, and whatever honor there will be in it, will be that I was right again. And there will be the end of it.

And knowing that sleep was gone, for he had often spent similar nights, being used to uneasiness in his own company, he rose and pulled on his boots, and dashed some water against his face, and swirled some in his mouth to take the taste of the bitter night away.

He opened the door that led out into the hall and soundlessly began to pad toward the stairs when he saw a small shape outlined against the tall windows at the head of the stairs. Knowing that he moved silently, he brushed against the wall to warn her so that he would not startle her too much.

"Really, Pickett," he said softly, "if you are going to wander at this ungodly hour, allow us to provide you with some chains to rattle so that your perambulations do not go to waste. The house needs a spectacular ghost to give it some pretensions."

"It is not an ungodly hour of the night," she countered. "It is, rather, an extremely godly hour of the morning. Old bones do not care for long rest, knowing that a longer one awaits. But you are up early, Jason. Are you so eager to attend matins?"

"No, my love," he smiled. "Have you forgotten? I am away today. I shall leave my house and my child in your capable hands. I trust you will keep them both free of small insects and large problems. Come, break bread with me, and I will give you my direction, and complete written authority to do as you wish."

"I would wish," she said, seeing in the increasing light the scars the long night had left beneath his eyes, "that you might give me the same license with your own person."

"Ah love," he said, bending and placing his hand along her cheek. "I do believe that when his Infernal Highness comes around at last to claim me, and lays his fiery collar about my neck, my own dear fierce Pickett will be there to challenge him, and swear, against the damnation of her own soul, that her poor misunderstood nursling has been wrongly accused, and stands innocent of all wrongdoing."

"I think you wrong yourself the most," she said sadly. "And look hourly for that gentleman to come and release you from yourself. And I do not think he could do half so good a job at torment as you have done."

"Torment?" He paused on the stair and threw his golden head back and roared with laughter. When he had recovered, he said merrily, "Pickett, you observe a gentleman in haste to be on the way to a gala ball, and on the way to collect on an important wager surely soon to be won, on the way to triumph, in fact."

She followed him silently down the long stairs, but in the hall she paused, and lay her hand upon his sleeve.

"When you were a boy," she said, watching him with troubled eyes, "we two had an important wager once. Do you remember? It was a picnic we were to go on, half a day's drive away. Oh, you were so excited, for we had your mama's permission to take a luncheon, we had an invitation to see some fine horses you had admired. We were to be allowed to be away until nightfall. For a week, you watched the skies, and noted the winds, and daily you wagered it would rain that day and cancel our trip. And I swore the sun would shine. And on that morning it poured rain, I believed it was the beginning of the flood. And you came to me, with tears in your eyes, and said, 'Pickett, at least congratulate me, for I've won.' Is it to be another such triumph?"

He stared down at her, his face gray as the uncertain light. "What matter?" he spoke softly. "It will be a wager won. And," he continued, "surely you do not begrudge me victory?"

And so I do, my lad, she thought silently as he gave her his arm to lead her in to breakfast. I begrudge you all such triumph, and all your bitter victories.

XII

The carriage moved almost silently through the night toward the broad entrance of the drive to Squire Hadley's manor house, but three of the occupants of the carriage were as silent as their conveyance. The only voice that chatted happily on was that of Lady Mary, who blissfully and without interruption prattled on about the forthcoming delights of the evening. The others sat quietly, each wrapped in their own silence of thought and speculation.

There had been a brief flurry of light chatter when they had all met in the hallway before they had left Fairleigh, Regina had been complimented fulsomely by both of the other ladies. She had been dressed with care, and Lady Burden's green satin ball gown had suited her unique coloring to perfection. Although she had been shocked, and then worried about the extremely low neck of the gown, low enough, she realized with some fear, to show the swelling rise of her breasts, her maid had assured her that contrary to her expectations, it would be considered a modest gown, and all the crack this season. When she had descended the stairs, she had seen that even the gown that the swollen Lady Mary wore had a more daring cut, and then her fears had been allayed completely by the slow and lingering smile that St. John had briefly worn when he had gazed upon her.

There was a brief roundelay of mutual compliments, Regina being quite careful to phrase her admiration for Lady Mary's quite inappropriately pink and white draped gown, and her very real esteem for Amelia's elegant amber velvet dress. St. John, she noticed, was looking so handsome in his severe black evening dress that she felt shy of turning a word of praise to him. Somehow, dressed as he was, she felt he was even more unapproachable than usual and his tightened expression as they entered the coach chased any lingering thought of easy conversation with him from her mind. Again, however, she mused, as she half listened to Mary's incessant chatter, she had caught the vestiges of a feeling of something she had forgotten, when she had first seen St. John this evening. But now her foremost worry was how she was to behave this evening.

Both St. John and Amelia had told her clearly that she had nothing to fear from the Duke. That she could, indeed, if she wished to, even speak with him as lightly as she wished. But that the best course of action would be to ignore him completely. But how, she wondered, wishing that she were not wearing long gloves so that she could comfortably nibble at a fingertip, could she ignore him? Or be sure that she would know how to act at a ball? For, under no circumstances did she wish to embarrass any one of her benefactors. But Amelia had only laughed, and heartlessly stated that there was no way in which she could disgrace herself at Squire Hadley's ball unless she became disguised and cavorted barefoot in the punchbowl, and even then, the Squire might think it all the rage to do so and join in her romp.

When she entered the large room to which they had been ushered when their wraps were removed, Regina was at first too dazzled by both the quantity of brightly burning candles and the panoply of dancers, to single out any individuals. Lord, she breathed to herself, as she half heard St. John introducing her to the largely beaming Squire and his breathless wife, there must be upward of a hundred people here! She had no way of knowing that what was to her an unimaginably elegant, brilliant, and crowded ball, was to her London-bred companions merely a dull, sparsely attended, inelegant local country dance.

Lady Mary was led to a comfortable chair among the dowagers, where, perceiving her interesting condition, she was immediately drawn into a—to her—delightful round of reminiscences of confinements and other homey discussions of mutual childbed experiences. St. John and Amelia stood watching the proceedings with Regina, until St. John, stifling a yawn, went off to fetch both ladies small glasses of ratafia.

"He does not seem to be here at all," Amelia said quietly to Regina, with just a trace of regret in her voice. "I suppose it was all a hum on his part, and after we were all expecting some ferocious confrontation. Ah, well," she went on, "he does have an odd sense of humor, at that."

Regina did not have to ask who "he" was, and scarcely trusting herself to do more than nod, she watched the dancers forming a country set. She had been so involved in searching the whirling room for the slight, familiar form that she had not noticed the stir that she herself had caused when she had entered. Her face, her form alone would have ensured a certain response in any male member of the company, but her mysterious reputation had preceded her, and mercifully, she was as yet unaware of the curiosity concerning herself. But when a tall young man detached himself from his fellows and bowed an introduction to Regina and Lady Burden, she gave a start as she heard herself being invited to join the dance now forming. But she didn't know how to dance, she thought with panic, and understood suddenly how a man who cannot swim feels when the water is closing over his head.

Amelia, smiling pleasantly, waited to hear Regina's response, but at the girl's stricken look suddenly remembered that it must have been true, that incredible claim that she could not dance, and with the quickness of mind and sure instinct for social grace that she was noted for, smiled sweetly and said, "Ah, but Mr. Birmingham, our dear visitor Lady Berry had the most unfortunate accident only this morning, oh nothing dire, but she did turn her ankle, and regretably cannot join us in the dance this evening. But, since you did journey all the way across the room for a dance, if you would not mind escorting Lady Berry to a seat, I will join you in her place."

Mr. Birmingham, repressing the keen disappointment he felt, bowed, and said, "But that would be beyond all goodness of your part, Lady Amelia," and, having deposited Regina in a comfortable chair on the sidelines next to the dowagers, chaperones, and mamas, gallantly escorted Amelia to the dancers.

Regina watched the dancers for a while, noticing that St. John had been snared by a burbling Miss Kitty, who was lisping and giggling and making play with her lashes in a manner that surprised even Regina. The ladies that Regina was seated among, after having murmured quiet introductions, eyed her suspiciously, and then turned back to Lady Mary, who was vying with the Squire's wife in detailing particularly dreadful parturitions.

After hearing the explicit details of a hopefully exaggerated difficult confinement on the part of one of the mamas, Regina began to feel uneasy. Watching Amelia whirl about with her third partner, and realizing that now that St. John had been captured by Miss Lottie, he would not soon make an escape, as Miss Kitty and even the betrothed Miss Betty were eyeing him as if he was to be their last supper, Regina began to feel increasingly the dreamlike aspect of her position.

She had bathed, and powdered, and dressed with care. She had come to this ball, but now felt as if there were a pane of glass separating her from all the others here. She could not speak with any authority about childbirth, and the only other young woman in her proximity was a poor young creature who was afflicted with a blighting galaxy of spots upon her face, and who glared with such ferocity at any young man whose mother had prompted him to approach her that he summarily retreated. No other young men approached Regina, and she felt that surely they all must think her of little consequence and less looks, or perhaps, in some supernatural way, had ascertained her deception.

She had no way of knowing that her beauty quite took their breath away, and coupled with the mysterious linkage she enjoyed with the powerful Marquis, they all felt she was far beyond their touch. Her refusal to dance had only fed the rapidly whispered rumors that she was of high social station and a complete snob, or a French émigré who could not yet master the language, and there were even some mean souls who whispered that she was part of a colossal joke the elegant Marquis was visiting upon his country hosts, and she was in actuality only an expensive bit of muslin brought down from London as a lark. Therefore, no girl of any reputation dared speak to her, and as no young man wished to be rejected by her, she was left quite alone.

The musicians played country dances, the young people formed sets, and Regina watched them lightly make their way through, what seemed to her, the impossible complicated forms of the dance. Slowly, her sure eye began to tell her what her experience could not. St. John and Amelia were certainly the best dressed, most elegant couple there. The other men seemed to her at once both too young and too old for fashionable attire, and their clothing seemed both too overly elaborate or too casual for the affair. The girls were often dressed in unsuitable colors, and their hair was dressed in styles which she intuitively knew were not correct. Occasionally a gentleman would glance in her direction and then either glance away or give her a calculating longer look. The women would either ignore her altogether or seek her out with a piercing look and then whisper some comment to their companions. Even while she admired the grace and precision of the dance, she was aware of their ill-concealed curiosity toward her.

After what seemed to Regina to be an interminable amount of time, she felt that she could bear the situation no longer. It is as if I didn't exist at all, she thought wildly, and beset by terrors brought on by her own trepidation, guilt at her false position in the Marquis's household, and fears of embarrassing her hosts, she, trying to keep a calm expression on her face, rose and went quietly toward the back of the rooms where she hoped to take refuge in the shadowy recesses of the window embrasures.

Once she had achieved the windows, she spied a small antechamber off the main room, where a large, curtained window stood slightly open to admit a few cool breezes to flicker the candles. Gratefully, she went swiftly to the window to stare out at the darkened, bare gardens.

It was with no real sense of shock, but rather with a

surprisingly pleasant feeling of expectation, that she heard the husky voice say from behind her, in velvety amused tones, "Come, this is no way to accept a challenge. Rather I expected to see you spinning about the room, causing me to fall into paroxysms of jealousy as I spied you dancing with delight, locked in Sinjin's arms."

"Ah, but I cannot dance," she replied, without looking around her. "Did not your extensive research tell you that?"

"No, really?" he said. "That I did not know. But wouldn't your gracious host have instructed you in the rudiments?"

"He did not think it necessary," she said primly. "My expectations are to teach young women in several regimens, dancing is not one of them."

"Dancing should certainly be one of them," he said, and placing one hand upon her waist, he swung her around toward him.

He outshone the candles tonight, she thought. Impeccable, his black evening clothes contrasting with his golden head, his eyes glinting like deep water in the refracted light. He seemed so full of life and vitality that, once again, her breath caught in her throat and all the clever, cutting things she had vowed she would say to him caught there and died on a sigh. He placed one warm strong hand on her waist and she felt the touch of him would crisp the sheer material of her gown through to her skin. He tightened his grip and caught her wavering protesting hand in his other. Then he began to pull her slightly toward himself.

She looked up into the laughing blue eyes and gasped, she had not expected such a frontal attack and was momentarily without words, only the color rushed to her cheeks.

"Oh no," he laughed with delight. "This is not rapine, my innocent. This is merely the prefiguring position for that lovely dance the Squire has so daringly allowed to be played. The Graces assured him it was all the style in London this year. And so it is. It is called a waltz, and it is very decadent, the dowagers insist, as it comes from the continent where all things decadent, save for your obedient servant, come from. But it is quite fashionable and the advantage of it is that a man may hold a woman in the same position he usually dreams of holding a woman in, except in full view and with the approval of all her protectors. So I must hold you thus if you wish to learn to dance it."

"But I do not wish to dance it," she protested, unnerved by his hand, which had swung her so dangerously close to him.

"But you must," he said quickly, "or else anyone spying us here, you in my arms, thus," he said, drawing her closer, "would think that we are lovers met in assignation, and since you haven't given out one little scream or protest, what would that young woman watching us, think?"

Regina was too thunderstruck to look about for the witness he spoke of, and, wanting to avoid any scandal, said quickly, "Then show me the dance, quickly, and let me go. You promised you would not attempt any . . . seduction here."

"And I am a man of my word," he said, beginning to move in the motions of the dance. "But if you think that this is how I begin seduction, I really must instruct you further in that art as well. But not here, certainly. Here I shall initiate you only to the wonders of the dance." And slowly, counting her steps for her, he eased her into the whirling grace of a waltz.

She found, to her surprise, that it was a simple thing for her, and, listening to the music, she soon discovered a certain delight in the dance. They spun and dipped and danced until she found a rare laughter about to bubble up in her throat. She had never danced, and it was a heady experience. When at last she heard the music end, she looked up to see him staring down at her with new interest.

Glancing over his shoulder, she saw that he had swept her into a different room, a smaller hall off the small antechamber she had originally fled to. Now that the music had ended, she made a small move to remove herself from his arms, and found herself, instead, drawn closer. And then closer still, and then discovered herself being kissed again. She fought free and was about either to deliver him a resounding slap or to tear away completely and run, but while these two excellent plans revolved in her head, she heard him laugh merrily and say, "But you don't even know how to kiss yet! Do you? Most unsatisfactory. Sinjin has been very remiss."

His comment stunned her so that she turned to stare back at him. The idea that one had to know how to kiss had never occurred to her, and was the last thing she had expected him to say. She instead only stared at him, with a look of real puzzlement.

"You see," he said, "you still kiss exactly like a small child thanking an elderly uncle for a birthday present. That is not how grown-ups kiss, Regina. No," he said gently, "not the thing at all. You see you cannot kiss with your lips locked so tightly together, as if there were some secret behind them that you must never divulge. A kiss must tender up all secrets. You must part your lips, thus," he said, placing a finger upon her full lower lip. "As if you were, indeed, about to impart some delightful secret at last to your lover, or as if you were about to partake of some rare wine, to sip something of fine bouquet. You cannot taste, or drink or kiss through sealed child's lips, Regina," he said, and seeing her bemused expression, her waiting lips, he lowered his head, and kissed her then, again.

But this time, she did not draw back, or fight free, she only leaned forward, as if bewitched, into the long sweet, entirely new experience he presented her with. But when his hands began to leave her waist and travel up slowly until they reached her breasts, she shuddered suddenly, and broke free.

"No!" she cried, looking into his depthless eyes. "You shall not. . . ."

"Oh I shall, Regina," he said quietly, strangely solemn. "But the point is, isn't it, that you shall? And you begin to know it now?"

"*No!*" she said, confused. "Let me return. Let me alone. You told me you would not——"

"I only said that I would not attempt to seduce you here, and although I don't know exactly how extensive your education has been along the lines which most interest me, I assure you that it is exceedingly difficult to complete a seduction of a young woman who is entirely dressed while she stands alongside of you in an anteroom. Not that it cannot be done." He seemed to speculate, with a laughing look in his eye. "But not done well at all, no, most unsatisfactory." He nodded with mock regret.

"I thought you were not here tonight," she went on, avoiding his eye, aware that he still had both arms locked about her waist, aware of his warmth and the subtle pull of her own body toward that slight, insistent frame that held her so close. "I truly felt that you were not here tonight. I only left the others because I needed to get away from the dancing. I did not . . . no, never intended to see you here."

"But I am here now, Regina," he said. "And now what do you intend to do?"

"She intends," came a cold voice from the doorway, "to come in to dinner with me."

St. John, his face white with suppressed anger, stood looking at them. Regina stared, with a guilty start, but the Duke only smiled his immovable seraphic smile.

"Regina," St. John said tersely, "Amelia is looking for you, go to her. I shall join you shortly. Go now!" he commanded, as he stood and stared at the Duke. Regina hesitated only a moment, until she saw that neither man had any eyes for her now, rather they stood quietly facing each other locked in some inner combat. She turned and left quickly, welcoming the blinding glitter of lights in the room she approached, even though they swam suspiciously in her now dewed vision.

"But Sinjin," the Duke said slowly, relaxing and smiling up at the taller man, "I did tell you that I had set my sights upon her, and you did decline my invitation to compete for her. You said, I believe, for I do have an excellent memory, 'I'll leave that field open for you.' Now all I am doing is cultivating my field: a thing which, to my complete amazement, judging from her response to that simple caress you so rudely interrupted, you have not begun, and you are become an unex-

pected impediment. As well as taking an unexpected
advantage. Sheltering her, clothing her, for all I know,
and even introducing her as 'Lady Berry.' Not at all the
thing, dear Sinjin. Very ungentlemanly behavior, passing off a poor penniless chit as nobility. Think of your
hosts tonight. Why, half of them think she is your new
mistress already, and the other half have been wagging
their tongues about her all night. They would not be
pleased to find out who she truly is. Unless, of course, I
am altogether mistaken, and you have serious intentions, in which case, I offer you my felicitations, wish
you joy, and will, of course, bow out completely. But in
that case, my dear boy, is the announcement to be made
tonight, or would you prefer that I remain mum until I
return to town?" And he smiled warmly.

St. John stood still, his face very white, his fists
clenched at his sides. All he could think of was how
much he destested this man before him, and how little
ammunition he had that he could battle with. Torquay's
last words, however, had sent a shiver of pure terror
through him, the soft words had held a volume of possible blackmail in them. He said then, in a placating tone
he did not feel,

"Come now, Torquay, you know that I have no serious intentions toward the girl at all. And neither have I
any long-term plans for her. It is only that you will
allow that she has some freedom of choice in the matter
herself. And if she seeks my company rather than yours,
you can hardly be spoilsport enough to blame me for her
preference?"

"Again, Sinjin," said the Duke softly, "I again understand what it is about you that so distresses me. So
very little of what you say has any truth at all. I may be
all sorts of a villain, but I do not try to dissemble at all.
What I do, I do in plain sight of the world. While all
that you do, you do in secret. I do believe, however," he
said, cocking his head to the side, "that you half believe
the lies that you tell, so that you tell yourself them at
the same time you tell others and it all comes out so
plausible both to yourself and to them. Oh, it's not a
dueling matter," he went on, waving a hand at the Mar-

quis's newly aggressive stance. "I am quite adept at pistols, even blades, as no doubt are you. But there's no point in naming the killing ground, because although the world will take a great deal from us, I doubt it would ignore the slaying of one's peer. And I don't care for the climate in Greece this time of the year, do you? No," he said calmly, seeing the effect of his words on the Marquis, "it's . . . a matter of fact. Do you enter heavily into trade? Ah, but then you do it in secret, on the sly, and let the world believe that you have an independence unsullied by the grubby touch of the shop and the ships and the slave trade. Oh I know, I know, you needn't stare so, there is little I don't know, my dear boy. While my own poor fortune has roots that any fool can trace.

"I know, as well as you, that money is not in the habit of breeding by itself in a vault, and that every well eventually has a dry bottom. I too, have played the merchant and the trader, in turn. But had you inquired, you would have easily found that out. I make no secret of it. And do you know, Sinjin, it is surprising, but most people, even from the very best families, see only the glitter of the gold, and give not one damn about which mine it has been quarried from? But do not fear that I will cry rope at you. If you wish it to remain a secret, let it be. But know that I know.

"I, too, find fleshly pleasures exceed most others, but I make no secret of my pastimes, while you slip and slide and evade a path to all your mistresses. I have not a damn for the world, and I flourish like a green bay tree. As you do. I think that, yes, it is that which so annoys me—your constant hypocrisy. That you are indeed to be my successor, I do not care. But that you are forever presenting such a puritan face to the world, as you do: that you pretend to be so repelled, so shocked, so disgraced at my activities, while all the time you emulate me—ah, that rankles. But that is not to the point tonight.

"Now what is this nonsense about Miss Berryman—pardon, 'Lady Berry'—preferring your company to mine? The child sees you only as a sanctuary, not as a lover. You've told her some nonsense about finding her a position, haven't you? Don't bother to deny it, I have it from her own delightful lips that you have. It's rather like a mouse seeking sanctuary in a snake pit, isn't it? I know only too well what 'position' you have in mind. But incredible though it seems to me, she does not. One of the things I dislike the most, save you, my friend, is admitting an error in judgment, but it does seem that she has misjudged you as completely as I have erred in my estimation of her. But you see, Sinjin," the Duke went on, "it is only fair. I claimed her first. She is mine. And the only other moral justification I have, if you must have one, is that I have never lied about it. I have been extremely candid about my intentions. While you, with the same intentions, are spinning a web of lies so complicated . . . ah it does not bear discussion any further. Have done, Sinjin, turn her loose. I come to claim her now."

St. John stood quietly, his calm belying the murderous rage that he felt. Then he spoke scornfully.

"If I choose to try to protect my good name, you consider it a fault? If I choose to conduct myself with some sort of dignity so that my family and eventually my heirs do not find their names synonymous with disgrace and improvident to mention in polite society, you consider that a sin? Well, Torquay, you and I are indeed different sorts of creatures. But you are right to leave it for now, for it is a discussion that can have no end. To the matter of Miss Berryman, then. Suppose you ask her which of us she prefers? Which of us is the one she chooses? Would you accept her own decision? After all, we both encountered her at the same moment. So you cannot say she is your prior property."

The Duke looked at St. John with a considering eye. "But that is foolish, Sinjin," he said coolly, "for at the moment, she sees you, of course, in only a most avuncular fashion. You are only a kindly benefactor, and I a vile seducer. But I tell you, Sinjin," he thought and then, smiling radiantly, he went on, "if you were to make the same proposition to her that I have done, then yes. Oh, yes," he laughed, "in that case, with all the scales dropped from her eyes, with all the subterfuge pushed aside, if then you asked her for her decision, I would, yes, certainly abide by it. Are you willing, Sinjin, to come into the open? To finally put the matter to her coldly and clearly, without all these trappings? For that is a wager I will take you up on. It is, if you recall, exactly the one I offered to you when we both first saw her."

The Marquis wavered, seeing all his carefully constructed plans crumbling, but the Duke put in,

"Of course, if you do not tell her, you understand that I will. I grow tired of waiting. I desire her now. She is blossoming into a rare beauty. I like to talk to her. It's a novelty. Unless you hesitate because you feel sure that she could not prefer your protection. You are, of course, younger, and taller . . . but then I have *such* address, and such lovely blue eyes."

"No," St. John said, "then it will be as you say. I will have done with the charade. I will tell her. She will be given the decision to make. Will you abide by it?"

"Of course." The Duke smiled. "I love a good game, you know."

"But give me a day," St. John said. "I cannot tell her this night, for obvious reasons."

"Certainly." The Duke bowed impassively and, turning to leave the room, he looked back at the Marquis and, seeking exactly the right words, drawled, "I have looked forward to this day, Sinjin. It is so very pleasant to be proven right, to find that at last, you are willing to play upon my field, according to my rules, and in my exact mode. Why, at this rate, it will not be long until we are sharing exactly the same pleasures, and I should not mind at all, Sinjin. Remember, I have long told you that we are birds of a feather. Very black birds, though, I fear."

The Marquis felt an internal chill at the words, and stood, for a long moment, drawing in a shuddering breath, before he could face the rest of the company. It was now more important than ever that he defeat Torquay's plans, although in some small part of his mind, there rang a small, steady alarm bell.

The Duke strolled back to the ballroom and, finding

his host, joined him in desultory conversation, which mainly consisted of a documentation of the virtues of his three daughters, especially the two not yet betrothed.

Jason Thomas, Duke of Torquay, was at his best that night, smooth, urbane, delightfully conversant and clever. There was not a female that danced with him, of any age, who did not leave his hands feeling infinitely more desirable, and slightly, but delightfully scandalized, although he did no more or less than was strictly proper. There was not a youth who stood and spoke with him who did not walk away feeling singularly more sophisticated, nor an elder who did not shake his hand as he left, who did not think that surely the chap's reputation was exaggerated, for here was a man of rare good sense and opinion. He was at his peak; blithe, conversant, and deeply interested in every one who spoke with him.

No one in the room, no, no one in the world, could have guessed at the cold fear that gripped him, or the sick dread anticipation of failure, and some other emotion that he dared not name, which caused him to sit awake the unblinking hours in the Squire's finest guest room, while the whole house, save for the steadily working servants, slept peacefully through the last hours of the remaining night.

XIII

It was a strangely subdued party that sat in the breakfast room at Fairleigh on that dim winter's morning. Mary, pleading fatigue, had sent word that she would breakfast in her rooms after the excitement of the previous night. Amelia sat quietly sipping her chocolate and watching St. John's strangely tense face under her lashes. Regina seemed impervious to them both and, distracted, tried to bring her thoughts back from the unsteadying remembrances of the last evening.

She had seen the Duke again, but for the balance of

the night, his behavior had been impeccable. He had amused his companions, flattered his host and raised his hopes for the future of at least one of his daughters, danced with Amelia until her face glowed with pleasure, and said hardly one word when he had been formally introduced to 'Lady Berry.' Only at the end of the evening had he allowed his lips to linger over her hand for an extra heartbeat, and had whispered so softly, "The game is almost at an end, my dear, and it will be winner take all."

She had lain awake that night, her unruly thoughts returning again and again to that strange embrace, and wondering with dismay and near panic at the reactions that he had drawn forth from her traitorous lips. How could it be, she had agonized, that she could hold a man in such contempt for his manners and lifestyle, and yet, and yet, long for his kiss? It was against all the precepts that she had governed her life by. So now, while she felt secure and safe from him here, protected by her two new friends, she knew that she was not at all safe from him within the confines of her own mind. It is time, she thought again, for me to leave here. It is of utmost importance that I go far, far away. Although, she wondered, with an unsquelchable honesty, how can I go far from my own self?

Amelia left the table first, saying something about completing some correspondence she had to reply to. It was then that St. John rose and, looking over at Regina, said softly, "Regina, please I should like to speak with you now. About that position I mentioned to you yesterday."

She rose gladly, and made as if to walk to the study, when he smiled sadly, and said, "No, not here. I feel the need for some fresh air after last night's revels. I know you do not ride, so will you accompany me for a little stroll about the grounds? Dress warmly, there is a chill in the air."

Regina hurriedly put on a warm pellisse and, securing her hair, tied on a warm furred hat that Amelia had donated to her and was looking for St. John in the breakfast room, and then the study, when a glance out the window showed her that he waited, pacing slowly, on the drive in front of the house.

St. John paced as he waited for her to join him. He was thinking furiously, as he had all night. Too soon, he mourned, too soon. He had not had time to prepare her. He had played a slow and waiting game, considering that he had all the time in the world. And he well knew that she needed time. She still thought of him as a kindly brother, or a friendly companion. He had felt it unwise to rush her along too quickly, seeing how completely Torquay's complete physical interest had repulsed her.

But had it repulsed her? he wondered. Last night, seeing her in Torquay's arms, he had felt a rush of purely murderous rage. Seeing that grinning devil holding that lush body to his own, almost devouring her in his embrace, had sent the blood rushing to his head. It had been an obscenely complete embrace, it had filled him with envy.

But upon further reflection, he remembered that she had not been struggling, not been crying out in alarm, but rather seemed rapt in his kiss. Perhaps Torquay had read her character better than he had. He had thought her uncommonly bright, uncommonly sensitive and shy. And had sternly repressed all his desires to kiss that incredibly pouting lip, to stroke that lovely form, because he had considered her, in some ridiculous way, a lady. He laughed to himself. Perhaps Torquay was right again, perhaps I half believed her to be the 'Lady Berry' I myself invented. But Torquay had shown him the light. She was obviously no lady, not sprung from her origins, and he had mistakenly treated her as if she were his social equal.

Still, now his hand had been forced by his rival, and he must put all his persuasiveness to the test. She trusted him, there he had the advantage of the Duke. She knew him better, there was another point in his favor, for had they not spent so many idle hours together? And he was younger, he did not have the reputation yet that Torquay had. It can be done, he assured himself, but he wished he did not have to be quite so precipitate. But then, he sighed, Torquay did call the tune.

She joined him quickly, and they walked to the dormant rose garden in back of the house. There, by a wintery frozen ornamental fish pond, he paused, and, looking about him to see if there was another being in the vicinity, he bade her to stand with him. Here, he thought, at least there is no one to overhear us. Although each word he spoke resulted in a little puff of smoke on the frosty air.

"Regina," he said, giving her his full attention, looking down into the worried eyes, "it is now time for us to speak about your future."

"You have heard from Miss Bekins?" she said hopefully, looking into his clear light gray eyes.

"No," he said, shaking his head, "not a word. But, there is a future before you separate from that good lady, Regina."

"Well, yes," she said doubtfully, "I do have an adequate education, Sinjin, but . . . no matter, if you have found me a position among your circle, I am sure it will be suitable. Please tell me about it."

"Regina," he said softly, "I fear you are not a very realistic young woman, for all your education. The sort of instructor that is required for young females in my circle is a young woman who can teach manners, and water colors, and etiquette, and . . . dance," he emphasized. "Very few of my acquaintances require a governess who will instruct their young daughters in Latin, or Greek, or World History. It is not even a desirable course of study for a young female. I think, to be honest, Regina, you must give up the thought of governessing."

"But then," Regina said desperately, "I have been thinking, perhaps you know of an elderly lady who requires a companion. . . ?"

"A companion," he said with regret, " to discuss balls and routs, and the old days with? No, my dear, your interests would suit you to become a companion to a retired gentleman, or army officer, not a lady. For what genteel old woman would wish to spend the long evenings discussing the Roman Empire or politics? No, Regina, your upbringing has been so unorthodox, I fear, that it would be impossible to place you in such a position."

She looked at him with despair, her green eyes, he thought suddenly, the only touch of color in the drab, winter garden.

"Then I shall have to find a place for myself," she said stubbornly, lifting her chin. "And I shall not be a charge upon your hospitality any longer. No, no," she said, brushing away his protests, "even my uncle would not have expected you to take charge of me forever. And enough time has passed, I have battened on you long enough."

"You forget Torquay," he said cruelly.

"No," she said, "I do not. But I cannot make you responsible for my condition any longer. You owe me no further obligation, My Lord, your debt to my uncle has been paid. You have been a friend when I have needed one, but it has been but a stopover. I must travel onward now." She turned to go, but he held her arm.

"Regina," he said softly, "then forget my debt to your uncle, though I never can. Do you not know that I now have an interest in your fate which transcends that of mere obligation?"

She looked at him with amazement. He had been gallant to her in the past, but never outright in an loverlike fashion, but now his softened expression and warm look confused her.

"Oh, I know," he said ruefully, "that I have played mock-uncle to you, been the soul of discretion in your presence, but do you think I have not noticed your face, your figure, your smiles and fears with more than an uncle's interest? It was only that I did not wish to presume upon your distress. I did not want to add to your confusions. I am not, after all, a man such as Torquay. There is such a thing as consideration for the fact of your youth and ignorance. And what I have to say now may come as a surprise, but I cannot contain it any longer."

She looked at him with growing astonishment. They

had spent many long hours in each other's company, and though she had wondered at times at some of his gallantries, she had never thought, or allowed herself to think of him, in the role of a lover. Their conversations had always been remote, and erudite and unemotional. He was, she thought irrelevantly, an exceedingly imposing and handsome man, but for some reason, none of his grace or charm of manner had ever touched upon her heart. It was difficult for her to think of him in the manner in which he now seemed to wish to be thought of.

"I only speak now," he said, "because our time is so quickly running out. Soon my sister will return home for her confinement, Amelia must leave for her own establishment, and it would not do, you know, for you to remain behind here at Fairleigh with me, unchaperoned. There would then be talk that would be unpleasant for both your, and my own, reputation.

"Regina," he said urgently, taking both her hands in his, "you do not know me too well yet, but you do know that your uncle both knew and trusted me. Indeed, he trusted me with his most precious possession . . . yourself. And I mean to continue to take care of you, for your own sake—not out of any debt of honor any longer—and for my own sake. For you delight my heart, Regina. I can speak with you with ease and intelligence, and, although I don't wish to shock you, I find that I can even understand that . . . creature . . . Torquay's desire for you as a woman. For you are very beautiful Regina, surely you know that. But you may not know how very much I desire both your mind . . . and your . . . womanly qualities.

"I ask you to give me the right to continue to look after you, for both your own and my sake," he breathed, looking at her intently.

She found a breath to speak, shaking her head.

"But . . . but what about Amelia?"

"Amelia?" he said. "What about Amelia? She is an old friend, a very dear and old friend, what about her?"

"But," Regina protested, "I thought she . . . and you . . . that is to say. . . ."

"Oh, no," he laughed. "Nothing of the sort, we are only old friends."

Poor Amelia, thought Regina sadly, but seeing that Sinjin was waiting for her answer she said quickly, in a little low voice,

"But Sinjin, although I like you very well, I don't, I cannot, oh dear, I am grateful to you, but I hardly really know you at all. And I know that I do not love you, Sinjin, no, not at all in the way one is supposed to."

"That will come in time," he said smoothly. "At least do you admit the possibility of its someday occurring?" he asked, growing impatient with her reluctance.

"I suppose," she began, and found to her embarrassment that he was drawing her closer. "But Sinjin," she protested, drawing back a little in his arms, "I have no family, no fortune, no background, and you are——"

"I am only a man," he said, gazing at her. "And I want only a woman, not her background and history. I can protect you, Regina. I can give you comforts, security, and love. Can you not accept my offer, if only out of pity at first, and then allow other emotions to grow?"

Comfort, she thought, security, and love, and the flickering vision of that other mocking face with its offer of desire and entrapment rose before her. She looked into the strong face before her and thought, he is so good, indeed I don't deserve such a good man, only a monster could refuse such a good man, and allowed him to draw her close.

She remembered to part her lips, as Torquay had insisted, and, feeling his mouth upon hers, she relaxed against him. But she was surprised to find no answering thrill, no seduction of her senses, only a peculiar sense of herself standing outside of his arms, watching the kiss that was transpiring between the elegant tall young man and the woman close in his arms, the woman who saw another face before her closed eyes and heard other laughter in her ears.

He is such a good man, she thought desperately, clinging to him now, trying to blot out the other face, as the chill wind cut at her.

He held her to himself and kissed her deeply, a growing sense of need overpowering him. God, he thought, she was a bewitching armful, if only he could take her somewhere and go further, she was in such a yielding mood. He fumbled with the buttons on her pelisse as he held her, and insinuated his hand through the opening he had created to stroke at one of her warm breasts. She did not back away, and he cursed his luck at finding her this acquiescent in this location. He held her close and looked over her shoulder at the abandoned summerhouse. Too exposed there, and someone might happen by. He knew he could not take her into the house for any purpose, because Mary and Amelia were walking about in search of amusement. Lord, he thought, his hand caressing her awakening breast, what luck to have no place to carry her to now. He thought of the warm, straw-filled stables, and his spirits rose.

"Regina," he whispered, his hand becoming bolder, holding tightly, taking care to breath deeply into her ear, "come with me now." She looked at him with surprise, she was having a hard time resolving the whirling train of her thoughts. He stared down at her with an avid expression, and she withdrew from him. He was about to take her back in his arms, when a slight movement of a white curtain in one of the lower windows of the house caught his attention. They had been observed. He wanted to curse, but only sighed heavily. "Forgive me," he said, releasing her, "I lost my head, but you have made me very happy. I understand that you are agreed?"

She turned from him and hastily buttoned her coat securely. Her mind was in an upheaval. Why had she felt nothing? Nothing but perhaps a sense of shock when he had caressed her. When surely, she owed him so much, and he was so very kind. But how could he be so stiffly formal, and yet so ardent at the same time? And all while he was asking her to be his wife? But no, she thought, she was not a fool. He could give her protection from all the cold winds of this world and he could protect her both from the Duke and from herself. She nodded.

"Good," he said briskly. "You understand, though,"

he continued, "that you are to say nothing? I cannot wait to have you to myself, to avoid this subterfuge, this . . . slipping about. But now, you understand, it is necessary."

She turned back to him, her eyes wide with amazement. "Say nothing?" she asked hesitantly.

He nodded. "We will simply tell them that your cousin found you a position in her house. You will leave, with appropriate farewells, in a hired coach, and then you can join me in London. I must go there at once," he went on, half to himself, his mind seething with plans, "to make arrangements . . . suitable house for you . . . near to my own, suitable clothes, all the arrangements. I will settle an adequate sum on you, Regina, although I know you will want to spend it more on books than on jewels and gowns. . . ." He paused, looking at her. She stood, stock-still, staring at him with an incredulous expression on her face. And then she began to laugh.

Her laughter rang out across the frozen landscape and brought tears to her misted eyes. "Oh, forgive me," she said, her voice curiously unsteady, caught between tears and laughter. "Oh, Sinjin, Torquay is right. I *am* a fool. A proper little fool."

He did not like the tone of her voice and, glancing quickly toward the house to see if any within had heard her peal of unseemly laughter, he asked her harshly, "Where is the joke, Regina?"

"It's a good one, I assure you," she said seriously. "Sinjin, would you believe," and she paused, realizing that for the first time she was speaking to him without that veneer of reserve and caution, speaking to him honestly and clearly, as she had spoken to Torquay, "that I thought, mind you, actually thought, that you were asking me to be your wife? Oh that is the cream of jests, isn't it? The mongrel Miss Berryman, or the infamous Lady Berry, whichever you prefer, thought that that show of passion and sentiment was a declaration of intentions? From a peer of the realm to a little beggar-maid. Oh my goodness," she said, wiping her eyes. "And then when you said I must say nothing, only then, mind you, only then did I understand. Why, you want me to be your mistress, Sinjin, just as Torquay does. Don't you?"

"Not just as Torquay does," he said tensely. "I really do admire you, Regina. I really do want only to be able to protect you. . . ."

"Only to protect me?" she asked quietly. "Not to make love to me?"

"That goes hand in hand with love, Regina," he said stiffly.

"Then where is the difference?" she asked.

"Torquay does not love you," he said solemnly. "He has never said so, has he? But I confess, I do. If the world . . . if my world, were different, I would marry you, Regina. But you would not understand. Could you bear to be rejected, out of hand, by all your friends, all your acquaintances, all your family, because of a misalliance? If it were true that we all only live for love and love alone, it would do. But in the harsh realities of this world, it would not do. And," he said, seeing her expression, "no, by no means is it only myself I am thinking of. How could I bear to see you rejected, refused entrees, refused invitations and snubbed in the street because my world thought you an adventuress? Because, be sure that Torquay would spread the story of your defection from your family, and the world would believe him. Your reputation would be in tatters, even my title could not protect you. But as my . . . secret companion, you could live in comfort, in security, wrapped about with consideration and love, your future assured. You have said that you do not love me, Regina, so your heart would not be involved. But use your head, and if you must use your heart, have some pity upon me. I could give you all that you have ever wanted, and you could give me the love I so desperately want of you."

She looked at him with a flash of something very close to hatred. But he was too intent upon his line of reasoning to see, and in a matter of seconds the look was gone, replaced by a closed, clear, calculating gaze.

"I know little of the life of mistresses, Sinjin," she said slowly. "Tell me, what becomes of a mistress when the . . . master grows tired of her?"

"I should never grow tired of you," he protested, but seeing her unblinking stare, he said quickly, "and as I said, there would be a sum paid. You would never be in need of anything for the rest of your life."

"And something else, Sinjin," she said, turning her footsteps to stroll back toward the house, keeping her hands tight together so that he would not see them shaking. "I know little of other . . . more important matters—in fact, I only learned how to kiss, I am told, the other day, but no matter—how can I be sure that my . . . lack of abilities in love would please you?"

He stopped her, with a hand on her shoulder. "I know you would please me, Regina," he said ardently. "Have I not given you proof of that just now? I would dearly love to teach you all you needed to know to please me."

She shook off his hand and strolled on. "But Sinjin," she said reasonably, "if I learn my lesson well, is there not the possibility of . . . children? I don't know certain aspects, but there are certain facts that are inescapable, even to me."

"Such possibilities can be avoided," he said, embarrassed by her tone. "There are ways."

"But not infallible ones?" she asked.

"Should such a thing occur," he said, feeling uncomfortable and eager to be away from her, to travel to London, to set the wheels of the arrangement in motion, "I am a gentleman. I would, of course, do the right thing, as regards money and care of the issue. But Regina," he said, "don't ruin this feeling we have for each other with such imaginings."

"But Sinjin," she said, pausing to look up at him with glittering eyes, "surely, the . . . issue, would not be a thing of my imaginings."

"I have told you," he said, unavoidably embarrassed, "that I will teach you many things. One of them will be a way to make such a possibility unlikely. But should the unlikely occur, I will continue to oversee your future, and the future of whatever else might result."

"But," she went on in a hard little voice, "how could you bear to contaminate your line . . . with mine? I am really such a mixed breed compared to you."

"I would do so gladly," he swore. "And if your world and mine weren't so dissimilar, I would do so legally. But what is a slip of paper to us, Regina? What is a five-minute ceremony to do with what I feel for you? I desire you, Regina, in every way a man can desire a woman."

"Except as a wife," she laughed. "But what about Amelia, and Lady Mary? What of their feelings when they discover the truth?"

"Why should they?" he asked. "Though you will all be in London, I assure you, your paths will not cross. You will live, as you did before, in different worlds. They will never know."

"But I should never see them again?" she insisted.

"Why should you?" he replied. "What are they to you?"

They walked in silence until they reached the door, and he halted.

"Go in, it is cold. I will go to London, I am impatient to go. I am eager to have you close to me, without deceit. Tell my sister and Lady Burden that some business has come up. I'll leave a similar message. You need only to say nothing. I will then send a note to you, purporting to be from—say, your new-found Cousin Sylvia, offering you a home and sanctuary until your majority is reached. Then all you need do is make your farewells, enter the carriage I will have waiting, and a new life will begin for us. I will send for you within a day. Think of nothing but our coming happiness."

She stood looking at him silently. He took her silence for acquiescence and, lifting her hand to his lips, he murmured, "You will not regret it." And, turning from her, he strode off.

Regina went into the house and walked quietly up to her room. She sank down upon a chair and buried her face in her hands. And stayed that way, unmoving, scarcely breathing, for a long time. The knock that finally came on the door was soft and hesitant. But after a moment, Regina rose and opened the door. Amelia stood there, unusually pale, with a small wavering smile on her usually composed face.

"May I come in, Regina?" she asked quietly.

Regina only nodded dumbly, and watched Amelia enter and find a small chair. She perched on the edge of it and looked up at Regina. Her gaze was fixed unwavering upon the younger girl.

"I don't mean to pry, I don't mean to interfere," she began, "but, no. That is not worthy of me. Of course, I mean to pry, else I would not be here. I confess. I did see you and St. John . . . out in the garden. Did he make you an offer, my dear?"

"An offer?" asked Regina, in a high, unnatural voice. "Ah yes, he did make me an offer. A most unexpected one."

Her worst fears confirmed, Amelia took a long breath and controlled herself.

"No, not unexpected to me. You see, I have noticed how he has looked at you, how he has deferred to you, how he has concerned himself about you." And Amelia, after one more shuddering sigh, sat silently. Both women stayed quiet for a few moments, Regina fighting for control of herself, Amelia finally allowing her last few vagrant hopes to die quietly.

"And," Amelia went on, as if there had been no lapse in the conversation, "what answer did you give him, Regina? I must know."

Regina stared at Amelia, and asked, cruelly, regretting the words the moment they were out, bald and curt, hanging in the air,

"What answer would you have given him, Amelia?"

"Ah," said Amelia, "then you do know? I was afraid of that. You have the habit of watching people, Regina. Not at all the thing, you know," she laughed unconvincingly. "I was afraid of that. But since you do know, then surely you know what my answer would have been."

"You would have said yes?" Regina asked in incredulity.

Amelia did not hear the note of horror in the other girl's voice, her emotions were riding too high now for her to pick up any nuance of speech. "You need not ask me that," she said unsteadily. "But I am a realist, Regina. And never, not really ever, did I really believe that he would ask me . . . no, not really. But your answer, Regina?"

"I gave him none," Regina said stiffly.

"But you must," Amelia said, now very agitated. "He has such a care for you. I have never seen him so truly concerned, so wholeheartedly involved. It would be a very good thing for him, it might be the making of him. For I do not delude myself as to his real character. Such a thing might be the very influence he needs to stabilize himself, to . . . allow himself to grow . . . to be complete."

"And do you think such a thing would be good for me too?" Regina asked, awestruck by Amelia's statement.

"Of course," Amelia said in excitement. "I am not a complete fool, Regina. I do not know who you are, or even what you are. But I do know that you are in some sort of difficulty, I do know that Jason is involved with you, I do know that Sinjin could not fail to make you happy. Ah Regina, you do not know him as I do. Beneath that veneer he affects, he is good. He is noble. Perhaps he has set his feet upon the wrong course for now, but all that can change. I would swear to it. Regina, please believe me, I do want the best for him. I so want the very best for him. And I feel that you could provide that. Whatever your history, you are young and very beautiful. But more than that, you are wise, and kind and loving. You could give him so much. So much that he needs. You must say 'yes,' Regina." Amelia stopped her discourse and searched for a handkerchief to stop the tears that had begun to flow. "Of all the women he has been involved with," she went on, muted by the cloth she held to her face, "only you have the soul and spirit he deserves."

Regina stood staring at Amelia, hating herself and St. John for what they had done to this usually careful and pleasantly composed woman. But still she could not accept what her ears had heard, still she could not understand Amelia's compliance with St. John's "offer."

"Amelia," she asked, curiously calm, "would you really accept the situation? Do you think it would be such a good thing . . . considering all the difficulties, not to mention the moral problems?"

But Amelia was almost beyond the limits of rational conversation. "Of course I do," she whispered, still clutching the handkerchief to her face. "I am trying to be honest, Regina. You know what I hope no other soul on earth knows, and I am trying to say the right thing for both you and St. John. But recollect, that I put his needs first. And I do believe he needs you. How can I in any honesty urge you to say anything but 'yes,' feeling as I do? It is what I would say. And as I love . . . as I have a care for him, I urge you to."

"Amelia," Regina asked, so softly she could scarcely hear the words herself, "would you say yes to being his . . . mistress?"

But Amelia had lost control, and did not understand Regina's question, or the purpose of it. She only sat weeping, flagellating herself for the despised tears, for the surge of sorrow she had felt when her fears, fears that she had harbored silently for almost a decade, had finally been confirmed. So she did not understand Regina's question, or the purpose behind it, and only took it as another symbol of her present debasement, an unaccountably cruel thrust by this friend and rival who had stolen all that she knew she could never have.

She rose and went quickly to the door, and answered through a sob, "His mistress, his slave, his footstool . . . yes to all, why do you do this to me, Regina?" And now weeping openly, she hurried out the door, thinking in her disarray, ah how shall I ever face Sinjin and his lady after this? How shall I greet Regina again, knowing that she knows all I have lost? How shall I be ever able to face the Marquis of Bessacarr and his new wife? And laughing a little madly, she thought as she reached her own room, What shall I wear to their wedding?

Regina shook her head, and shook it again, as if to clear it, like a dazed creature. Then she went slowly to the little inlaid wood desk in her room. She carefully extracted two sheets of paper and, without hesitation, began to write upon one. An hour later she looked down at the two notes, and the six others she had discarded. The one addressed to Amelia began;

"My Dear Lady Burden, I had never until this day understood the vast gulf that separates our two worlds. No, I had never understood that fact, that to all intents and purposes, we did live in different worlds. So I must ignore your advice, for though it might be applicable to a Young Woman of your world, it would not suit mine. My upbringing, perhaps, my petty moral sense, perhaps, but. . . ."

The letter to St. John was shorter, and more direct. It comprised only a few lines:

"Your Grace, A very wise man recently told me that there are some men who prefer relationships that are clear-cut, like that of employer and employee. I do not think I could be your employee. I do not think that either your or my spirit could grow in such a relationship. I am not such a person. Therefore, I would not be right for you either. I thank you for all past favors. I am afraid I cannot remain to be your Obedient Servant, Regina Analise Berryman."

And then, wearily, like a very old woman, she began to pack only those clothes that she had brought with her in the worn suitcase she had brought when first she arrived at Fairleigh.

XIV

St. John let himself into the small house quietly. It was still early in the morning by his standards, not even ten o'clock, and the ladies who dwelt in such large numbers upon this street were obviously still abed, since there was so little activity upon the pavements. How many years, he thought idly, as he opened the door, had he himself wakened, dressed, let himself out silently this early, to find the exterior world of this street so deserted at an hour when the rest of London was bustling with commerce. It was one of the pleasanter attributes of this discrete address, one of the primary reasons why the names of the actual owners of the houses was such a select roster of the peerage.

He felt curiously refreshed and alert for a man who had had so little sleep, who had ridden such a long way in the last afternoon and night. But after only a brief rest and a change of clothes, he had taken himself out on the streets at this ungodly hour to hasten the preparations he was making. He felt some small trepidation at the immediate task before him. Maria had only been installed here for a very little while and might be difficult to dislodge, but he could not suppress the small rush of joy he felt when he allowed himself to imagine her successor.

His reflections were rudely cut off when he entered the small hallway and heard a babble of voices. There was much laughter and giggling coming from the small sitting room to his left and, without a pause, he strode in the doorway, stopping the voices short. He looked at the assemblage before him with surprise. He had thought that Maria would still be in bed. Certainly, he had never known any of his mistresses to be early risers. But there, seated comfortably in the room, was Maria, in somewhat sloppy disarray, he thought fastidiously, her ample form carelessly wrapped in a feathered dressing gown, and her companions were two older, brilliantly dressed, highly made-up women.

One, a spectacularly raddled blonde with enormous black eyes, he immediately recognized as Lilli Clare, who was, if his memory served, the long-time consort of an elderly infirm Baron of his acquaintance. The other, a tiny curly-headed brunette, was Genevieve Crane, a giddy young woman whom he himself had enjoyed under his patronage a year or two ago. They looked up at him like guilty children, startled at his presence.

He had interrupted their poor version of morning tea, he imagined. He had blundered into one of their cozy chats. He had not thought of them as having a life apart from his nocturnal visits. But he shrugged and allowed himself to smile as he looked at them. After all, he thought with some charity, it was, for the time being, Maria's house, and she had no way of knowing that he was returned to town. It was not as if she were being unfaithful to their bargain; no male was present. And though he might deplore her choice of companions in his absence, it was really none of his business. As she would soon be none, either.

"Sinjin," she cried, gathering her gown together, "you did not tell me you were in town. It is too bad of you," she went on, giving her rapt companions furious looks and little waving motions of her hands.

Catching her eye, they rose promptly and, muttering little apologies, gathered up their belongings and left with admirable speed, leaving only a potpourri of assorted heady scents behind them.

"I had not planned to return so soon," he said casually, flinging off his cape, "but a certain change in plans has occurred."

She eyed him thoughtfully for a moment, and then, allowing her dressing gown to fall open more fully, walked toward him with the slow, seductive walk he had found so entrancing before and now watched only with amusement as he saw how her rather elongated breasts moved independently of each other as she paced toward him. Too much, he thought to himself, eyeing her rounded abdomen and the deeply defined bulge of her pubis. She wrapped two arms around his neck and sighed into his ear, "But *such* a pleasant surprise, St. John, such a pleasant surprise."

He took her arms away from his neck and stood back, looking at her sympathetically. All the mystery of her, he found, was gone. He could only feel a certain small sorrow for the confused looking woman who surely was running to a premature stoutness, and whose fading dark good looks would soon take her to other sorts of establishments, far from this fashionable street.

"I'm afraid," he said, "it is not too pleasant a surprise." He withdrew a check from his inner pocket and laid it in her hands. I'm afraid," he went on, "that my plans have changed in many ways, and that you will have to find a new abode. But you will see that I have been generous, and that you have profited from our acquaintance."

She looked, unbelieving, at the paper in her hands.

"But it's only been a few weeks," she shrilled. "You haven't even given me a chance! It's not fair. I've hardly even settled in. I haven't shown you all that I can do . . . there's lots more I can do," she continued, but he put up his hand.

"I'm afraid not," he said, and turned from her to look out the window.

"If it's the ladies who were here this morning," she said hurriedly, "well, you never told me I couldn't have in a few friends. We weren't talking about you really. We were just chatting. They are my neighbors, and all we do is chat. . . ."

"It's not that", he said in a bored voice. "It's only over, Maria. I ask that you remove yourself before the day is out."

"What have I done?" she wailed. "What will people think, you tossing me out so soon?"

"Say what you will about that," he said. "Blame it on my well-known capriciousness. But remove yourself from the premises, Maria. Our association is over."

But Maria Dunstable had been around the course too long not to know that her dismissal, so soon after her having acquired such a choice place, would look bad. And she was growing a little too old to be able to bounce back easily. She, too, had seen all the signs of her looks' decline. She, too, had seen the inevitable signs of where her path would soon lead her, and had been ecstatic at having attracted the interest of a fashionable parti like the Marquis. Her rage and disappointment got the better of her innate good sense, and she did what she knew was unforgiveable in a woman of her trade. She lost her temper.

"You poxy bastard!" she shrieked, losing all the soft throaty cadence to her voice that she hoped she was famous for. "All right, I'll go, but it won't be a hardship. I'd rather sell it to a spotty grocer boy in the streets than put up with your fumbling grunting any more. I've had better. I've had ones who could make me feel something, too! Even poor Lilli's palsied old man can do it better! And even Genevieve's better off. She had you and she don't regret losing you! Not for a minute! I've had schoolboys who were——"

But he cut her off by turning and dealing her a hard slap across her face. White-faced, he gritted his teeth. "You will leave, Maria," he said coldly.

She looked at him, wide-eyed. She had slipped. He would never recommend her to his friends. He would call her a common doxy. She would never again have the comfort of her own apartment, she would have to work in a houseful of women, and then, as the other women became younger and more desireable, she would have to take to the streets. The enormity of her crime sank in slowly. She dropped to her knees and, throwing her arms around his boots, she wept, "Oh don't be angry. Oh God, I'm sorry. I didn't mean it. There was never no better than you, I swear it. I was only angry. Oh, forgive me."

Sinjin's lip curled in distaste. She was weeping uncontrollably into his legs. He forced himself to pat her head once. "I have forgotten it," he said grimly. "Now go and pack before I remember again."

When she had left the room and he could only hear her snuffling as she gathered her possessions together, he relaxed. He could see Regina here. He could see her sitting on the couch and smiling. He could hear her soft voice. Feel her lips. He thought of the evenings they could spend here, talking, playing at cards, discussing. . . . He caught himself up short and frowned. Daydreaming about a mistress who would talk and play cards with him? This was a flight of fancy, indeed! And yet, he remembered that there were those of his acquaintance whose mistresses served just such purposes. Men who maintained duel households, and seemed to treat their mistresses almost as they did their wives. There was, for example, poor foolish old Lord Reeves, whose weekly perambulations with his equally ancient mistress of many years was the cause of much amusement to all his acquaintances. For thirty years, as faithfully as a footman would wind an old clock, doddering

Lord Reeves would appear to take his now senile mistress for an hour-long stroll. A mistress until death did them part, St. John thought uncomfortably.

Yet he himself had never chosen his women for anything else but sensual pleasures. The Cyprians who enjoyed his patronage were always chosen only for their face, form, or reputation. Conversation was the one thing he never attempted with any of them. But, he mused, perhaps, just perhaps, if he were to set up another household, he would in time find himself in his dotage, making his unsteady way back to this little house every week, to visit with an equally infirm Regina. The thought caused his lips to curl in an unpleasant smile. He grew impatient, and tapped one booted foot as he waited for Maria to complete her packing so that he could then lock the door behind her. The door to his, and Regina's, new home.

When Maria had left, after giving him one long, last imploring glance, St. John let out his drawn-in breath. The fight had gone out of her. She had been docile and accepting of her fate at last. He noticed again, with distaste, as she had left, how sagging her body had been, how rumpled that face that he had found acceptable only a few weeks before. How entracing her somewhat humid lovemaking had been. But now he could only think of clear green eyes, of a long, slender, elegant female form. Of a soft, lemony perfume.

But, looking about the house before he locked up again, he felt a tremor of unease as he thought of the other women who lived on this street. Would Regina be willing to take tea with Lilli and Genevieve, or even Maria, if she were fortunate enough to find another wealthy protector? Would she take delight in comparing notes about their noble patrons, as surely Maria and her friends were doing? What would she discuss with them? Gowns? Their past? Their men? How could she even understand them? Who would her friends be? He shrugged off the unwelcome thoughts and left the house quickly. It was done. It had been an unsettling experience, that was all. But now, at least, the house was ready.

He had planned to go to visit Melissa Wellsley next, to let her know that he was back in town, to pursue that friendship a little further. Perhaps to the furthest. For now that he had Regina, he could contemplate marriage with a clearer eye. With Regina waiting for him each night on Curzon Street, he could easily tolerate a fashionable wife raising his family away, far away, at some country address such as Fairleigh. It was part of his plan and, he reasoned, a good one. It was, after all, time that he set about the business of ordering his own house, and providing himself with an heir. He would no longer have to search about for an amiable companion, as he felt sure that the liaison with Regina would never deteriorate to something as sordid and unpleasant as his recent scene with Maria. No, he would last with her for a long time, and take his ease, at last, with a delightful companion. One he could speak with as a lady. Make love to as a courtesan. He would teach her. It was all working out so smoothly.

But still, he did not, he mused, as he walked down the street, for some reason, feel like visiting with Melissa and her delightfully anxious mama as yet. It was not yet time to send Lady Wellsley into ecstacies. He laughed to himself, wondering if all men felt that way on the eve of a serious declaration. Did they all experience this . . . lack of enthusiasm at the prospect of holy matrimony? No matter, he reasoned, it would be easier done on a full stomach. He would take himself off to his club for luncheon first.

But luncheon did not sit well. And even the wine he sipped tasted slightly off. He was pushing the winestain from his glass into a series of little circular patterns on the snowy cloth when he became aware of someone settling down, heavily, into a chair beside him.

"Greetings, Sinjin," James slurred as he sat down abruptly.

St. John looked at his friend with some annoyance. James was red-faced, his eyes slightly unfocused, and his neckcloth in some slight disarray, that, along with the unavoidable fact that he had seated himself without

even a polite by-your-leave, all confirmed the fact that
his old friend was slightly disguised.

"At this hour?" drawled St. John, lifting an eyebrow.
"Really, James, does one squalling infant reduce you to
this? I confess you give me second thoughts about the
delights of matrimony and patrimony, my friend."

"Never say you've finally been caught, old man?"
James said in delight. "Who's the lucky lady? Do I know
her?"

"No such lady as yet, not quite yet," St. John laughed.
"But how do you come to such a state, James? The sun
hasn't even begun to set and you are already in no state
to be seen."

"Not so bad as that," James said with an attempt at
bluster. "Just breached an extra bottle of wine. But I'm
devilish glad to see you, Sinjin. Thought you'd rusticate
forever. It's good to see you," he said, his round face
shining. "I've been searching for you. It's been dull here
in Town without you."

"Now, James," St. John said, smiling, "I've known
you for too long to be too touched by your welcome.
What is it you want of me, old friend? No, don't bother
to protest, you are at your most charming, James, and
always have been, when there is something you desire
of me. Whether it was a pen wiper at school, or the
name of some Cyprian when you were on the town, I do
know that look in your eye."

"Put your finger on it," James muttered, looking around
the almost deserted dining room, "That's it exactly."

"A pen wiper?" laughed St. John.

"Don't play coy, you dog," James whispered, sending
out a heady breath of claret. "I need your advice . . .
on a matter of some female."

"Really, James," St. John said in annoyance, "when
will you begin to acquire your own amusements? It
seems, no more than seems, to me that you are forever
acquiring my cast-offs. And losing them as quickly as
you acquire them. What became of Annabelle? I thought
it was all settled with you."

"Drank, my boy," said James with ponderous import.
"The woman drank constantly. Got sloppy about it. I

had to give her a congé. But, Sinjin, you never told me about it," he said with an accusing whisper so redolent of wine that it drove all thoughts of dessert from the Marquis's mind.

"James," St. John said, drawing back from his friend's reddened face, "I only introduced you. I do not think it my obligation, or occupation to provide you with feminine companionship. Why don't you find your own divertisements?"

"Look at me," James said hopelessly, with wine-emboldened candor, spreading his plump hands wide. "Am I the sort to be able to dig up those dashing creatures you find with such ease? Don't know the first thing about how to go about it."

"Your money alone is enough, James," St. John said in a bored voice. "They are none of them in search of an Adonis. Merely an ample purse. Don't tell me you've been lying in wait for me to come back to find you another female?"

"But I have," protested James. "I've tried. But I don't want just any drab. The choice ones don't even seem to see me. And I won't settle for less. You've got a talent for it, my man. But look at me, I'm insignificant. Fattish, baldish, not tall or good looking. No, no, it don't matter how much blunt I've got. I don't attract the high fliers that you do. I count on you, my boy, to get me some worth for my money."

"James," St. John said with a flash of annoyance, "you're a married man now. Why don't you just disport yourself with your wife?"

James drew himself up to his full height, and a terrible look came into his eye.

"I won't have you insult my wife, Sinjin," he said so loudly that the few others in the room turned to look at him. "I won't have you saying such things about her."

St. John looked at his friend in alarm, and hastily put his hand upon his shoulder and said in a low voice,

"No. Don't fly into the boughs, James. I never thought to impugn the name of Lady Hoyland. Indeed, I did not. Whatever gave you such a thought?"

"Well," James said in a quietened voice, somewhat

mollified, "you suggested that I seek . . . that I visit my baser desires upon her. I can't have that, my man. No. I cannot countenance such talk. I know you're unmarried St. John, and perhaps that explains it, but one doesn't think of one's wife in that fashion, no, one doesn't," he said, shaking his head ponderously.

The Marquis looked at his friend in amazement.

"What are you talking about, James?" he asked.

"I suppose," James began, with the somewhat heavy sentimentality that came easily to him in his condition, "that it's because you never knew your father. But I was fortunate to have mine for some years, Sinjin. And he gave me excellent advice. Fatherly advice. As a father should. Which is what you missed, I suppose. So I shall impart it to you. 'James,' he said to me, 'James, remember well when you marry, that your wife is a precious thing!' He told me that, Sinjin," James said mistily.

"Of course," Sinjin said, with a longing glance toward the door, "but I do have another engagement now, James, so if you will excuse me. . . ."

"No, no," James said insistently. "It's only right that I should tell you what my father told me, seeing as you had no father to tell you, Sinjin. You don't understand."

He dropped his voice to a conspiratorial whisper, and draped an arm over St. John's shoulder as he edged closer and breathed:

"Wives are not like other females, Sinjin. No female of our class is like those other women. They don't like it, you see. Can't blame them. They don't feel a thing, you know, except a notion to please their husbands. They hate the whole nasty business. You've got to be quick and neat about it. Got to get yourself nerved up for it, and have a drink and go right to it with no fooling about. And all along they'll just lie there and look upward, or aside at the bed curtains, and wait for you to be done with the whole nasty business. . . . Wait so patiently and with such fortitude for you to puff your way through the disgusting thing. They're not bred to it. They don't feel a thing. Aren't meant to. My father told me so, and he was right. If it's sport you want, there are those other women . . . not a wife. You try any of that sort of thing with a wife, and she'd die right there, Sinjin. Just expire from shame and shock. Can you imagine your mother or sister liking it? They don't expect it . . . don't want it. Can't blame them. It's base, Sinjin. Base."

"I see," St. John said, casting a pitying look at his friend and disengaging his outflung arm. "But I really do have to go now, James."

"Not before you give me a name," James insisted. "I know it's base, but that sort of woman expects it. Likes it. Got to give me a name. What about that Maria . . . whatshername? You done with her, Sinjin? Or any other. I'm . . . in need, Sinjin. But too much of a dull sort to search out my own. They don't notice chaps like me, with all my blunt. I don't do a thing for their reputations. Sinjin, please," he said, reddened now with both wine and some internal struggle.

"Maria Dunstable," St. John said with asperity, eager to be away. "Seek her out. I think she will greet you with open arms, James, I really do."

"Sinjin," James went on, driven now by some other forces and leaning his flushed face close to his friend, "only tell me, because I can't ask her, you see, I simply can't—I don't want a slut to laugh at me—but, does she . . . does she . . . do the French?"

St. John hesitated. There was a new, sick feeling in his stomach. He wished only to be away from James and his drunken pleading.

"Does she do the French?" James insisted in a deep whisper.

St. John thought briefly. "The French" that his friend was shamefacedly whispering might be any one of a dozen variations that he could think of off hand, variations that here and now he would rather not think of in relation to James, but he thought, yes, Maria would be glad to do any one of them for a new protector, she would be desperate to.

"Yes," he said curtly, "yes and yes." And rising abruptly, seeing his friend beginning to speak, said only, "She was at the Opera. You can ask after her whereabouts there. Good-bye, James. Good luck," and turned from his friend coldly, to signify dismissal. James rose as well, and having the name he had sought, left hurriedly, muttering somewhat incoherent thanks.

St. John stood, curiously shaken, in a window embrasure and watched James make his unsteady way out to the street. The confrontation with his friend was really only a repetition of similar scenes that they had played out together on other occasions, albeit, this one was less subtle, more out in the open, due to James's condition. But he had never felt his own nerve endings as raw on the subject of his hidden life as they were now. Fleetingly, the unbidden thought of Regina came to him. The covetous, greedy look that he knew would be on James's face when he saw her in her regal splendor. The calculating look that would appear on other faces when he was seen with her on his arm, their silent calculations as to how long it would last, how long before they would have an opportunity to have her; how expensive would she be. St. John felt strangely unhappy at the prospect. He wanted to keep her to himself, all knowledge of their intimacies to himself. He would, he promised, if it meant never taking her out in public.

He looked up from these oddly unpleasant thoughts to see an intent face watching him from the depths of an armchair that faced the street. It was the last person he wanted to see, although only a few moments ago it was the very person he had wanted to gloat over. It was the blandly smiling Duke of Torquay.

"I see you have heard," he heard himself saying as he strolled over to a chair next to the Duke's.

"Heard what, Sinjin?" the Duke said in a rich whisper.

"The outcome of our wager, of course."

"No," Torquay said softly, his wide eyes losing nothing of their innocence, "I've heard nothing. Only when I heard of your posting to London with such haste, I too remembered some business in town. Country squires with eligible daughters can make the pleasantest holidays seem tedious, you know. Did you know, for example, Sinjin, that whereas the eldest was as beautiful as Athena, the youngest was as graceful as Terpsichore, and the middle one was so lovely that she brought tears to the eye? I confess I hadn't noticed it, but the Squire is an honest man, so perhaps age had dimmed my eye. Had you noticed their magnificence, Sinjin? I had myself been in the habit of identifying one by a rather continuous giggle, another by an extremely tedious lisp, and the third by the portly young man she seemed to constantly wear, like a bracelet, upon her arm. It disturbs me that I might have missed such great beauty. Now, had you noticed their beauty, Sinjin? For it occurred to me, much to my chagrin, of course, that if the Squire could not net a Duke, he would be equally overcome by a Marquis."

St. John made a motion of a man brushing away a fly.

"It's too bad you didn't linger there longer, Torquay, or you would have heard. I've won. I really have won, you know. I'm here only to make arrangements for her. She's chosen me, after all."

He hadn't really expected the Duke's reaction. It was as sudden and as unexpected as a bright light blowing out. The man recoiled as though he had been slapped. The smiling eyes glazed over as if with a frost, the smile was gone, leaving the face white and bereft of expression. "Ah," said the Duke with a sigh as if he had been wounded in battle, "ah then.

"Where is she now?" he asked, almost involuntarily, with none of the customary lilt to his voice.

"At Fairleigh, awaiting my message. Awaiting my discretion," St. John replied carelessly, watching the other man's expression.

But in that moment, the Duke had recovered himself, and a new, strangely sad smile was posed unconvincingly upon the ashen face.

"Then I wish you well. I must confess that I am strangely disappointed. In more ways than I can explain. In more than simply losing a wager. But then you know, Sinjin, I was ever a poor loser. How did you do it, I wonder? Prose on about the poetry of her instep and her eyelashes? But I thought her impervious to flattery. Offer her a goodly sum? But I thought her . . . unimaginative about money. Make love to her? But I thought her unacquainted with the art. I do grow old, Sinjin."

He paused and glanced down at his long white hands, which had gripped the arms of his chair till they were white-knuckled. He relaxed and flexed the fingers and then said softly,

"But I comfort myself with the expectation of watching the younger ones come to take my place. Perhaps I will then follow your ascendance with as much envy as any of the other novices to our arts. Perhaps I will become like poor James, and wait for your discard before I add her to my pack. Perhaps. . . . But I do go on. One of the disadvantages of age, Sinjin, this rambling on. I congratulate you, in any event. No," he said rising, "I more than congratulate you, you know. From the pinnacle of my five and thirty years, I salute you. I am lost in admiration." And, sweeping an elaborate bow that was a mockery, dredged up from some other lost generation of cavaliers, he made as if to go.

Some last vestige of vengefulness made St. John stop him.

"But what about the amount of our wager, Torquay?"

The Duke wheeled around, an ugly expression momentarily upon his face, before he said, sweetly,

"But how remiss of us. We never named it. Name it then, Sinjin. The game is yours, so the forfeit must be yours to decide. Name it."

St. John stood thinking for a moment. The Duke waited, standing rigidly still, then signaled for his coat.

When the footman came up to him, he bore both the long cape and a slip of paper on a silver salver. As he was assisted into the garment, the Duke rapidly scanned the message. His body stiffened for a moment, but then he crumpled the message into a tight ball in his fist and thrust his hand deep into his pocket. When he turned to St. John again, there was a sparkling light in his eyes, a dancing joy ill-contained in an otherwise impassive countenance.

"Name it," he said again, but St. John could scent his impatience, his newly fortified almost vaunting delight.

Some niggling fear at this rapid turnabout in the

midst of what he had thought was total victory made
him say, although even as he said it he was vaguely
ashamed of it:

"Oh nothing for me. But perhaps Regina would like
some trinket. Some bracelet, some token to remember
you by. For surely, it was you that brought us together,
after all."

"Done," said Torquay, with a disturbing sidewise look
at St. John. "Pardon my leaving with such unseemly
haste," he said over his shoulder as he walked to the
door, "but remember, I did admit that I was a poor
loser. A trinket, then." He laughed. "A token to remember me by. Oh certainly," he promised, and with
one more strangely illuminated look, he left.

It was some time before St. John recovered himself
enough to leave. He had sat, lost in thought, for hours
after Torquay had left. He suspected his rival's ambitions, but after all, he was, despite everything, a gentleman. No, he would not sink so low as to abduct
Regina now that she was spoken for. Now that the
wager was won. If he did, he would never be able to
show his face in any of their circles again. No, he was
not so lost in dishonor as to bring that fate down upon
his head. No matter what the impetus. He was too
conversant with the proprieties. And there was no doubt
that he had been badly stricken by his loss of the wager.
So that could not be in his mind. Still, something in his
affect had disturbed St. John.

But more than that had disturbed him. He sat in the
chair for long hours. Till it was too late to pay a polite
call upon the Wellsleys. Indeed, he felt he would defer
his visit to the Wellsleys. The girl would keep. Perhaps
it would be better to be settled with Regina before he
set up another establishment with Melissa Wellsley.
After all, a man could only do so much at one time. He
sat and rationalized, and thought, and was profoundly
disturbed. So that finally, when evening fell, he went
around to Madame Felice's, but found to his absolute
dismay that even the earnest blandishments of her newest recruit, a rosy-cheeked young simpleton from Sus-
sex, could not inspire him to anything remotely resem-

bling lust. He paid her anyway, and walked, lost in thought, all the way home.

But even in his own wide clean bed, the voices persisted. James's hoarsely imperative question, "Does she do the French?" whirled in his head, along with Maria's shrill screams about his lack of prowess as a lover. Torquay's maddening smile drifted over Maria's tear-stained face, and the dumbly questioning look of failure on the girl's face this night. He heard James repeat again and again his matrimonial advice, and heard Melissa's little brittle, "Oh la, Your Grace,' and throughout it all, always, in the background, was the sound of a soft, cultured voice, and the sight of two clear green questioning eyes. And lying sleepless, in the small hours, he wondered how it was that in winning, he felt such an abysmal sense of loss.

He thought of her then, living in that snug little house with the discreet address that he had been preparing for her. He saw her standing there, looking around her with incomprehension. He saw her on his arm, looking up at him in confusion, as all the others ogled and whispered about her. He saw then, as if for the first time, although he could have sworn he had never seen it, that briefly seen and suppressed look of hatred that she had flashed at him.

He felt her cool hand in his again, her lips against his, her laughter meeting his as it sometimes had when the same ridiculous thought had occurred to them both at the same time. He remembered why it was that she was such a poor player at cards, and why she had been so grateful to him for his role that he had played in her life. He saw what his motives had been, and were, and for the first time, saw clearly what they would eventually lead her to.

Until slowly, and with maddening certainty, he came to realize that in winning, he had indeed lost. Lost something of unclear, but inestimable value to himself. And rising from his bed and pacing, he began to put all the bits and pieces together, until he stopped short in the middle of the room and reached a startling conclusion. And though he felt at last a little light-headed, and certainly a little mad, he also felt almost as a schoolboy in his glee and relief.

And then he began to plan his way clear to winning. Winning all, finally and with sureness, and with a sense of honor.

XV

The attic bedroom was shabby, the furniture in it well used, and the gabled ceiling was too full of chinks to completely keep out the sharp wind, but still Regina was as grateful for the room as if it were a palatial chamber. She sat in a small chair that seemed to long to tilt sideways and collapse under the accumulated weight of its years, and in the dim morning light the little window permitted, counted and recounted the small hoard of coins of her purse.

"Walking about money," Uncle George had termed it when he had pressed it into her hands while she had laughingly protested his gesture. But now, she thought wryly, that was exactly what it was turning out to be. For if she did not husband it carefully, she would, indeed, have to walk the rest of the way along her journey.

There had only been enough to take her for a little way along the coach route, that was, if she expected to both eat and sleep along the way. She had been lucky enough to encounter a farm family on their way to town on the previous morning when she had let herself out of the house at sunrise. If they had been curious about her, they had soon forgotten all their questions when she had begun to admire the youngest of their tow-headed brood, and for the rest of the ride in their wagon, she had been treated to stories about the virtues and escapades of their entire family. And since they rejoiced in a family of nine children, there had been enough conversation to last until they had finally let her off at the posting house.

Again, she thought, she had been lucky in disembarking here after a few stops, for the night.

For though the inn had been rather shabby and down at the heels, the landlord's empty rooms had been enough to convince him to admit the well-dressed lady, even though she had no escort, no maid, and paltry luggage with her. After a suspicious sniff, he had let her pay in advance, and had given her shelter in this dreary room under his ancient roof.

But now morning was come again. And her jot had been paid for only the one night, and somehow she must find a way to continue her travels. It was, she reasoned, what she ought to have done in the first place. Although Miss Bekins had never replied to her letters, she was the one and only other human left on the earth who could be trusted. All the niceties that she had worried about, as to whether Miss Bekins could afford her presence, whether she could find a position at the school, or would even be genuinely welcomed there, were forgotten now. There was no other place to go.

But how? she sighed, rising. There was only enough money left for either a few more stops on the coach, or a few more meals and nights' lodgings.

"An excellent game," she could almost hear that hoarse voice laughing. Indeed excellent, Regina thought, rising and taking up her traveling bag again. Oh yes, Your Grace, an excellent game.

She asked only for coffee in the inn's main coffeeroom, although the scent of good country ham and bread that the few other travelers were indulging in caused her nostrils to widen. While she sipped at it, she eyed the others in the room. There were only four of them: two solid looking country men, avidly eating and discussing livestock in broad loudly interested tones; a morose looking shabby pedlar who seemed lost in some internal revery; and one stout overly dressed old farmer, obviously on some family business. They had all glanced up at her when she had entered, with varying degrees of curiosity, and then had lost interest in her. She was

clearly, their attitudes said, neither of their world or
concern.

When the bored-looking young serving maid began to
clear their now deserted tables, Regina rose and went
over to her. "Excuse me," she said in a hushed tone,
"but I wondered if you could be of some assistance to
me."

The girl stopped her stacking of plates and looked at
her with ill-concealed suspicion. Ladies of quality, her
expression clearly read, did not stop to converse with
kitchen wenches. Not when there was both a landlord
and landlady, and fellow travelers to be approached.
But Regina had been fearful of the sharp-eyed landlady,
and had felt that perhaps only someone in similar financial circumstances would understand her request.

"I'm in rather . . . an awkward position," she began,
quietly, for she did not want the only remaining patron,
the old pedlar, to hear her. "It seems, due to circumstances that are too tedious to go into, that my funds
are running low. Oh, I have enough, I assure you, to
pay my way here, but . . . I shall need to find some
sort of . . . employment, for a brief space, so that I can
continue my journey. I have many miles to go. To
Canterbury, as a matter of fact," she went on, dismayed
at the girl's blank expression. Was it possible that the
girl was a deaf-mute? "And I was wondering if you
could tell me if there were any . . . positions available
in this town, or the next along the route?"

"What sorta 'position'?" the girl asked in a loud, hos-
tile voice, straightening and pushing back a lock of her
lank hair.

"Well," said Regina desperately, "perhaps teaching,
or . . . companion, or sewing, or. . . ."

But the girl laughed, flinging back her head and guf-
fawing. "Teaching?" she laughed. "Not likely, and the
onliest companions any of our folk might be looking for
from you would be as a companion of the night, if you
get my meaning. And why should anyone pay good
money for a stranger to sew for 'em? This isn't London
Town, my dear," she said in a mock accent, swinging
her hips.

Regina flushed when she saw how quickly even the serving girl held her in contempt, and caught the pedlar's interested glance at her. She backed away in confusion.

"Hold on, Clary," called the pedlar, rising and coming toward them both. "Remember what the preacher says about Christian charity."

"I assure you," Regina stammered, aghast, "that I do not require charity."

"Naw, naw, you don't get my drift," the pedlar smiled, his long thin face showing animation. "Now Clary, my paw told me to cast bread upon the waters . . . specially if it don't cost nothing to do it. Listen, my whole business depends on good feelings. 'Good feelings'll sell more thread and gee-gaws than good prices,' he said, 'and don't forget it my lad.' Now," he said holding up two none-too-clean hands, "I don't need to hear your story, nor do I want to either—the less you know," he winked, "the less to regret. But my business is people, y'see, and I read people like the gentry reads books, and I say there's no harm in her, Clary. No harm atall. And if she were about the sort of business you mean, Clary, a guinea to your shilling she wouldn't be after asking you where to find it."

The girl flushed and ducked her head.

"Not that you're not a lovely little thing," the pedlar grinned to the sallow little maid, "but any fool can see that you're a good girl. But now listen, miss, it's a lucky thing you did run into us, Clary and me. For if it's work you're after, someone will have to set you straight, and Clary and me, why, we've worked all our lives, and likely will continue to do so, you're right to ask us. But no," he said, shaking his head, "no one hereabouts is going to be looking for a teacher, nor a companion . . . and even if they was," he added kindly, "they wouldn't be looking for one   off the street, if you get my drift. So you have to set your sights different-like. You see?"

"Now," he said, thinking, "Clary, what about Mrs. Stors in Witney? Didn't I hear that that wench of hers Gilly was coming to her time? And wouldn't she be needing another girl to serve in the taproom and main room? Why there's your opportunity, miss," he said, seeing Clary's little nod, "for Mrs. Stors is a good woman, she is that. And if you carry a tankard, and set down a plate, she can use you I reckon. Now the pay's not tremendous, mind, but there'll be good food, and lodging, and a good steady job for you. So if you can forget about all that teaching, and companioning, if you've got the stomach for real work, there's your chance."

"Witney?" Regina asked, thinking of her diminishing coins. "How far is that . . . on the coach, or can I walk to it?"

"Well," considered the pedlar, looking at her shrewdly, "I suppose I could advance you a few——"

"No, no, I assure you," Regina began, "that won't be necessary. It is only advice that I require now, please," she said gazing at him intently. "Only advice."

The pedlar sighed; she was such a beautiful girl, and he was a sentimental fool—he would not mind her being in his debt, even if he never saw her again, but he understood her look of horror. She was a lady, after all, and he took his hand out of his pocket again.

"Well," he said brusquely, "the stage ain't due for some hours yet, so if you take shanks' mare, strolling along under your own power, if you take my meaning, and walk straight along the road, you'll likely get to the next stop by late afternoon. Then it'll be only two more stops till Witney and the Crown and Gaiter. That's where Mrs. Stors will be. And tell her that Old Jack Potter sent you. That'll be recommendation enough. And good luck to you."

Regina thanked him and, picking up her case, put a few coins on the tabletop, and left.

Jack Potter watched her leave and, seeing her turn in the right direction, waved a farewell to her.

"You see, Clary girl," he sighed, "looks don't necessarily mean happiness. No, my old dad was right when he said that a beautiful woman attracts trouble like an old oak attracts lightning. So remember that the next time you wish you had big green eyes and a complexion like cream."

But Clary, who was scrubbing the tabletops with more vigor that she had shown in two years of work, did not find his advice comforting, at all.

It was late at night when the coach, with its customary flourishing of blowing horns and bustle, stopped in front of the Crown and Gaiter. The walk to the next stop along the coach line had left Regina weary beyond belief. Her slippers had not been made for a long tramp along a country road. But she had refused the offer of a ride from both a cat-calling group of young men in a farm cart and an overly hearty middle-aged man in a curricle. When she had seen any equipage approaching that looked well enough to contain any member of the gentry, she had quickly taken to the brush at the side of the road. She still wished to cover her traces.

But now she was lightheaded from hunger. When she had finally reached the next inn, she had splurged on a muffin and tea, and had been almost grateful that the coach was late so that she could sit and warm herself by the fire in the coffeeroom. She had been badly frightened by a slightly tipsy young man who had been ogling her, and who had looked as if he was gathering up enough courage to approach her, and had sat stiff and, she hoped, unapproachable looking until she had heard the clatter and rattle that signified the coach was approaching.

Once inside, she shut her eyes tightly and began to wonder, for the first time since she had begun her flight, what actually could happen to a young woman who had neither home, nor friends, nor family, nor trade. The thought had never really occurred to her before. There were, she knew, work houses for debtors, and poor houses for the old and destitute, but where they were located, and how one applied to them, she did not know. London, she reasoned, would be where they were found, but she could not go back there. But what did the friendless and homeless do in the countryside?

Women could work in trade, she knew, as milliners, market-mongers, and dressmakers, or in homes as serving girls, housekeepers, and servants. But one had to have skills or opportunities for the first, and references for even the meanest sort of employment in the second case. Even Belinda, her own maid in her uncle's house, had come with references. But she had neither a trade, nor friends in trade, nor references. She almost laughed to herself when she thought of what St. John's expression would have been had she asked him for references so that she could find employment as a parlor maid. But no, she soberly thought, she did not want to think of him at all. She had left Sinjin and Amelia and the Duke, and their whole world behind her.

Thus, when she saw the shingle with the Crown upon it swinging in the cold night breeze, she stepped out of the coach with mixed hopes for her future. It was late, she was cold, and she had only a few more coins between herself and whatever the unimaginable fate was for a homeless woman.

Mrs. Stors was a large broad elderly woman with a blunted face, whose skin clearly showed that at some time in her past she had been fortunate enough to live through an affliction of the smallpox. She listened to Regina impatiently as they spoke in the steamy kitchens. The inn was crowded to the doors. Today had been market day, and merchants, pedlars, farmers, and visitors from miles around the locality had crammed the inn full.

"Well," she said, staring at Regina sharply, "you don't look like a serving wench to me. But I do need an extra pair of hands tonight. And Jack Potter's a fair man. Still, I don't know what to make of you at all, I don't. You talk like a lady, you look like a lady, but your face and figure could get you a snugger bed than the one you'll have to share with Lucy, I can tell you. But I don't have time to jabber with you. So if you're not a thief, or a slut with a new game, I'll use you tonight, and we'll see what happens. But take off that fancy coat and put on one of Lucy's dresses, because I can tell you, my customers won't half believe you waiting on them with that Paris gown or whatever it is you're wearing. *Lucy!*" she bellowed.

A stout young smiling girl with black curls clustered

all around her broad red face appeared in the doorway, laden with tankards of ale.

"This here is Regina. Stop gawping. Take her to your room double quick and give her a dress to wear, and tell her the lay of the land. Quick. For she's to help you out tonight in the taproom. And be quick about it," she roared, and spinning on her heel, she rushed off into the kitchens.

Regina felt a bizarre sense of disbelief when she surveyed herself in the small mirror in Lucy's little room. The dress she had been given to wear was none too clean, and far too low cut and too short at the ankle.

Lucy's dress was an absurd costume for her. It was too brightly colored, of a cheap material, tight at the waist, and shockingly low at the neck. But a quick glance at Lucy's approving stare sank her hopes of crying off and donning her own severe blue walking dress again. Still, when she noticed with alarm how any little inhalation threatened the security of her precariously concealed breasts, she knew that she could never leave the room in it. But Lucy just grinned, and said, "Won't you be the sensation tonight," and after insisting that Regina unfasten the tight chignon she was wearing and "Fluff out yer hair a bit, love, so they won't think you're going to bite them," she left to the bellowing echoes of Mrs. Stors's *"Lucy!"* that rang through even the incredible hub-bub that rose from the inn.

Regina drew her hair back and tied it at the nape of her neck and, after resisting an impulse to tear off the dress and change back into her own clothes, she ruefully remembered the three coins that clung together for comfort in the bottom of her purse and, straightening her posture, she went wearily down the narrow flight of dark stairs and into the taproom.

It seemed to her that it was almost fantastic how the uproar seemed to quieten when she stepped into the room. The customers, a roiling sea of hearty country-men, with a few rough-voiced women sprinkled among them, appeared to blur before her eyes. She looked down in confusion.

When she closed her eyes and waited for the earth to

swallow her up, the noise level began to rise again. She
had no idea of how out of context she had looked,
gliding into the crowded, smoky room, with her gleaming chestnut hair pulled back from her pale-finely fea-
tured face, her gently curved figure clearly delineated
in the ill-fitting gown, her slender form hesitantly entering the room. But when she opened her wide green
eyes, she saw the tables full of men beckoning, "Aye
girl, some service," "Two bitters," "Some food here,
Lass," and remembering Lucy's hurried instructions,
she tried to place their faces and their orders correctly.

It seemed to be going well, it is not so difficult, she
thought, when she could think, as she rushed from the
tap to the tables, from the steaming kitchens to the
uproarious tables. It was hot, there was a strong mix-
ture of scents, of ale, of human sweat, of woodsmoke.
But the patrons here were a casual lot, she thought.
They were considerate enough, she thought, returning
to the room with her eighth tray of small beer, for when
she got an order wrong, they only laughed and handed
the food about themselves. She could not distinguish
one face from another, nor one voice from another in the
uproar. But Lucy had passed her in her travels and had
whispered, "Keep it going, love, you'll do fine."

The heat of the room had brought a pink flush to her
cheeks, the drawn-back hair had escaped from its confines and drifted along her neck, and she was looking in
confusion for the rightful recipient of her tray of bever-
ages when she felt a strong arm clasp her around her
waist and a merrily drunken voice slur, "Aye, here's the
best thing I've seen in the market today."

She looked down in horror at the widely grinning man
who had captured her and, trying to keep the liquids
from tipping over, tried to escape his embrace. But a
moment later he had risen and, taking her with his
other arm, he held her still and pushed his sweaty,
grinning face close to hers. "Give us a kiss, girl," he
chortled. "Spice up the brew." A second later, she was
swung away from him by another man, older and with
the dirty face of a working farmer. "Don't be a pig,
Harry," he laughed. "I did see her first, and I'm the one

she's longing for," and with that, he captured her waist, groped at her buttocks with his free hand, and pressed her toward him for a kiss. As she felt his mouth upon her own, she gave a little shriek and tipped the tray, sending it splashing down on the table, and on all its occupants. Laughter rose up around her, and she pushed away from the man who had grasped her and, without thinking, swung her hand around and slapped him soundly on the face. The laughter rose even higher at that, and, tears in her eyes, she rushed from the room.

Mrs. Stors found her standing in the hallway, trembling. "It won't do," the woman said half regretfully. "It won't do at all. You don't have it in you, my girl. A serving wench can't behave like a debutante. There's no harm in the men, none at all. But they do expect a kiss and a tweak, or a cuddle and a saucy word with their victuals. Won't do to discourage trade. Oh they'll forget this soon enough, but you won't do. You'll never get used to it."

An unexpected light of sympathy came into the other woman's eyes.

"I don't know your game, and I don't want to. But there's a bed here for you tonight. And some victuals as well. And a few shillings for your night's work, but you'll have to be going in the morning. Try something else, my dear."

"No," said Regina stiffly. "Thank you for your efforts. But I don't deserve pay for this night. Nor will I disturb Lucy any further. If I may wait for the coach in your . . . parlor, I'll be gone in the morning."

The woman's face turned stony.

"Too much the fine lady for my charity, are you? Well suit yourself, but the private parlor's engaged by a gentleman. So if you don't want Lucy's bed, you'll wait in the street, my dear," and she turned and left.

Regina, regretting her rash words, went back to Lucy's room and, leaving the detested dress neatly upon the bed, dressed as warmly as she could.

Then, wrapping her cloak securely around herself, she quietly left the inn. She could see, in the fitful moonlight, that there was a place to sit on the side of

the building, a long low bench there, she thought, for
indigent coach travelers to rest upon. She sighed, grateful for the secluded spot, and settled down. Here, no
one entering or leaving the inn could see her. She felt
rather like a leper anyway, tonight. As she sat back and
closed her eyes, the foolishness of her rash actions came
to her. She was still hungry, still homeless, and still a
long way from wherever her new home was to be. She
would, she thought, take the coach however far she
could still afford to go. And then she would have to see
how she could fare. At least, she thought wearily, I
shall finally know what exactly does happen to homeless
young women.

And she closed her eyes and tried to doze until morning would bring the coach and the last leg of the journey
that she could envision. So she did not see the slight
cloaked figure leave the inn and, after a moment, walk
quietly up behind her. Nor did she see the moment of
hesitation, when it raised one hand to touch her shoulder, and then, after a pause, withdrew it. The figure
stood, irresolute, while a cloud chased away from the
moon only long enough to light the fair hair like a
beacon. Then, with a small shrug, the figure turned and
walked silently back into the Crown and Gaiter again,
and with one last long glance at the shadowy recess
where Regina sat, quietly closed the door again.

XVI

One more stop, Regina thought to herself as the coach
bounced noisily through the morning mists. Only one
more stop, time to linger in the warmth over one more
cup of some hot liquid, before her purse emptied, and
then she would have to do something. Only what, she
still wondered.

She was now beyond hunger, beyond weariness, in
that strange state of mind that exhaustion and depriva-

tion brings. She felt enormously older and wiser than anyone else in her world, in that peculiarly exalted state of mind that extended sleeplessness can bring. She had not slept on the hard bench last night, rather she had sat awake as the night cold had seeped into her body until she embraced it as naturally as the warmth of a fire. She felt cold no more. And she could now review her future as dispassionately as if it were someone else's, with an Olympian detachment. Whatever else she did, she vowed, at last she would make no more pretense. At last she would be herself.

For, it had occurred to her during the long night, from the moment that her uncle had brought her to town, she had been untrue to herself. She had been living up to other people's expectations. First, she had pretended to be her uncle's cosseted and loved niece, when, if she had been honest, she would have realized that they scarcely knew each other. And she should have, she condemned herself, been setting about the task of finding her own place in the world. When Aunt Harriet had come, she should have been firm in her resolve; not for a moment should she have encouraged the woman to hope that she might eventually settle upon poor benighted Cousin Harry. She should not even have accepted his invitation to the theater simply for the expedient pleasure of being taken out for a night on the town. She should rather have taken the money that she was offered and fled to Miss Bekins, without standing on any ceremony.

In a veritable orgy of self-disgust, she had sat upon the hard bench in the inn courtyard and condemned herself like a prisoner in the dock. She should not have nodded dumbly and accepted the Duke's mad game plan. She should have forgotten about her dignity and screamed and shrieked and run free, without sitting like a fool and listening to his bizarre theories of self-respect and honor.

Indeed, in the case of the Duke, and her every encounter with him, she had been wrong. She had allowed herself to become caught in his web, to be fascinated by him, to almost welcome the verbal jousts she had with him, and, she realized with sinking heart, to enjoy other contacts with him as well. What arrogance she had had, she bitterly flailed herself, to think for a moment that she could deal with him as an equal. He had bested her every step of the way.

And then to cap it all, she should never, never have accepted the Marquis's protection. Never have pretended to be 'Lady Berry' simply for a safe harbor to rest in.

In all, she had pretended. In all, she had taken the easy way. She fairly hated herself now. And when she thought of those few moments in the frozen garden with Sinjin, how she allowed herself to be deluded into imagining he was going to make her an offer! Then the shame she felt when she remembered how she had rationalized her feelings in his embrace overrode all else. Even her appearance in poor Lucy's foolish little serving dress could not approach the self-disgust she felt at that. No, she had had enough of pretense. But, she thought, as the coach slowed at the gray stone inn, The Lion Crest, she had come to that particular conclusion too late.

When she stepped down and had her bag handed to her, she offered the coachman the next to last coins that she had. But he shook his head and declared loudly, much to the interest of the fellow passengers that were listening, that the sum wasn't enough. She had misunderstood, she thought sadly, and offered him the last coins in her purse, shaking her head to signify that there was naught else. He gave her a long hard look of regret. For, he declared in an undervoice, if he had known she hadn't the whole fare, he would have arranged some other way for her to pay him his due. But the objections of the passengers on the coach as to the delay merely caused him to drop the money into his pocket and sigh about lost opportunities. And the coach rattled off into the dim gray morning.

The mist was turning to a soft, sullen cold rain, and Regina turned to face the inn. She felt no further fear or trepidation. It seemed that there were few other depredations that she could suffer. She merely picked up her case and walked slowly, taking shelter under the overhanging eaves in front of the inn. She stood silently for a few moment, knowing that she could not go into the inn without the money for even a dish of tea. So she stood quietly, wondering with a strange sense of inappropriate laughter, about where she was to run to from here.

A moment later the door swung open, and the landlord, a huge bear of a man with bristling sideburns and a completely bald head, stepped out and looked at her with a welcoming smile. Yet he looked the sort of man who did not often smile, it was a forced expression for him. Regina was taken aback by the false welcome that seemed pasted onto his beefy face.

"Oh do come in, m'am," he said, bowing low. "I never thought you would just stand and wait outside in the rain."

She looked at him with amazement. What sort of new game was this?

"I'm afraid," she said quietly, "that you have mistaken me. I . . . I am simply waiting for the rain to let up before I continue down the road."

"Oh no," he said, picking up her traveling case. "I was expecting you, m'am."

"No," she said, seeking to get her case back as he turned toward the door. "I have no bookings here. You mistake me, I tell you."

But she had to follow him in as he simply walked off with her case of clothes.

He stood in the hallway and grinned at her. "If you'll permit me," he said, seeking to remove her dripping cloak.

"No," she said in exasperation, clutching the sodden garment to her, "I tell you I am the wrong woman."

"Oh no, m'am," he said pleasantly. "I was waiting for you to come off the coach from Witney."

Regina's numbed mind began to respond. Could it be possible that Mrs. Stors had regretted her harsh words and had contacted this man? Could there be a new position for her here? She followed the landlord as he led her to the back of the stairs to a private parlor. There, he paused and knocked softly on the door.

He opened it slowly and bowed her in.

"The lady you was waiting for, Your Grace," he said.

She stopped on the doorsill when she saw him. He was standing by the fire, and when he looked up, she found it hard to read the expression in his large blue eyes. But oddly, she felt only a vast sense of relief at seeing him. Seeing him, she thought irrationally, she felt a strange sense of homecoming.

He frowned, and came toward her.

"But you are frozen," he said, and taking the cloak from her, he led her to the fire. Once she was seated, he signaled to the landlord. "Some good hot soup, I think," he said imperatively, "and some other tempting foods."

"At once, Your Grace," the landlord replied, and bowing his way out, he closed the door behind him.

Regina lay her head back against the chair and relaxed. The fire was almost painful in its warmth. She felt a wave of tiredness sweep over her, but she opened her eyes to find him still frowning as he watched her. Somehow, he looked vaguely weary himself, she thought, the sensitive face looked paler, more thoughtful than usual, the cornflower eyes looked shadowed and were not lit with his usual inner humor.

"Yes," she breathed. "Yes, Your Grace, you were right. You do win. I have lost. I am a long way from Canterbury. A very long way indeed."

He did not reply, but stood close to her wordlessly until the landlord entered again with a full tray of dishes.

"First," he said, in his distinctive whisper, "eat and drink a few things. Then you can rail at me. I often find that vituperation is difficult on an empty stomach."

He guided her to the table, and she did eat some of the foods there, and drank some wine, at his insistence. But she found herself curiously lacking in appetite, and could not eat more than a few bites of any other of the array of foods before her. Then she sat back and looked at him again.

"I hope you haven't sickened, Regina," he said lightly, taking her hand and guiding her back to the chair by the fire.

"That would impair some of my plans, you know. It would be most inconsiderate of you. But you don't know how to take care of yourself, do you? Why did you turn down the offer of Lucy's bed? Foolish pride again?" he asked as he saw her eyes widen in surprise. "Or more of that sense of honor you do go on about? Oh yes, I was there. Snug as you can imagine, in the good lady's best parlor. But I imagined that if you refused poor innocent Lucy's bed, you could definitely refuse mine. And oh it was so warm and wide, but lonely, Regina. Alas, Lucy didn't tempt me at all. But I watched over you. I saw you wrapped in little else but your much discussed honor, sitting up all the cold night. I could have discovered myself to you then and there. But I decided, instead, to let you run your string out. And so you have, haven't you? For I know that you didn't even have enough money left to pay the coachman. You made quite an impression on Jack Potter, and he guessed truly enough that you, as he so succinctly put it, had hardly enough coins to jingle together. But I played it out to the end, that you can't argue. I waited to see if you could conjure up another Sinjin," he paused as he saw her wince, "or Lady Amelia, before I drew the final curtain.

"But now it is ended. It is over. Or have you any further protestations?"

"No," she said softly, "you are right. It is over."

"What," he asked gently, "no furious defense of virtue? No glowing plans for independence? No aspersions upon my character? I am disappointed. Truly. And here I looked forward to some superb operatic scenes. Perhaps you are too tired? Perhaps you would like to rest a while before you begin a tirade?"

"No," she said again. "No, I am beyond tired. But you have won."

He looked at her for another long moment. And she simply sat and gazed sadly back at him. He looked so complete, she thought, so elegant and in command. And so apart. His dark blue close-fitting jacket accentuated the fairness of his hair, the dazzling white of his neckcloth showed the purity of his skin. A fallen angel, she thought again, amazed again at how none of his career was written upon that disturbing and clever face.

"Why?" he asked, turning to gaze into the fire and prodding a wayward log with his booted foot, "were you on your way to Canterbury?"

"I thought you knew all," she said.

"Why, so I do, but even I have some limitations. I knew all the facts, but there was no way of my guessing your intent."

"I was on my way to join Miss Bekins," she said. "But you knew that."

"But surely you received her message." He frowned, turning to face her. "I heard that it was glowing congratulations to you on having landed such an estimable position. She was so delighted to hear of your good fortune. Imagine, finding a position in a Duke's household.

"But, never fear, I was careful not to specify exactly what sort of position it was, and since I rejoice in having fathered one small (although sadly trampled) creature to carry on my noble line, her assumptions about your future duties were of the most benign. And she could hardly have withheld the news of the good fortune that had fallen her way."

Regina only looked up in stupefaction.

"I never received any message, she never replied to my letters at all. What good fortune?"

"Only that your estimable Miss Bekins is even now as we speak on her way to a marvelous job as a teacher in the New World, passage paid. Did you know that she always wanted to travel? A learned woman, your Miss Bekins, but a trifle too sober-sided for my tastes. A keen-edged hatchet mind like my own dear Miss Pickett is more to my taste. Still, she was adventuresome enough to leap at the chance to travel. You know, my love, it is an ill wind that blows no good at all. At least, my . . . arrangement with you resulted in some good. Miss Bekins would never have secured that exciting position in ah . . . Massachusetts, I believe, if it were not for certain intervention. And it was fortunate, imagine, she had only five hapless brow-beaten young ladies under her charge when I located her. No," he said, watching her closely, "I never did promise that I play a fair game. I do tend to try to cover all exits and entrances."

"But I never heard from her," Regina cried in a small voice.

He turned to the fire again and asked in a low voice, "Who posted your letters, my dear?"

"Why, I gave them all to Sinjin and he——" She stopped and closed her eyes.

"Ah well," he sighed. After a moment's silence, he spoke again in a livelier, mocking voice.

"So it's been out of the frying pan and into the fire for you, Regina, hasn't it? You changed your mind about Sinjin's vile offer, and escaped only to find yourself forced to comply with mine."

"He told you about that?" she asked.

"Why no," he answered, "rather I told him about it. It seems that St. John agreed to join our little game, to see if he could win you from me. Or from yourself. No matter, but it had become a three-sided venture. Did you not know? Then I imagine you made your choice out of affection alone. Whatever caused you to change your mind? The eternal fickleness of women? But you might have done better to stay with your original choice. He has a fine house in Curzon Street, you know. And I, well, I am erratic, I might just decide to incarcerate you in some pokey country abode, ringed around with daisies, far from the Opera, and balls and flash of the city. For I am very possessive, of my . . . possessions."

"I didn't change my mind," she said, rising and walking hesitantly toward him so that she might better read his expression. "I never chose Sinjin, you know."

He gave a little involuntary start. "No," he said, "I didn't know. Sinjin seemed to feel that you had, though."

"No," she said, "I gave him no answer at all. He took that for 'yes.' I suppose he couldn't understand my not saying 'yes.' "

"Neither can I," he said quietly.

"I told you. I told you that I would never sell myself. Although," she said, shaking her head, "I do see now that it was a foolish thing to say. You were right, I think. It is very easy to make claims, to say 'never,' when you don't really know hunger, or desolation, or fear. Then it is very simple to say 'never,' very difficult to mean it. You were right."

"No!" he exclaimed roughly, and swinging around, held her shoulders with his hands, seeming to have been shaken out of some rigid inner control. "No, Regina, I was not right. Not at all. I may be in control now. I may have the power, and the authority, and the facilities, but I do not have the right. Give up all else to me, but not that. I know full well that I do not have the right, and never did."

She did not shrink back from him, or avoid his blazing eyes, only swayed a little, and said firmly,

"No. You are wrong, Your Grace. I was such a pompous little fool that night in your carriage. 'I shall never sell myself, not for jewels, or comforts, or fine clothes. I shall not live a life of servitude.' I said that, didn't I? But I was wrong. I was, in the end, quite willing to sell myself—for security, for safety. You were right, you know."

"I see," he said, releasing his grip upon her, a look of infinite sadness upon his face, and turned from her again and remarked, in a hoarsely sorrowful voice, "So you do not come to me . . . precisely 'intact,' do you? What was it? I am surprised," he went on, wheeling around to face her and saying in a savagely mocking voice, "at Sinjin's ineptitude. Did he hurt you? Shock you? Have his tastes grown so bizarre that he put you off the idea of your new career entirely? It's really rather too bad, now I shall have the task of reeducating you. It can be very pleasant, you know, if it is done right."

"My Lord, Your Grace," she laughed, putting her hands to her head, really the food and the warmth were making her dizzy with weariness. "You do have a lovely picture of me, don't you? No, I'm sorry to disappoint you, Your Grace, but no, I did not . . . no, yours was the only lesson I received in . . . no, I am yet 'intact,' as you put it, in body. But, not in spirit. No, neither in principle."

"What are you talking about?" he whispered furiously.

"I was, in the end, willing to sell myself," she wept.

"Do you know, Your Grace, I was. I thought, now this is a jest you will appreciate, I actually thought, when he said he had an offer for me, that it was an Offer. I thought he was asking me to marry him! And even though I did not love him, or really even know him, I was willing to say yes. For all those reasons I discredited earlier. For comfort, for security," she wept openly now, "for safety."

"Ah Regina," he said, and gathered her close to him, and held her closely, and stroked her hair as she wept.

"But that is not," he spoke softly as he comforted her as a brother might, "such a terrible thing. No, rather that is the way of the world. That is very acceptable, you know. Why half of England would not be wed today if that were not such a normal thing. There was no crime in that.

"And," he said, holding her a little away from him and touching her teary cheeks, "every young woman has her heart broken at least once, you know. It makes you quite fashionable," he said with a sweetly sad smile.

"No," she smiled back—impossible, she thought, impossible not to smile back at him—"my heart was not touched. You do not understand. I did not love him. But my pride in myself, ah, that was broken. How could I have contemplated . . . allowing kisses, embraces . . . deceiving myself—all for only comforts and security?"

But he only gazed at her, his face unreadable, until he lowered his head and, holding her head between two hands, like a man holding a delicate cup, he kissed her long and longingly. "You learn quickly," he murmured in an unsteady voice, raising his lips from hers. "Is it that I am such an extraordinary teacher, or is that you are such an apt pupil?"

Regina could only stand and wonder at the emotions he could so swiftly raise in her. He kissed her again and then put her away from him reluctantly.

When he stepped back, his eyes were dark and solemn. He pulled himself away from her and, walking to the mantel, struck a pose, one leg negligently thrust out on a low stool in front of it, his head thrown back, and that damnable mocking smile again in place.

"I would wish," he began theatrically, "that at least there were a scribe here, or a witness. For I am about to do something so entirely noble, so full of lovingkindness and bravery, that I expect at any moment to hear a choir of heavenly angels. Or at least see a brilliant shaft of sunlight suddenly appear. My dear Pickett would swoon with rapture and anyone of my acquaintance would dine out on it for a year. For I am about to make an enormous sacrifice, you know, and no one, no one would believe it. Least of all myself. But you have quite turned me around. You have evidently magicked me."

"Regina," he said in a softer tone, "the bargain I made with you was an unfair one. An evil one, if you will. But I was rather like that Chinese emperor who proudly trotted about his kingdom stark naked until one day, one innocent little boy pointed out the fact that he wore no clothes. And only then did he feel shame. Not that I can feel shame, mind you, for I don't think I can call up that emotion at all, being a nobleman, you know. Yet I think I can still dimly perceive that elusive thing called 'Honor,' " he smiled. "For you turned down Sinjin's offer and mine as well, preferring to work at anything, even as a common kitchen wench, rather than accept our largesse for far less work, at least in our humble estimation. I did misjudge you, Regina, but then," he mused, "females such as yourself are not thick upon the ground, at least not in the circles I have been traveling in. And they have been circles, it seems, all coming around eventually to the same starting point."

He stared at her for one brief moment and then went on more briskly, "I did, I know, some quite unforgiveable things, but then I do not wish to be forgiven. I cannot say I'm sorry for what I've done. How can I feel remorse when I had not done it, you would not be here with me now? And I cannot turn back the clock. I can hardly go back to your aunt and Cousin Harry, and bow, and say, "By and by, I was lying, I have never touched Regina at all. I am, after all, only a blackguard." No, I cannot. And I don't think I would want to. You didn't belong with them, you know. And I can't stop Miss Bekins on the high seas and pirate her back to her pitiful little school in Canterbury. But I can make restitution. For you see, Regina, a good friend of mine," he paused and laughed and went on, "But I exaggerate even now. Rather say, my one good friend recently reminded me of another wager I once made. A wager in which the winning was far more bitter than the losing. I think I am done with wagers for a space. Regina, our game is canceled. I have not won, but neither have you lost. I shall give you a certain sum of money, and you may do as you please with it. You will be free. And somewhat wealthy. So you can finally discover what it is you want of life, and what it is life wants of you. There, it is done in a stroke. All done. But curiously, unlike what the preachers all say, I do not feel instantly cleansed, or one whit better. But it is done. I am the rulemaker of this game. And I have ended it as a draw. You can establish your own school, or travel and join your Miss Bekins. Or become a patron of lost causes. Or even go back and take over little Lucy's job. Whatever you wish. You will be completely free."

But Regina, looking at the pale and tormented face before her, only felt dizzy with the realization that had suddenly come to her. That all along she had felt drawn to him. That each time she encountered him she felt truly alive. That his mocking face had intruded on all her thoughts, awake or asleep, since she had met him. She looked at him and wanted to be close in his arms again. She wanted to hear him rage, and mock, and discourse. She wanted to laugh and cry with him. He had entered her life and brought with him life, and she had the feeling that if he left now, he would take with him part of her life. She no more understood him than she understood herself, but now, in the heightened state of awareness that she had reached through turmoil and weariness, only her instincts still worked for her. And she knew that she did not want to leave him.

She walked close to him. "I do not want your money," she said slowly, "nor do I accept your charity. I consider that I have lost the game. I accept only that."

"Damn you!" he said savagely, and drew her close to him. "What are you trying to do to me, Regina? What other new defense are you breaching now? How far will you go before you destroy me entirely? You are leaving me nothing, you know," he breathed into her hair. She felt his body shudder, and then he spoke softly again.

"Then you will have to marry me, Regina. You could do worse, but I don't see how."

All her exhaustion suddenly vanished, and she pulled away from him.

"Marry you?" she cried.

"Yes, it is not Sinjin's 'offer,' you know. I make you a true offer. Marry me."

"So that you can complete your degradation!" she cried to his astounded look. "So that you can finally prove to all and sundry that you have no care for your rank or name? So that you can snap you fingers and say, 'See what I have done now? See how I am married to a nothing, to a no one, to a nonentity?' Oh no, you shall not use me thus."

"No, no, Regina," he said, his voice between laughter and tears. "What sort of nonsense is this? If I wished to marry for that reason, I assure you . . . oh, I assure you that there are others far more suitable to those purposes than you. Others of my much more intimate acquaintance, Regina."

"But I am not a lady," Regina protested.

"But you will be a Duchess," he smiled, "and if I wished to find someone unsuitable . . . oh Regina, you have no idea of how many unsuitable females I have managed to know. You, at least, can speak, and read, and write, and reason. You have not lived in the gutter. Oh, if I wanted to astound the world with a wife, I could do far better than you. But you are wrong, Regina, you *are* a lady, you know."

"But Sinjin said," she began, "that if I married . . . him, I would be sneered at, snubbed, avoided . . . it would be a scandal."

"Oh," he laughed, holding her close again and rocking her. "It will be a scandal, my love, to see how many, how very many will trip over themselves to become acquainted with you, to issue invitations, to include you in their every affair of consequence. For you will have a title, but more than that, you will have money and power. It is marvelous what a social equalizer that is. Oh you will be accepted. That is, if you wish to be. But I somehow doubt that it will be important to you. But if it is, you will have that. My birth, if not my worth, will give that to you, if you want it. And as for me, why I never cared about my acceptance and, strangely enough, neither has the world. And for those others who insist on being high sticklers, why, you wouldn't like them anyway. But for your children, love, why distance lends acceptability—they will be as acceptable socially as golden guineas, I assure you."

"Why do you ask me to marry you," she asked, holding him tightly, "when I have already agreed to your bargain?"

"Because it is best for you," he said, giving her a light kiss for each reply, "because I have a softness for green eyes, because you are lovely, because I wish to be envied, because I want to."

"No, why?" she asked again.

"Would you unman me entirely?" he smiled. "Would you win all, sweep up all the winnings and leave me without a cent in my pocket? Ah, Regina, you grow greedy."

"But I must know," she protested.

"First answer me," he said. "First give me your answer. For unlike Sinjin, I do not take your silence for 'yes.' Oh no, your silences are too loud for that. First answer—but know now," he said, "I do not offer you a marriage of convenience. I am too selfish for that. If you take me, you must take me completely. My money and my life, you little highwayman, for it would be a real marriage, of mind and body. Now answer, just one syllable, but answer," he said. And then prevented any answer by covering her lips with his own. She clung to him, staggered by her avid response to him, as though through no will of her own, as though her body had more wisdom than her brain. Here at last, she felt warm, protected, and at peace. Yet his lips, his clever hands, and the taut strength of his body brought her everything but peace. And then, when she felt she must somehow get even closer to him although she did not know how that could be achieved when she was locked to him already, he raised his head suddenly, seemingly to listen. He drew away from her, and walked to the window and stood staring out. His shoulders seemed to slump. She stood wavering, feeling bereft, as though a part of herself had gone with him.

Now that he had left her and she could admit the world again, she too heard the muted stampings of horses, the rattle of a vehicle, the sound of voices, the inn doors opening, the sounds of fresh activity.

"You are saved again," he said wearily, still looking out of the window. "For see, enter the deus ex machina. Comes the conquering hero. The shining knight. Again, Regina, you are saved from me. Perhaps it is best," he mused, almost to himself. "It was a mad idea at any rate. It was not remotely noble. I was only taking advantage again. It is poetic justice, it is deserved."

He swung about from the window.

"Come in, Sinjin," he called pleasantly as the knock came upon the door, "We await your pleasure."

XVII

St. John stood in the doorway. He saw Regina immediately. Her pallor, her exhaustion, the state of her dress, still crushed and damp from the rain and her travels, and her wide green eyes a little frantic, struck him to the heart. Ignoring the Duke's low bow, he strode to her side.

"Regina," he said, "you are all right? You are safe?"

"Untouched," Torquay laughed. "Ah, but you arrive in a good time. In but a moment more, she would have been foully ravished. Cruelly used. Lancelot, you arrive in time. In a good hour."

"I am well, Sinjin," Regina replied, and looked up at him with disbelief. "Why did you follow me here?"

"But I had to," he said urgently. "I had to find you and speak with you. You were right, Regina. Right to leave when you did. It was the best thing you could have done. It . . . confirmed all that I felt about you. Regina, look at me, I must speak with you."

"But take off your coat, Sinjin," the Duke said lightly, "for you are dripping rain all over Regina, and I have only just dried her out."

"Leave us alone, Torquay," St. John said roughly, casting off his dripping cloak and staring down at Regina.

"So that I do not awaken love's young dream? Yes, I am *de trop* now, obviously," the Duke said, walking toward the door.

"No," cried Regina. "Do not leave, Your Grace, please, please stay here."

"But Regina," St. John said in a deep low voice, "I must speak with you . . . alone."

"His Grace has the right to hear anything that you might say to me. Is he not a player in your game?" Regina insisted with unfamiliar harshness. "Please stay," she asked again of the Duke, who stood by the door.

He smiled, and shrugged, and closed the door. He stationed himself by the window, watching her with a bemused expression.

"Regina," said St. John, taking both of her hands in his, "it was wrong of me to presume both upon your innocence and the situation that you found yourself in. When I read your note, I had already realized that fact. I came home from London to tell you so. I have been following your traces since you left us. I have inquired at every inn along the route. I have been frantic. Amelia is with me. She is just outside the door. She . . . she berated me too, Regina," he said, remembering the cold fury with which Amelia had greeted him, the contempt in her voice, the icy quiet that she had maintained throughout the days of their journey. And the curious thing that she had said when she had handed him the note Regina had left for him. "It was a cruel thing to do, St. John, no, more than cruel, it was unforgiveable. But at least I think you have set me free." But his search for Regina had been so desperate that he had not had time

to think further about Amelia's strange remark. "She
has come along with me so that you might be . . .
adequately chaperoned on our return trip. For you are
coming home with me, Regina. You are returning with
me. To be my wife. It cannot be otherwise."

"An embarrassment of riches," the Duke laughed from
his position at the window.

"You," St. John said through gritted teeth, "you are
the author of all these difficulties. You are in no position
to comment on this. No, Torquay, you shall not have
her."

"You are almost as bad a loser as I am," the Duke
said, "but you are right, I shall not have her. I only
mention the curious fact that she finds herself in the
unique position of being offered the name and fortune of
two noblemen within the hour. What a lovely pair she
has to choose from! A dissipated Duke, and a slightly
used Marquis. What a noble pair! And what a demand
there seems to be for your hand today, Regina. Are you
using a new scent? You see, Sinjin, I made her the same
offer myself, only moments ago."

"You?" St. John exclaimed, giving a short ugly laugh.
"You married to her? Must you try to contaminate everything you touch? Is there no thing you hold in honor?
No matter, Regina, you are safe now, from him, and
from me."

"Yet remember, Regina," the Duke said quickly, "I
did make you yet another offer, another choice. You can
go completely and the devil take the pair of us. You can
go completely free of us."

"Never free from me, I swear it," Sinjin said furiously.

Regina looked from one man to the other.

"But Sinjin," she asked, "what of the social suicide
that you spoke of? How can you now offer me what you
said was impossible before?"

"That is the news I bring you," Sinjin smiled, "for I
have discovered that it is easily enough solved. We can
get around it, Regina."

St. John took a packet of beribboned papers from his
pocket and spread them out on a table before her. They
were creased, and in some cases dirty and tattered

parchments, but he handled them with great care, as though they were priceless.

"I spent many long hours with my solicitor in London, before I came here. He is a canny and, surprisingly, very socially correct man. I confided in him, and I am glad of it. For he has devised a simple plan for us to win free of our problem, Regina. There are many émigrés now, from across the channel. People of birth and title and rank but who have been separated from their fortune and lands, penniless but considering themselves lucky to have not been separated from their heads, by Madame Guillotine. There are those willing to sell their titles, for a consideration. We will have papers—take your pick. Choose a name. Choose a rank. You can have any, or all." He laughed in delight.

"We will put it about that you are an émigré who has been educated in this country, that would explain your lack of an accent. No one has really ever known you, Regina. Even at the Squire's ball, you remained incognito. It will do. It will serve. You must see that."

"Oh I shall keep mum," the Duke drawled. "Never fear that I shall divulge the truth," he said, intercepting Regina's quick glance toward him. "It is a neat solution. Remember I told you, Regina, that most people will sell anything in order to find comfort in life, even their birthright."

"You must see," St. John said, his gray eyes pleading with her, "I need you, Regina. I will make a good husband to you. It will be only a little thing to do to ensure our happiness. What matter it what name you are known by? You will change your name when you marry me, anyway."

"But not myself, Sinjin," she said calmly. "I did tell you that I didn't love you, Sinjin. And I still do not."

"But you shall," he insisted, cursing the circumstances that led to Torquay's standing there, silhouetted against the window, for if he could only hold her, embrace her, he could convince her. He thought of his sick shock when, having made all his plans, he had returned to Fairleigh in triumph, only to find her gone. To find her note. Each word that she had written to him had caused

him another stab of remorse. He wanted her now as his
wife and mistress in one. He would not live in the
double world of James, nor in the despised one of the
Duke. With Regina, he saw, he could be complete. And
he now saw how he could accomplish it. But there again
was the omnipresent shadow of Torquay.

"If we were alone, I could convince you," he said
huskily.

"How ungracious, Sinjin," the Duke said. "You are
making me feel like an interloper, rather than another
aspirant to her hand."

"Then leave," snarled the Marquis.

"Sinjin," Regina said rapidly, seeing him start toward
the Duke with fists clenched, "I would never, no never
consent to having my name changed in order to have my
name changed. Berryman is no noble name. I have no
title. But I am Regina Berryman. If I were to pretend,
even if only for a little while, that I were a French
countess, or lady, soon I would come to believe it. I
would be living a lie. You too, Sinjin, would, in some
small part of your mind, come to believe it. And somewhere in all the deception, I would lose track of my real
self. It would not do. No, never. At least His Grace was
willing to have me, common name and all."

" 'Love is not love which . . . alteration finds,' " the
Duke quoted softly.

"Love!" St. John shouted. "What does he know of
love? Is that the name he gives to all his pastimes?
Don't be deceived by his glibness. If I could tell you,
Regina, of what he has done in the name of his 'love.' "
He stared down at her. "He is a byword for licentious-
ness. You are too young to understand what lengths he
has gone to. How he has sullied his name and his body.
What he has lain with . . . what women . . . what——"

"Creatures," the Duke put in in an oddly subdued
voice. "Almost a bestiary full, in fact. Everything save
for giraffes and donkeys. I fear he is right, Regina. I
have ranged far. I have done things which, for all my
honesty, I would rather you did not know of. I might
say that it is all done. That I expect I could become an
uncommonly dull husband. That I grow old, and weary

of such amusements, especially since they never did amuse me the way I expected them to. I might say that with such a wife, I would feel no need of them. I might say that you would leave no room in my admittedly small heart for any others. There simply would be no more room. That I yearn for some truth. Some end to this unending game I have played with my life. All that I might say. But he is right. Understand that completely. He is right. I can only offer you an unclean hand, and a slightly tattered title."

"But," she said, freeing her hands from St. John's grip and walking toward him, where he stood rigid, close to the window with a rigid smile upon his drawn face, "you offer it in honesty. Do you not?"

"That yes," he said seriously, for once unsmiling, cold, and curiously defenseless. "But Sinjin offers you a great deal more, Regina. Be aware of that. He offers youth, a name that is not half so shocking as mine, a title, and a fortune. It was not he who plunged you into this situation. It was not he who sent your Miss Bekins halfway across the world. It was not he who invented this cruel chase we both have led you. Yes, he became a player, he dealt himself in. At first, I believe, only to annoy me, but he soon played in earnest. But he did not invent the game. Remember, Regina, I abducted you. I harrassed you. I sought to corrupt you. I am the originator of the game, even though I was the one eventually captured by my own devices."

"Do you withdraw your offer, then?" she asked, her eyes searching his face.

"I do wish I could," he said regretfully. "But no. I am not, at last, so noble. I cannot change so much. It would not be possible. I still offer you, for whatever use you wish to put them to, my name, my fortune, myself."

"Why?" she insisted, in a choked voice. "Out of guilt? A sense of reparations? To compete with Sinjin? I must know why."

He put up both his hands in a gesture of defense, and smiling only with his lips, he said hoarsely,

"Will you play for such high stakes then? Will you leave me nothing? No little vestige of myself? I see you will not. Say then, because you are the most honorable creature I have ever found."

"Honor." She shook her head.

"Why do you wish to marry me, Sinjin?" she turned to ask.

"If only we were alone," he swore, "I should show you. But why? Because I love you, Regina. I must have you with me. I can speak with you. I can commune with you. I desire you. And need you." He tried to think of what else she would want him to say, and helplessly asked, "What else do you require of me?"

"Perhaps, honesty," she said. And turning again to the Duke, she asked, "Do you need me, Your Grace?"

"Your Grace?" He laughed. "It is a little late in the day for that, isn't it? At least let me hear 'Jason' from your lips, once."

"Jason, then," she said. "Leave off the game, I pray you. I must know. Do you need me? Why?"

"Have done," he sighed. "Who would not need you?"

"Do you?" she insisted.

St. John stood still and watched them incredulously, unwilling to believe the look he saw upon her face for Torquay. She never took her eyes from his face.

The Duke, at last, so pale that she feared for him, smiled once again, only this time with real humor and tenderness.

"I need you," he said quietly in his hoarse voice. "Indeed, more than any other man on earth could. And yes, I want you. And yes, damn it, I love you, insofar as I can understand the word. For I do not use it overmuch, as I am not sure I understand it altogether. But I am a selfish man, Regina. I think that if I really understood what love was, I would deny you. And insist that you leave at once, with Sinjin. I would renounce you. But I cannot. As I said, I am not a good man. But how foolish I am become. How can you wish to come with me, knowing what you do? I see your move now, Regina. Your victory is complete. Go to Sinjin, then. Collect all your winnings and go."

"I want to go with you, Jason," Regina said after a pause, hoping never again in her life to see that blanched, sick look upon his face, and wanting to erase it with her lips or her words. She stepped toward him and looked full into his face. "Whatever you have been or done. I do not know either what love is. But, to begin, I like you, Jason. Even when you frightened me, I could not help thinking of how much I could like you. I am happy with you when you cease to be on guard against me. I think of you constantly, and have done for weeks, it seems. And for some reason, I only want to be with you. And yes," she said softly, forgetting St. John's standing so close to the two of them, seeing only her world in the Duke's intent eyes, "I desire you, too. You did teach me what desire is, and I find I want only you to teach me more. All of that. Is that love?"

"Let us attempt to find out," he said gravely, catching up her hand in his.

"You cannot do this, Regina," St. John choked. "You do not know what you are doing."

"She is marrying me, Sinjin," Torquay said softly, his gaze never leaving Regina, his hold on her tightening. "That is what she is doing."

"No," St. John began, but Regina spoke swiftly, cutting off his words.

"Yes," she said. "But Sinjin, do not grieve. For I think you have not lost anything. I think you do not know yet what it was that you had asked of me, or whom it was that you asked it of. You wanted me to lie, and lie again, to myself and to you. You asked me to marry into a lie. No. It is you who must yet discover what love is. It is more than desire, I know. More than possession or passion, although I know that is a part of it. It is rather, in the end, I think, a part of friendship. Look to your friends for it," she said.

"Is Amelia just outside?" the Duke said softly. "Then I must have a word with her. She must ride back with us and stay for a while at Grace Hall. For I want you well chaperoned, Regina. At least, I will begin this right. And she will want to witness our marriage. I know she will want to. But we shall invite a great many people, Regina. And you shall see how many will stumble over themselves to come to us."

He held her hand tightly and took her to the door with him, but she paused to look up at St. John.

He stood still, his finely chiseled face seemingly graven in stone.

"Some day you will find it, Sinjin," she said carefully, "but you were deceived. It was not I. No, never was it Regina Analise Berryman. For her, there was only desire. For 'Lady Berry,' there was love, and only for her. But that is . . . that was . . . never me."

St. John stood for a long while, only staring down at the hard-won papers he had brought with him. The names: Mme. de Roche, Mme. Vicare, Mme. Chambord, swam before him. He had lost, the thought kept repeating. Lost all.

The door opened and Torquay came in once again, moving with the noiseless grace he always appeared with. St. John felt a hand upon his arm. And a soft voice said:

"We would like you to come too, Sinjin. To wish us happy. Regina would like that very well. As I would. No, Sinjin, understand. You are yet young with a world of women ahead for you. Regina is the only woman in the world for me, indeed my only hope left for love . . . for honor, if you will. But understand, I do not gloat in triumph. I do not caper and fling your loss in your face. I, of all men, understand what a loss it is. I have long since ceased to regard this as a game. But you must pardon me for singing. For that is what I am doing, Sinjin. Forgive me. But I must sing," and as noiselessly as he had come, he left.

St. John heard, as from a distance, the sound of a carriage in front of the inn. He walked, dazed, to the window, and saw through the rain-misted little squares, that Amelia was entering the dark coach with the distinctive crest. A moment later, he saw Jason Edward Thomas, Duke of Torquay, his distinctive bright hair dewed with rain, drape his long cloak about a small figure that stood close to him, as if welded to his side, to shelter it from the downpour. He saw the bright head dip for a moment, down under the cape-draped arm, and for a long moment the figures clung together. And then he handed her up into the coach. A moment later he entered. And then the equipage took off, the horses moving briskly down the darkened road.

But St. John Basil St. Charles, Marquis of Bessacarr, stood at the window looking out into the deserted road, some purple beribboned papers crushed in his hands, his arm against the window, his head lowered on his arm, for a long while, a very long while, after the dark coach had gone.

Lord
of Dishonor

Lord of Dishonor

Edith Layton

A SIGNET BOOK

Indisputably, for Michael . . .

I

It was a cold, still night. No breath of wind stirred the bare tree branches that stood upturned like freezing beggar's hands beside the quiet road. The sky had a milky cast, the air a metallic tang, and the night lay heavy with the promise of snow. But the traveler sat folded deep within his greatcoat and rode at a leisurely amble. There were no onlookers to shake their heads at his folly, for cautious men stayed by their fires on such a night, and even incautious ones did not venture forth unless there were some urgent reason.

He had felt urgency, he thought, as he pulled his collar closer about his neck, when he had left the docks this dawn. He had felt such vaulting, surging impatience that he had abandoned his carriage and most of his belongings to the hands of others and given them directions to his destination, for he had felt a carriage ride too slow a pace to set for himself. He had packed a few items in his bags and set out at once, alone and on horseback, so that he could arrive ahead of them, so that he could gallop as his ambitions had. But now the urgency had faded, now that he was, at last, within a few leagues of home, he found himself tarrying.

It was amazing, he thought, permitting himself a smile that almost hurt in the frigid air, how he always forgot. For two years he had dreamed of home, and now that he was so close, the old memories came crowding back. Curious how those memories became dull and blunted when he was so far away that there was no possibility of a swift

7

return, but when he was actually so near as to make desire a reality, reality blunted desire.

He felt his mount's great body heave a great shudder that almost matched his own. The thought of the beast's discomfort goaded him as his own had not. He nudged the animal into a grateful trot. The stallion had made his mind up for him. He would seek some other shelter tonight. And perhaps tomorrow night. There was no great hurry, after all. Two years or twenty, when one came right down to the point, it made no difference at all when he returned home.

The inn was small and snug. The warmth that greeted him was such a contrast to the bitter night that it caused pain as he stepped through the door. An experienced traveler, he did not whip off his iced and leaden coat and rush to the fireside to thaw his constricted hands. That would only cause more discomfort. He stayed, instead, a moment to chat with the landlord and agree that it was, indeed, a very cold night. Then he walked slowly to a table in the common room. Only when he had ordered some hot repast, and only after he had warmed his gloved hands against his mug of hot grog, did he begin to divest himself of his gloves and scarf.

Only then, when he had absorbed some of the heat of the room and freed himself of bodily distress, was he able to fully take note of his surroundings. It was a simple, pleasant place, he decided. A typical English inn, built by the side of the road to accommodate travelers. The floors were scrubbed wood, the tables and chairs simple hand-hewn things, the fireplace ample, the serving girl casual and cheeky. Nothing elaborate, nothing for the Quality, it was merely one of a hundred such places strewn about the countryside. He had discovered himself longing for the sight of just such a place in the last months.

There were not many patrons this night. Those with homes clearly were in them. Nevertheless, there was custom. An elderly couple seated near him seemed to be a farmer and his wife. Forced to attend the unexpected birth of their grandchild, he thought, as he sipped his drink and listened absently as they consoled themselves about being so far from home this night with the expectations of a gay family reunion once they reached their destination. A fellow who looked to be an unsuccessful peddler counted and recounted his small store of coins at a far table, while three young local lads laughed and traded heavy-handed innuendos with the serving girl.

When he drew off his coat at last and draped it over the back of an empty chair, he became aware of a sudden silence falling over the room. The quiet lasted only a second and then the various talk picked up again. But the landlord appeared at his table as if by magic, even as he settled back in his chair once again.

"Why sir," the landlord said unhappily, his round face all concern, "you ought to have asked me for a private room. We have such, you know. And as Nan's not brought you your food as yet, it wouldn't take a minute to set you up there."

Clothes do make the man, he thought, leaning back and smiling at his host. For his garb had marked him as a member of the Quality, and the landlord was clearly worrying about the insult of having placed him in the common room. He had not bothered to change for travel; indeed, he had not even thought of it. But now he thought of what the landlord could see. In his high polished boots, with his dark gray pantaloons, gleaming white shirt, and well fitting black jacket, he was as exotic as a parrot among pigeons. Looking down at his green and gold embroidered waistcoat and carefully arranged neckcloth, he amended, no, he was as exotic as a peacock among geese.

"No, no," he said in his soft voice, "I am well content to be here. I've been abroad, you see, for a very long while and am glad to be among Englishmen again."

His host still seemed uneasy, although he backed away. When the serving girl brought dinner, beef and dumplings and ale, fare as simple and warm and ample as herself, the landlord bustled forth once again to line up his guest's tableware, fuss over his napery, and dart censorious glances at the wench for lingering over the table. The gentleman ate in silence, noting that a small pool of quiet seemed to have settled over his corner of the room, as though the others were aware of him but determined not to allow him to know it. He was, in that warm and simple place, as apart as if he had been in his own parlor. But as it was a circumstance he was accustomed to, he finished his meal in charity with his world.

When he had done and the sense of a well-being that the warmth and the food had brought had evaporated, as all comforts do when one becomes accustomed to them, he pondered his next move. He could stay where he was, he thought, looking about him. The landlord surely had several rooms vacant this night. The serving girl had made such a symphony of movement over the clearing of his table that he knew he could have company to while away the small hours of the bitter night with, and a warm bed even if his host had no thought of using a hot brick to take the chill off his sheets. And as he was not expected, it did not matter how long it took him to complete his journey home.

But, he thought perversely, for all its pleasures, the inn was not a home. And a home was what he had promised himself. This was only one of a succession of clean, comfortable places where he had sojourned recently. Though the serving girl was willing and familiar, she was too familiar. In fact, he wondered if he had not already sometime, somewhere passed a night with her. And even if he were expected, it still would make no difference when he arrived at home. He made his mind up quickly, as he so often did.

He beckoned the landlord to his side and asked, "I've ridden most of the day and at the last was too frozen to take note of the signposts. What town is this?"

"Why, Oakham, sir," the landlord replied, with as much amazement as if he had asked if it were night.

"So far?" the gentleman said, as if to himself, for he had not realized how far he had gotten before his will had begun to flag.

"Oakham," he murmured, "Oakham. Tell me, is that not close by Leicester?"

"Very near, sir," the landlord replied, with some worry now apparent, as it seemed, incredibly, as though his elegant guest were preparing to depart. "But it's a bitter night, sir, bitter."

"And is not Kettering Manor in Leicester?" his guest asked, taking some coin from his pocket.

"Kettering Manor?" the landlord gasped, as if he had been asked if the seventh circle of hell lay across the road. "Aye, sir, it is," he finally admitted, as he saw amusement register in the gentleman's eye.

"And would you happen to know if the countess is in residence now?" his guest asked imperturbably.

"Aye, she is," the landlord mumbled, now avoiding his patron's eye. But that was commonplace, too.

"Then for all your hospitality, thank you," the gentleman said smoothly. "And further thanks if you can give me a swift route there. For I am expected, I think."

As the landlord gave directions, his guest noted that all attempt at conversation in the room had ceased and that he was being watched with an admixture of shock and envy. It was as if he had announced that he was about to dine with the devil. He shrugged into his now warm greatcoat once again and left a larger amount of coin upon the table than was strictly necessary. It was to compensate the serving girl, who looked after him reproachfully as he left. He tipped her a sweet smile as he paused at the door, which only seemed to sink her spirits further.

Even as he closed the door behind him, he could hear the babble of voices rise in his wake. He strode to the stables and apologized silently to his mount as he prepared to travel again. "Only a little farther tonight," he thought, for himself and his horse.

"Ah Nan," cried one of the three young fellows as soon as the gentleman had left, "seems you've got to pick one of us after all. The fine gent's off to the countess, the more fool he, for he'll not find a prettier wench in all the land than you."

The compliment did not seem to content the young woman, as she savagely swept the gentleman's largesse into her pocket.

"Maybe not, Jem," another of the fellows chortled. "But

maybe he's after quantity, not quality. He'll have at least three ladies to share his bed at the countess's."

"Three?" roared the third fellow, who had taken on so much to ward off the chill he could now feel neither heat nor cold. "Why, I hear tell it's no fewer than six that share a likely lad there. Aye, and the countess herself, as well. 'He's expected,' he thinks. Why such a pretty fellow would always be welcome there."

"Oh, stop nattering," the girl said angrily. "Especially about your betters."

"Betters?" cried one of the fellows in such comical amazement that the entire room joined in the girl's abashed laughter.

The gentleman outside heard the burst of laughter even through the tightly closed doors and windows. He gazed back at the inn, seeing the light glowing from out the fogged windows and scenting the wood smoke that poured from the chimney. For a moment, he regretted his hasty decision. Then, realizing that he would have been discontent with whatever his course of action might have been this night, he sighed and spurred his horse forward toward the road again.

He was not expected, but he would be admitted. And if the countess was notorious, if even her name caused shock and her whole set caused scandalized comment in the simplest of country inns, why then, he would most assuredly be welcomed. As the cold took hold again and he hurried the last weary miles, he thought that he was making haste to a home, at least, where his presence would be greeted by its mistress with glad welcome. Which was, he thought as he spurred his horse to a bracing gallop, a good deal more than what could have been said for his original destination.

"North!" the lady cried, clapping two little hands together as a child might when her butler brought the news. "Here? It's the very thing! Just what was needed. Show him in, Gilby, at once. Only think," she said to the room at large, "North has come to visit us."

While a murmur went up among her company at her

words, the lady turned to a tall, heavy-set elderly man at her side.

"Robert, it is North who's arrived. I haven't thought of him in ages. And now, he comes in the dead of night, in the most inclement of weathers. Never let it be said that there isn't a divine providence, Robert, never," she said fervently.

"Don't know why you're making such a to-do," the elderly gentleman said crossly. "He's a good enough chap. But I thought you were enjoying our little party just as it was. Don't see why you're carrying on like he was your savior. You could have told me if you were bored. We could have taken ourselves off somewhere or the other."

"No, no, dearest," the lady said, calming herself. "Do not misunderstand me. I was enjoying myself enormously. It is only that . . ." but here she hesitated and then went on swiftly, peeking up at the gentleman winsomely, "He will make the party complete. For now we have fourteen, such a pleasant number."

"Fifteen," the gentleman corrected her, "for I wouldn't have been easy with thirteen present in all. I take note of such things. Not that I'm superstitious, Fanny, but a chap notes things like that."

"Oh fie, Bobby, you know how wretched I am with numbers," the lady said peevishly, fanning herself in her agitation. "It's only that now all will go perfectly."

" 'Course it will," the gentleman said in a placating manner. He forgot the matter immediately as he turned to speak with one of his guests, just as he forgot all matters that were even slightly troublesome. His lady took herself apart from the others, however, and stood expectantly waiting for her new guest to be ushered into the salon.

She was an exceedingly diminutive female to bear such a great load of names as Fanny Juliana Octavia Amberly, Countess of Clovelly. And if words bore physical weight, and one added to her title the measures of notoriety which had been heaped upon that name, she would have been unable to move at all. But as it was, she moved with as light a tread as a child, though she had left that estate behind decades ago.

The Countess of Clovelly was one of the few middle-aged females whose admirers did not exaggerate wildly when they swore she resembled a girl. She was wise enough to enhance the imposture where she could and clever enough to deny it where she could not. Thus, if she allowed gray to creep into her golden curls, it was only because it enhanced her fairness. If she permitted a few extra pounds to round out her once well defined curves, why then, they also helped to smooth out wrinkles upon her merry countenance. She denied herself heavy powder and paint not to make a point of her youthfulness, but because she knew that accentuating her features *too* clearly would only point out the passages of time. She wore colors fit for an ingenue when she realized dark tones made her look hagged, and she smiled constantly because she discovered that when laugh lines cannot be hidden, they might as well be called into constant play. At fifty years and counting forward quite slowly, the Countess of Clovelly was a charming, cuddly miniature temptress, still capable of causing stableboys to sigh as she passed.

Now she stood atip with delight, like a cherub on a Christmas morning, in her grand salon awaiting her new guest. When he appeared in the doorway, she did not hesitate. She flew to his side and impetuously brushed her cheek against his before he could properly take her hand. When he did lift that little white hand, she blushed prettily and then said only one word, breathlessly and dramatically.

"North!"

"Countess!" he breathed, twinning her utterance with just a faint undernote of mockery.

"Here at last?" she asked in more normal tones.

"You have asked me to visit for years, and I have been churlish enough to deny you. But tonight, I chanced to be passing through, I confess on my way to some other port of call. But when I saw your house ablaze with light, it looked to me on that lonely heath like some great bright ship sailing through the seas of night. So I chanced to stop and hail it. Am I welcome aboard, countess?"

"Always!" she said fervently, as his speech had been just

the sort of poetical nonsense she adored. "You need no special invitation."

"Look everyone," she cried, taking his cold hand and leading him into the room, "it is North at last!"

Her words were unnecessary, for the others in the room had ceased to speak the moment he stepped into their midst. As he greeted them, he was smiling widely at the interior thought that he need only to step over a doorsill this night to effectively cut off all conversation. All those present were known to him, although he had not seen them in several years. There was a middle-aged baron and his temporary lady, a light female known to consort only with the wealthiest protectors; a beaming, aged French count and his ancient dame, with a handsome young couple one might take for their children if one did not note to which bedrooms they repaired each night; a tulip of the *ton* and his flushed, bibulous wife; a minor poet with a major appetite for fame; and two slender young scions of the nobility with a famous divorcée in tow for show purposes only, as the pair well knew the penalty for their mode of friendship if it should ever be discovered and attempted discretion even in a circle such as this.

It was their host who took it upon himself to ask his new guest all the questions the others might have cared to inquire about. Robert, Duke of Laxey, fired query after query at the new arrival. And so Lord Christian Jarrow, Viscount North, a practiced guest, stood in the center of the room, cradling a snifter of brandy that had been pressed upon him, and told them of his past two years' adventuring. He spoke of the present conditions in Vienna, in Italy, in France, and even upon the tiny island of Elba.

Lord North stood at his ease and chatted amiably, parrying questions and asking some of his own as though he had just risen from his armchair to greet unexpected visitors. There was no way either from his speech or manner that one could guess he had spent the better part of three days in arduous travel, or that he had breakfasted at sea, had luncheon upon the road, and had only just arrived hoping for no more than a few words and a suitable bed. He stood in the center of the bright, warm room as though he were host himself, and no eye strayed from him.

The countess stood at the edge of the company grouped around him and said not a word. Usually she would have been in full spate by now, for she dearly loved attention and would normally have made the most of presenting such a glittering guest. But she only watched him. If there had been any in the room who would have taken the trouble to observe her similarly, they would have seen her small white teeth worrying at a corner of her delightfully rosy lips.

She could not blame any of them for neglecting her, not even her dead Bobby, who hovered at the viscount's shoulder and would not have noticed if she had sunk to the floor in a dead faint at this moment. North was a gentleman worth noticing. Even if he were not, the rarity and brevity of most of his appearances would have made him so. For he never stayed too long in one place, or within one set. He was the quintessential traveler, a bright, wandering comet that briefly lit each corner of his world and then left all his acquaintance in comparative darkness by his absence. He was witty, he was clever, he was reputed to be heartless, and he was undeniably beautiful.

It was not only the two young noblemen whose eyes covertly studied his graceful, well-made form, and neither was it only the baron's expensive playmate who watched the play of expression on his face with the soft, rapt breathing of a predator. His was the sort of physical beauty that attracted even as any great work of art ensnared the eye. One did not have to wish to own such a creation, often it was enough just to study and appreciate it.

Only a little above average height, his form was well proportioned and well muscled, with not an extra jot of flesh. He had a fencer's easy play of movement. But it was his face that first and last attached the eye. It was a lean countenance, the ivory white skin so taut across the fine bone structure as to appear to have been stretched to fit. Feature by feature, it was not a classic visage, but the sum more than compensated for the parts. His cheekbones were high and perhaps too pronounced. The nose was straight, a trifle too long and thin, the mouth not at all the full, plump standard of Greek statuary, for while well cut it was thin as well, and bore at times a half-quirked, sensuous smile. The eyes were long and almond-shaped and pulled down slightly at the corners, rather than tilting upward in classical fashion. But despite the astonishing thick, bright-silver-tipped gilt hair and slightly darker brows, it was the eyes that one's gaze returned to again and again.

From afar, or even in shadow, Lord North's eyes were unexceptional save for their keen expression. But in clear light and up close it could be seen that they were extraordinary. For to speak with the nobleman from his right side, one would look for answer in his grave gray eye. Yet to approach him from the left, one would seek response from his cool blue orb. His eyes were not so dissimilar as to shock, but seeing him once, the viewer would be troubled by some nagging discrepancy and turn to search his face until his varicolored eyes were at last discovered, and the viewer amazed and enchanted.

To see him once was to remember him forever, to hear his name was to recall him instantly. His reputation was as varied and colorful as his strange countenance. He was said to be a libertine, he was whispered to be beyond mere libertine. If the ladies were enthralled by him, it was said that he reciprocated their interest, often and variously. He was wealthy, attractive, and titled, and shared only his fortune and person freely, but never his title, as he was rumored to have foresworn the idea of wedlock. As he entered his third decade, he had given himself, but never his heart, to whomever he fancied, and it was well known that he entertained some unusual fancies.

The countess watched him closely, but with more of deep calculation than of desire in her expression. This was not surprising, for though she bore an infamous name, her constancy was never questioned. She had been with Robert, Duke of Laxey, for over a decade, and it was hardly likely that she would sunder such a settled relationship merely for the excitement of dallying with an exotic young gentleman, no matter how compelling he might be. Still, she remained silent as her guests thronged about Lord North, and only broke from her reverie when she noted the merest hint of fatigue upon him as he closed his remarkable eyes for a moment, and seemed to have just a second's difficulty in reopening them.

"But Christian," she said pouting, pushing through the others and coming to his side at once, "what brutes we all are. For if you have only just arrived today, you must have been traveling leagues. And in such inclement weathers! Why Bobby, we have treated poor North's horse better than we have himself. I'm sure the animal must have been fed, well rubbed down, and put to bed already, and here is poor North forced to hold forth on the state of the world for us."

"My dear countess," Lord North smiled, "I've already dined, but I would have foregone even that if I knew what further treats you had in store for me. Surely I deserve no less than a mere animal?" he went on as the company roared with laughter and the countess called him a "wicked boy" for misconstruing her remarks. But the laughter did not reach either Lord North's weary eyes or the countess's mock-shocked ones, as they both were well aware of the sort of sallies they were expected to trade with each other for civility's sake.

"Enough of this," the countess cried, all abustle, ringing for her butler with a great show of concern. "North, we must get you to your room, and you must promise to sleep half the day away tomorrow."

"You do not leave us at once, do you?" she asked after he had made his good nights to the assembled company and followed her and the butler out of the room to the wide staircase.

"Not at once, no," he replied, "not if you do not wish me to do so. I only return home, and there is no great hurry."

"Oh wonderful," she answered, with the happy enthusiasm of a child. She spoke to the butler absently as she gazed up into her guest's eyes.

"Gilby, give Lord North the gray room—no, no, not

the gray, it is not at all what it should be. Give him the blue, yes, the blue."

"But my lady . . ." the butler began.

She cut across his hesitation quickly. "No, Gilby, the blue it is. It is the only suitable one."

As the servitor stood in confused fashion, she abandoned her air of charming infant and spoke in a voice of command.

"The blue, Gilby. Oh bother," she said angrily, "to tell the thing takes longer than the doing of it. Come along, Christian, I've got to have my maid repair my hair, for if you are only bound for bed, we have a full night ahead of us. That is all, Gilby, only see that his lordship is not disturbed further tonight."

"Only think, Christian," she prattled softly as they went up the long, circular staircase, "I was just dreading the possibility of snow, for the company's becoming rather flat—don't breathe a word that I've said so, my love, but there it is. And then you chance to come along. It's providence, I vow it is," she said as she led Lord North and the footman with his portmanteau past the head of the stairs. Her guest listened with half an ear, for now that he was arrived at his destination, he was in truth, almost drugged with weariness in the way that one is when one at last admits to it.

"Do have a good night's rest," she whispered as they came to a halt before a doorway. "And pray be quiet as a wee mouse, Christian, for Lady Alcott is down the hall and she was up half last night with a dreadful toothache and the poor old dear is resting at last."

"I shall restrain my tendency to drunken revelry," he said softly.

He took her hand for a good night, and watched with a half-smile as she prodded the hesitant footman and hurried off with him down the dim hallway.

Lord North sighed and cracked the door open. He took up his bag and went quietly within. The room was in darkness, the only available light a dull red gleam from the embers of a dying fire in an ornate central fireplace. He paused for a moment, for in her haste his hostess had neglected to ask the butler to have a new fire lit, and the room was striking chill. But he was so exhausted now that he merely placed his portmanteau upon the floor and walked to the pitcher and basin he could discern on a washstand to his right. It was obvious that the room had recently been in use but had not been refurbished due to his sudden arrival. That was not unusual; the countess's guests often treated her accommodations as a superior sort of hotel, arriving and departing at their whim. He hoped the sheets at least were clean, but was too tired in any case to quibble. It would be enough that they were there, and upon a soft bed.

He stripped off his jacket and shirt and hastily washed, grimacing as the cool water struck his skin, realizing that his frivolous hostess had also forgotten to ask that hot water be brought for him. But he thought, as he clenched his teeth and soaped himself, he was fortunate to have found a warm welcome at least. For while shocking, the countess was no fool and did not consort with just any rag-tag that chose to land himself upon her. For all her notoriety, she had birth and title and, even yet, some social sway because of them. In London, she had access to many in the *ton*, and if at home she chose to disport herself with rather more raffish company, she never lowered herself completely from society's view.

Like the Duchess of Oxford, who also flaunted society's conventions but remained within its orbit, Fanny Juliana Octavia Amberly, Countess of Clovelly, was in many ways circumspect. And if, also like that infamous lady, the countess's six children reputedly came from so many various fathers that wits named them "the Amberly Assortment," why then, she lived after all with only one of those purported gentleman at a time. Her legal husband, the earl, might drink in morose solitude in the countryside, but she and the Duke of Laxey had lived in open, comfortable domesticity for ages now and were one of society's most devoted couples.

Lord North toweled himself dry but found the room grown so chill that he snatched up his shirt and wore it unbuttoned as he made his way toward the great four-postered bed. He was about to abandon all thoughts of his flighty hostess and her hospitality and give himself complete and utter rest. He pulled off the shirt and tossed it upon the counterpane before he swept back the high-piled comforters with a huge yawn. And then he stood still and instantly wide awake as he stared down at the bed. For it was, he discovered, already occupied.

With sudden stealth and neatness of motion the viscount drew back. He studied the sleeping form for a moment. The scratch of the tinder box was the loudest sound in the room. By the vague light of the one candle he had lit, he stared down at what lay before him.

She was young, he had almost mistaken her for a child. The close-cropped tangle of shadowy curls upon the pillow certainly bespoke the schoolboy. But by the candle's light he could now see the outline of full breasts beneath the modest white gown and one outflung leg had eluded the material enough for him to judge it very shapely indeed. The face was beguiling, with delicate features and soft parted young lips.

Lord North relaxed and chuckled softly to himself. There could only be three reasons for her presence in his bed, and all were amusing. His hostess could, in her fashion, have considered the chit a gift, and left her as an elegant host might leave a book or a mint upon a valued guest's pillow. Or she could have been a female who had become enamored of him and had slipped into his bed to surprise and delight him. Or, more ominously, she might be of good birth and he party to a time-worn trap for matrimony.

He stood and considered. For all her reputation, the countess was not such a care-for-nothing as to leave such a scandalous souvenir. No one had known he was coming, and in any case, he had never seen the girl, so it was doubtful she had been impelled by reckless desire. And certainly, there was no one so proper of good birth within this house who would seek such a crude solution to a daughter's spinsterhood. In any event, he thought regretfully, watching the slow rise and fall of her sleeping breast, he was tired.

And, he thought, with a touch of fastidiousness, he did not choose to lie with a female he had not chosen. Whatever her reason for occupying his bed, he would leave quietly and whisper the predicament into his hostess's ear.

He sighed again and reached across the still form to pluck up his shirt, and had his hand upon it when a cool, low voice said unexpectedly in the silent room,

"One more move, sir, and I shall be forced to put a ball through your heart."

He drew back slowly and looked first into a pair of wide dark eyes, and then into the bore of a small but serviceable pistol. The girl sat upright now, having raised herself in one quick motion. She gripped the pistol tightly and, he noted peripherally, her hand was steady though she propped it with her other for insurance.

He smiled at her words and looked at her with growing attention, but he did not move at all, and only stood arrested, half bent, before her.

"Leave at once or I shall be forced to fire," she said adamantly.

"I was only just reaching for my shirt," he explained reasonably, not moving at all, so close to her that the barrel of the weapon almost touched his chest.

"I cannot miss from this close," she said, her voice now becoming quite anxious.

"But I do not know you!" he said with interest, lowering himself to sit upon the bed in front of her.

"I cannot think," she said a little wildly, "that the chance for a few moments of carnal pleasure is worth your life."

"And clearly," he said, with much delight, "you cannot know me."

II

Lady Amanda had known none of the guests at Kettering Manor when she had come to visit. Now, three days after her arrival, she devoutly wished that were still the case. For if some of the guests frankly startled her by their bold interest, some of the others distressed her with their constant spite.

The aged Comte de Florac had seemed a dear, grandfatherly sort of fellow until she understood the general gist of some of his suggestions for future friendship. Amy Farrow had appeared to be a charming young female even though she traveled with the sensational Baron Hyde. But then Amy had begun to make sly comments about her new friend's hair, form, and upbringing whenever the baron had taken an interest in their conversation. The only two whose company Lady Amanda rather enjoyed were the young lords, Jeffrey and Skyler. But there again, it was distressing to be chatting with them in jesting fashion and to suddenly interrupt some of the warm, long, meaningful glances that so often passed between them.

She had set aside a week for her visit, and now it seemed as if even one day more was too much. She was not homesick, that was never the case, but again, never had she so longed for home and the security of familiar surroundings. It was one thing to go to bed each night secure in the knowledge that she had been right, that this trip ought never to have been embarked upon. It was quite another to wake and remember with a sinking heart that there was yet another dreadful day to somehow be gotten through. Being right was cold comfort when one was constantly being wronged.

She had been craven this night. She had decided to escape the revels that passed for pleasant society and pleaded a headache for an early bedtime. The thought of even one more evening spent ignoring innuendos, smiling in brittle fashion at things that were not amusing, and playing ignorant gooseberry while the two young gentlemen sighed over the top of her head at each other was unendurable. The thought of having another pleasant coze with her hostess was positively unthinkable. So she had crept to a sickbed when she felt as fit as a fiddle, and heartily detested herself for it. She soon found, as she lay awake in the dark (for if she read a book, there was always the chance that her solicitous hostess would discover the sham), that self-disgust was even worse than self-sacrifice.

She had been lying there counting sheep and stiles and stars in an effort to court sleep when her door had opened and, incredibly, a gentleman had stolen into the room. Her first reaction had been horrified shock, her second had been grim awareness. Her hand had stolen immediately beneath her pillow to feel the reassuring shape there. It had been a mad start to include a pistol in her baggage, and she recalled that even as she had secreted it there she had laughed at herself for doing so. But she had known in what sort of a house she was to be a guest, and had sworn to be prepared this time. What had seemed to her then to have been a bad example of old-maidenly fluttering, now appeared to have been sound common sense.

She could have challenged him immediately, in the first instant that his shadow had appeared in the doorway. But she had given him the benefit of doubt. It was, she reasoned, gripping the pistol tightly, entirely possible that he had imbibed too much and had mistaken the room. In fact, when he had headed straightaway for the washbasin she had been sure of it. When he had stripped off his shirt she had drawn in her breath, to be sure, but when she had heard the water pouring she had felt easier. She could not imagine so fastidious a rapist.

So she had lain absolutely still. It would be far better,

she reasoned, if he were to think she was sleeping. Then they both could be spared embarrassment and he could leave, sure that no one had witnessed his foolish mistake. It had been difficult to keep her eyes half-shuttered and her breathing even when he had approached the bed, and almost impossible when he had lit the candle. But she felt that in his cast-away state he had needed the clear light of verification before he departed. But then, once he had decidedly seen that he was not alone and yet he had begun to reach toward her, she had acted immediately.

Now she sat up before him, her pistol primed and ready and almost touching his heart, and still he did not stir. In fact, he sat beside her and smiled easily at her. She did not really want to kill a fellow being, and her finger froze over the triggering mechanism. Maddeningly, in that moment, the only thing she could think of was of the amount of noise and subsequent gore that would fill the room if he pushed her too far.

"Please leave at once," she managed to say, hoping that it would not sound too much like pleading.

"A charming request," he said softly. "Where do you propose that I go?"

Certainly, he must have drunk too much, she thought. They were so close she could hear his every exhalation, and yet she could scent only the faintest breath of brandy upon his lips. She considered herself an expert on the matters of degrees of intoxication; it was, after all, how she had learned when and where her father was capable of having coherent speech with her. If the gentleman was half sprung, he must indeed be very susceptible.

"To your room," she replied tightly.

"Why then," he said sweetly, "there is no problem. For I have already arrived there."

"This," she said very patiently, deciding that he must be, however he had achieved it, very drunk indeed, "is my room. You are mistaken."

"I do not think so," he said thoughtfully, cocking his head to one side, "for my hostess specifically assigned me to this one. In fact, she led me to the very door."

She drew in her breath in a gasp. This was far worse

than she had first thought. Seeing her consternation, he looked at her keenly.

"We have two choices," he said after a moment's thought. "Our hostess clearly was remiss, though I think it more than likely the excitement of the evening scattered her brains, for she is, no matter how she attempts to conceal it, a most singularly acute female. We can either share this comfortable bed . . ."

At her wide-eyed alarm and the sudden raising of the pistol, he smiled and went on, "Or I can simply nip downstairs and demand another room, explaining that I found this one already taken."

"No," she said at once, thinking of the reaction of the company when they discovered he had come upon her in her bed. Their minds would leap to so many conclusions that she was sure her reputation would be in tatters, no matter how they construed it.

"I could say that I find it too cold, and I do, I do," he said, looking at her with such mock sorrow that to her surprise she had to restrain the impulse to giggle.

"But then," he added blithely, "no doubt our hostess would wish to come up and see for herself. Or at the very least, send someone to light the fire. Of course," he said triumphantly, "you could just as easily trot downstairs and lodge a complaint."

Her teeth worried at her lip as he spoke, for she began to see that even if the gentleman were blameless in this, it would not be an easy situation to extricate herself from.

He began to reach toward her once again, and she left off her ruminations and raised the pistol till the barrel actually lay against his skin.

"My shirt," he said softly. "My dear, I only reached for my shirt. It is deucedly cold in here and it may have escaped your notice, but I am half naked."

Incredibly, in all her distress, that had not occurred to her. But now, looking at him, she became slowly aware of the breadth and shape of the undraped form before her. She did not lower her weapon, but only stared at him, finally taking careful note of the actual man she had surprised.

He was, she thought, so spectacularly handsome that it might yet be that she had actually drifted off to sleep and was now only dreaming his presence. For surely she had never seen such a radiantly attractive male in a waking state. She did not take the time to minutely inspect every detail of his brilliant aspect, it was enough that she noted the imperfect, yet striking face, the glow from his flaxen hair, and the strong, almost sculpted torso. It was when she noted the very human golden down upon that torso that she momentarily dropped her gaze in confusion. It was, she thought with embarrassment, hardly likely that such a specimen needed to creep into unsuspecting females' bedchambers to have his way with them.

As though echoing her thoughts, he said then, with deep amusement apparent in his low voice, causing her to open her eyes wide and look upward hastily, "You see? I make no effort to wrest your very fine pistol away as you weigh your options. Really my dear, I find rapine a very tiresome business. There's all that thrashing about, and caterwauling, not to mention the distinct possibility of getting oneself bitten, or worse, in the process. No, love-making should be a slow process; one should at the very least be able to relax when one attempts it. Should you like to see?" he asked suddenly, charmingly, shattering her momentary calm.

"No?" he said softly. "Ah, well, I thought I might at least try, for you will grant the circumstances are most unusual and I thought that perhaps the difficulty lay in the fact that I had not asked."

She glowered at him because, in truth, his earlier words had been so seductive that she had indeed dropped her guard and no doubt had been gaping at him like a smitten ninny.

"Do you think it possible," he asked calmly then, "that you could put the pistol down? Not only am I cold, but I am now beginning to entertain the unpleasant notion that the force of your emotions might force your finger. It's a very fine weapon, with no doubt a hair-trigger mechanism. I should hate to think that I've ended my days simply because you had to sneeze. I promise you, for what it's worth, that I shall not attempt you. But I hesitate to say a thing that might make you laugh, or even shudder, for a lively fear of what those reactions might do for my remaining span upon the planet. And if we are to find a solution for our present difficulties, we must be able to communicate."

She looked hard at him once again, and then sighed and lowered the pistol. If he had been a less comely gentleman, she would not have. But it was undeniable that if he had been ill looking, she would have immediately shouted the rafters down. If he had even been only well enough looking, she might have not even bothered to hold rational discourse with him.

But seeing him was to believe him. It was not possible to assume he was a lurking deviate. She could not imagine that such a gentleman would even desire her, or note her at all, if he had not found her in what he thought was his bed. Such an exotic fellow, she decided, would only consort with females who could match his splendor. Although she had often been told that she was well enough looking, and even had a little vanity about herself, she could not think that she fell into such an exquisite class.

It seemed that he matched her sigh. Then he took up the pistol from where she had placed it on the bed and examined it.

"A breech loader. A very nice weapon," he concluded, and handed it back to her. "I suggest you put it away now, so you are not tempted to do mayhem for anything I might say. Only *say*," he said emphatically, and then laughed as she slipped it back beneath her pillow.

"Now," he said decisively, "I am going to reach for my shirt. I am going to pick it up. Then I shall first put one arm into it, then another. You understand? There will be nothing alarming in that, will there?"

She nodded, faintly smiling. He reached across her, almost touching her in the action. As his lean, nude torso blocked her vision for a moment, she did not see the door open. But he did, and stopped in mid-motion again. She could, however, hear the voices.

"Oh! Oh my heavens!" cried the Countess of Clovelly as

she paused in the doorway, a branch of candles held high enough to illuminate both the room and the avidly interested collection of persons behind her.

"Oh lud!" cried the countess in failing accents. "Amanda! North! I never imagined . . ."

Everything was in motion now, Lady Amanda thought, squeezing her eyes shut for the moment as if that would make it all go away. The countess hurried into the room, five or six other persons popped their heads through the entrance, and the gentleman upon her bed merely sat down again with an oddly forced smile upon his lips.

"I only came to see if your headache was better, Amanda," the countess said in agitation. "I never suspected. But I am not too late, for North, you are only half undressed. Or am I, and are you only half dressed? Oh lud, that is never what I meant to say."

Amanda could say nothing. All the reasons and excuses died in her throat. The gentleman that had been called North similarly sat still, but with a look of wry expectation upon his face. Then the countess took a deep breath. She turned to the rest of the company who stood on the threshold with looks of unholy appreciation readily apparent.

"If you please, friends, find your way back to your rooms without me. I have some business here."

With much tittering and whispering, the guests evaporated into the dark hall, for the countess had used an imperially imperative tone. Then she turned to the couple upon the bed.

"North, I must ask you to leave. Your room, as I said, is the gray room, just down the hall. But in light of the circumstances, I think, if you don't mind, I should rather you took the bishop's chamber for the remainder of your stay with us. It is very commodious and is at the end, then around the corner of the hall. A footman will show you there. And then, I think, you and I and Robert should have a little talk in the morning. And Amanda, as for your behavior . . ." The countess seemed to find herself speechless, and only let out a loud exasperated exhalation.

"But Mama . . ." Lady Amanda began, and then stopped

as the gentleman, who had been slowly buttoning his shirt, paused and wheeled about to stare at her.

"Ah, 'Mama,' " he breathed. "That tells all."

"Amanda," the countess cut in brusquely, "I shall speak with you in the morning as well. I am just too distraught at the moment. But I am staggered, I am confused, Amanda. For with all your high morals and principles, I am . . . There is no way I can speak tonight," she finished, and turned toward the door, gesturing with the candles dramatically as though she were the angel sent to drive Adam and Eve from the garden.

"Are you coming, North?" she demanded.

"At once," the viscount said through tight lips.

But he paused a moment to look down at the girl in the bed. And then said in a whisper so low, she could not be sure she heard it, "Perfect sense, my dear. The pistol, I take it, was not insurance for you against my advances. Rather it was to ensure that I did not get away."

Then he straightened, strode to his portmanteau and, taking it, followed the countess and her candles out of the room. The door shut, leaving Amanda in relative darkness, in all respects.

The clock in the hall tolled three strokes when Lady Amanda Amberly at last decided to desert her bed entirely. Lying down, she discovered, only made her feel more vulnerable; thinking was a thing that ought to be done on one's feet. Still, after pacing the carpet for a space, she took up a position upon the window seat in her room and discovered it to be the best choice of all. For there, she could stare out into the night and watch it become lighter as the snow slowly turned the dark shadows to milk.

Sleep was, in any event, out of the question, as was any attempt at rational converse with her mother. Even if she did dare seek out that lady in her rooms, and risked the embarrassment of finding her there with her Robert, she could not think she could as yet make coherent comment on the happenings this night.

She would have to have been born under a cabbage leaf not to know what the penalty for an unwed female's being discovered with a half-dressed gentleman in her bedroom was. As she had been born, in fact, as one of the detestedly named Amberly Assortment, she knew full well what the consequences were. If the gentleman were unmarried, then one would have to marry him straightaway or be shunned by polite society from thenceforth. If he were married, one might as well pack for the continent immediately.

Even in her mother's wild set, which could be called "polite society" in only the loosest construction of the term, there were certain limits beyond which one did not go. If certain of her own brothers and sisters were known to be only her half-brothers and half-sisters, still her mother was, after all, married. Marriage was a license, in many cases, for free license. Once a lady had presented a legitimate heir or two for her husband, she could live her own life according to her own whims and society would politely look the other way. Perhaps, Amanda thought with a grimace, that was why it was called "polite" society.

But that was precisely the sort of life that Amanda had been trying so desperately to evade since she had come to the age of reason. She was not the sort of person to go about feeling sorry for herself, but it was undeniably true that it had been difficult growing up as one of the Assortment. Jerome and Amanda had been born to the earl and his countess while they still lived together. Mama had left her husband's home before Amanda could even properly enunciate her name. And although she was herself legitimate, as her subsequent siblings came into the world the fact of her own legitimacy mattered less and less. Mama had come home each time to bear forth Mary, Alicia, and James. But by the time Cecil was brought into the world, Mama had removed herself forever from Caldwell Hall.

All of the children were sent to school as soon as they were able to be packed off; perhaps even Mama had thought it hard to have them about to constantly remind the earl of his wife's inconstancy. Not that that seemed to matter greatly to her husband; he seemed happy or unhappy enough with his port, his hounds, and his hunting. In fact, the only spark of interest he ever showed in fatherhood was in his eldest, his legitimate heir, Jerome. There were times when Amanda thought that her father himself scarcely remembered that she was, indeed, his own child.

But the whispers had begun in boarding school. The sly asides, the little jibes had increased until she scarcely heard them any longer. It was only unfortunate, she often thought, that if another girl wished to win an argument and had clearly lost the battle, she could be counted on to bring up Amanda's history to her as a final coup de grace. She had learned to live with that, which made the shock of her first Season difficult to explain.

Amanda shivered as she sat and watched the snow, but it was not from the cold. She had been eighteen, Mama had prevailed, and she had allowed herself to be talked into making a debut in London when she left school. Her title was, after all, valid. Her fortune was an absolute reality, though her beauty and grace were things that Mama nattered on about but Amanda had tended to doubt. Yet it seemed from the moment that she made her bows that she was enormously popular. It had been delightful, those first few weeks, those assemblies, balls, and routs. She had received flowers and compliments and invitations and compliments and gowns, and she had the hope for proposals. It had been nothing short of wonderful to have been so very much wanted at last.

It was young Charles Dearborne, a baron's son, who had at last opened her eyes to the truth. For he was her first taste of calf-love. He had been tall, very dark, slender, and clever. Socially adroit, with impeccable breeding, he had completely overwhelmed her with his constant attentions. She had begun to dream of a future with him. Then one night, he had smilingly lured her out onto the terrace at a great ball. It had been a perfect lover's night, with a great chalk moon staring above them, and she had dared to hope that it was the night he had chosen to make his offer.

For all his wit and habit of light jest, he had spoken not one word, but only gathered her up in his arms and kissed her. She remembered it still; she had only been able to sigh with gratification at how lovely it was. Then he had pressed another kiss upon her willing lips, and again she was speechless with sheer happiness at the perfection of it. He had drawn back a moment and she waited for his utterance, but he had only captured her once more and kissed her again. And then yet again, with more fervor. As his hands strayed to her bodice, she began to wonder when he would declare himself; as his hands began to reach within her white debutante's frock, she began to grow confused.

She had pulled back and whispered hurriedly, fearing for her own boldness, "Charles, haven't you anything to say?"

"What else is there to say?" he had grinned, pulling her toward him again.

"But what are your intentions?" she had said witlessly.

"Aren't they apparent?" he laughed.

"No," she had cried, wresting herself from him. "No, they are not."

"Then I will make them so," he had chortled, and kissed her once again, this time quite savagely.

She pushed him away and stood staring at him aghast.

"Charles," she had finally gotten the courage to gasp, "aren't you going to declare yourself?"

He had gotten some of his composure back and stood facing her, his face grown suddenly very cold in the moonlight.

"Declare myself?" he had mumbled, and then he laughed again. "I declare myself very much entranced with you. Very much in lust for you, puss, but that is all. Did you think me ready to declare anything else?"

"Yes," she had said quietly, "yes, I did."

"Are you serious?" he asked incredulously. She could only nod. "My Lady Amberly," he said finally, after a moment's thought, "I declare that I should very much like to make love to you, but only that. Your kisses led me to believe you would very much like to do that as well. But if you think I am willing to offer for you, you are wrong. And do not cry that I have led you on. For you have led me on just as much."

Then he seemed ill at ease and said defensively, "And if you think to trap me by having me compromise you here,

I tell you it won't wash. I expected no more from you than your mama is so famous for giving. And there's no one who'll believe otherwise. Do you think me such a flat that I want to have you mother "The Dearborne Collection" or some such lot for me? Now come, puss, let's drop this nonsense. It was a good try. Now come to me and we'll continue."

She had left him where he was standing. She had gone back to the ball and danced until her toes were numb, for she would not give him the satisfaction of knowing what he had done to her. But she had never spoken to him again.

After her encounter with Charles, she had looked carefully at all her suitors and listened closely to all that they were saying. What she had taken for gentle raillery, she discovered, was always a good deal warmer in content than that which she heard addressed to other girls. The looks she received were always more speculative and leering than were directed at other girls. Most damning of all, she suddenly realized that no other young females making their debuts had offered her friendship. To prove her worst suspicions, the Season ended, and for all her popularity she had received no offers.

She went to her father's home after that, and never returned for another Season in London.

Life went relatively placidly for her, then. Though she was in her father's constant sight, she was never on his mind. He had his bottles, his hunting cronies, and his housekeeper-mistress, in that order, to keep him amused. From time to time, some errant whim would remind Mama of her yet unwed eldest daughter and she would be summoned and quizzed about her matrimonial prospects. She would stay at Kettering Manor and spend her time with various of her other visiting half-brothers and -sisters. They liked each other well enough, for all that there could be no bond between them. Sometimes they would laugh at their appearance when they were all assembled, and it was fitting, for they were the only ones who had a right to do so. But it *was* amusing for them to see dark-eyed, dark-complected James, freckled and fair Mary, tall and hearty Alicia, delicate Cecil and Jerome and herself together.

Mama had offered her a home, but she had swiftly refused. On her infrequent visits, Mama always offered her prospective husbands too, but she was quick to discourage them as well. For although she was old enough to know better, she again had hopes. They were all embodied in one man, her near neighbor Sir Giles Boothe. He reminded her a little of the perfidious Charles, but only in appearance. He too was tall and, though his hair was as brown as her own, he was slender and as irreproachable in appearance as he was in birth. But if he was not so dramatic and dashing as Charles, he was also not such a rattle, nor near so flippant and ardent.

Giles was a prudent man. He had come to know her when she had returned from London. It had taken a year for him to stop and chat with her when they encountered each other in the village or when they were out riding. It was another year before he came to pay her formal calls. Only of late had he begun to make those calls with frequency, only recently had he started to invite her to all the assemblies and fetes in the district as his guest. She could not blame him for being such a hesitant suitor. Perhaps he, too, thought her capable of eventually presenting her husband with "The Boothe Bevy" or some such burden, she thought.

Obviously, Giles was wary of her even as he was attracted to her. As she was above the age of consent, he had kissed her, though never as thoroughly as Charles had done. But when she reciprocated, or even seemed to lean toward him in encouragement, he would back away from her. She did not suffer from conceit, but she did not believe the problem lay in her looking glass.

She was not a large person, as so many of the stately fashionable beauties were, but neither was she quite so tiny as her mama. Her form, she knew, was pleasing, Charles had often told her so. Her hair was not just a common brown, rather Charles had often said it resembled, as well as bore the scent of, cinnamon. When she had had a raging fever at seventeen, her nurse had shorn off all her hair so that it would not sap her remaining strength. Looking into the glass when she had recovered, she had been delighted to see the mass of tumbled curls the crop had given her, and kept her hair that way when Mama had said admiringly that it was just the mode that Caro Lamb had adopted and looked delightfully. At any rate, Amanda thought, it needed little care and spared her the tortures of curl papers, so it would do. Her eyes were large and gray, though she thought them too long, and while well formed, she considered her mouth too generous. She had no complaints about her nose, which was straight and unexceptional. If she were not the stuff of ballads, she reasoned, at least she would not give a viewer a disgust of her.

But likely, she thought on a sigh, as she sat and kept watch in the night, it was the blood beneath her pale complexion which distressed Giles the most. When she met his advances with enthusiasm, he must wonder if she were not signaling that she shared the same tastes as her mother. As always, Amanda felt her stomach knot up when she herself wondered at the truth in that.

Now, she thought in despair, what would Giles think when he heard of what had transpired here? There was no hope in heaven that such a collection of reckless people could keep the secret. It was the sort of gossip that they would gladly dine out upon. She would not blame Giles if he did not believe a word of her innocence. She was an Amberly, and blood would tell.

She had come to Kettering Manor this time much against her wishes. Mama had made it clear that as her daughter was about to turn three and twenty she wished to felicitate her. None of Amanda's siblings were in residence, and when Amanda arrived she received not only congratulations but a lengthy lecture on the evils of remaining unwed at her great age. When she had, at last, mentioned the possibility of an offer from Giles, her mother had only sniffed. "Is he going to tarry until you are thirty to be sure?" she had demanded. Amanda had remained silent, for it was true, and she had often mused upon it, that Giles's father had wed only when he reached forty. If his son emulated him in that, she would be in fact thirty and past it, if and when he offered. Her mama had finally left off and given her a golden locket for the occasion. And for the crime of coming to collect that golden trifle, she had lost all hope for her future, and all the respectability that Giles embodied.

Where had she erred? Amanda almost cried in vexation. She had done all she could to prevent such a crisis. Once before when she had visited, the stout Sir Crosly had tracked her to her room filled with whiskey-brave amours. She had repulsed him with a candelabra and sent him groaning to his room. This time she had taken a pistol with her, but it had only earned her disgrace.

Her past might be muddled, but at least her way forward was clear. If all her ambitions were thwarted, she yet could have serenity. Even if the gentleman who had entered her room were married, she could still return home and live there as quietly as possible to the end of her days. Father wouldn't mind, even if he noticed. If the gentleman were unwed, it made little difference. She would not have him. If he were beautiful as an archangel and clever as satan, it would not matter. To wed a gentleman from her mother's wild set would be to be absolutely sure to follow her footsteps. She could not lead such a life. She would not have him, she resolved, though her name be blackened to pitch for refusing him. It hardly mattered, she laughed bitterly at last, for had not her art mistress at school once taught her that black cannot be made blacker?

The gentleman that Amanda so resolutely denied lay fully clothed in his room upon a great canopied bed and slept the sleep of the thoroughly exhausted. While Amanda paced and prowled and flailed herself and then sat sadly to weigh her options, he slept dreamlessly. This might have made her very angry had she known it, but she would undoubtedly have been cheered if she could have been privy to his last waking thought before sleep overtook him. For he had muttered aloud to the empty room before he lay his weary golden head upon his pillow,

"I shall not have her."

III

Lord North arose early and much refreshed after his deep and deserved sleep. He went to the window to assess the amount of the snow that had fallen. No great amount had accumulated, and the sun glinted brilliantly on the few inches that had. He nodded to himself and then went about his morning ablutions with the swift, sure motions of a gentleman who had often awakened in strange surroundings and who had done for himself many times before. As he washed, shaved himself, and dressed, there was an expression of smooth unconcern upon his face. When he went to check his appearance once in the glass before he went belowstairs, there was a cold and placid set to his expression. No one would guess that this was a gentleman about to be at the very least lectured, at the very most condemned, by his hosts.

The viscount seemed to be self-assured and calm as he took the great stairs lightly and made his way to the center of the vast house. It was no imposture, for he was totally resolved. He had decided upon his course of action before he had closed his eyes the night before. Though he remembered no dreams or decisions coming to him in the night, it was as though some ever-wakeful portion of his mind had worked upon the dilemma as he lay sleeping. For now that morning had come, he was sure of his course of action. There were no conflicting emotions to forestall him. The thing was simplicity itself.

It was a shoddy trick for his hostess to have played, but he could not blame her overmuch. It could be no easy feat to bring one of her Assortment to the altar. It was merely that she had miscalculated, for he was not green enough to sacrifice himself on that altar for respectability's sake. A gentleman should, of course, offer his hand to a young lady of quality whose reputation he had deliberately or mistakenly jeopardized. That, Lord North mused, permitting himself a little smile as he halted in the great hall, seeking the direction of his breakfast, was decidedly what a gentleman should do for a lady. But, he thought, scenting the unmistakable odor of ham and coffee coming from a long way off, he was not precisely a gentleman and the Amberly female was certainly not a lady.

His hosts were in for a crushing disappointment. He would not do the acceptable thing; he was not, after all, an acceptable gentleman. No one would be surprised to hear of his refusal even if the lady had been a lady. As she was one of this household, no one would even turn a hair at hearing the tale. It had been a foolish, desperate attempt, the viscount decided, and it would only make the mating of the young woman a harder thing to achieve in future. The circumstances of the young lady might even become in time, he thought with real amusement, a tale to be savored at London clubs; the stuff of epic tales, a legendary pitfall for unwary male travelers, like the sirens, or in this case and more aptly, like the Procrustean bed.

The viscount made his way to the breakfast room. Pausing for a moment in the doorway, he spied his hostess seated bolt erect at a laden table with an untouched plate before her, her consort at her side, sleepily perusing a paper as he sipped at his coffee.

The countess saw the viscount first, and rose to her feet.

"North," she said sternly, trying to place the same expression of censoriousness upon her face as she had in that syllable. The duke looked up, then down, then at his paper, as though profoundly embarrassed and discomfitted by the entire scene.

"Good morning, my lady," her guest said sweetly, making his bow and then coming up to his hostess to take her hand. "What a comfortable room. I passed the most restful night, thank you so much. I had not hoped to see you quite so early, for I often rise with the birds and am surprised to see you do the same. What a happy coincidence! Now I shall not have to breakfast alone."

"I could not close my eyes all the night," the countess said in dire accents. She looked rested enough, her guest thought, although it was obvious that she had put on a great deal of powder in order to accentuate or simulate pallor.

"Ah, too bad," the viscount sympathized, looking over to his host.

That gentleman squirmed beneath the viscount's benign, inquiring gaze and then mumbled, "Slept like a dead man myself."

Then encountering his lady's baleful stare, he added unconvincingly, "But that's m'way. Not like the dear lady. I'm not sensitive in the least. She prowled all night, like a damned tabby." Then unsure of whether he ought to be commenting on the lady's nocturnal habits with a gentleman who was supposed to be doing the right thing by her daughter, he subsided into a sort of anguished silence by biting off far more than he could chew of a fruit scone and rendered himself incapable of further speech.

"We must talk," the countess said in accents of high emotion, holding her clasped hands before her in a noble posture. Unfortunately for her intent, the viscount thought her size, form, and face made her resemble more of a field mouse at bay than a valiant tiger defending her cub.

"Certainly," her guest replied smoothly, raising a brow and directing one brief glance at the butler's impassive face, "but before breakfast?"

"Why no, of course not," the countess faltered, seating herself again.

The duke shot her as much of a look of caution as he could, as his cheeks bulged with half-chewed scone. She waved her guest to the buffet table and bade him select his breakfast. As he did so with alacrity, the duke managed to swallow enough of his mouthful to whisper somewhat thickly to her, "Told you so. The fellow knows the right thing to do. Man of the world. A bother about nothing, m'dear."

The viscount chose his repast with concentration and then sat down with his hosts. While he ate, he put them further at their ease by holding light converse about the weather, the state of the nation, and the excellence of fresh eggs. Not one of the attentive footmen, nor the butler, nor after a space, his hosts themselves could quite believe that this collected gentleman had anything on his mind except the business of breakfast. For one horrible moment, the countess herself had the insane notion that the previous night had happened only in her imagination.

But then the young lords Jeffrey and Skyler wandered in, in search of sustenance, and were visibly startled to see the viscount engaged in such equitable discourse with his host and hostess. They then made such a failure at trying to conceal the looks of shock, awe, and disappointment that they constantly darted toward the golden-haired guest that the countess felt herself upon firm ground again. So it was that she was able to say, in the most casual of tones, "Oh, North, now you've finished your breakfast, do you think you might have time to have a private coze with Robert and me?"

Lord North only rose and bowed slightly, and with the most charming smile, said affably, "Of course, I am at your service, my lady."

It was when they were out in the hall again, safely out of earshot of any retainers or guests, that the viscount spoke again. The unhappy duke, lagging behind his guest and the countess, his gaze riveted upon the floor as though he had lost a valuable coin and was searching for it, picked up his head at the utterance.

"I should like to speak with you and the duke my lady, at any time, but do you not think it best if I speak with the young lady—your daughter, I take it—first? After all, she, you will admit, has the most to either gain or lose by this morning's business."

"But you have it wrong way around, Christian, I'm sure, for first you are supposed to address her——" the countess began catching herself just before she uttered the word *father*, as she realized that the word was singularly inappropriate in this instance. Instead, she made a feeble recovery by saying, "mother."

At the polite but disbelieving look upon her guest's cool countenance, she fell silent. The duke at once leaped in to say bluffly,

"Of course, dear fellow. Just the thing. You two ought to have a get-acquainted chat. That is," he said, beginning to see the deep waters he had plunged into, "if you have not already, last night, I mean. Devil take it," he foundered.

"I do believe," the countess said winsomely, discreetly putting her tiny foot down upon the duke's boot tip, "that is a most excellent suggestion, Christian. Amanda has been fretting all morning. She hasn't even had breakfast. She's in the small salon awaiting our discretion. A conference alone, between the two of you, would certainly be in order now. I shall not even insist on staying with you to play chaperon, in light of the circumstances," the countess added with stress underlying every syllable.

"Robert and I will be in the study, when you have done," she said pointedly, as she led the viscount to the small salon. "And will be waiting your announcement."

She could do no more, the countess thought in exasperation, without writing the thing out in bold letters and picking them out with a pointer for him. North had been so adroit at setting a mood of civilized commonplace that there was no way she could state the thing more firmly without seeming to be an underbred boor.

"Don't fret," the duke said happily as they watched the viscount enter the salon after tapping lightly upon the door and being bade to enter. "The thing will go off swimmingly. North's got a head on his shoulders. Not a nodcock, after all. Trust him to know the right thing."

But the countess paused to stare at the closed door for a moment and sighed. She did not bother to dispute dear Robert, but the thing was that even if the viscount knew the right thing, one did not trust him to do it at all, if one were at all wise.

"Good morning," Lord North said pleasantly as he entered the room. He saw the young woman start to her feet as he approached.

He wore an easy, amiable smile, and as he took the young woman's icy hand, he gazed into her fearful eyes and said, without changing his expression at all, "You look very well, even with your clothes on, my dear."

She stepped back as though he had struck out at her. But it was true, he thought with detachment, she had no need of candlelight to flatter her. For even here, where the tall glass windows of the french doors admitted the harsh light of the sun's reflection upon snow, she looked very well. Delicately made, perhaps, he thought, but not so diminutive as her mama, and nothing like her mama in aspect or attitude. She was, rather than openly seductive, almost a gamine. He thought her curls charming, her form delicious, her face enchanting. He would have been delighted to become her protector, but he was determined she should not become his bride.

He had decided to put the matter to her openly, before he ever broached it to her parent and her noble consort. Then, of course, he would have to pack and leave. But he thought it only fair that he should inform the young woman of his decision first, as he would doubtless not have had the opportunity to do if he stated his case straightaway to his host and hostess. She deserved to know of the failure of the plot from his own lips at least; some honor must be dredged from this sorry incident. The viscount, as his hostess had suspected, knew the right thing to do.

"Your mama," he went on to say, noting that she was gazing at him with something like horror manifest in her expression, "agreed that I should have a word with you before I spoke with her. I could talk the thing up and down for hours, but that would be hardly kind to her, as I'm sure she's on pins and needles to hear my decision. I'm convinced it would be equally distasteful for you."

As she made no reply, but only stood gazing up at him with her features so immobile now that he could not read them, he said a bit more abruptly, "I'm sorry, my lady, but it won't do. I'm sorry to have kept you up so late last night on such a fruitless mission, and to have kept you from your breakfast this morning as well. By the by," he smiled, trying to elicit some response from her as it began to seem that he was addressing empty air, "the eggs were excellent. Very well," he sighed as the pleasantry died upon his lips unnoticed, "no more attempts at dressing the thing up. I won't have you, my dear, I won't offer for you, and wouldn't have even if you had accommodated me immediately last night, rather than waiting for your mama's fortuitous entry."

He braced himself for a slap, prepared himself for an outburst of fury, and waited for her to storm or weep or fling herself upon his chest to beat at him with her fists. He was taken aback, then, by the one thing she did do.

She sank to sit upon a divan and let out all her pent-up breath in a gusty sigh. "Thank heavens," she breathed. Then she turned a radiant face up to him and said happily, as though they had come to some most agreeable terms, "I am so glad. I sat here wondering just what sort of scene there would be when Mama and the duke called me in to hear your offer. I didn't know how you would take it, but I was dreading their response. I'm so very glad that you flew in the face of custom."

"You are glad?" he repeated slowly, playing for time, trying to fathom what new gambit she had come up with to snare him.

"Of course," she answered promptly, "for I had no notion of accepting your offer, my lord. The whole thing is bizarre. Someone played a trick on us. I don't care to think of whom it might have been," she said frowning for a moment, "but it makes no matter. I would not live out the rest of my life with a stranger who had wandered into my rooms one night unless I was wandering in my wits. The entire idea is ludicrous. I don't blame you in the least for thinking me partner to such a scheme, but I assure you I was as appalled as you were when Mama came marching in. The pistol, you see, was not to hold you there, it was to discourage any gentleman who might have had similar ideas. But it doesn't matter what you believe actually," she said, as if to herself. "Good day, my lord."

The viscount, a gentleman famous for his quick wit and decision, stood quite still. If he could believe the lady, the situation tickled him enormously. If he could not, whatever further scheme she was hatching challenged him.

"But what will your mama say?" he asked softly, playing devil's advocate to get to the crux of the matter.

"Just what you would think," the young woman answered, shaking her head. "But I shall not let that change my mind. I'll be leaving for home almost immediately, so it won't sink me entirely."

"You do not reside here?" he asked in surprise.

"Oh no," she replied, half attending to him. "I make my home in Doncaster with my papa."

"And it will not matter what society says of you?" the viscount said very softly.

Her shoulders went up at that, a little defensive shrug as though to ward off a blow, which touched him as no words could have done. But her words were mundane enough.

"Oh that. But I do not travel in society, you see."

"Miss Amberly, or Lady . . . I do not even know your proper name," he said on a laugh as he came closer to her. "I really do think we stand in need of an introduction. I am Christian Jarrow, Viscount North. And you are . . ."

"Amanda, Lady Amanda Amberly," she said, gazing up at him as though for the first time.

"May I sit?" he asked carefully.

At her nod, he sat in a chair near to her.

"My lady," he began, "in truth, when I first came in here I had you painted as some sort of villainess. If I can believe you, then I become some sort of villain. Since so much rests upon the outcome of this, our only chance at private speech, can you not be plain with me? If this is all some sort of machination to force me to declare myself through guilt or pity, I repeat, it won't do. I shall not marry you. It has not so much to do with the method of our meeting, although that certainly makes it impossible for me to offer, since I am remarkably resistant to blackmail, but a great deal to do with the fact that I do not care to be wed. Not now. To anyone. And most probably, not in future. I am a determined bachelor. So please, with that idea firmly fixed in mind, speak plainly to me."

Amanda looked up at the cold, exquisite countenance before her and laughed, although the sound had more anger than merriment in it.

"And I tell you, my lord," she said through clenched teeth, "and have told you, that I do not want you. Not now. Not any time. So, if you will be so good as to stop telling me in every sort of way not to angle for your person, I will tell you to leave, please. Immediately."

The viscount relaxed. He sat back and beamed at her.

"Is that all you ever say?" he asked pleasantly. "I seem to recall that phrase from when we first met. Accept my apologies," he laughed. "But you will admit I had little cause to believe you then. For what it is worth, I do now. Come, tell me what you know of the matter and we will see what we can make of it. You see, I was very weary when I arrived last night, and extremely surprised to find I had a bedmate assigned to me. The rest you know. Now tell me what part of it do I not know? I deserve at least that," he added as she turned her head away. "It will be not only your reputation that will be extinguished when I give your mama the sad tidings; whatever little is left of mine will be swept away as well."

Amanda considered the viscount openly now. She had had no speech with her mother in the morning, she had only been told curtly to go and sit in the salon till she was called. When he had come walking in, she had been prepared to make her speech of denial and had been startled by his own rejection coming first. Worse than that, the moment she had seen him in the cold light of day, she had taken a long look at that remarkably beautiful face. When at last she had discovered the secret of those astonishing eyes as they fixed a chill stare upon her, she had known his identity at once. There could not be two such noblemen in the kingdom.

He was fully as infamous as her own mama. Even if one took exaggeration into account, his reputation was as stunning as his physical presence. If she had feared association with the rakish set that revolved about Kettering Manor, she had found herself confronted by perhaps the most prime example of a rake in that or any other set. The thought of being manipulated into wedlock with exactly the sort of gentleman she most reviled had struck her speechless, and the enormity of the idea took even the sting and sense of his first words from her.

But now, perceiving that he was at least as eager as she to elude the consequences of their accidental meeting, she subsided into relief. She still could not believe such a dazzling creature could have any designs upon her. Such an exotic's interest could only be for curiosity's sake. Thus, there could be nothing lost by putting their heads together to seek a way out of this coil.

Briefly, then, she told him of her situation. Very briefly, in fact, for there was a great deal she did not mention. So it was that she gaped at him like a kitchen maid at a fortune teller at the county fair when he said slowly, when she had done,

"So it is not only that you don't wish to marry a stray who happened into your bedroom at your mama's instigation, but you also have hopes for another match."

Since she had said nothing of Giles, or any other possible suitor, and did not want to think of Mama's possible culpability, Amanda was at a loss for a reply. Before she could think of one, he smiled and said gently,

"Come, my lady, circumstances lead to an obvious conclusion. You are past the age of a come-out and are still unwed. It's enough to terrify any mama."

"Past my last prayers, you mean to say then," she shot back, stung at his cavalier assessment of her years and unmarried state.

"I mean precisely what I say," he said, a bored look coming into his eyes. "I did not seek you out this morning to pay you pretty compliments and engage in light flirtation. You know full well you are an enticing baggage, and as you have title, wit, and dowry, it becomes obvious that your single state is more a matter of choice than chance."

Amanda did not know whether to be complimented or infuriated by his calm appraisal, but before she could decide what reaction to present him with, he went on obliviously,

"So it only follows that you have been biding your time,

and no female ever bides her time without some object in
view. I take it, then, that this object does not meet with
your family's full approval? Is he so unacceptable then? A
smithy, or is he only that cliché, an impecunious dancing
master?"

She was very gratified to see his surprise when her only
reply was a peal of laughter. Before he could ask why she
was so amused, her laughter stopped and she said with a
coolness to match his own, "Oh yes, biding my time. Of
course. There are so many gentlemen falling over themselves to declare for me. And why not? After all, I am an
Amberly, and one of the famous Assortment, as well.
What fellow would not wish for the thrill of wedlock with
me? Which of them could bear to pass up the chance to
spend a lifetime with me, and wait with baited breath each
time I present him with an heir? What fun he would have
scrutinizing every infant I produce, looking at eyes and
hair color and bone structure, wondering which of his
acquaintance sired which of his offspring. Their mamas
and noble relatives as well, earnestly long for such a union.
And as for smithys and dancing masters, why, they are no
less eager to vie for my hand. What sort of fellows could
deny themselves such a treat?"

"I see," Lord North said reflectively, ignoring her
outburst. "But then, who is the fellow? For you took such
great care not to mention him, I am quite sure he exists.
You seem too realistic a young woman to have plucked
him from between the pages of a book. Come, my lady,"
he said with the merest trace of sympathy, "it may matter.
It may help to tell me all."

It was that vague hint of fellow feeling that undid
Amanda. She capitulated.

"He is a near neighbor at home. But we are not lovers,
nor is there any understanding between us as yet. But I
have known him for several years and, I confess, I had
. . ." She bit off her next words and then said, head held
high, "And there is no question of his being unacceptable.
He is only, I imagine, somewhat slow to offer, at least in
Mama's view."

"But not in yours," he replied with a smile. "Since any

young woman dreams of a suitor who makes up his mind with the speed of a glacier. In any event," he said with a lightening of his countenance, "you can scrape by well enough, I see. You have only to return home, tell him of your narrow escape from disgrace, and he will speedily restore you to respectability."

The viscount rose and straightened himself, pleased with the outcome of the conversation. He would doubtless, he thought, remain in the countess's bad graces, and his reputation, such as it was, would bear yet another blot. But at least the young woman who, he could see now, was only victim to her mama's impatience, would be well out of the situation. Her next words, spoken as quietly and thoughtfully as if he had already left the room, caused him to sit again.

"Oh yes, I'll scrape by," Amanda said sadly. "I shall go home and live with Father. But as for Giles, I doubt I shall see him ever again."

"What a delightful suitor," the viscount said enthusiastically. "Slow to make up his mind, quick to change it at the faintest breath of scandal. No wonder you yearn for him."

"I could not blame him," Amanda cried, stung from her mood of sad reflection. "How would you feel if you heard that the lady you were considering marriage with was found in her bed with the most disreputable libertine in the land, he half-clad and she an Amberly?"

After her outburst had cleared her head as well as her vision of the murky fog of self pity, Amanda noted that the viscount sat silently looking at her with a quizzical expression.

"Oh," she gasped, "I am so sorry."

"Not at all," Lord North said calmly. "I was half clad."

Amanda began to make hurried excuse, but the viscount waved his hand dismissively.

"There's no one who will dispute your reading of my character," he said. "I think, however, that you undervalue your own attractions. You are, if we are to speak perfectly frankly, one of the legitimate ones, I take it?"

"Yes," she said quietly, still very sorry for having touched his feelings, although he gave no sign of having any.

"But," she added, "I am my mama's daughter, and people set great store by such things."

"Well I know it," the viscount murmured, showing some genuine emotion for the first time, though it was too fleeting to be readable to Amanda.

Lord North rose again, but this time he only paced to the long windows and stood, his back to her, gazing out at the brilliant day. Then he turned and spoke again. The sunlight behind him was so bright that it seemed to Amanda that he spoke as a disembodied voice, for all she could see was a dark shape of his form and a nimbus of fair hair.

"I feel somewhat responsible, though lord knows why. Frankly, it makes no matter if I were discovered, half, fully, or totally unclad in a bed with a dozen fair ladies, and their pug dogs as well, for that matter. I am, as you so rightly put it, a libertine, after all. But you, my child, seem to me to be in for a hard time if I just waltz forth from here with another naughty anecdote attached to my biography. And, I haven't even earned that particular tale of conquest," he mused. "Perhaps that's what nags at me. No matter," he went on briskly.

"There is a way out of this, Lady Amanda. It is very devious, very underhanded, and totally delightful. It serves both my purposes and yours as well. It will make your mama ecstatic and nudge your laggard suitor to his destiny, if we play it in tune."

Amanda cocked her head to one side as she listened to him. Her look of total confusion was so pronounced, as were all the expressions that flickered over her winsome face, that he laughed. He came to her then, and sat beside her. He took her hand in his and said,

"My lady, you will have to lend me your hand for this, as well as your ears. We will become engaged. Oh, don't startle like that, you'll do yourself an injury. 'Engaged' I said. Note, I did not say 'married.' The announcement will be put in the papers, your mama will be triumphant, and your name will be cleared. It is one of society's niceties that an engagement wipes the slate clean. It would not matter what precisely I had been found in last night, so long as it was followed up by an engagement."

Seeing her look of incomprehension, he laughed to himself and went on, "you will come with me to my own home, and meet my own dear mama and family. But," he said with emphasis, "you will commence to write a series of letters home to dear . . . whatever is that hesitant fellow's name?"

"Giles," whispered Amanda, gazing at her would-be fiancé as though he had run mad.

"Giles, then. Your first letters will be filled with girlish glee at having found such romance, such a princely fellow. But even that first letter will be touched with a slight note of hesitation. Giles will understand that emotion right enough. You will wonder, only in an aside, if you are doing the right thing to throw yourself into such a hasty marriage. Each subsequent letter will contain more self-doubt. By the time he has received six of them, he will, if he has any wit at all, be wondering whether he ought to come to advise you. By the time he has received a dozen, he will, if he has any spine at all, post away instantly to rescue you from my toils. We will say, for I will help you if you wish in the composition, that I am fickle, that I am lewd and licentious, and that I am unprincipled. We will not need to strain for invention, we will only write the truth. Then, he will come to free you from your unholy pact with me, and you will have all that you originally desired."

"But I don't wish to deceive him," Amanda said in hesitation.

"Yet, what choice have you? You've said he will not believe the truth," he answered reasonably.

"But if he does not come?" Amanda asked, awestruck at the possibility of his proposal.

"Then you are well quit of him, for if he fails to be moved by your distress, he would make a most disastrous match. But still, you will be free again. Breaking off from an engagement with me would be certain to win you approval in the most austere reaches of society. What say you, Lady Amanda? Shall we give it a try? It seems your only course."

"But won't your family be disturbed by my masquerade?" she asked in a wavering voice, unsure that this master stroke of strategy could be the godsend she saw it.

"They will know no more of it than your enchanting mama," he said calmly.

"But won't they be disappointed at its outcome?" she asked.

"Not in the least," he answered smoothly. "They will applaud your good sense."

"But why should you do this for me?" she asked at last.

"Why, I have nothing better to do at the moment," he explained as though surprised by the question. "And it promises to be quite entertaining."

It was only a short while later, when the Countess of Clovelly had trod around the edges of her Turkish carpet so many times that the duke feared for the rose design at its edges, that a knock came upon the door of the study. The countess stopped and shot a look of high tension toward the duke.

When the door opened, she had her hand posed dramatically against her heart. The viscount came into the room and poised himself at the entrance. Then he opened his arms wide and said, smiling hugely,

"Mama!"

The countess dropped her hand and flew to embrace him.

As the couple met, the duke had a few seconds of hesitation as he hurriedly did mathematics in his head and frowned. But when the countess cried, "I am so happy for you both," the duke at last understood and, chuckling to himself at the constant rightness of the world, went to congratulate his lady's new prospective son-in-law.

IV

There would have to be a party. It was in vain that Amanda tried to explain that she had no liking for parties and hadn't prepared herself for one. Vainly too, her new fiancé hinted and then flatly stated that as he had been from home for all of two years, he was all haste to return. There simply must be a party, the countess exclaimed. It was inevitable, the duke chuckled fondly as his lady had her secretary scribble a growing sheaf of invitations. The only concession to the guests of honor's requests was that the party would be held sooner than the countess would wish, and that some of her plans would have to go by the board for reasons of expediency.

A great many hostesses would have been handicapped by the suddenness of the event, a great many more would have been defeated by the pressing lack of time. But the countess was undaunted. Kettering Manor, after all, was made for festivity. She and the duke lived for gaiety, and the entire establishment was in a perpetual state of readiness for guests and entertainment. Even more happily for her, those of her set were equally always available for celebration. If galas had been known to have been arranged for such occasions as dogs' birthdays and winning derby horses, a genuine engagement party was certainly enough cause for a major fete.

No sooner had the viscount extricated himself from his prospective mama-in-law's gleeful embrace than she announced her intentions. After hearing all the objections to her scheme, she conceded only that the ball she planned would have to be held two weeks rather than three hence. And immediately after she had looked in on her daughter and bestowed an ecstatic smile upon her, she wiped away a happy tear and rushed off to compile her guest list. The duke, of course, was called into conference with her, and as they arose one by one, her present guests were invited to come and offer up suggestions as to the make-up of the great celebration. By late afternoon, the only persons aside from the household staff who were not merrily planning the forthcoming ball were the two for whom it was to be given.

Now that his name had been offered and promptly accepted, the viscount decided that a conference with his newly coined fiancé might be in order. At least, he thought, he might get to know her a little better. But when he presented himself in the same salon where he had made his offer, she only sat and blinked at him. It seemed as if she had not stirred from the moment when he had left. When he came in to pass the time of day with her, she shook herself as one coming out of a dream might do, and then rose.

"I think," she said dazedly, "that I must think this thing out, my lord. This has all been so sudden." Then, realizing from his twisted smile that the cliché she had uttered was unfortunate in this instance, she flushed and begged his pardon, and then begged his leave to return to her room. At his slight nod, she fled. Not having any desire to be pressed into service for compiling the guest list for his engagement ball, as there was no one whose presence he wanted, the viscount found that he and his horse required exercise and spent the better part of the afternoon riding and thinking alone. He was not, as so many newly promised men were, occupied with second thoughts, for, he thought as he rode over the snowy landscape, he had never had any but second thoughts from the first.

As the days wore on, he had a great deal of time to entertain those thoughts as his hostess and her household prepared to entertain his nominal guests. Now that he was netted, the announcement sent to the papers, and cards of invitation sent throughout the land, he was left to his own devices. His blushing bride-to-be stayed as far from him as from a contagion. The only conversation he had with her was the polite sort, at meal times. But he did not pass all his time in solitary pursuits, for it could be noted that as well as riding the viscount spent a great deal of time roaming through Kettering Manor, conversing idly with stablemen and even, on occasion, with the housekeeper.

He did see a great deal of his future bride, though. Each evening he sat with her, and each evening he found that he conversed a good deal if not with, then about her. For he discovered the chit was singularly unable to defend herself against her mama's guests and their unique methods of communicating their good wishes. He found himself in the position of being a sort of verbal Lancelot, as he nightly slew social dragons for his fair lady.

The very first evening, after their engagement had been declared and a dozen toasts drunk to it, he had come in from the dining room where the gentlemen had offered him another half dozen ribald toasts with their port. He had scarcely noted nor taken offense at the growing sexual innuendos of their comments. He was, after all, as his hostess had claimed, a man of the world. But when he had joined the ladies he had seen his fiancée white-faced and dumbstruck as the ancient Lady Alcott and the tipsy young Mrs. Small cackled together over Amanda's head. He caught only the tail end of their comments, but enough to know that they were quizzing her about what other idiosyncrasies she had discovered about her fiancé aside from the disparate hue of his eyes. The other unusual attributes they suppositioned were physical as well, but rather of a more intimate nature.

He was well used to such banter, but the look he surprised on his future bride's face was one of sick shame. He made his bows to the other females and, with the most winning smile, asked if he could not have just one private word with Lady Amanda. With knowing chuckles they agreed, and he was able to lead the ashen girl to one side of the room.

"You mustn't take too much note of what they say," he said off-handedly. "Lady Alcott's giddy with the height of her years, you know, and the Small woman's cast away most of the time."

Amanda ignored his words. Her lips, he saw, were trembling. He thought that she might weep and was about to suggest she retire to her rooms with that time-worn excuse of a headache, when she spoke. Her voice was not trembling, rather it was one of shaken wonder.

"I almost struck her! Just think, I was about to do physical injury to a female old enough to be my grandmother! And I looked about for an escape and saw a vase of flowers and was tempted to empty it over that other dreadful female. I did not know I could be so angry," she said, her fine gray eyes searching his as if for an answer.

"I shouldn't, you know," he said carefully, his lips twitching, "for they'd adore it. Come, collect yourself. Let me do the honors. I'll quite enjoy it."

For the rest of the evening, he kept close by her side. His seeming devotion spurred even more comment. He parried comments about their unusual meeting with sly references about the speakers' own companions, he met witticisms about Amanda's attractions with amusing gossip about females upon the continent, he avoided discussion of his own history by oblique references to his inquisitors' pasts. He must have done it well, he thought, for they continued to call upon him to perform for the rest of the week as coachload after coachload of new guests arrived. But his new lady, at least, was able to calm herself and sit by his side, mute and observant.

His hostess was so occupied with her upcoming fete that he had at last to insist upon speech with her. He had time only for one rational discussion, and that on the subject closest to his heart. But, she protested when he taxed her with it, he must be mistaken. And if he were right, she finally conceded ruefully, it must have been only because of her own flightiness, her excitement at seeing him, her eagerness to oblige him. It was his unusual eyes, of course, she admitted. Seeing him standing there before her that night, she had meant sincerely to appoint him the gray room, which was a charming chamber, but had said *blue* only because she had been wondering aloud at his delightfully strange eyes. Thinking *blue*, she simpered, she had led him to the blue bedroom in error, such was her haste to see him comfortably settled.

Comfortably settled, indeed, he thought as the two weeks wound to a close; so might a capon be comfortably settled for a feast. His prospective bride had kept so far from him that all his suspicions were reawakened. When he first spoke with her, she had been so reasonable a female that he conceded she might have been as much a sacrificial victim as himself. Her current absence from his presence fed the meanest forebodings. But though he might feel a twinge of disappointment now, it was directed solely at himself. For he was seldom gulled, and was vaguely displeased that she might have actually succeeded in deceiving him with her affect of innocence. Still, it made little difference to him.

As he dressed with care the night of the ball, he amused himself by thinking that this night's festivities had even less valid reasons for being than had the famous soiree for the Pekingese's birthday. Whether the girl were a cheat or sincere, it would not tie him to matrimony. Being possessed of a base reputation, he could basely step from the arrangement any time it suited him to do so. At present he was content to let matters go forth.

The ball promised to be a bore, his hostess had frankly betrayed him, and his future wife appeared to be a conniving slut, still the viscount wore a pleased smile as he stepped from his room. He was, in fact, very glad at all that had transpired. Taking his spurious fiancée home with him was a charming way of taking the curse from his own homecoming. She would bear all the attention, not he. Her name would stagger them. The Amberly female's plot, he thought, as he at last deemed himself ready to enter the spirit of the evening, suited his needs exactly. It was a thoroughly diverting way to divert his thoughts from home and all that awaited him there.

He could hear the music as he stepped to the head of the stairs. The great house had been thrumming with activity all week, and tonight it had reached a crescendo. Guests had arrived with monotonous regularity since the invitations had gone out, and this night even more came crowding in. There were so many that even the capacious house could not hold the lot, and many had had to stay with nearby friends or failing that, at inns. The countess had aimed her missives well; such a festivity could not be missed by those who had been summoned.

When Lord North reached the bottom of the stairs, he found himself thronged with the company. He was offered felicitations, congratulations, and looks of ill-concealed surprise. But even as they took in every detail of his composed face to assure themselves that he was not distressed with the circumstances of the incredible engagement they had heard of, their eyes were searching beyond him for a glimpse of the lady clever enough to snare such an elusive bird of passage.

There were upward of two hundred people pressed into the lower portion of Kettering Manor, and most were known to the viscount either by face, name, or repute. The countess's guests were culled from the ranks of the nobility, the *ton*, the military, the merely wealthy, the acting profession, and professions never spoken of in polite company. Although guests of every rank were present, there were no royals in attendance. Even noblesse oblige could only extend so far. For this was an infamous set, and though some of its members might be of the highest society, their sport took place in the shadows of those lofty realms.

Thus, a gentleman who would make sure he measured each word in the House of Lords, might relax here tonight and trumpet the worst sort of slanders or silliness knowing that whoever quoted him would have to admit to having been in a similar case and condition to have heard him. A lady who would be accustomed to taking tea in atmospheres so strict that she dare not utter any but the most blameless sentiments, might tonight either gather up or contribute to gossip so scurrilous that even her lowliest maid would be shocked to repeat it in a tavern. But there was safety here as well. For the countess did not entertain scramblers or mushrooms, only the *crème de la crème* of the *ton*, who just happened to wish for occasional lapses into the dregs of their cups of privilege.

There were noblemen without their wives or with another's wife. There were mistresses who had to have good memories to remember to whose side they must return after a dance. There were gentlemen whose strange proclivities could not bear the light of day and ladies whose faces had not been seen by light of day for decades. There was great wealth here and breeding, and the wealth changed hands rapidly and a great deal of inbreeding was natural.

Lord North stood and acknowledged the company while his eyes searched, too, for his lady. Since his valet had been traveling at a slower pace, it had been a simple thing to summon him to the countess's to attend him for the duration of his stay. Thus he was immaculately and soberly dressed as usual, in close-fitting black coat, white cravat, and formal black satin pantaloons. His waistcoat was blue and gray and gold, and even from a distance his golden hair made him unmistakable. So it was that Amanda was able to focus upon him alone in that vast crowd of guests, as the duke and her mother led her down the stairs.

It was as grand an entrance as the countess could have wished, and in that hushed moment, even Lord North could forgive his fiancée her weeks' long excuse that she could never tarry while her mama's dressmaker was fuming. The countess wore a lavender frock, the duke was commonplace in black and white. There was no other spot of color to take the advantage from Amanda's spectacular dressing. She wore a deceptively simple gown of light yellow edged with white and sashed around with deeper saffron. As her curls were cropped too close to dress, they had been bound with a ribboned circlet of white and yellow flowers that seemed to glow against her spice-brown hair. The hue of her frock gave a creamy glow to her triangular, elfin face and her long lashed eyes were wide with expectation. She looked young, hesitant, and delectable.

As the voices around him picked up their excited conversations again, Lord North smiled in approval. It had been very clever of the countess not to deck the girl out in white, for she was no debutante, and he had to applaud the restraint in not permitting her to wear jewels. Almost, it might appear that she was as she claimed, springtime innocent of her mother's schemes. As she approached him, he gazed thoughtfully at her, taking in the whole of her appearance, from her flushed cheeks to her white neck to her small high breasts and gently curved waist. He took her hand and breathed, "You look enchanting, my dear," while he thought, "And now the play begins."

He led her into the dance and soon others followed and the ball was officially in session. She did not speak as they waltzed, nor seem to note the way his eyes never left off gazing into her face. In due course, he surrendered her to the duke and then noted as she was taken up by the ancient comte and then again by Lord Skyler. Those few who were part of the original company when he had arrived at Kettering Manor now enjoyed the status of celebrities, and the order in which they claimed Amanda for the dance showed that they were anxious to remind the others of this. When he saw Amanda claimed by a dashing major in His Majesty's horse regiment, Lord North turned to enjoy the ball upon his own terms.

He found that he was in even greater demand tonight than he usually was. He danced with two females who had fleetingly been under his protection, and five would-be candidates for the honor. He listened gravely to gossip of the doings of various of his acquaintance, and at the last, stationed himself quietly by the punchbowl, taking refuge from the rest by pretending to attend with great interest to the never-ending narratives of a totally foxed duke. Napoleon might be on Elba, indeed he had seen the fellow there, and normalcy might be returning to the whole of Europe, but the pleasure-starved swarm that frolicked before him were yet wary of travel upon the continent. That was why they were here in such great numbers. Some of their set were already in Vienna and with the coming of spring, he was sure the majority of these present now would be off again about the world, but for now they were grateful for the local pleasures of one of the Amberly Assortment's engagement ball.

When dinner was announced, Lord North strolled toward

his fiancée and, with quiet authority, disengaged her from the knot of admirers that had enveloped her when she had left off dancing with an elderly rogue. He gave her his arm and conducted her to a small table that had been set somewhat out of the common way behind an arbor of flowers. The theme of the ball had been springtime in winter, and the countess, knowing her company well, had devised several such bowers for privacy's sake.

"I'll procure you some tidbits and then you can rest for a space," he said. "You're a raging success. In fact, if you'd like to break off our engagement immediately, I'm sure you can net three other fellows within the hour."

He had meant it as a pleasantry and was surprised to hear her say with some loathing, "I cannot eat a thing. And I should like to leave this moment."

He began to make assurances that he had only been speaking in jest when she cut him off abruptly by saying wearily, "Oh I know, I know, you cannot say a thing in earnest. But I cannot abide a moment more of this, or these people. They smile at me and flatter me and wish me well, while I know that they do not think of me for a moment. They're all thinking of what advantage they can make of me or this evening. It's all such a charade. Not only on my part, but on theirs. When can I leave, my lord? But I've asked Mama and she expects me to dance till dawn. For I shall not. You know of such things, when can I respectably quit this company?"

"Respectably?" he asked, arching a brow. "Why never. But after midnight, you can make your good nights to a chosen few who will then filter the word down to the others, if you wish."

"I wish," she agreed fervently.

When he had brought her a plate laden with expensive out-of-season trifles, he said softly,

"You must expect them to be curious. You've come from nowhere to make a catch from their waters."

"They all know the story," she said abruptly, laying her fork down with a tiny prawn still impaled upon it.

"If it comforts you," he said pleasantly, "they would

have most probably made up the same tale if they did not know. Or worse."

"How I wish we were at your home," she said on a gusty sigh.

"I shouldn't," he said quietly, and as she looked up, startled, he went on, ". . . refine upon it too much."

After the dinner they went around the room with her mother, being introduced to the entire company.

"The clock has chimed twelve, sit-by-the-cinders," he whispered amiably when they were done. "And after this measure, I can escort you to your rooms. They've satisfied their curiosity and now they'll be content to let you go."

By the time he had cleared their passage to the stairs, it was almost an hour into the new day. It seemed that the company could not leave off exclaiming over what a glamorous couple the young woman in her buttercup dress and the gentleman with the hair the color of sunshine appeared to make. Though North was known to them, no female present this night could honestly claim to have held his attention above the changing of the moon. No gentleman could even hint that he had held the countess's delightful daughter for more than the space of a dance. The compliments were effusive. "Such a perfect match," they murmured. "So well suited," they cooed. It would have all been quite gratifying, Lord North thought, if he could be oblivious to their underlying meaning and the frankly avid eyes of the gentlemen as they estimated the charms of his bride-to-be, and if she could ignore the less than subtle invitation upon the lips of the ladies as they saluted her new fiancé. But at last he stood before her door with her.

"Thank you," she said sincerely, "Mama would have had me stay in the midst of all that until dawn if you had not gotten me free."

"I have my uses," he conceded.

They stood alone in the dim corridor and she found that, to her surprise, she was at last nervous with him. For he stood watching her with an expectant expression.

"What shall you do now?" she asked, not really caring, but wanting him to at least speak.

"You mean," he queried softly, "if you are not going to ask me in?"

"I am certainly not going to ask you in," she snapped.

"Pity," he murmured in a voice that belied the words. "I expect then that I shall have to go back to the ball, and presently I shall escape to the library where I shall have a rousing time listening to those few gentlemen who consider themselves political pundits. Or I can go to the salon and trade warm stories with a few fellows. Really, my lady, you are condemning me to seeing the party out to its last breaths. This respectability is a heavy thing."

She looked so perplexed that he laughed at last.

"You see, my dear fiancée," he said, reaching out to tuck one wilting flower back into her ribbon and letting his finger test a curl, "if I should just disappear into my own comfortable, innocently empty bed now, all those assembled belowstairs will doubtless believe that I have, instead, repaired to yours."

At her wide-eyed shock, he went on, "No, you didn't think on that, did you? But they would, my dear, they doubtless would. As I doubtless would if only I were asked. But as I have not been," he smiled at her dismay, "I shall go below and make myself most in sight until the last guest has reeled to bed, while you take to your comfortable bed for slumber. Selfish one," he chided gently, drawing nearer.

"I shall not be sleeping," she said with resolve, stepping backward with her hand upon the door. "I shall be packing. We will leave tomorrow, will we not?"

"Oh no," he said, "I'm afraid it will take yet another day."

"Why?" she cried, putting so much mournful disappointment into that one question that she was embarrassed by her own eagerness to be gone from her mother's house.

"It's not that I want to leave Mama, though it is, for I confess I don't believe that faradiddle she told me about blue and gray eyes and blue and gray rooms, though I suppose it *is* possible," she said, her words and her thoughts all jumbled on the subject of her mama's possible perfidy. "But it's all these other people. I have never wanted to associate with them before, and I confess I can scarcely bear it now. Do you know that three gentlemen have hinted at possible liaisons with me this night alone? And at my own engagement party," she said, almost forgetting her counterfeit status in her annoyance.

"Only three?" He smiled. "I'm sure you misunderstood, it must have been far more. But if we leave tomorrow, who do you suggest come with us as chaperon? Just tell me her name and I swear, I'll be prepared to order up the coaches instantly."

Amanda stood stricken. She had never thought of it, and of course, Mama had not. Mama had only assigned a maid to her for her trip. But he was entirely right. She would need the escort of some respectable female on the journey. Even though the viscount was now named her fiancé, there would be no hope of any eventual reunion with Giles if it were known that she had traveled overnight across the countryside alone with such a man as he. And, to save her immortal soul, she could not think of one respectable female among the hundreds of persons presently within the walls of Kettering Manor.

"Exactly," Lord North said, watching her reaction to his words. "But fortunately, since I was left to my own devices for all these days," he glanced at her wryly as he spoke, but she was still too overwrought to notice, "I had the time to think about it. With your permission, my lady, I have sent a message off to an elderly relative of my mother's who resides in the next county. A very respectable female. So respectable, in fact, that she would never recognize one face in the company here this night. She's a bit long in the tooth, but very fond of my mama and doubtless eager to be in her debt. She will arrive, I understand, two days from now. Does that suit you?"

"Oh, yes," Amanda said with relief. "Oh, thank you."

"Then I bid you a good night," he said, and leaned forward slightly to her. But at that, she took in her breath sharply and said hurriedly, "Oh, wait. Just one moment, please." She vanished within the room.

As the time went on and he could hear her moving within the room, Lord North permitted himself a vague hope of what was going to transpire next. Whatever his ruminations, however, he was not expecting her to thrust several closely written sheets of paper into his hands.

"I've written two versions of a letter to Giles," she said nervously, "and was wondering if you'd go over them and see which is the better to send."

He laughed then, took the papers from her, and promised he'd cast an eye over them. Then he half-seriously cautioned her to lock her doors and prime her pistol again. At her look of distress, he smilingly allowed that while he would in future be most cautious as to which chamber he retired to, there was no telling if all the other members of the present gathering would be so circumspect. Then, bidding her a lighthearted good night, he went to rejoin the company.

As the night wore on, Lord North was not bereft of attention. Though he did not dance another step, he was offered partnership in many other diversions, by many other sportive persons. He denied them all. He attempted to visit the gaming room, but after listening to Lady Slade's complaints about how chill her own room undoubtedly was since she was alone, Mary Whitmore fretting about how cool he had grown toward her, and Mrs. Abernathy whispering over an excellent hand about how cold her own husband unfortunately was, he escaped from the room and from further female companionship. He did not join the other gentlemen either. Not the group trading risqué stories, nor the political gentlemen, nor even the lords Skyler and Jeffrey's select invited guests and their various subtle invitations to amusement.

Instead, as the sky slowly turned to the light of true morning, Lord North sat at ease in the deserted library entertaining himself by reading with interest two different, closely written letters to a disbelieving gentleman named Giles.

V

The Honorable Miss Emily Atkinson arrived at Kettering Manor at the unfashionable hour of ten in the morning, two days after the countess's lavish ball. Her time of arrival was not the least fashionable aspect of her person. For when Amanda hastily abandoned her breakfast to make the acquaintance of the lady who would be her nominal chaperon on the journey to her fiancé's home, she was, for a moment, convinced that it was just another jibe on that disreputable gentleman's part.

The Honorable Miss Emily looked, at first stare, exactly like some sort of elderly indigent who had been plucked from her flower stand in the Covent Garden markets of London. At any moment, Amanda expected her to open her mouth to say, "Violets for my lady?" Instead, she said, "Charmed," in a most unexceptional manner, and displayed no further desire for speech until a light breakfast was offered to her, when she said with as much enthusiasm as was possible to place in so few words, "I think I shall, thank you so much."

For such a meager person, Amanda thought, the Honorable Miss Emily consumed as much sustenance as an army trooper might. Miss Emily was very aged, very small, and extremely thin. Her out-of-fashion jet dress hung upon her as slackly as her threadbare purse hung upon her bony arm. Amanda had always somehow associated small spare elderly persons with wit as acute and sharp as their looks. But Miss Emily was as scant with speech as she was with person, and those few words that escaped her were commonplace and complimentary to a fault. Watching Miss Emily consume her "light breakfast" with the rapacity of a wolf, nodding complaisant agreement to every bit of prattle the countess presented in her eagerness to make a good impression on her daughter's prospective relative, Amanda could not shake the ridiculous notion that somehow an enormously fat, indolent person had become trapped in Miss Emily's insubstantial body.

But Mama had been agog when she had been told the identity of her daughter's chaperon. "Miss Emily Atkinson!" she had cried. "Trust North to do the right thing. Irreproachable, my dear, she is totally irreproachable. She was once lady of the chamber to the old queen, and not a breath of scandal has ever been attached to her. The most amiable of souls, the epitome of good *ton*." Perhaps it was all those years at court, Amanda thought, that accounted for Miss Emily's unhesitant, pleased acceptance of every scrap of information that was fed to her, along with every morsel of food.

Amanda's bags were packed and were already loaded into the coach that would bear them and her maid to Windham House, Lord North's home. She sat in agonies of impatience while Miss Emily enjoyed her repast and her mama burbled on about how delightful the unexpected alliance was, and painted pictures of her daughter that would have been extravagant in describing a martyred saint. Lord North toyed with his cutlery with a look of great amusement upon his face. But Amanda kept note only of the time and wished her mama were wise enough to do the same and let their party make an escape before the other guests awoke and joined them.

Most of the guests at the ball had stayed on, for an invitation to a ball at a country home was readily understood to be an invitation for a week or more, since travel was so tedious and such an onerous task. The guests had been occupied with hunting, dancing, playing parlor games, giving musical recitals, and nipping in and out of various bedrooms since the day of their arrival. Amanda had found herself slinking and creeping about the house in futile attempts to avoid their jovial attentions. Despite her care, she had been the recipient of congratulatory pinches on the cheek and less mentionable parts of her person more than a few times from the gentlemen, and had received more candid and shocking advice about the state of wedlock from the ladies than she could bear.

The most embarrassing counsel had come from her own mama. It was inevitable, she thought later, that her scatter-wit parent should suddenly decide that a daughter might need some maternal advice on certain intricacies of the married state before her wedding date. Amanda had tried to forestall the conversation that day when she had been sought out in her own bedroom by saying that it was, after all, not quite her wedding night, but her mama had said, knowingly,

"Precisely. I'll have quite good advice for you then. But for now, all that I want to impress upon you, Amanda, is the importance of not celebrating that night prematurely."

Mama had the uncanny ability every so often to leave off her fluttery affect and speak with such decisiveness that one was compelled to listen. Amanda sank back onto her bed without further protest as the countess went on, "I am not saying that Roger has not been a good papa to you, but I doubt he has ever given you any idea of how a female should go on in such affairs. Indeed, it would be most reprehensible if he had. But no matter. I assume that you and this Giles person have never . . . ah . . . ." Her mother faltered, and Amanda had quickly put in "Never," for fear of hearing anything more explicit.

"I thought not," her mother said with satisfaction, "for I believe I should have seen it in your face if he did, or you had."

Amanda very much doubted this claim of prescience, but as she did not want the conversation to dwell on such matters, said nothing, only hoping it would be over quickly.

"North is a compelling man," her mother said, now avoiding her daughter's eye. "And very clever when it comes to our frail sex. I only wanted to stress, Amanda, that I think it would be very unwise if you allowed yourself to be eased into a more intimate relationship before the knot is tied. Knowing North, I am quite sure nothing too advanced transpired before I stepped into your room; he is not the sort of fellow to rush his fences or even enjoy covering ground too quickly . . ." And here her mother lingered for a moment, the expression of wistful musing upon her face more shocking to her daughter than anything she had yet said.

"At any rate," the countess went on, shaking herself from her distraction abruptly, "I only wanted to say, with no further frills upon it, that it would be a bad idea to consummate this marriage before it has taken place. North is a fellow who grows bored quickly, and who has, alas, little faith in your innocence. You do know what I am saying, don't you?" she asked suddenly, suspicious of her daughter's silence.

"Of course," Amanda shot back with heartfelt truth. "And I assure you, I have no intention of allowing any intimacies with my Lord North."

"That is not precisely what I meant," her mama said thoughtfully, "for a few tantalizing hints of what is to come would not go amiss. I only advise against fulfillment of those promises. Do you take my meaning? Oh dear, how complete is your knowledge of the married state, Amanda?" she asked with a look of trepidation.

"Quite extensive, Mama," Amanda said, laughing. "After all, I did go to boarding school, and there is little that we did not discuss among ourselves of the matter."

"Lud," her mama said, aghast, "then we really must have a good long talk before you actually marry."

Although Amanda had agreed, she had privately resolved from the moment she had shown her mama to the door, that if she did manage to retrieve something from this tangle and actually marry Giles, she would not return for that chat until she had presented him with at least two infants.

For all her confused wondering about her mama and that lady's motives in the mix-up of bedchambers that had resulted in her present engagement, she still could not like deceiving her. But truth to tell, she did not know her parent too well, and feared that if any hint of the truth of the odd arrangement with the viscount slipped out, her mama's hand might be forced to even more disastrous lengths. Although, she thought, it would be difficult for her to be compromised more firmly than she had already been, unless Mama actually drugged her and dragged her to that gentleman's sheets. Nonetheless, the sooner she was quit of Kettering Manor, the better. Then she thought, brightening for a scant moment, the only persons she would have to keep the truth from would be the Honorable Miss Emily, the viscount's mama, his other relatives, and his entire household staff.

It might have been her doleful expression that prompted Lord North to say idly, cutting into Mama's comments about how cunning an infant Amanda had been, "But dear cousin Emily! Just look at the hour. Why, if we tarry here any longer, it will be past dinner time when we arrive at the Fox and Grapes. I did book us there, since I recall the inn has a marvelous reputation for its cuisine."

Miss Emily ingested the last crumb of her toast and stood up in one rapid motion.

"How delightful it has been," she said.

The countess gave Amanda a tearful and fulsome good-bye, entreating Lord North again and again "to take good care of my little girl," while the duke beamed and Lady Emily said "Delighted" with the regularity of a clock counting hours.

Amanda and Miss Emily climbed into the first coach, their maids into a following vehicle. Lord North swung up upon his horse and they were at last away as the sun rose directly overhead. Amanda waved through the rapidly fogging window, and noted that a few persons in the house had pulled back their curtains to see their departure.

As the coaches disappeared down the curving drive, the countess turned to her dear Robert and said happily, "The wedding, of course, shall not be such a paltry affair as the engagement party was. I shall have time to sit and plan, and with any luck, Robert, it will be the social affair of the season."

The duke lost his habitual smile and then answered, somewhat tentatively, knowing he was treading upon very thin ground, "Did North say it was to be here, then? Not that I'd mind, be delighted, puss, as you well know. But his mama—ah, his family, that is to say . . ." He let his words trail off unhappily.

His lady gave him one of her rare sharp looks.

"Don't be nonsensical, Robert. They may well not like it, but there's no other rational course. I am her mama."

"Ah well," the duke said, growing expansive once again, "we shall make it memorable then, never fear. When's it to be, puss, May or June?"

But at those innocuous words, the countess paled. Her step faltered and she looked back fearfully at the faint traces the departing carriage wheels had left upon the last trace of snow.

"I don't know!" she cried. And then, squinting her eyes as if to shield them from glare of the snow which was no longer there, she said slowly, thoughtfully, "They did not say."

They had only traveled a little while when Amanda collected herself, gave a final discreet sniffle, and then turned her attention fully to her companion, the estimable Miss Atkinson. That lady sat across from her comfortably peering out the window, although Amanda could not guess what she was seeing there. The hot bricks that had been placed at their feet, combined with the warmth of their breath, had succeeded in making the interior of the carriage cozy, and the resultant steam effectively blurred the windows completely.

Amanda had prepared herself for being quizzed or openly confronted with myriad questions from the viscount's honored relative the moment they were alone, but she soon found that the lady seemed to have no intention of breaking the silence within the swaying carriage. Since any extended silence in the close company of another human discomforted Amanda, and as she read both condemnation and accusation into this absence of conversation, she began to prepare the way for discussion.

But she discovered that comments upon the weather drew only an immediate pleased response of agreement on the fact that winter was generally cold. When that subject was exhausted, Amanda found as the miles slipped by that Miss Emily agreed that the carriage was well-sprung but that travel was indeed tiring, and that she too was anxious to arrive at their destination. The only information Miss Emily volunteered, and that hesitantly, as though she did not wish to give offense by holding such bold opinions, was that Lord North was a delightful fellow, and Amanda's own parents were similarly so. As she lapsed into defeated quiet again, Amanda did not seek to disabuse the lady of the notion that the duke was her parent, and wondered sadly if her companion knew any other word but the omnipresent "delightful."

Presently, Miss Emily dozed with a delighted little smile upon her lips. Amanda cleared a circle of fog from the window with her sleeve and when the road turned, gazed wistfully at the straight figure of Lord North as he rode ahead of the coach. When they stopped at last for tea, Amanda felt a relief that had nothing to do with the prospect of stretching her cramped legs or being able to use the ladies' convenience.

As Miss Emily disappeared into the inn, Lord North gave his horse to the stable boy and strolled over to Amanda with a secret smile.

"She is, as you have doubtless discovered," he said into Amanda's ear, "little better than an idiot, is she not? But very high *ton*, my dear. She was in great demand socially in her youth, for she could be counted on to never see what was beneath her nose, and thus to never spread a bit of tattle. But, you will note, she never uses the wrong fork or says an unpleasant word. And she has a great fortune, as well. The only reason such a paragon never married, I suspect," he added in a low voice as he held the door open for Amanda, "is that she doubtless never realized she was being proposed to. An excellent chaperon, is she not?"

Amanda refused him answer to that. But as they took their tea and sat and watched Miss Emily devour every bit of cake and cream they had not consumed, they chatted pleasantly upon a multitude of entertaining, nonimportant subjects. He was, Amanda thought, a charming companion when he desired to be. But, she reminded herself as she recovered from her mirth over his account of a tea he had suffered through aboard a ship in a storm off the coast of France, he would have to be facile at such things if all she had heard of him were true. It could not have been only his striking good looks that had earned him his infamy.

As he threw on his greatcoat once again and turned to her to offer his arm, Amanda understood all at once why he was considered so dangerously compelling. His bright hair seemed silver-tipped in the sunlight, his ivory face bore a faint gold glow from the cold, and his odd, jeweled eyes held a secret amused recognition of her unwanted, unwittingly sudden reaction to his splendor. She quickly lowered her gaze and made haste to enter the coach again and to gratefully endure the undemanding company of Miss Emily.

Amanda had deliberately avoided her fiancé assiduously since the morning they had struck their strange bargain. It was clear that his offer had been an act of charity. Offered out of boredom, or mischief of some strange sort perhaps, but nevertheless she knew very well that their bargain had been struck largely as a donation to the needy. She *had* been in need, and was very grateful to him. Therefore, she had decided that she would not presume upon him any more than she absolutely had to; it would simply not be fair. After hearing Mama's lame excuses for the incident, she had known that he had been as grievously wronged as she, and if she were to constantly trail after him, he would be sure to suppose her Mama's willing accomplice. If he had been kind enough to suffer her being foisted upon him, even for a short time, it would be poor payment to him for her to hang upon his sleeve.

But as they began their journey again, she saw that she could not avoid him any longer. For the viscount left off riding alone and now it pleased him to stay within the carriage with the two ladies for the last of their ride to the evening stopover at the Fox and Grapes.

As Miss Emily dozed, he sat back and bent himself entirely to the task of entertaining his fiancée. At first, he began to comment upon the engagement party they had just endured, and soon Amanda found that she was laugh-

ing merrily at all that she had felt fear and revulsion for.
When seen in the light of his clever words, the huge
sinister marquess who had offered her strange delights
during their dance became only a baggy-pantalooned
buffoon; the acid-tongued dame who had made her squirm
with pointed questions became an inept witch from a
skewed fairy story. Soon, she was adding her own ridiculous comments as counterpoint and they were laughing so
heartily that Miss Emily opened her eyes to smile and
whisper, "Charming."

As the carriage horses began to tire and plod more
slowly to their destination, he sobered and with her constantly fascinated questions to spur him on, told her tales
of the Vienna woods and streets and society. Then he held
her spellbound with his tale of how he had dined with
Bonaparte himself in that island retreat that the erstwhile
master of Europe clearly regarded as a hell on earth.
Amanda listened and grew strangely sad and subdued as
he described how the former eagle had been transmuted to
kitchen-cock in his exile. He saw her disquiet, and soon
had her gurgling with laughter again with his narrative
about a bungling spy at that dinner who had sought to get
his companions and himself foxed enough to spill state
secrets they did not possess.

He paced her moods with subtle skill so that the journey
of miles seemed to have been accomplished in mere
moments. It was only when Amanda was alone in her
snug room at the Fox and Grapes dressing for dinner that
she realized how well he had gauged her responses, and
how pleased he had been at the result of his efforts. Now
that she was, given the conversational gifts of Miss Emily,
to all intents alone with him while away from Mama's
house, she was amazed both at him and her own reaction
to him. It was as if, she thought, some great cataclysm of
nature had marooned her with Edmund Kean or some
other gifted actor. She knew full well that she was not the
viscount's usual sort of company and that he had, on a
whim, decided to make do with a chance companion. She
felt he was playing to an audience that was not there and

could not help the fact that some of his vast appeal and talent had dazzled her.

But it made no difference to their scheme, she reasoned as her maid tugged a comb through her curls. Because for all that he was scintillating and glamorous, she could honestly say that he had never been natural with her. For all she knew, he could not be so with anyone. She would do well to remember that. In that way she would be spared any foolish fears that might embarrass herself or him. She would have to constantly remind herself that she stood in no danger from his attentions. His easy seductiveness was not aimed particularly toward her, it was only an integral part of his personality, and would only mean that her position would not be quite so difficult a one as she had envisioned.

Amanda dressed in a thin but warm sapphire blue woolen frock. She threw a pale blue paisley shawl over her shoulders since the walls of the old inn admitted as much cold as the several blazing fireplaces sought to dispel. Miss Emily, she perceived when they met downstairs, had either not changed at all, or had an entire wardrobe of tired shapeless black dresses. The viscount was, as ever, an exquisite, even in his simple buckskins and dark gray hacking jacket.

They dined on the justly celebrated viands of the Fox and Grapes in a private paneled room with a comfortable fire roaring in the grate, and thick curtains pulled across the tiny windows shut out the bitter night.

The food was delicious, the wine incomparable, and the conversation even better than the fare. Soon Amanda felt that she was a privileged person on a gay holiday, rather than an exiled and disgraced young female, tolerated only through the good graces of a notorious stranger. She felt a distinct pang of regret when Miss Emily cleared the last bit from her dessert plate and announced that, while it had all been quite delightful, she was off to bed. Amanda rose to accompany the lady upstairs to their rooms, when she was forestalled by a languid comment from the viscount.

"But it is early hours yet, dear cousin. It has only just struck nine. As Lady Amanda and I have some family business to discuss, do you think you could allow her to remain here with me for a while? It is, I will admit, a private parlor, but as the landlord will soon send servants in to clear there can be no disgrace in a young woman and her fiancé lingering over their dessert, can there be?"

"Why certainly not," Miss Emily agreed at once. "There cannot be."

Miss Emily bestowed her usual benign smile upon them both and left, murmuring "Delightful" so often that the landlord, who chanced to be passing by as she mounted the stair, smiled in gratification at her obvious approval of his inn.

As Amanda settled back, the viscount leaned back in his own chair and grinned at her,

"You understand, of course," he said, "that she would have replied the same way if I had said, 'But as it is early hours yet, there can be no harm if Lady Amanda and I throw off all our clothes and make mad passionate love upon the floor until morning, can there be?' "

His words startled her, but the look in his eye had her giggling until he added, in an undertone, "There would be no harm in that either, you know."

But even as she drew in her breath, he changed his manner abruptly and sat upright and said in a businesslike fashion, "Now as to those letters, my lady . . . do you mind if I call you merely Amanda? I think that we have reached the stage in our acquaintance where even such a strict arbiter of fashion as Miss Emily would agree it was proper."

At her consenting nod, he went on, drawing her letters from his jacket, "Now, as I see it, the first letter is far too enthusiastic. The fellow will think you're crowing over your achievement, and the last little hint, let me see . . . 'I wonder at my precipitous judgment of the viscount, as I hardly know him . . .' is far too tame. You seem to be more like a lady who has discovered a diamond in her knitting basket and wonders only if it is entirely flawless. No, the tone is too bright, entirely too self-congratulatory. As for the second effort, it is too morose. Giles will think there's something smoky afoot if he reads it carefully. Too many, 'I wonder' and 'Whatever came over me, I do not know' sort of digressions. You need a letter that is a combination of the two. Come, let us ask the landlord for some clean sheets and we will put our heads together to compose the perfect first shot in our battle with the fine compunctions of Sir Giles Boothe."

After the table was cleared, they bent their heads literally, the sun-struck golden one and the curly brown one, over the sheets of paper the landlord provided. The hours went on unheeded as they labored over the letter they collaborated on. There were many times during its composition when the pen had to be laid down, as the lady who held it was laughing too hard to write a straight line. And many times when the pen was laid aside absently, as she explained pensively what she imagined Giles's thoughts, emotions, and character to really be. Though she thought that she was explaining only Giles, her co-author sat and watched as her expressive face and soft words told him a great deal more of herself than she ever imagined.

Two hours had gone by when she finally laid her pen down with a gratified sigh.

"It's done," she said. And then she looked up into his strange eyes, now less strange through constant association and because in the candlelight their oddity was unnoticeable, and said with wonder, "But look! I've only written two pages. It seems as though we've composed a saga together, and there's only these few pages."

"But there's a great deal in them closely packed," he commented, taking the letter from her. "I'll have the landlord hold it for the mail coach. Unless Giles is made of sheer granite, this little effort of ours will give him much to think upon. He does not even need to read between the lines to understand that you went to your mama's to receive a birthday gift and found yourself receiving instead the thrillingly complete and close attentions of a practiced seducer. Your mama, however, was nervous about such a devious fellow and, indeed, surprised him entering her dear daughter's boudoir. Now, you've committed yourself to the evil fellow, for you're a good girl. But you wonder if you've done the right thing by such a sacrifice to propriety, and hope he can advise you. Since you're so set on being as truthful as possible, you'll agree the only things we've fudged are your dear mama's and my intentions."

Amanda nodded, thinking back on the words she had put down on paper.

"And," the viscount went on, "to cap it all off, you find yourself attracted to the fellow, even though you know full well that he has no constancy, nor any morals at all."

"Yes," she breathed abstractedly, still thinking of the letter.

They sat quietly for a moment as he regarded her closely and she thought of their efforts. Then Amanda reluctantly rose from her seat. The wind was howling outside the windows and the fire, having been fed again while they were busily writing, crackled pleasantly. Again, she was reluctant to leave for the chill hallway.

"Ah, but it is early yet," the viscount said, rising as well, but only so that he could reseat himself in one of a pair of comfortable chairs by the fire.

"Come," he gestured. "Stay a while; don't rush off simply because dull work is done. There can be no harm in lingering over a cordial. You can even rouse dear Cousin Emily from her slumbers, if you want, to ask permission."

Amanda laughed, and feeling more pleased with herself than she had in days because the letter was at last written and about to be sent off to Giles, walked toward the other chair and sank back happily into it.

"A good day's work," she said with satisfaction.

"Yes," the viscount agreed, smiling happily back at her. "And just think," he added, "the day is not even done yet."

VI

Amanda leaned her head back against her chair and closed her eyes for a few moments. It was quiet in the room, save for the singing of the logs in the fireplace and the faint click of glasses and gurgle of liquid as her benefactor, Lord North, poured her the promised cordial. As he had said, the day was not yet done, yet she felt as though she had come a long way further than a mere count of hours could encompass. She was far from her home now, far from her mama, and equally distanced from Lord North's residence. She felt safe in her cocoon of comfort, in that limbo between the onset of her troubles and the resolution of them.

She accepted the fragile glass of clear liquid and drank a measure without thinking. A moment later, she was sitting erect, breathing with difficulty and gasping a plea for water.

"No, no," Lord North laughed from behind her, "water would ruin the effect. Just sit back again and take a small sip, then open your lips and breathe out from your mouth. No, don't look daggers at me," he chided her as she swung her head around to glower at him. "Just try to do as I say. Then you can rail at me."

Amanda sat back again reluctantly, and after she had her respiration under control, did as he suggested. The first shock of the little bit she sampled produced the same burning effect upon her palate, but as she parted her lips and breathed out, she slowly became aware of the overwhelming taste and fragrance of raspberries filling her mouth and nostrils. She stopped in wonder and gazed down at the glass.

"Yes," Lord North said in agreement with her unspoken thought, "it is quite marvelous, isn't it? A distillation of raspberries the good friars invented. A subtle thing, like so many other pleasures. First the fire, then the slow flooding of the senses. As Cousin Emily would say, 'Delightful.' "

Amanda took another sip and another breath, and found herself smiling. The viscount's voice came from directly behind her, as though he bent to speak into her ear.

"A singularly good feeling, is it not, to sip berries brewed in flame, while the cold, hard outside world fades away? There is nothing evil in such pleasure, is there, Amanda?"

This time, Amanda distinctly felt his warm breath upon her ear. She began to grow very wary and her muscles began to tense, until she realized that again, it was probably no more than his usual banter. If friendliness moved him to couch his conversation in such rich, ripe, seductive terms, he could hardly be aware of its effect upon an untried, unripe chit such as herself. But then, she felt his hand gently touch the back of her neck and begin to stroke the vulnerable region her curls did not cover.

He spoke softly, coaxingly now, but she could scarcely hear his words about "pleasures" and "joys," while her anger grew until it seemed to overflood her reason.

"What did you say?" she finally managed to ask, scarcely able to believe that which she thought she had heard through her veil of fury.

"I merely suggested," he said softly, now so close to her ear that she could feel each warm breath, as well as the light caress of his lips upon her earlobe, "that as it is yet early, and as we are unoccupied, and as I know it will bring you pleasure, as well as my poor self, that you accompany me to my room now."

When she did not answer at once, he went on softly, "Dear Cousin Emily will not know, nor care, unless we repair to her own room, if that is what makes you hesitant. Come, 'Manda, we have hours of blank night to spend deliciously."

"How dare you?" Amanda finally exploded, shooting up from her chair and wheeling about to face him.

He straightened, his face as bland as if he had just suggested they go for a stroll, and answered her calmly, "How dare I what, Amanda?"

She thought for a moment that the liquor had disordered her wits. But she could not have imagined his words even after ingesting a quart of alcohol-soaked berries.

"How dare you ask me, just coldly ask me to . . . to . . ." Amanda cried, unable in her disbelieving anger to vocalize his suggestion.

"Make love to me?" he supplied helpfully, much to her relief and appalled disbelief. "Well, I suppose that it might have seemed rather blunt, but really, my lady, I did not think you so wet behind the ears that you required the entire artificial scene: the light touch, the few hesitant kisses, the bolder embraces, and then finally, triumphantly, the finale, with me catching you up in my strong arms and bearing you off, protesting futilely that it is against your better judgment, to my bed. I thought you a female of rare good sense. I paid you the compliment of honesty. I'm sorry if I displeased you, but really my dear, it would have been rather difficult for me to tote you out of the room, off into the corridor, and up the stairs under the eyes of the innkeeper, his servants, and other clientele. And while this is a private parlor, at any moment just as I told Cousin Emily, some sort of servant might wander in. I do not approve of lovemaking as a spectator sport," he said reprovingly.

Amanda was in such a state of anger now, about all he had said and all he had left unsaid, that she found herself in the position of having so many things to declare that they all rushed to her lips and, finding a bottleneck there, struggled fruitlessly to get out.

She was furious at his estimate of her state of grace and curiously also enraged that this aloof and elegant gentleman should bring all the forces of his considerable charm to bear against one small unworldly girl. It was unfair, as though a sorcerer should conjure up a tidal wave to extinguish one little candle. And paradoxically, she was equally insulted at the vague idea that he had not, after all, exerted himself to bring forth quite as much persuasion as he could have done. She struggled for words to express some of this, while he stood waiting patiently for her next utterance.

"How dare you," she cried ringingly, sure that her face was red as a berry, "think that was what I wished, think I was that sort of female, think that I was someone you could while away a boring night with?"

"Is it that you are insulted that I did not painstakingly go down the list of your charms?" he asked curiously.

Since that, Amanda discovered suddenly, had been one of the grievances that she had not admitted even to herself—the thought that he was only making do on a tedious night with a female who was not up to his usual standard—she denied it hotly.

"No," she almost shrilled in her vexation, but he went on as though she had not spoken.

"But of course. I thought you were aware of your fine points. You are a lovely creature. I thought you hardly needed me to state the obvious. I could, of course, go on about your form, which is magnificent, your eyes, which are beguiling, your perfume, which has made my head swim more than the Framboise ever could have, your skin, which is as smooth as——"

But she did not wait for him to tick any further items from his seemingly never-ending list, as the soft cadence of his voice and the astonishingly complimentary things he was saying discomforted her almost as much as his touch had. She instead only cut him short by saying bluntly, "You are being deliberately obtuse." Growing calmer now, as the seduction he had attempted seemed to be dwindling to a discussion, she added, "I meant to say, how could you have thought that I was the sort of female who would just take to a gentleman's bed when asked?"

He made no reply to that and only stood head cocked slightly to one side. She did not give him time to answer, in any case, but went on in cold anger, "It is because my name is Amberly. It is because even though I am legitimate, I am nonetheless one of the Assortment. It is because of where I come from and the reasons why I am here tonight, is it not? You thought me just as base as yourself."

He picked up a bottle and refilled his glass, not meeting her angry stare.

"As you say," he whispered.

"Well, I shall trouble you no longer," she said bitterly. "I shall take the post back immediately in the morning. I will not stay a moment longer."

As she turned from him and gathered up her shawl, he said quietly, "Come, Amanda, do not leave in anger now. There is no further cause for it. I am suitably chastened. No purpose can be served by your flight. We shall go on as planned. You stand in no danger from me now."

She hesitated, for in truth, she feared the repercussions of a precipitate flight from him. She could even now hear the excited, scandalized comments she would receive from all the guests at her mother's house. Giles would be lost to her forever, she would be ruined, and most likely her mother would stop at nothing to achieve her connection with yet another wandering gentleman.

"No, I speak the truth, my lady, this is a safe retreat for you. I only attempted your seduction. As I mentioned at our first meeting, I do not champion rape. There is nothing I can think of at the moment which repels me more. And you may stay and sip your raspberries until dawn, for I do not take advantage of drunken or fuddled females, especially not drunken females," he said feelingly. "For that is a brute activity for swinish men. I may well not be a moral fellow, but I do have standards," he said in wounded tones. "We vile seducers have gotten a very bad name, I can see," he laughed, his swiftly changing mood lightening. "But I can think of few things more antipathetic to pleasure than either coercion or force. You do not wish to lie with me, that's clear. Let's have done with the notion then."

She paused, for his words did not ease her mood, rather they made her feel both childish and rude.

"It is not that I don't wish to . . . stay with you," she said, scarcely believing the sort of conversation she was entering into. "It is that I would not with any man. That is to say . . . why should I have to explain myself," she wondered aloud, "when any properly brought-up young woman in the land would not have to do so? Because I am an Amberly does not mean that I behave as you might have imagined. I am really quite a conventional creature, my lord. Quite as straight-laced as any female of a good family might be. I'm sorry if my name led you to believe otherwise. It has been a stigma to me all my life. I have always attempted to ignore it and thought others might do the same, but I see that I have erred."

"Of course," he said smoothly, offering her another glass of the heady liquor. "You are completely to blame. You should have informed me of your reluctance to bed me the moment you clapped eyes on me. In fact, you might even have held a pistol to my heart as you told me so."

Amanda had been seating herself, but stopped to stare at him at his words.

"No, my innocent, you see the fault does not lie in you, if indeed, fault there is in this. I presumed you were 'up to snuff,' as discreet gentlemen say, precisely for the reasons you so sweetly shouted at me before. I was a doubting Thomas, and was served the same as that unfortunate fellow for my disbelief."

He sat in the chair across from her and raised his glass in a salute.

"To peace, Amanda. I promise I will not make the same mistake twice. But," he added as he noted she did not raise her glass as well, "if I am to be completely honest, I cannot promise I will not make similar suggestions in future. I am, after all, a creature of habit. And you are, as I have said, a very taking little article. You cannot put a doe in a lion's cage and expect the creature not to swipe at her with his paw every now and again," he complained. "Some men play at hunting, some collect rare gems. I have my own methods of diversion. But if it makes you feel any better, I shall not lunge at you and you need only to put me firmly in my place, should I err again. Of course, if you ever feel so inclined at any time until the good Giles comes to claim you, to invite me to such an encounter, pray do not hesitate to mention it," he added on a hopeful note.

At that, she laughed at last and gravely lifted her glass to him. After she had taken a sip, she said earnestly, "But please, my lord——"

"Christian," he said. "At least that much forgiveness, please."

"Christian, I should feel easier in mind if you would not make such a request," she said a little plaintively.

"Don't fret. I shall honestly try." He smiled gently, watching her, his light eyes strangely luminous in the wavering firelight.

"I think," he said carefully after they had sat quietly for a space, "that we ought to talk, Amanda. As you see, I hardly know you at all. And if we are to fly the flag of an engaged couple, it would be helpful if we knew each other better, don't you agree?"

She quickly concurred, but as nothing dries up conversation faster than the all-encompassing request to tell someone about yourself, she sat dumbly, pondering what precisely she should mention first. As though he knew her predicament, he said easily, "The name has always given you trouble then?"

"Yes," she admitted, but again, as she had already told him that in quite emphatic fashion, she subsided and stared down into her glass.

"I have found," he commented idly, "that though a person grows up with a thing, there is always that precise moment when one becomes acutely aware of it. Was it that way with you?"

"Why yes," she said, "it did happen just that way."

Now she looked into the fire and avoided his eyes and let herself think back as she had not in years, for in truth, she realized that no one had ever spoken frankly with her about her infamous name. Charles had only flung it at her. Giles never did or would name the very thing that kept them apart. It was far too sensitive a subject for them both, for him to broach to her. Mama certainly never had. Father scarcely spoke to her at all. Jerome ignored it and the other children somehow avoided actually speaking of the obvious topic after their initial embarrassed laughter whenever they met. But here, sitting in the semi-dark with this libertine gentleman the subject once brought up, would not stay down again. It was now necessary that he understand her. It was now important that she hear her own explanation. The words seemed to spill forth from her, and it seemed quite a natural subject to converse about in this bizarre situation.

"I always knew that there was scandal attached to our family," she said reflectively. "I was four years old when Mama left for the first time, and five when she returned home to have Mary. I was seven when Alicia was born and by the time James came along, I was used to the fact that there was something out of the ordinary going on. But it is curious, you know, rather like growing up with a handicap. In some fashion you believe that there is nothing truly exceptional in your condition and you are constantly surprised at other people's reaction to it."

"But you were aware that it was irregular?" he prodded gently.

She scarcely attended his words as she was attempting to frame her deepest feelings in proper words. It was a novelty and a relief to at last speak freely about her burden.

"What? Oh yes," she said ruefully. "Servants chatter, you know, and all adults seem to believe that children do not grow functional ears till they attain adulthood. I knew, in the words of Cook, that we were all a 'parcel of bastards.' "

She looked up in shock at her words, as though someone else had uttered them, for she had never spoken so about her family, and thought she saw him wince slightly at her utterance. She began to utter shamefaced apologies, but he stopped her at once by saying softly,

"No, no. I can see it was what you must have heard. But there are gentler words you can use if you like. 'Wrong side of the blanket' I can see is a bit cumbersome, but 'natural child' is a kind euphemism. 'Base-born' is a bit harsh, 'illegitimate' too much of a legal phrase. 'By-blow' is altogether too violent, and 'love child' is too sentimental. Perhaps the most poetic term I ever heard was the appellation 'child of the mist.' But I can see that would be a difficult phrase to slip into easy conversation. 'Bastard' is, after all, most definitive, I fear. But go on. I am not easily shocked; in fact, I should very much like to be, just to experience the sensation again, you understand."

Over her laughter, he asked again, "But when did you understand precisely what the problem was?"

"Curiously, it was not at school," she said, slipping back into her vocal reverie. "Although other girls often alluded to my family and though it rankled, it never quite 'hit,' do you understand?" she asked, curious as to the phenomenon herself.

"Oh yes," he sighed.

"It was when I was fifteen and at Mama's for the holidays with my best friend Martha Applegate," Amanda said decisively, seeing it for herself now. "I do believe that was the first time I fully understood the matter, and fully the worst time ever before or since." And so it was, she thought in amazement, even worse than the episode with Charles had been.

She paused, looking up at him, oddly afraid to go into the matter again for her own sake as well as for reasons of propriety. He sat, still as stone, his face, what she could make of it in the shadows and fitful light of the candles and fire, unreadable.

"Oh, don't stop now," he said in a voice as low as her own thoughts, "or I shall think far worse than the truth, I promise you. I am a member of your mama's set, you know."

"It was not so shocking, I suppose," Amanda said at last, "except to me. It was simply that Martha and I were at loose ends one day. Martha's father, you see, was an admiral in His Majesty's service, and as she had no mama, and her father had been at sea a very long time, he had no objection to her staying over vacation at Kettering Manor with me. He had never heard of it, I expect. Jerome was at his friend's home and our own house would have been most inhospitable for us, father being the way he is. And the other children were younger, and we were bored with them, you see."

"I see," the viscount said in a gentle tone, "that you are reluctant to tell me what precisely happened."

"Oh," Amanda replied, surprised to discover that he was right again. "Well," she said in a rush, "we wandered into the library one afternoon in search of some books with bright pictures to copy out. Martha fancied herself an artist then. When we dragged out a huge, dusty volume from a high shelf, we discovered several identical volumes behind it. There were six of them at least, all gilt-edge, slim, green-calf-bound, expensive-looking little books. We picked one up to look at it and were amazed. They were profusely illustrated, with a picture facing each little poem— limerick actually—on every other page. The pictures were staggering to us—that is to say, they were unseemly, they . . . were to do with matters not usually illustrated," Amanda explained lamely.

"Pornographic, in short," the viscount said with laughter in his voice.

"Yes," Amanda said, relieved that she did not have to dredge up any more similes. "And we looked at them. No," she admitted fiercely, "we did not, we simply devoured them. When we saw that all the volumes were the same, Martha slipped one into her skirts and we tore upstairs to my rooms, bolted the door, and occupied ourselves with the book for hours."

Amanda looked up at her inquisitor defiantly then. But he only answered languidly, "If you were to show me a fifteen-year-old who would not do so, I should recommend him or her for canonization instantly."

She giggled at that, as though she were fifteen again, and went on a bit more confidently. "The pictures were amazing. We did not bother to read the book itself for several hours."

Amanda paused as she remembered how it had been. The room so warm (or had that been just from the flush upon her cheeks?), Martha and she stretched out upon her bed studying the illustrations. At first they had been too awed to see them aright, and then when they had done emitting their little shrieks and cries and false laughs and pummeling each other with pillows, they had gotten down to scrutinizing the details. Some were caricatures, some workmanlike, some quite well executed. They had decided at the last, though, that they all were a combination of truth and blatant lie. But now she only said, "We decided, at last, that they were exaggerated."

"Oh?" was all the reply she heard.

"That is to say," Amanda said, feeling her cheeks heating up again, as though the intervening eight years had never passed, "some of the drawings might well have been factual, but the majority of them were grossly exaggerated for effect. The females, you see, though crudely depicted, were within the realm of possibility, but the males . . . and some of the activities they were engaged in were clearly impossible because . . ."

But here Amanda's good sense returned and she left off, very dismayed at what she had almost said, lulled as she had been by the strange conversation, the late hour, and her ready listener. She could not, not even if the viscount sprouted a great pair of gossamer wings and a halo, say what she had been about to disclose. For what Martha had said actually, with all her five months' seniority for credence, was that the gentlemen could never really look so. Why, they would have to have special clothes made up to accommodate such clearly fraudulent appointments as they had been given, for they could never fit into everyday attire as they were depicted. They had then both soberly considered all the males of their acquaintance and had agreed, with much mutual relief, that such details that the artists had shown were patently ridiculous.

"It's a wonder," the viscount said in emotionless tones when she did not speak, "that the two of you didn't take yourselves off to a nunnery at once."

"Ah well, but we had surmised that all the illustrations in the entire book were similarly nonsensical," Amanda said reasonably.

"I see," the viscount replied in a stifled voice. "Do go on."

"After a while," Amanda said thoughtfully, her voice becoming rather low, "we tired of the illustrations and began to read some of the verses. We discovered from the introduction that the poems had been written as part of a contest dreamed up one night at a fashionable gentleman's club in London and had been privately printed as a joke."

"It's a common enough diversion when the brandy palls and there are no good wagers running," her listener commented.

"We took turns reading them, and those we understood were actually amusing. We didn't know half the names mentioned, though. For, you see, the book was written about all of the acquaintances of the gentlemen," Amanda said.

"I begin to understand," the viscount said as if to himself.

"First Martha read one, and then I read another," Amanda continued, surprised to note that her lips were trembling even now. "Then Martha began to read one and suddenly closed the book, looking quite conscious. I rallied her, taunted her in fact for her timidity. But she began to lecture me about what a shameful thing we were doing. When that did not stop me, she cried that she was bored with the entire project and made as if to throw the book into the fire. I flew at her, laughing, and snatched it from her hands. I began to read the poem and then I understood."

"It was, of course, about your mama," the viscount said softly.

"You read it?" Amanda asked, returning from that overheated bedroom of the past to this cozy parlor.

"No, no," he said, "I only inferred as much."

"Well, it was," she said sadly. "I read it the once and then I did fling the book into the fire. I don't remember the poem now, but the illustration showed a line of remarkable gentlemen tarrying outside a ladies' chamber. No, that's not true," Amanda said brokenly. "They were doing rather more than that. And I do remember the last two lines at least. I have never been able to forget them." Amanda recited them woodenly now, speaking them aloud for the first time since she had read them all those years ago.

". . . But she told the gentleman it wasn't important, she'd just have another one for her assortment."

"At least it scans nicely," the viscount said, handing her

a large white handkerchief as she discovered to her astonishment that she was weeping. When she had left off dabbing her face, he spoke again.

"Did you ever mention the incident to your mama?" he asked.

"How could I?" Amanda asked in shock.

"I rather think you ought to have done," he mused. "But no matter. Did you discuss it ever again with your good friend Martha?"

"Oh no," she said matter-of-factly, having gotten herself under control again, "for her father returned from the sea the following year and married some lady he had been corresponding with for years. She took Martha out of school. And as she had been in the country and was, in fact, quite social, Martha was never permitted to visit me again. I did hear that she married some few years ago herself."

"You certainly should discuss the book with her in that case. Or at least the illustrations," the viscount said obliquely.

"I always did wonder," Amanda said, suppressing a yawn as the heat of the room and the effect of the liquor was making her drowsy, "why Mama had so many copies at hand."

"I expect that she had the duke buy them up so that they could do the same thing with them that you did . . . burn them. And knowing your mama, it's reasonable to assume that she simply forgot where she had placed the remaining volumes. I'm not keeping you awake, am I?" he asked with mock affront.

"Oh no," Amanda said, "but you know, it is odd. It was such a difficult thing for me to relate, and I had never done so before. But now I've told the tale, I find it was not such a dreadful thing after all. I feel much better about the incident, in fact."

"A shared burden is always lighter," he said, rising. "Lord, you make me sound, as well as feel, like a graybeard, Amanda. But I think it is time for you to sleep. We must be up early tomorrow if we are to leave time for Cousin Emily to consume our breakfasts and still reach a

comfortable inn by evening. I think we've achieved our
purpose. I do know a great deal more about you now, and
for what it is worth, you have presented me with an
entirely new experience—embarrassment. For my own
behavior, my lady, never yours," he added as she sat up
sharply. "Now come along, let us allow our landlord to
close up."

"But you have told me nothing of yourself," Amanda
argued as she rose and went to the door with him.

"Why, there is little more to tell," he said gaily. "I am
noble, I am generous, I am truthful, I am entirely honorable,
just as you supposed."

He stood at the door with her and looked down at her.
She bore a sleepy, tousled look, like a child newly awakened from dreams.

"Now, to bed," he said adamantly.

"Yes," she agreed, gazing up at him, "let us go to bed."

"Shocking stuff, Lady Amanda," he laughed. "How
dare you suggest such a thing? How dare you attempt to
sully my honor? It must be all that scandalous literature
you read."

As he grumbled on about her attempt to smirch his
honor, she giggled. He saw her to her door, and then
bowed and left for his own room. She did not waken her
maid to attend her, as she scarcely had time to draw off
her dress and throw on her nightshift before sleep claimed
her. He went slowly into his room and lay down upon his
bed. He lay there a long while in unblinking concentration.
For he had gotten to know his fiancée very well indeed,
and he did not like the result at all.

VII

The morning came too soon to suit Amanda. She had wanted a bit of time to herself so she could sort out her feelings about her confessions to the viscount. But she had awakened late, with only enough time to spare to dress rapidly and join him and her chaperon at breakfast. While Miss Emily plowed steadily and soundlessly through a massive country breakfast, pausing in her consumption of it only to wipe her lips delicately now and again, Lord North chatted on about merry, inconsequential trivialities. His relaxed, amused attitude dispelled any doubts Amanda had harbored about her precipitous unveiling of those dark memories that she had felt would be so damning to her name and reputation. Rather than avoiding his gaze and fearing his judgment, she found herself instead very eager to continue the journey as well as any conversation with him.

In that expectation, however, she was disappointed. When the time came to resume their journey and she and Miss Emily had settled themselves in the lead carriage, the viscount saluted them, closed the carriage door, and mounted his horse alone again. Since it was a lowering day, with thick gray clouds scuttling overhead, propelled by icy blasts of wind, Amanda worried that her narrative had given him such a distaste for her that he preferred to risk pneumonia rather than to continue to abide her company. But after a half hour's travel, in which she was only able to extract such information from Miss Emily as the conditions of her bed and the excellence of the breakfast, Amanda readily understood the viscount's reluctance to sit with them. Indeed, when Miss Emily, in a rare burst of conversational bravery, volunteered unbidden that the repast she had just partaken of was—dared she say it—delightful, Amanda found herself envying the solitude of Lord North, storm-tossed and wind-blown though he was.

That gentleman did not think himself an object of envy, however; neither did he enjoy the cutting wind and cold. But it was not Miss Emily's deadening presence that made him eschew transport within the warm carriage, no matter what his sham fiancée might imagine. She would have been, in fact, devastated to learn that her worst fears were founded on solid truth. For it was her own person that the viscount wished to avoid, and he would at this moment endure the bite of a blizzard's teeth, rather than hear one more syllable dropped from her own soft lips.

He had thought that he would get to know her at their stopover at the Fox and Grapes, and that he had. But he had imagined their method of acquaintance would be achieved in a more physical manner. He had accepted that she might not wish to bed him when he was an unknown thrust upon her by her impatient mama. If he had balked at such a deed, he could certainly understand her doing so. Similarly, he understood very well that she might not wish to marry him, especially if she were aiming for another's declaration as well as feeling coerced. But he had been genuinely staggered to discover that she was an innocent, and fully as circumspect as any properly brought-up young female.

It was not often that he misjudged a woman, and the thought of it gnawed at him. She was obviously no chit straight from the schoolroom, she had seemed up to all the rigs. She was bright and lovely. He had thought she was, inescapably, her mother's daughter. It was clear from her reactions to him that she was well aware of him, and she had seemed to be playing the game just the way she ought, in just the way that most delighted him. She had gazed at him when he wasn't looking, had dropped her lashes over her large gray eyes when he turned to return her interested stare. She had sat close to him while they composed that ridiculous letter, letting her curls brush against his cheek, while appearing to be heedlessly letting other parts of her enchanting person brush against him as well. Her spicy perfume had filled his nostrils, as she laughed appreciatively at sallies that were too warm for conventional misses. And all of this, it transpired, instead of being the coy prelude to the bliss he had imagined, had been unknowing acts of friendship.

Lord North shook his head, as though to throw off the first flakes of snow that had settled upon his cheeks. She had not been provocative, she had merely been candid. There was no doubt of that now in his mind. He had been able to fill in most of the gaps in her narration, and no experienced female could have told her tale the way that she had done. Though the story had begun by titillating him enormously, it had ended with his realization of the fact that she had not planned that effect. Bizarre as it might be, he had come to the incredible but inescapable conclusion that the Countess of Clovelly's eldest daughter was as pure as the snow that was now driving into his face.

He shrugged, dislodging some of the flakes that had covered his shoulders. His mistake was explicable, he supposed, only because it had been so many years since he had any dealings with unworldly misses that they were as exotic a breed to him as unicorns were. And that was why he rode on alone and safely apart from her, pondering what his future course of action should be toward her, rather than taking refuge in the warm carriage.

It was not that he was sulking over her refusal of his intimate attentions, for he was experienced enough to take rejection philosophically, and seldom personally. But then, he seldom encountered refusal. He was not a vain fellow, but he would have had to have been a deaf and dumb one not to have long since realized the effect he had upon persons of Amanda's gender. And unlike most beautiful men, he was a skillful lover, well able to attach a female beyond the stages of first attraction. Too often beautiful specimens of both sexes thought it enough to simply present their splendid selves in a state of readiness to their admirers in order to bring about blissful mutual satisfaction.

The viscount, for all his famous physical attributes, knew better. Amanda herself had reminded him that he had learned the truth in a very hard school.

He had been eighteen and home from school on a vacation, at loose ends just as Amanda and her curious friend Martha had been when they discovered their educational volume, and almost as naive as they were, when he had discovered a good deal more explicit compendium of sexual information. All of it had been encompassed in the one compact shape of Helena Burnham's ripe person. Squire Burnham was a near neighbor and young Christian Jarrow had noted his wife's blond beauty from afar for most of his green years. Yet, for all of a young man's arrogance, he still would never have dared to include Helena in any of his fevered dreams of future conquest, as she was a friend of his parents. Although she was a decade younger than his own mama, he was at an age that considered any beings above the age of consent to be teetering upon the brink of eternity. In fact, he recalled now as he rode forward in the snow, and backward in his musings, he had even called her "Mrs. Burnham" the first time he lay in her arms.

He had arrived in those smooth bonds speedily enough, though through no efforts of his own. He had encountered her while out riding. He had accepted an invitation to tea politely, though privately dreading the idea of a nice long coze with one of his parents' contemporaries as only a lad of his age could have done. But he had instead surprised himself by ending up upon her silken sheets and body before a proper tea had had time to brew. Her husband had been away, the servants were trained to her command, and the seduction was effortlessly accomplished.

Although, he thought now with the accumulated wisdom of over a decade's experience, the only task more difficult than seducing a lad of eighteen might be that of breathing in and out, still she had been adept. She had soothed his fears by expressing her need for him, and quelled his conscience by telling of her husband's inabilities. In the main, she had prevailed through the sheer rapidity and expertise of her assault. He left her home dazzled and more delighted than even Cousin Emily could have expressed. He had known that such encounters might be pleasurable; indeed, at eighteen he had thought of little else. But aside from a few unsatisfactory embraces with serving girls, he had not yet accomplished his goals for further education in that area. Helena Burnham taught him what a truly overwhelming experience such sport could provide. Aside from the genuine joy derived from his encounter, he rode homeward feeling omnipotent, whole, and totally a man at last. He grinned now at the thought of how very young he had been.

Yet, even as his visits to her increased at her demand, he discovered his belief in himself shaken by her demands. At first she required only his cooperation, which was then all that he could give to her. But she soon began to require him to attain more polish. As the summer dragged on, she drilled him in the arts of love as a stern nanny might train a toddler in the art of table manners. The young Christian Jarrow had been by turns abashed at his lack of skill, appalled at some of the lessons, ashamed of his reluctance to apply himself, and finally resolved to do better.

He had been glad of a consuming interest away from home and willingly became her apprentice. Long July twilights were passed tracing her lush curves with the focused intent of a navigator studying complex charts of strange sea lanes, whole drowsy August afternoons elapsed as he labored to cull each last secret from her well memorized body. If he wondered at her husband's convenient absence or at her tutorial skills, the issues were soon forgotten in the narcotic haze of the wonder of her lessons. They spent the summer together, locked every stolen moment in mute and concentrated effort.

It was on a late August afternoon, while preparing for a tryst, that he noted he had retied his cravat six times because of his shaking fingers. He had dropped his hands and gazed into space. He was, he realized, facing an amorous encounter with anxiety and stomach-churning dread. He discovered himself suddenly no more eager to embrace her than he was to have a tooth drawn. Visions of her stretched out upon her bed brought equal parts of arousal and apprehension, and he knew that he could predict her future sighs of contentment as surely as he could foretell her terse, strained orders of command. At once, he saw that, for him at least, desire had coupled with duty. She had become, at last, a chore.

He had been many things in his brief span, but never insensitive to the feelings of others. He was puzzled that this discovery of distaste and an ache to be free of his lover should be a relief untainted by guilt or sentiment. But even at the age of eighteen he had come to the understanding that they had no thing to bind them together beyond the adhesive of physical desire. They had no laughter to bind up lapses, no mutual sympathy to gloss over mistakes, no conversation to fill up resting spaces, no affection to spur on desire past repletion. He strove to acquit himself well, she strove to teach him to please her, and that was the sum of their relationship. It was both not enough and far too much for him.

He completed his toilet speedily that evening, suddenly all haste to keep his appointment with her and, by meeting with her, end their meetings forever.

She evidently had not expected him so soon. She obviously had not expected the malice of her servants. But after the oddly sympathetic butler had shown him into a parlor to await his mistress's pleasure, he could clearly hear the conversation she was having with her husband in the adjacent room through a conveniently carelessly open door. It was a revelation to him to hear his abilities being discussed frankly in dispassionate detail. It was almost as though he had eavesdropped on two of his dons debating whether or not he was to have a passing grade in a difficult course of study. Squire Burnham clearly derived as much pleasure from the telling of his wife's experiences as she did from the having of them.

He was, at least, pleased to hear that he had done well. Better, in fact, than young Graham, their steward's son, had done the previous spring. It was flattering to know that she found his performance matched his appearance. But it was decidedly unpleasant to learn of their byzantine plans for his further enjoyment and enlightenment. When he appeared in the doorway, they broke off at once, and turned to him in guilty amazement, like footpads caught squabbling over the contents of a corpse's purse. He bade them good evening, told them he was afraid that he had pressing engagements that made his visit impossible to extend, bowed, and left them there almost as astonished as he was by his aplomb.

Although he deliberately avoided both Burnhams scrupulously on every subsequent visit home, as the years passed he discovered that he was grateful to them. He was enormously successful with women, for he had learned a great deal from his eighteenth summer. He never pursued a married lady again, no matter how delicious she might appear to be, but that was advantageous only to his fellow man. Most beneficial to his own well-being, he had learned that the arts of love were intricate and important, but useless to employ without some vestige at least of fellow feeling between the participants. Though he did not consider himself remotely moral, he shrank from ever using any individual for his own needs as he had been used. So he could easily understand Amanda's anger at his intentions for their evening's entertainment. If she were not so inclined, it would be unthinkable for him to harass her to join him.

The viscount frowned now, and not because of the steadily falling snow. He had offered the chit his support partially because he found her desirable and had thought they might have an amusing time of it together for so long as their bogus betrothal lasted. Now he found himself in the unpleasant situation of entertaining fully as charming and amiable a companion as he could have wished, but one who was unexpectedly chaste as well. He was like a man who had acquired a thirst for a vintage wine he could not afford. Yet he could not place blame upon her for deceiving him, nor even any upon himself for self-deception. It was a maddening business.

When the snow had powdered his hair enough to make him resemble some exquisite fop from a long vanished court, he shook his head to clear it within and without. Though she was blameless, he could not repress a surge of impatience with her. But as it was growing cold enough to turn his thoughts from his dilemma to his comforts again, he prepared to leave off his solitary introspection and face her again. He would help to write such compelling letters to her damned doubting Giles, he determined, that he would soon have her off his hands. Yet, he reminded himself lightly as he signaled the coachman to halt so that he could effect entry into warmer precincts, it might yet be true that blood would tell. And if by some happy chance, the viscount decided as he greeted his cousin and his fiancée with a broad grin, all that dubious Giles feared were to materialize, and the young Lady Amanda's heritage should manifest itself at last, why then, he would be please to accommodate her and help her to fulfill her destiny.

No matter what his intentions, the viscount did not have a great deal of time to tarry in light conversation within the snug confines of the carriage. It was not long before the coachman staged an unscheduled halt to their journey to have conference as to the advisability of traveling much further onward in the snow. The sloping hills of the lake district were scenic enough in summer, but treacherous when coated with the rimes of winter. The driver of the lead coach swore on his forty years of man and boy that the snowfall would not last, even as the handler of the second coach maintained that his four and fifty years of experience, along with his aching bones, told him that their world would be white wilderness by evening.

The viscount, fearing that they all would freeze to death while the argument raged on, settled matters by declaring they would stop at once at the King's Arms a few miles further along the pike rather than pushing on to their scheduled accommodations. The hostelry, he confided to the ladies, while never so fine as the Fox and Grapes, would at least provide shelter and food for the wayfarers.

It provided little else, Amanda sighed, that evening at dinner. Only Miss Emily seemed to be making any headway with the stringy roast, and not even she could swallow the vinegar that passed for wine.

There was no uncomfortable reminscence before the fire that night. Nor was there any comfortable chat either.

The fireplace in the private parlor gave off foul exhalations of black smoke whenever the wind changed, which it did with frequency. It was small consolation to the travelers that the winds now did little more than toy with the snow that had ceased to fall, for they were committed to stay the night. It was then as much to avoid Miss Emily's constant gentle lamentations over their faulty decision to stop at such an insalubrious place as it was to escape the stifling puffs of wood smoke, that both Amanda and her fiancé resolved to retire early. Despite her icy bed and a breakfast fit only for livestock, however, Amanda had cause to be grateful for the viscount's decision. Because of their unscheduled stop and even earlier departure, when she came at last to Windham House, it was a shining morning.

She would always, she thought, remember the house as it was in that first moment that she saw it. Windham House stood high on a gentle hill and as the trees around it were bare, she could see its entire face with its myriad windows glittering like bits of ice in the dazzling light. The house was old, and as each succeeding generation had indulged its whims upon its form, it now rose high and stretched wide, the only unifying thing about it the soft golden hue of its stone facade. Beyond and behind, the absence of foliage permitted the viewer to see the brilliant blue of the long lake the house's terraced grounds rambled down to meet.

Amanda did not even hear Miss Emily's excited prattle as the viscount assisted her from the coach. She walked bemused as he led her through the doors of his home. She said nothing as she surrendered her wraps to a footman and followed her host to a high-ceilinged salon. While Miss Emily nattered on, the viscount stayed silent as well, watching Amanda as she stood and gazed out the long windows, looking out over the wide lake to the gray and purple mountains in the distance. When she tore her rapt gaze from the scenery and looked around herself with an expression of awe, he thought her enthralled by the spectacular scenery.

But he could never have guessed at her thoughts. For as she stood and took in her surroundings, she thought that

she might have known that such a unique man would have
sprung from such a magical place. The room, she thought,
the entire bright house, was the perfect setting for its
master. This house, his home, was equally as much an
idiosyncratic blend of sunlight and grace as he himself was.
It was as though his heritage had given him his own
unique facade. The hues of the lake were reflected in his
odd eyes, his flaxen hair was like the glint of sunlight
upon its changing waters. As he was a creature com-
pounded of light and air, so was Windham House. Never
had she seen or imagined such a perfect blending, such a
sympathetic aspect of dwelling and resident spirit.

Miss Emily kept reassuring them that their hostess would
be along presently, and Amanda sat on the edge of a
chair to await her entrance. The viscount, however, seemed
restless, and he wandered from table to window to mantel,
like a mote of golden light trapped within the sparkling
room. Amanda was so anxious about how she would be
received that when a person she took to be the housekeeper
entered the room, she stood at once. She was glad she had
done so when Miss Emily cried out, "Oh, Augusta, how
good to see you again."

As Amanda tried to hide her surprise, Miss Emily went
on to congratulate her hostess on how well she looked, and
to inform her of how pleasant a journey it had been.
Amanda was grateful for the steady flow of meaningless
compliments and tedious detail of their travels, for she
never would have guessed that this woman was the Viscountess North and might have only greeted her and asked
which room she should repair to if she had not been told of
her identity.

The Viscountess North stood rooted to the spot as Miss
Emily talked, and though she seemed to attend to what
was being said, her eyes sought her son, who gave a
helpless shrug along with a wry smile of greeting, and then
she looked quickly at Amanda and then quickly away
again. She was a short, solidly made female, of a height with
Amanda's own mama, but lacking that lady's pleasant
configurations. She also possessed some decades' more years
than the countess counted. Her hair might have been black

in youth, but now was mottled with gray. Her face was
lined and broad, olive-skinned with thick brows above
alert dark black eyes. She made no concession to fashion
and wore a simple heavy purple garment, partially covered
with a beige fringed shawl. Lord North, Amanda thought,
must have taken after his father's side of the family, for
there was no feature of the viscountess's that could trans-
late to her son's appearance.

When Miss Emily paused for breath, Lord North took
advantage of the lapse in conversation and went to his
mother's side.

"Mama," he said softly, raising her hand to bow over it,
"behold the prodigal son."

Before she could greet him, he went on smoothly, "It is
obvious that you have not received my letter. May I present to you then my fiancée, whom I have brought to visit
with us? Yes, it is true. I have been nabbed at last. I do
not know if word of mouth travels faster than my poor
missive, but I assure you that it is the talk of the town. I
returned from the continent, stopped off for a space at my
dear friend the Countess of Clovelly's charming abode,
and there I met and lost my heart to this dear lady."

Lord North came to Amanda's side, took her hand, and
brought her face to face with the viscountess. That lady
stood stock-still, expressionless, as her son continued.

"And here is the young woman who captured my heart
in one blinding assault upon it. Can you blame me for my
precipitous action? Her face, her form, her person are all
that one could wish for in a wife. How could I bear to wait
upon events? I had to act with haste. May I present my
lady, Lady Amanda Amberly."

Amanda was so close to the viscountess that she could
perceive her slightest expression. But the change Lord
North's words brought upon his mama's controlled countenance was not difficult to ascertain even from afar. Un-
mistakably, Amanda saw the lady wince.

VIII

There is a suitable time of day for every human purpose. The glare of full sunlight is best reserved for those acts of decency, honor, and valor. Most clandestine meetings are better left to be carried out in the dark of night, and twilight is an excellent time for romance. There is a good cause for this division of activity. It is easier to plan deeds of secrecy or commit acts requiring fantasy when there is some difficulty reading one's companion's face clearly. It is no coincidence then that sermons are best given on Sunday mornings and that actors prefer the inconstant flickering flare of footlights in which to create their illusions. Therefore, it was unfortunate, Amanda was to think many times later, that the viscount chose the sunniest spot in the brilliantly lit room in which to tell his mama of his fiancée's identity.

But her governess had the right of it, Amanda thought sadly, as she stood dumbly and waited for the viscountess to acknowledge her existence, breeding will tell. For if in one moment, her fiancé's mama looked so ill at the announcement of her son's betrothal that her dark face became several shades lighter and her lips compressed to a thin line, within the passage of two heartbeats the lady had erased the fleeting expression of pain. She soon was in control again and even in the unrelenting light her expression was unreadable. It was well that the viscountess had such great powers of recovery, Amanda thought, for she herself cringed at Lord North's next careless words.

"Yes, just so, Mama. The dear countess's own daughter.

How singularly convenient for me, don't you agree? But come, aren't you going to wish us happy?" he asked sweetly.

The viscountess put out a blunt little hand and took Amanda's.

"I am pleased to meet you, Lady Amanda," she said in a low, emotionless voice, "and hope that you find Windham House most comfortable."

While Amanda was glad that she hadn't been subjected to false cries of happiness, the patently artificial smile that the lady now wore made her sick to the heart. She was tempted to cry out, "It's none of it true, he is safe from me," but found that she could only take the older woman's hand and shake it politely.

The viscountess seemed about to speak again, but whatever she might have said was lost when a hearty voice cut through her hesitant beginning words. A stocky young man bustled into the room and headed directly for Lord North.

"Chris!" he shouted, and then tumbled upon the viscount, hugging him and pummeling him upon the back, while saying in a loud and happy voice, "Chris, you devil. How good it is to have you back!"

The young man was a head shorter than the viscount, but almost twice as broad. Although not fat, he was compact and seemed to be of hearty stock, resembling a smith or yeoman farmer rather than the gentleman his neat clothing denoted. When he turned his attention from Lord North to look at Amanda, she could see his resemblance to the viscountess was so singular as to be almost caricatured. His complexion was swarthier as he seemed to have been tanned from the sun, but his broad face, jet hair, and dark eyes marked him as her descendant as surely as if she had decided to manufacture a masculine replica of herself.

"And here's the pretty lady, eh?" the young gentleman cried. "Make me known to her at once, Chris, so I can buss her soundly. I won't have another chance till the wedding, I vow. For I don't want you coming to cuffs with me. When I heard the news—we had it from Boggins, you know, the fellow takes all the London papers, not like us rustics—I thought I would burst with impatience till I saw her. I know she'd have to be a stunner to nobble such a care-for-nothing as you. And so she is, Chris, so she is."

The young man stood, hands linked behind himself, rocking back and forth upon his heels, smiling hugely.

"Amanda, let me make you known to my mannerless bother of a brother, Gilbert, for he won't leave off talking until I do. Gil, my impetuous friend, this is Lady Amanda Amberly, my intended wife."

Amanda found herself engulfed in a bearlike embrace just as Lord North had been, even down to the detail of being thumped soundly upon the back as well, as Gilbert chortled in her ear, "Delightful. Lovely. Chris has found himself a charmer, all right and tight."

"Leave off, Gilbert, do," Lord North said languidly, "or the poor lady will not survive until her wedding day. She's not used to such enthusiasm."

Gilbert released her reluctantly.

"Very well, Chris. She's yours to command, but what sort of welcome is this, Mama?" he demanded. "Break out the champagne, let's have a toast. Chris, you must tell me what you've been doing these last years, aside from winning yourself such a prize. Are you going to take up residence here at last? Or are you going to hop off about the world again with poor Amanda in tow? And did you really meet with Bonaparte? What was Vienna like?"

As all these questions were asked imperatively, with appropriate changes of expression for each, Amanda was relieved that she could giggle under cover of Lord North's genuine laughter.

"Have done, Gilbert. We'll have time enough to talk. For now, aren't you going to feed us? For we've had to make a stopover at the King's Arms, and we're dwindling to skeletons after being treated to their fare."

As Gilbert made an outsize grimace of distaste, his mother spoke quietly, "Of course, Christian. In fact, I was about to ask that you join us for luncheon. Perhaps, Lady Amanda, you will want to go to your room to change? And Emily, I'll have your usual room prepared."

*   *   *

Luncheon was lavish, and Amanda was relieved to discover that between Gilbert's constant questioning of his brother and Miss Emily's rambling discourse on their journey with her hostess, she herself was required to contribute little to the conversation. Things had gone more smoothly than she could have hoped. Her hostess was polite, no pointed questions had been asked, her room was cheerful and pleasantly appointed, nothing could have been more congenial than this family meal. Yet still, she could not shake her feelings of disquiet.

She turned her attention to her plate, telling herself that if she looked for unpleasantness, she would surely find it. Gilbert continued to quiz his brother, and she realized as she listened to them that she was learning a great deal about the viscount that she had never thought to ask, or ever thought she had the right to ask. She had not known the extent to which he had traveled or the many famous persons he had encountered and called friend. When Gilbert saw that his questions had her attention as well, he left off his inquisition of his brother long enough for that gentleman to attend to his soup.

"He thinks he's such a sly boots," Gilbert said with enthusiasm, "but just think of the places he has visited, Amanda. Paris, Venice, Vienna, and Elba itself. He cannot pull the wool over my eyes; he was in His Majesty's service unless I miss my guess. What I wouldn't have given to have been there, but I doubt I could have kept my mission secret, I haven't the knack for deception he's got."

"For your somewhat skewed compliment, I thank you," his brother drawled, laying down his spoon. "But though I dislike puncturing your bubble, old fellow, I beg you to think on how successful a spy a fellow with my rather distinctive phiz could be. Can you not just hear one agent whispering to another, 'Oh yes, North has the plans, he's the fellow with the pied eyes and the yellow hair.' No, Gilbert, I'd make too fine a target for army service and far too noticeable a one for any havey-cavey business with cloaks and daggers."

"As you say," Gilbert replied gaily, laying a finger aside his nose and winking hugely at Amanda.

If the viscount was uncomfortable with the topic, it was not apparent, but as he swiftly and adroitly turned the subject to the party where he had met Amanda, she wondered if his brother had not indeed hit upon a clue to his wanderings about on the face of the continent. She did not refine upon it too much for she was soon too fixed in her embarrassment at the tale he told. As he described her mama's house party to his avid listener, Gilbert, Amanda became aware that as Miss Emily attacked her repast in silent concentration, her hostess was now listening carefully to his discourse as well.

"Oh yes," the viscount carelessly continued to answer to his brother's queries, helping himself to a cut of lamb, "the Marquess of Bessacarr was there as well, but only for the one night of the engagement ball. He's far too slippery a fellow to linger longer. But Baron Hightower was there, as you'd expect, as well as the vicar, the lords Skyler and Jeffrey and their set, Prendergast and his latest female, Melissa Careaux, Julia Johnson and her cronies, a few fillies from the opera, Hartford, Barrymore, Cumberland, the lords Lambert, Hunt, and Lawrence, and Count Voronov. Oh, masses of people. Have I left anyone out, my dear?" he asked Amanda.

As she sat, too mortified to speak, for he had just named some of the most notorious rakes, roués and lightskirts in the land, he went on blithely, "I must have. There were hundreds, Gil, hundreds there to celebrate our betrothal. Suffice it to say, almost everyone that I know was there."

From the grim set of the viscountess's lips, Amanda knew that lady was well aware of the nature of each of the guests her son had named. Surely, Amanda thought, the viscount perceived that fact as well, but he continued to speak in just as easy a fashion.

"Oh, the Dowager Duchess of Crewe was not there. Pity, for she and her companions do liven a party. But I hear that she's planning to go to Paris, and doubtless her preparations for the journey accounted for her missing out on such a gala. But almost all of them are to be off for a jaunt on the continent soon. I question their judgment. From what I saw of Bonaparte, I should think there's a dance left in the old boy yet. But luckily, most of my other acquaintances were still in town and able to come to us for the festivities. How delightful it was," he mused, while his brother sat red-faced. It was not from embarrassment upon his part, but Amanda could not know that. It was only that there were several other questions he yearned to ask, but knew were improper to broach among the ladies. In fact, he wondered if some of the mere names his brother had stated were proper to mention in his mother's presence. He quickly brought up the topic of estate matters that he believed the viscount had not been informed of by their agent in their usual exchanges of letters and the conversation went forth easily once more.

The only other uncomfortable moment during the luncheon was for Gilbert alone, when the viscount inquired sweetly, at the one moment when his brother had put so much cutlet into his mouth that he had to pause in his steady stream of questioning, "Not that I'm not ecstatic at seeing you, dear boy, but oughtn't you be up at school now?"

Amanda was equally as taken aback as Gilbert at the question. For though the gentleman was clearly youthful, there was so much in his manner of hearty, bluff country squire that she had forgotten that he was indeed still of an age to require schooling.

"Deuce take it, Chris," Gilbert answered when he was able to both frame the words and swallow his morsel, "I thought you knew. Well, the sum of it is that the university and I agreed to part company. That is to say, fiend seize it, Chris, I ain't no scholar and never will be. Mama agrees, and even Papa said as much when I was a tyke. You're the astute one in the family, Chris, and a lucky thing that one of us is, at that. I've no head for Greek or Latin. I help to run the estates now, you know, and I've a flair for it," he said defensively.

"We'll discuss it later," the viscount promised coolly, as his mama sat up stiffly and his brother squirmed.

But clearly, no one thing could depress Gilbert's spirits for too long, and the luncheon continued as he dominated the conversation with his constant questioning of his brother.

When the last dish had been cleared, the viscountess rose. "I think we ought to allow Lady Amanda to become acquainted with Windham House," she began to say, when Gilbert leaped to his feet and cried with approval,

"The very thing! Come, Amanda, I'll show you around the place."

"I think," the viscountess continued, as though she had not been interrupted, "that Christian should do so."

"An excellent suggestion, Mama," Lord North said with equal coolness. "Gilbert, we'll speak later, but as her fiancé, I do think I should have the honor of introducing my lady to our house."

At Gilbert's totally crestfallen aspect, the viscount continued more gently, "You shall, no doubt, grow to know her even better than I do now, for I can't think how anyone can resist your exuberance. But I can't risk having you steal her out from under my nose on her very first day with us, can I?"

As Gilbert protested his innocence in the matter of attempting to turn the affections of beautiful young affianced females, albeit with a gratified flush at the compliment upon his cheeks, Lord North went to Amanda and offered her his arm.

"Shall we take a tour, my lady?" he asked quietly, but with such underlying meaning larded into those few simple words that Amanda nodded and took his arm at once.

But she thought later, she had misread him, for there was no undercurrent of double meaning in his conversation as they strolled through the house, nor did he ever attempt to take her aside for any private conversation. He greeted the household staff cordially, and took the congratulations of cook, housekeeper, butler, and maids with the same pleased containment as they wandered through the rooms. He was at ease with them as if he had been gone only a day. But Amanda could see from their wide smiles and shining eyes that he was genuinely and warmly welcomed back to his home.

He led her through the entire house, pausing only to point out interesting or historical data as they toured. They went from wine cellar to kitchens, from state bedrooms to ballroom, with his knowledgeable commentary given in as detached and informative a fashion as any paid tour guide at the London tower.

When they had seen almost the whole of the house, and Amanda was dizzy with wonder, and hoarse with exclaiming over the beauty of the red salon or the orangery or the Chinese room or the music room, he at last paused.

"Shall we go outside?" he asked, as though to himself. "Ah no, for there is still a great deal of snow underfoot and I notice you have no pattens. I doubt my Wellington's would fit you, and I hesitate to waken your hostess from her afternoon nap to borrow hers. We shall have to leave the maze and the rose gardens for another day. I think then," he said as though the idea had just occurred to him and amused him deeply, "that I will show you to the portrait gallery. I know," he went on as he led her out of the conservatory to a long gallery lined with alternate mirrors and portraits, "that such a gallery ought to be viewed at night with the aid of a flickering taper, for dramatic emphasis. But we shall have to make do with afternoon light."

The gallery was situated in the very heart of the house, constructed parallel to so many of the rooms they had visited that Amanda was surprised that they had not happened upon it before. It seemed to her that he had deliberately saved it for last, avoiding it until their tour around the rest of the house had been completed.

There were no dark or gloomy chambers in all of Windham House. It was as if each person who had dwelt there had loved the land so much that they insisted their house open its eyes constantly to the beauty that surrounded it. Every room had windows either facing the landscape, or cantilevered so as to admit the light from every angle and direction. But even so, the force of the light in the narrow hall was so strong as to hurt the eye, for the row of mirrors threw back the afternoon sunlight in almost blinding fashion.

"This passage is the result of some ancestor's attempt to bring Versailles to the lake district," Lord North said on a smile. "Our squint lines pay the price of his ambition. The family, at least, does not hang in some deserted, musty, forgotten hallway. I find it a bit overwhelming, but they must approve of their condition, for we never have had so much as one disgruntled spirit prowling about disturbing our slumbers demanding further shade."

Amanda left his side and slowly paced the gallery, scrutinizing each portrait. There were gentlemen in ruffs, powder and patch with their ladies in opulent dresses, ball gowns, and morning robes. There were faces from every past period of history, in every condition and stage of life. Haughty faces, delicate poetical visages, happy and thoughtful studies, proud and shy subjects; the rows of ladies and gentlemen, with their infants and lap dogs, stared out of the canvases at the lake and grounds around them.

Lord North watched as Amanda sought something from each encounter with the ancestrial portraits.

"The title," he commented as he walked along with her, "came late. It wasn't till James sat upon the throne that we could boast a viscountcy. There, that's the fortunate fellow who won it for us, the chap all in mustard yellow and flounces. He was thick as thieves with our royal highness and I shudder to think what price he paid for the honors. But there were Jarrows here upon this site, I imagine, from the beginning. I expect there were some hiding in the marshes, painted blue, and muttering darkly as the Romans first came marching across the land. It is a pity that none of the druids were handy with a brush and palette, isn't it?"

Amanda scarcely attended him. She had been gazing at each representative of his family attempting to find a match with his own unique visage. There were some gentlemen with his light musculature, a few of both genders with fair hair, but no face with his eyes, nor any with his crown of dandelion hair. As if he had overheard her thoughts, he said, from close by her elbow, "No, you won't have the distinctive thrill of seeing me, or what appears to be me, decked out in the costume of an earlier era. I know that's the staple stuff of eerie romantic novels, but as we lack ghosts, alas, so I must deny you that treat as well. But you should have expected that."

She turned to him in puzzlement but he went on, "Thi

last fellow here is the last viscount, fittingly enough. I came into the title when I was twenty and have never had the leisure nor the inclination to pose for any portrait. But here is his lady wife as well. Gilbert will doubtless hang beside them with the rest, 'ere long, that is, if anyone can get him to sit still long enough."

The viscountess, Amanda noted, had never been fashionable, not even in her youth when the portrait had been executed, and the artist had wisely not attempted to make her so. The portrait showed her sitting serene and dignified, her black hair about her shoulders, her figure even then wisely concealed beneath a great many folds of apricot fabric. But it was while she was looking at the painting of the gentleman Lord North had designated his father that Amanda began unwittingly to frown. The gentleman was slim, tall, and lightly made. But his hair was a light brown and in the clear light of the outdoors that he had been posed against, she could see, by peering into the picture, that his eyes were a deep chocolate brown.

Lord North had been observing Amanda's face as closely as she had scrutinized the portrait.

"Didn't you know?" he asked suddenly, in a strangely altered voice. She tore her gaze from the portrait and looked at him questioningly. He stood before her now, blotting out the sun.

"No?" he asked tauntingly. "No, I should have guessed as much. It's all of a piece, isn't it? Lady Clovelly's daughter is indeed nothing like her mother or her mother's boon companions. Then it is well that I took you for this little tour today."

He lowered his voice and looked down at her with something very much like cold anger in his gaze.

"Have you no ears, child?" he demanded. "Do you hear no evil as well as never seeing or doing it? Dear Amanda, why did you think your estimable mother was so quick to bundle me into your bed? Why me, of all the light lads she entertains? And why, little Amanda, did you think all our well-wishers were quick to cry, 'How suitable!' 'How perfect!' and comment upon how well matched we were? Did you never ponder it?"

Amanda could only shake her head. She could not understand his bitter mockery, for his face was as chill and composed as that of any painted portrait upon the wall, and his voice was heavy with sarcasm.

She looked at him in alarm, as he seemed so furious with her. She did recall random tatters of gossip about him that had come to her ears, but they were only bits and pieces of talk that she had forgotten, or caused herself to forget after they had made their plans. She knew he was said to be profligate, immoral, and abandoned. She had refused to countenance a true alliance with him for that reason. And as all the members of his wild set had a nickname, she also knew that he was referred to jestingly as "The Vice-Count North." But although she now had a glimmering of a dreadful idea, she still dared not imagine what he was implying, not here with him staring at her as though into her very mind.

She stood before him, twisting her hands in the folds of her azure skirts, her huge tilted eyes blank with dread, her curly head raised to meet his gaze. She seemed to him like some fragile sprite pinioned by the shafts of sunlight as she awaited his next words. He found himself perversely growing even angrier as he realized that in this, too, he had misjudged her.

"Why it's a delicious bit of tattle, Lady Amanda," he said savagely, "this business of our engagement. One of the Amberly Assortment to wed the base Lord North. Exquisite irony. You have totally missed the joy of it. It was there in my mama's face, and if you had tried, you could have certainly read it in Gilbert's open countenance. It is here for you to see, Amanda, only open those great gray eyes of yours to look at it."

He swept his hand to encompass the whole of the passage, then he took her tousled head between his two hands to hold her fast and look down into her apprehensive eyes.

"Amanda, my dear fiancée," he said with a twisted smile, "my reputation is based on more than mere rumor. You ought to have paid attention to those rumors instead of holding yourself above them, for they are nothing but the truth. I can see now that you know it, but you dare not voice it. Yes, I am one of those unfortunates we were discussing so amiably the other night. One of those you were so quick to disassociate yourself from. Twice you denied it, I believe. But I admit it. I am one of those chaps from your little picture book. I am a by-blow, sweet, a fellow from the wrong side of the blanket, a child of the mist. No, as I am a viscount, I expect I am rather higher than that, I am a lord of the mist. And all the world knows it but you. That is the great jest we've all shared. Amanda, my dear, don't shrink from me, for I am already like a member of your famous family," he said caressingly now, as he lowered his head. "Dear 'Manda, I am a bastard," he whispered against her lips.

IX

The study had a large bow window which presented a fine view of the lake and the mountains in the distance. Since the lady seated at the rosewood desk paused, pen in hand, while she gazed out at the few birds that wheeled and spun in the distance, a viewer could be forgiven if he guessed her a poetess waiting patiently for inspiration to strike from the blue. As the young woman also wore an abstracted air, while her petal-pink gown bore spatters of ink and almost a sheaf of papers lay crumpled about her, one might also have concluded that her muse was not in a cooperative mood.

Amanda at last turned her head resolutely from the bright winter prospect and set her pen to paper again. For all her morning's labors, the letter to Giles had only progressed to a total of two pages and there was more, so much more she wanted to include. But she could not write the simple two lines that would have said it all and had instead to couch those plain phrases in so much roundabout that she was only half done with her chore. She found herself wishing that she had the sort of bond of communion with Giles that could have enabled her to merely write: "I have made a dreadful mistake. Please come and fetch me home immediately. All my love, Amanda."

She sighed so heavily the piece of paper she was writing upon stirred beneath her hand. It was so much simpler for her to simply say a thing directly rather than to attempt all this subterfuge. That night at the Fox and Grapes, Lord North had written an excellent letter with ease. But then, she thought, frowning at the very idea of her mock fiancé, hidden meanings and deceptive wordings seemed to come to him as naturally as breathing. So it was that the words that intruded upon the silence exactly matched her unspoken complaints.

"Wouldn't it be simpler and less time-consuming to simply scrawl 'Help!' in huge letters, sign the thing in tears, and post it to Giles immediately?" Lord North said, as he strolled into the room and over to her desk. "But that, alas, would most likely cause the poor fellow to run for cover thinking you'd lost your wits entirely. It's clear you need my assistance, for you haven't the least knack for deception. You've been mewed up in here for hours and all you've done is to create enough kindling to keep the fire blazing merrily for the rest of the afternoon. I waited patiently for your summons. And when you didn't emerge, I began to entertain the nervous notion that you'd hung yourself from a convenient rafter. So pleased to see that you're not in that much distress," he added, smiling down at her as he picked up one completed sheet of paper.

"I scratched upon the door, and rapped it soundly when you didn't answer," he explained. "But I see now that you were simply too deep in the throes of creation, not self-destruction, to attend to me. Let me see what you've accomplished," he said, ignoring her glare as he began to read what she had written.

Amanda ran her ink-stained fingers through her hair and then daubed unsuccessfully at her dress as he perused her letter. Though he wore near country garb, buff breeches, high boots, and a fawn jacket, he looked so immaculate that he made her feel a drab.

" 'Windham House is a delightful home!' I see that association with Cousin Emily has affected your speech to its detriment," he commented. "But 'beautifully situated' is nicely put. There is a great deal here about mountains, lakes, and views, Amanda; the letter smacks more of a travel brochure than a billet doux. It isn't till we are done with all the geographical detail, here at the bottom of the page, that we come to some little hint of personal distress. And 'Though the viscountess is amiable, I cannot help but think she entertains some of the same doubts that I myself have been occupied with,' is rather tame stuff, isn't it? Come, Amanda, Giles cannot be such a complete stick. Where's the fire, the longing, the regret that should be peeking through each phrase?"

Amanda glowered at him. "I am not so good at double-thinking as you, my lord," she managed to say angrily.

"Ah, so we are not forgiving, are we? I'll admit it pleases me to see you're not a complete paragon, 'Manda. I'd be most uncomfortable entertaining a saint. But allow me to point out that I never misrepresented myself. I assumed you knew the odd circumstances of my birth. It was never my fault that you did not heed the common gossip," he replied calmly.

"It isn't that," Amanda cried, stung that he could so misunderstand her. "It was that . . . it was—" she faltered—"it was that you promised you would not attempt to . . . seduce me," she concluded, abandoning missishness in her righteous rage.

"Seduce you?" he answered, raising an eyebrow, and looking genuinely blank before the light of understanding dawned upon his face. "Ah, that kiss. You consider that seduction? My dear 'Manda, I may well be haphazard in my morality, but I am not such a fool as to attempt a seduction in the family portrait gallery. Servants swarm about the house, my dear, and even if I had ordered them all away in order to commit the foul deed, I would hardly attempt to engender another such as myself beneath the very eyes of all the ancestral spirits of this house. And, 'Manda, my dear," he went on, drawing a white square of linen from his pocket, "I promise you that when I attempt your ruination, there will be no doubt in your mind as to what I am up to. I am not so oblique in my methods as I am in my letters. There's an ink smudge on your cheek," he added helpfully, handing her the handkerchief.

She scrubbed at her cheek, hoping the large white square would cover the color rising in her cheeks. It was both reassuring and lowering to hear how lightly he had dismissed that kiss. Even though she had been horrified and frightened of his anger at herself and his own state, she had forgotten her trepidations at the mere touch of his mouth. Her own lips had tingled at once and her eyes had widened at how that simple contact had scattered her wits. It had been a curiously delicious moment, those seconds before she had recovered, pulled away, and fled from him.

He seemed oddly pleased now, and said, eyeing her confusion, "So it was my actions that displeased you, not my situation? But you will have to learn to hide your feelings, my dear. It is Giles who is to think something is amiss, not my mama and brother. You clung to Cousin Emily so closely at breakfast this morning in an effort to avoid me that you almost ended up buttering her toast and getting your fingers bitten off in the process. It looks decidedly odd that you should come to visit my home and pass every moment without me. But it's not too late to remedy. Let's write something tantalizing to Giles, and then I'll take you for a stroll about the grounds. For the wind has died down and it's a clear and cloudless day we ought to make the most of."

Lord North drew up a chair and signaled for Amanda to seat herself again. "Now," he said with determination, "admittedly I'm flattered at your estimate of my home, but let's leave your appreciation of it to a sentence or two. I rather like the phrase on page two, 'North is a compelling fellow, and now I can see why he was so successful at winning my trust.' Could we not substitute 'heart' for 'trust'? So much more compelling," he concluded, while Amanda ducked her head to hide her flush, and commenced to write at his direction.

Amanda wore a thick red pellise with a stout hood, and was glad of it. For though the wind had ceased to blow with force, even the slight breeze from the lake was chillingly cold on such a winter's day. The viscount had donned a greatcoat, but his golden head was bare. He seemed to thrive on the bracing air, and after they had strolled about for a while, Amanda discovered that the motion of their walking warmed her own limbs. Soon she shrugged back her hood and let the sun warm her head as she paced in step with him.

The grounds to the house sloped down by gentle terraced degrees, to the shores of the lake. One level held a
winter-barren rose garden and maze, the next some formal
gardens and an ornamental pond, the third had a stone
balcony that looked over the lake. Here there was a white
wooden summer house, open to the air on all sides, protected only by a latticework cupola, and here Lord North
and Amanda rested. It was not until she stood, her arms
against the stone wall, peering over, that she realized how
far they had come. Behind her, the house seemed distant
as the lake itself was. Her cheeks were reddened from the
cold, her eyes sparkled, and she laughed up at the viscount
when he suggested that they tarry a while, as it was
doubtful Cousin Emily would follow since there was nothing digestible in sight.

"Much better," he commented, noting her air of relaxa-
tion. "After our impetuous decision to wed, my family
must have thought it curious that my affianced treated me
like a leper."

"But won't it be more difficult when I leave if they
believe me infatuated with you now?" Amanda asked.

"If they do not believe you infatuated, they will know
the whole of it," he answered, leaning over the balcony
and gazing down at a stand of winter-darkened evergreens,
"and that would be ruinous to our plans."

Amanda did not reply, and he went on blandly, "Don't
fret, 'Manda. I am not so noble as to turn my life and my
family inside out just for the sake of your plight. I am
enjoying this mockery for my own reasons."

When she still said nothing, he turned to face her to
read her reaction. He grinned at the sight of her, for she
was eyeing him dubiously, looking, he thought, very much
like a curious elfin creature out of one of the books he had
read as a child.

"I cannot," she said, shaking her head, "imagine why
you should derive any pleasure from this imposture. Most
gentlemen would have nightmares about finding themselves in such a situation. I dislike every moment of it
myself, although I know it is necessary."

"Ah, but I am not most gentlemen, as you should have

realized by now," he said placidly. "And whether you acknowledge it or not, you are certainly not like most ladies. Why, Amanda, you should have been appalled by my disclosure to you yesterday. I cannot believe it is only your good breeding that keeps you from approaching the subject of my illegitimacy again. But you've accepted it as calmly as if I had told you about a birthmark, rather than a birthright."

Amanda was taken aback by his words. She had in fact spent many hours of the night thinking about his condition. But she realized he was right, the facts of his birth had not distressed her half so much as her own lack of perception had done. So she blurted, "No, but why should it upset me? I have, after all, been raised up in a family that makes light of such matters. Well, not 'light' precisely," she offered after a moment's thought. "But we have always accepted that circumstances of birth do not alter a person. I don't like Mary any the less because we didn't have the same father, and I very much doubt if she and Cecil and Alicia and James would even want to claim my papa as their true sire."

"A most unusual family," the viscount commented, as if to himself. Then he smiled at her, caught up her hand, and said, "Let us sit for a space. The summer house doesn't shield from the cold, but I should give you a chance to rest before I march you down to the lake shore."

Amanda seated herself upon a rustic wooden bench within the skeletal frame of the little house and watched as Lord North prowled its perimeters, and listened closely as he spoke to her. He did not rest at all, but paced as he pointed out details of the structure and described its summer aspect for her. His gift of speech was so vivid that soon she could almost see the heavy purple heads of drooping wisteria that hung from the roof in summer, hear the merry light chatter over the dishes of rainbow ices, and scent the fresh, cooling breezes that blew in from the lake. But he returned her abruptly to winter when he said in as casual a tone as he had related all the rest,

"I believe I owe you some sort of explanation, Amanda, for you accepted your false betrothal under false pretenses.

It's only right that you know the whole of it, for I think that Giles, indeed everyone else in the kingdom, knows of my false position."

"It's not important!" Amanda said staunchly, gazing at him where he had come momentarily to rest, with one booted foot up against a bench. She was going to go on about how she well knew how ridiculous matters of reputation were when he cut her off abruptly.

"Don't speak as a child," he said sternly, "it is very important. Should you have to go to such lengths, such twistings and turnings of the truth, if you were born to an unexceptional family? Why, you and your beloved Giles would have two in the cradle and another on the way if your mama did not have a penchant for bearing children from diverse affairs of the heart."

Amanda looked at him with awe. He spoke seriously and was bereft of humor.

"It is very refreshing to see such familial loyalty, my dear," he said roughly, "but as you should know, the world is very hard on those of us who are the result of human frailty. It is amusing," he went on, though he did not seem at all amused, "how very forgiving they can be of those who stray, provided they at last reform. But they are not quite so forgiving of the by-products of those lapses. Those living reminders are indelibly stained. Their existence recalls to mind weakness of human nature; they are regarded as somehow obscene, as though their breathing presence constantly conjures up the act that begot them. Let me tell you, my sheltered darling, that if Giles has forebodings about your sudden flight of romance with a rake-hell, he will without doubt be aghast at your particular choice of rake-hell. The reason we have had to be so nice in our choice of words in letters to him is that he doubtless thinks it a case of like calling to like. Even though," he said with pointed sarcasm, "you have papers and certificates and sworn testimony to the fact that you, at least, are legitimate."

Amanda could not think of an answer to this, and realized that in any case, any words she might utter now would be like an application of a poultice upon a gaping mortal wound.

"My title," the viscount said, rising to pace the interior of the summer house again, as though he found it difficult to be contained within it, "is as spurious as our loving relationship is. Oh, I am legally the viscount; my adoptive father was punctilious about that, at least. Never fear that we both stand in danger of being ordered from the house," he added, throwing a bright glance to her. "But I am not even a rash mistake of the late viscount's. In fact, I do not know what fellow is accountable for my presence upon this earth. And, as I did not even have the good grace to grow to remotely resemble any one of the family, the world knows of my condition as surely as if it had been announced from the rooftops."

Lord North walked as he spoke, and it seemed to Amanda that he had to speak. What had begun as light banter had clearly become something he could no longer contain. Wisely, she did not offer platitudes or sympathy as he told her of his state, but only listened closely to what he said and more closely to what he chose not to say. As he had clothed the naked structure in which they rested in the soft lineaments of summer with his words, so now he was able to let her see the past players and their performances upon that stage of his life that had also vanished after its brief season.

His childhood had been unexceptional, save for its having been perhaps even more pleasant than for most lads from a privileged family. He had come to his parents after ten barren years, and as an only child he had been adored by his father and cosseted by his mother. He could recall nothing that jarred his comfortable boyhood. But yes, he told Amanda with a rueful grin, there were those moments he could cull from his infancy that now stood out like markers on an otherwise pristine landscape. But they had only ruffled the surface of his content.

There was the governess dismissed when she was overheard telling him how fortunate he was and how he should always practice to show his parents his deep gratitude. There was the cook given marching orders when she took to serving him queer stories with his gingerbread, tales of changeling children, goblin creatures exchanged for true human babes stolen from their cradles by mischievous fairies.

At eight, he had been sent tearfully off to school, to be trained up as befitted a young heir to title and fortune. When he had returned for his vacation the following year, he was told that his mother was increasing. His parents were jubilant and he returned to school elated, not so much at the idea of having a sibling, but at his parents' profound joy.

Gilbert had been born when he was ten, and he could still recall the look upon his mother's face when she exhibited his wrinkled, rather disappointing-looking brother. She wore an expression of mingled triumph and ecstatic vindication. He had neither been unduly worried nor cast down when he was not allowed to pass much time with the infant. He had only been surprised at how protective she had become of the babe, and how disinterested she suddenly was in him and his school experiences. But his papa had redoubled his attentions so even that had not disturbed him.

It was when he was twelve and home for the summer, that his life had been changed forever. His papa had been ailing, the lingering illness that would eventually claim him had begun to show its teeth. Through boredom the schoolboy had taken to playing with the infant, now a rotund, willful toddler, albeit always under his mother's watchful eye.

It was on a rainy Saturday morning that the first incident had occurred. Mama had some matters to settle with the housekeeper and Gilbert's nurse was abed with a streaming cold. He had been attempting to entertain his infant brother with some sleight of hand involving a red ball. Gilbert was monstrously spoiled, Lord North said with a reminiscent smile to Amanda; it was a wonder to him how well the lad had grown despite it. But then, because Gilbert could not have the ball, he had fallen into a rage. The child had at that time the habit of flinging himself face downward and kicking and thrashing at the ground when frustrated, while screeching continuously until he got his way. While Gilbert had been in this state, teary, red-face, and squalling, Mama had come running into the room. She had caught the wailing boy to her breast, and spat at his elder brother,

"What have you done to my son?"

He had explained the circumstance, but she had only stared at him and then marched out with the weeping child in her arms. He had thought then of what a strange thing she had said, but had put it down to her agitation and thought no more upon it.

"I was," he now said ruefully, as much to the ether as to Amanda, "an uncommonly dense boy."

Silence descended upon the summer house and Amanda stirred slightly, aware that she was growing cold from inactivity but not daring to move lest she break the train of the silent viscount's thoughts, lest she cause him to abandon his tale. But it seemed that he was only collecting the threads of it together, for soon he continued.

The next morning had dawned clear and sunny. This time, he had romped out into the rose gardens with Gilbert. Mama had fallen into a light doze upon her chair in the sunlight. Again, some small thing thwarted Gilbert, but this time when he flung himself down, he landed directly in the thorny rose bushes. "Lord," the viscount said, shaking his head in wonderment even now, almost two decades later in the icy cold of the abandoned gazebo, as he recalled that blazing August afternoon. "He served himself well for his folly." For now Gilbert had reason enough and more to squall. He arose from the bushes streaming gore from a dozen scratches, looking as though he had been flayed alive.

Mama had roused from her nap and shrieked with dismay. She clutched the shrilling, bleeding boy to her bosom and rose to face his brother. They were then of a height and he could recall, would always recall, the look of hatred and horror in her eyes. She did not shout, nor even raise her voice. But she trembled as she spoke, and her words tumbled out as though long-pent pressure released them.

"What evil have you done to my baby now?" she said in

a voice of iron. "Be wary, Christian. I will not let you harm my son."

This time he had risen to the bait.

"But I haven't harmed him," he explained reasonably. "He pitched himself into the bushes headfirst in one of his tempers. He wanted this rose I had plucked. He hasn't taken much hurt, it just looks fearful, and I am your son too, Mama," he had added, almost as an afterthought.

"Indeed, you are not," she had said.

They had stood arrested in the summer sunlight that had grown cold, the two of them so silent that even Gilbert ceased screeching and only lay, lower lip puffed out in fear, as the silence of their confrontation lingered.

"Explain yourself, Mama," he had answered, in a tone he had heard his father use, as though he had grown suddenly from twelve to forty years.

"You are not my son," she had whispered, her words loud in the quiet of the garden. "We acquired you when you were born. We had no children. We needed a son. Your father did not want Windham House falling to his brother and that wretched lot. His brother was a wastrel. Have you never looked in the glass, Christian?"

"What are you saying? Who else is my mother, then?" he had asked, not believing what he asked, nor what she answered, and having difficulty hearing anything above the roaring in his ears.

"A slut," she hissed, "a common woman. A farmwoman. Glad to sell her son for a crust of bread."

He had been as horrified by the furious, venomous attitude she projected as he was by her speech. But still he could not believe her. He thought her only angry at him and vengeful, and in his confusion he reverted to a child again.

"I don't believe you," he said, remembering that his lips had quavered almost as much as Gilbert's had. "I have never seen her. Where is she, who is she?"

"We sent her away so that her presence would not shame us. Her name is Annie Withers. She lives at a place called Land's End now. In Ashbourne. We still support her. Shall, for all her wicked life," his mama said wildly.

It might have been the telltale quiver of his mouth, or it might have been Gilbert's uncharacteristic silence, but she suddenly fell still as though understanding her words at last. A look of terror had come over her and she had fled with Gilbert, leaving him dumbstruck in the garden filled with roses and birdsong.

"She came to me the next day and apologized," the viscount said, resting now, leaning against the bare lattice frame of the summer house, "and begged me to never tell my father of her words. No, she pleaded with me not to."

Amanda dared speak tentatively. "And you never did?"

"No, he was ill. In any case, there was no need. I went to Land's End in Ashbourne and she had told me no more than the truth."

His coachman had waited in the carriage on the main road as he had walked the miles to the little cottage. A few extra shillings had bought the fellow's silence and the detour from the journey back to school. It had been a neat little cottage, set off by itself at the end of a lane with roses, more roses, growing in the front garden. There had been sheep, and cattle and chickens, and it had seemed a pleasant enough small farm holding. A boy, scant years older than himself, had been working in the garden when he had stopped to ask directions. The lad had looked up at him, and he had been shocked to see his own distinctive eyes gazing back curiously at himself. One blue and one gray eye had widened in the other's face even as his own had, when he asked, "Is this Land's End?"

"Aye," the lad had said.

They had been of a height, of a sameness, except for the fact that one head was fair and the other dark. One was dressed in collar and jacket of a gentleman and the other wore the full and baggy trousers, oversized doublet, and patched coat of a farm youth.

It was years of training and privilege that spoke next, in a voice of command. "And where is your father?"

"Got no father," the lad had said in sullen tones. "Never set eyes on him, leastwise."

The woman had come out of the house as they spoke and stood riveted as she watched them. She was a good

looking, flaxen-haired female. Even at the age of twelve he
could see that she had been beautiful, and still bore traces
of that loveliness although her form was too bulky and her
clothes, simple countrywoman's working garments.

She held a washcloth to her breasts and stared at him.

"Christian?" she asked in a low voice. "Can it be Christian Jarrow?"

Heedless now of the gaping boy, he had walked to her,
dared one glance at her wide blue eyes, then dropped his
gaze to the ground as he summoned up his courage to
demand, "Are you my mother?"

"They told you?" the woman gasped. "All of it?"

"All," he said.

"His lordship sent you?" she then asked again, stupid
with amazement.

"No, he knows nothing of it, and he is not to know. He
is ill," he had answered, and then impatient, and ill himself,
he only asked again, "Is it true?"

"Yes," she said.

He had not waited for a reply, had not even said "Good
day." He had only turned upon his heel and left. He could
hear her call after him, falteringly, "Christian," and then
more weakly, "My lord. Wait, only wait and listen," but
he had gone on.

"I have gone on a long way since then," the viscount
commented now, "and never returned. Oh, I've come back
to Windham House, for it is nominally my home, but it
has never been very comfortable for me since. Mama does
not like me very well," he said with a twisted smile. "It's
not that we fight, no, for that would be underbred. Say
only that she contrives to make me aware that I am an
interloper."

He paused, thinking on how he scarcely needed reminder,
remembering those years when he had first learned of his
condition and how he had struggled with it. He had been
drawn to creeping down to the portrait gallery at night
with a branch of candles, searching those mute and painted
faces painstakingly in the hopes that by some magical
means, he might discover it had all been a mistake. Then
there had been the confrontations he had endured at school

when he came to understand comments he had previously ignored. After he had blacked a few eyes, these accusations had become submerged, only to flow in a constant whispered underground even as his thoughts now ran. He had ceased speaking as he thought back. As Amanda dared not venture a word, it was the complete silence which prodded him back to the present.

He seemed to recall himself and gave Amanda a brilliant, winsome smile.

"Rather a better story than the tale of a naughty illustrated book, don't you think? And I have dozens more. I should have paid them back by being an excellent son as my governess suggested, but I have only gone on to illustrate how true the saying is that blood will tell. But come," he said, his mood veering again, "I have frozen you to ice, bored you to bits, and terrorized you as well, by the look upon your face."

He walked to Amanda and offered her his arm.

"No more of the past then, my dear. You've told me your tale, I've told you mine. Now we can be true co-conspirators, each with a tale to hold over the other's head. I suggest that you contrive to have Giles dredge up some personal shame to relate to you as soon as you have him in your company again. Nothing holds a relationship together so well as mutual confession. And," he added, smiling in his normal fashion again, "mutual fear of retaliation. Now I shall trot you down to our famous lake and regale you with merry stories so that you return to the house looking as though you had passed the entire afternoon in blissful communion with your beloved. Should you like to pass it that way, by the by?" he asked with such exaggerated interest that she was forced to laugh as she took the arm he offered and stepped down the flagged steps toward the lake.

There were details Amanda thought to ask him about his tale, several facts she wished to have him elaborate upon, but he gave her no chance to dwell upon them. They walked down the steep stairs and ambled along the winding paths, and he kept her constantly entertained. It was as though he had never spoken of his intimate life to her, so complete was his absorption now in their merriment.

He displayed yet another aspect of his quicksilver personality as he boyishly mimicked the fat, plodding sheep and assigned them nonsensical names and histories. When he was done with that, he mocked the soaring bird's cries so well that they circled back again and again to discover what manner of creature it was that had called to them.

When he guided Amanda to the shore, they tested the thin ice at the brink with their toe tips and then he showed her how to skip stones across the lake's broad blue back. It was not until the sun had begun its early descent that they paused in their wanderings to watch the echoing glow of its light trailing across the water.

They were far from the house and from any human habitation. As they stood upon the shore, they laughed together and their laughter met and echoed until it sounded as though the whole winter-locked world was amused with them. Amanda had thrown back her head in gaiety, and in that second she perceived that his face had grown still and thoughtful. She saw the way the sun had been captured in his hair and the way his strange eyes shone like the billowing crests of the waters, and she grew still as well. He gazed attentively at her rapt face and smiled as though he had seen something enormously pleasing to him.

He said only the one word, "Yes," and then suddenly drew her toward him and lowered his head to kiss her. Taken by surprise by the abruptness of his action, she surprised herself even further by allowing herself to be pulled into his complete embrace. She rested against him, drawing warmth, incredibly sweet warmth from his lips and sheltering body. It was as if there in the icy grip of winter she had found the heat of the lowering sun upon his lips and in his blazing mouth. But then, even as it seemed that he had thawed every part of her, she recalled herself. She drew back, aghast at her unsought response.

"No," she said, shaking her head in denial, "you promised you would not."

He held her fast and brushed his lips against her cheek. "I lied, you know," he whispered.

When she broke his hold by stepping back a pace, he dropped his arms to his sides. She stared at him, amazed at both his and her own betrayal of herself.

"I do lie, you understand," he said sweetly. "That is the truth."

Then he laughed and shrugged off the expression of concentrated ardor as easily as he had adopted it.

"First lesson, sweet Amanda," he said, now only speaking as dryly as a tutor might, "seducers always lie, your nanny was quite right about that. Second lesson, they soften your heart by enlisting your sympathy. Thirdly, they lower your defenses by wanting, seemingly, only your friendship. But they don't mean well by you, Amanda," he said seriously now, "and that they never lie about."

He put out a hand and caressed the side of her face as she stared back at him, disbelieving his chameleon qualities; so changeable, changing even as she gazed at him from lover, to liar, to sympathetic companion.

"Let us go back to the house now. You really ought to get started on another letter. And Amanda," he added in friendly fashion as he took her hand, "do tell Giles to hurry."

The letter lay open upon a broad oaken desk, and the gentleman who had just done with reading it for the fourth time stood with his back to the room, hands linked behind his back, staring out at the snowy grounds. At length, he turned and walked decisively to the desk. He was a tall, well-set-up gentleman, dressed soberly and comfortably. Although not a handsome fellow, there was that in his plain open countenance that drew the eye and inspired confidence. He took up the letter and read it briefly once again, and then took it to the hearth where a fire rumbled comfortably against the chill of the day. With one exasperated gesture he crumpled the letter and flung it upon the flames. But in the next moment, he dropped to one knee swiftly and snatched it out again. He blew the flames from its margins and lay it back upon the desk to straighten it.

He was never a fanciful fellow, but as he attempted to brush the cinders off its singed edges, he could not help but think that so might a letter appear if it had been composed and sent by the devil's own hand.

X

The guests seated at the long dining table sipped their wine, pronounced it excellent, and dutifully waited for the servants to fill their cups again for yet another toast. As Gilbert had given the first to his brother and his fiancée, now it was the prospective groom who stood to raise his glass. He held his head high and flourished his goblet.

"To my singular stroke of good luck at finding such a treasure," he said as he gazed at Amanda. "A treasure that I did not know I was searching for, but discovered I could not live without. A treasure that lay waiting for me like some priceless pearl upon its rich sea bed. To Amanda," he concluded with a quirked smile.

"Here, here," some of the gentlemen concurred as they rose to salute his lady as well.

Amanda ducked her head and prayed that it appeared as though she were overcome with the idiotic shyness commonly attributed to future brides. It was too much to hope that he would have left off mentioning beds in his public praise of her. She wished that she did not flush so readily, for by now she knew him well enough to know that her aghast reaction to his hint at the truth of their meeting was precisely what he had been angling for. She could only hope that the other guests would attribute the twin spots of high color upon her pale cheeks to coy pleasure rather than the fact that she felt like a thief caught with her hands dripping stolen gems.

For if she had felt unhappy about their imposture before, when she had first arrived at Windham House, the subsequent weeks she had passed here made those first moments seem as innocent as a schoolroom prank. It was, she had discovered to her sorrow, no easy thing to live a lie. And as her worst sins, before the viscount had entered her bedroom and her life, had been only those of omission, the commission on a continuing basis of a monstrous deception had made her supremely sensitive. She felt as though her sensibilities had been sandpapered, so acutely did she respond to every nuance of speech directed to her.

Amanda looked to her hostess, who was now nodding politely to the toast being made by their vicar. It was curious that the one person she had imagined she would feel the most uneasiness with was the one whose opinion, it transpired, made the least difference to her. For the viscountess, while unfailingly polite, had never exchanged more than a bare minimum of words with Amanda in the time that she had sojourned here. And even the most exquisitely sensitive ear could not have picked a wrong note from any of her comments. The viscountess had accepted her as it seemed she accepted all that was about her. Her demeanor was equally flat with Lord North as it was with Amanda and all her servants and guests. Only Gilbert could draw some spark of emotion from her eyes or lips.

It was that young gentleman, who now seized up his glass to toast his brother once again, who made Amanda feel the most wretched. For Gilbert was as honestly and openly thrilled about the forthcoming marriage that was never to be, as she imagined he might be about his own. He obviously doted upon Lord North and approved of Amanda as wholly as he approved of a sunny day. He had attached himself to the two of them, and as Lord North dryly commented, could only be peeled off when they had cause to be alone by outright threats or bold appeals for the right of privacy enjoyed by a besotted couple.

Amanda liked young Gilbert enormously, and thought of him very much as she did one of her own younger brothers. The thought of his dismay when she parted from Lord North sank her spirits. Now, as she watched him beaming upon his brother, she wondered again as she often did, just what his reaction might be if he knew the truth not only of the falsity of her position, but of the absence of any real physical relationship between himself and Lord North as well.

Very much like a player at charades who wonders why the others have not guessed the answer to a riddle that seems obvious once one has been told the answer, Amanda, glancing about the long table, wondered how anyone could not instantly discern the truth of Lord North's position. The discrepancies of face, form, and personality between the two supposed brothers was so stark as to be almost comical.

The viscount, at the head of the table trading quips with Gilbert, was a stereotypically lean and elegant figure of a nobleman. He, the false son, was the one with the patrician bearing and personality. Gilbert, who sat facing him, was as swart and stocky as a plowman, and while he had a good enough head for figures and a heart as wide as his great chest, his conversation and demeanor were as rough and honest as that of any worker in the fields. As they stood thus, the golden-haired rapier-witted viscount born to a farmwoman, and the last of a long line of gentlemen looking even in his evening finery as though he had just come in from the barnyard, Amanda realized that if it were not for the viscountess, it would have been Gilbert who would have been labeled as an imposter.

Which of the guests, Amanda mused as she drank her wine, realized that their host was not born to his position? Then, looking up as if in response to an unspoken command and meeting the viscount's mocking glance, she wondered which of the guests did not.

The dinner had been given this night in order to celebrate their engagement. Aside from the obvious difference in the number of invited guests, it would have been hard to find two more dissimilar parties than this and the one that Amanda's mother had presided over. Although the countess's party had included those souls whose very presence might have staggered most gently reared young females, Amanda had been able to sail through it with a minimum of discomfort. She might not have greatly cared for those in attendance, but they were the stuff of her childhood experience and she accepted them as one accepts a duty visit to an unpleasant relative.

But though there were only sixteen in all at the viscountess's dinner table, in contrast to the hundreds at Kettering Manor, they amazed Amanda all out of proportion to their actual number. There was not a famous name among them, and no one of a rank higher than their hosts'. No gentleman present leered at Amanda, much less dared a pinch. Though some of the females were comely, not one ogled a masculine tablemate, nor fluttered her lashes or fan in unmistakable invitation.

As the dinner wore on through soup, fish, and fowl, the conversation tended toward crops and politics, never touching upon license or indiscretion. As the lamb gave way to beef and rolled forward toward veal, sermons and fashions were discussed, with never a mention of scandal or folly. When the last sweet had been nibbled and the ladies retired to the parlor, the gentlemen raised their glasses of port to congratulate the viscount on his charming lady and future happiness with never a speculative word about her desirability and past experiences. And the ladies clustered about Amanda and quizzed her about her dressmaker with not a whisper about her fiancé's sexual prowess. Amanda was astonished.

As she listened to the wives and daughters of the local landowners, she could scarcely believe her ears. These gentle well-bred creatures were realized objects from her most fervent dreams of future peace. Such were the friends she imagined she would have herself when she was at last wed to Giles. These were the sort of people whose existence she had envisioned solely from her talks with her schoolmates. For a certainty, Mama had never entertained such proper ladies, and as for Papa, he had long since abandoned entertaining anyone but hunting cronies as apt to drink themselves into sullen oblivion as he himself. So it was that when the gentlemen joined them at last the viscount was surprised to see Amanda, her face blissful, blooming among the local flora as a rose among common thistles.

They passed the evening in listening to little Miss Protherow playing at the spinet, while in turn Gilbert, Sir Butterworth, and Major Wells sang accompaniment. After Mrs. Whitchurch had sung a particularly affecting air having to do with love and sacrifice, the vicar, Mr. Morley, told an amusing story that was almost a parable about marital fidelity. After gentle applause, the company split into little groups and the chatter became more general.

Amanda enjoyed herself thoroughly. It was toward the close of the evening when she found herself alone with Mrs. Burnham, the squire's wife. Mrs. Burnham was of an age with Amanda's own mama, and of all the ladies present, she was the one who most resembled those females that Amanda was best acquainted with. For Mrs. Burnham, although stout, had a gown cut less for function than fashion, and her hair was of a vibrant golden hue that hinted more of an origin in bottles than birth. As the lady came close to chat with Amanda, it could be seen that she was older than she had appeared from across the table, as her skin was covered with a great deal of powder to conceal its lines, and her lips were more encarmined than the ingestion of strawberry ices could have accounted for.

When Amanda had done with telling the lady the tale about meeting with Christian, the one that he had approved and that she had never deviated from, Mrs. Burnham smiled pleasantly.

"What a fortunate young woman you are, to be sure," she said softly. "Christian is unique, is he not?"

As Amanda nodded her agreement, peripherally disturbed by some note in the other lady's voice, Mrs. Burnham went on, "As I have good cause to know—" she sighed reminiscently— "for we were once very good friends, he and I."

"And no longer?" Amanda asked, wondering whether this lady had exchanged some harsh words with her neighbor and sought now to repair the matter through his fiancée.

"Oh, we are yet friends," the lady sighed, and then

added further in a low voice, although she and Amanda
were far from the other guests, "but mere friendship is sad
stuff indeed, compared to what we once were to each
other."

The viscount was across the room from Amanda and the
squire's wife, discussing village affairs with some of the
other gentlemen, but his gaze had never wandered from
the pair. Now, as Mrs. Burnham bent her majestically
coiffed blond head to confide to Amanda and he saw the
younger woman's face slowly leached of color and gladness,
he stiffened. Murmuring a half audible excuse, he left the
gentlemen and made his way rapidly to the ladies. As he
approached them, he could not hear what Helena Burnham
was saying, but from the aspect of the couple, he could not
shake the image of a great tawny lioness bringing down
some delicate, fleet-footed creature to feed upon.

The squire's wife noted his approach and she broke off
her conversation with Amanda, to cry, with patently false
enthusiasm, "Ah, North. Lady Amanda and I have been
having the most delightful *tête-à-tête*. You are a lucky fellow,
and you must be sure to bring her around to our home
frequently so that we can strengthen our friendship, for
we have such a commonality of interests."

"I doubt that, Mrs. Burnham," the viscount said with a
charming smile that caused the lady's eyes to widen, even
as his words froze the smile upon her parted lips, "for
Amanda, sad to tell, has little interest in ancient history
and I know that is your specialty. Now, she has quite a
flair for writing, in fact spends hours at her desk composing the most delightful fictions," he went on, oblivious of
the squire's glowering wife, as well as Amanda's guilty
start, "and if we can get her to give up the composition of
letters and begin some more major work, we may yet hear
her praises sung by the highest critics. But alas, writing is
such a solitary persuasion, I doubt she will have any time
for purely social visits," he concluded with an expression
of remorse, as he tucked Amanda's clenched fist under his
arm.

Mrs. Burnham stood for a moment, and then inclined

her head with a wry smile as though to acknowledge a true hit.

"Ah, well," she said with resignation, "so be it. I did but try. I see that dear Henry requires my attention. Good evening, North, Lady Amanda." And nodding her head, she made her way with great dignity to her husband's side.

The viscount did not even pause to gauge Amanda's reaction. He led her immediately to the window enclosure where there were no other guests to overhear. Only then did he say ruefully, "Come, Amanda, you can skewer me later. But for now, I beg you, let it pass. I'll have conference with you when the guests have gone, but Helena will have been triumphant if you look so stricken. This is a country set and their revels will soon be ended. Bear with it only a little while longer and attempt to show some gladness, please."

But when he looked down at her, he saw, to his surprise, that all traces of her dismay were vanished. She only betrayed her emotions when she spoke to him through tightly clenched teeth.

"But, Christian," she said sweetly, "only prepare me please. How many other of your lights of love shall I encounter this evening? Is the vicar's wife among their number? And the major's daughter and Sir Humbert's mama?"

The viscount grimaced, but as the first lady mentioned was such a pillar of respectability that the entire village wondered how she had produced her five children, and the other two were variously a dewlapped female resembling nothing so much as a turnip wrapped in purple gauze and an ancient so debilitated that the company drew in its breath whenever she paused in conversation for fear that she had breathed her last, he soon grinned happily.

"Of course they are," he answered calmly, as he led her toward the center of the room. "How could I have passed them over?"

Amanda, Lord North, Gilbert, and the viscountess stood at the door and bade their guests good-bye as the ancient tall-case clock in the hall struck eleven. The viscountess paused to exchange a few words with the others but left

for her own rooms before the minute hand had crept far
past its zenith. Though Gilbert, still buoyed by the
festivities, announced that he was ravenous, wide-awake,
and eager to exchange impressions of the evening, his elder
brother told him simply that he desired some time alone
with Amanda. Gilbert shrugged philosophically, made a
few sallies about discretion, reminding them of the servants who would be swarming about the place setting it to
rights, and then took himself off to the kitchens to see
what tidbits he could forage that he hadn't had time to
devote proper attention to in the course of the evening.

It was not until Lord North had escorted Amanda to the
study that he spoke.

"I was very young, you know," he said without preamble,
as he shut the door.

As she did not answer, he went on, wandering to the
desk and picking up yet another sheet of yet another letter
to Giles, "And though it might be ungentlemanly to say it,
Helena was both the instigator and the games master. But
then, I am hardly a gentleman, so I shall say it."

He chanced a glance toward Amanda and noted that she
stood and scarcely attended to him, an expression of anger
now clearly discernible upon her face.

"Come, Amanda," he said with some annoyance, "surely
the fact that I had a misspent youth, which you surely
could have guessed, cannot have cast you into a rage? It
was an eternity ago and I have not, would not, embarrass
you by similar entanglements while you are under my
roof. Credit me with discretion, if not with proper
deportment. I'm amazed at your reaction. I'll swear I did
not think you such a prig."

"Prig?" cried Amanda with such force that the viscount
found himself taking a pace back. Her piquant face, which
he had seen in attitudes of quizzical amusement, curiosity,
and even sorrow, was now set in an aspect of fury. But
since, he reflected, it was not a countenance made for such
a vehement emotion, she looked not half so menacing as
tempting to him, though he was wise enough not to comment upon that fact.

"I tell you, my lord," she raged, now giving her emotions full sway, "that it takes a great deal to shock an Amberly."

Privately, the viscount doubted this very much, but he said nothing, knowing she must go on to her full length of anger, uninterrupted. He readied himelf for accusations about his licentiousness and profligacy evinced from the cradle and fostered onward. But her next words caused him to drop his cold, amused aspect.

"I saw the cut of that particular article when I first laid eyes upon her," Amanda lied, "and what she said did not discompose me in the least, I assure you. In fact, had she told me that you and she headed up a hellfire club in the local church, I should have not turned a hair."

Realizing that she had perhaps gone a bit too far in her protestations of sophistication, Amanda dropped her gaze from the viscount's amazed eyes and bit her lip.

"But then why are you so enraged?" he asked, dumbfounded, for once with none of the amused certainty he affected.

"Because she ruined the evening," Amanda blurted.

"Ruined the evening?" the viscount echoed. "But what was there to ruin? I thought you bored to extinction, and who could have blamed you? Only Cousin Emily could enjoy such a gathering. Even Mama, I assure you, held it for propriety's sake alone. Gilbert, of course, finds pleasure in any gathering of more than three, if there is enough food present. But this was merely a simple country evening passed with neighbors and local lights. There was not a witty word uttered nor a new tale told. I can see that Helena's spiteful confession might have overset you, although that occurred in my heedless youth rather than my heedless adulthood, but I cannot envision what you considered ruined."

"It was not tedious to me," Amanda said earnestly, attempting to make him understand her never-spoken vision of content. "I had the most pleasant time until she spoke. It was just the sort of evening I had always dreamed about. Surrounded by neighbors and friends, talking about inconsequential stuff of everyday life, with no one trying to top another's anecdote or attempting to add a scurrilous detail, and no one vilely drunk, and nothing but the kindest construction placed upon one's words or actions. They were all so respectable," she said at last, still feeling that she had not explained the whole of it, "and they treated each other with respect. Can't you see?"

He stood very still and then said, as though from a great distance, "I am beginning to, Amanda."

"And then when that overblown creature began to whisper about your liaison with her, she quite shattered it all," Amanda said sadly.

"But my dear," the viscount replied softly, "they are not paper people. You have idealized them far too much. I should think that there is as much baseness and secret shame in their make-up as in any other person's. Just as there must be some unspoken decency and value in the affairs of those you most dislike and are accustomed to meet."

"Perhaps," Amanda retorted, "but I hadn't wished to know if it were true. And surely it cannot always be so. There must be those people who live their lives in tranquillity, with loyalty and honor." She was annoyed at what she perceived to be his patronizing tone and so went on heedlessly, "I can fully understand that you may not wish to admit it, my lord, but I prefer to believe that all the world is not so vile as you would have it."

The viscount bent his glowing head as Amanda gasped at the way her words had come out. Before she could soften them, he said mockingly,

"Perhaps. But then, you certainly can understand that I don't wish to know it, if it is true."

Amanda attempted to amend her rash statement, but he cut her off.

"Think nothing of it, 'Manda. I have made my own bed, it is only natural that I should choose to have the whole world lie in it with me. At any rate," he went on, with that worldly bored note in his voice that made her feel like a chattering child, "your illusions about my neighbors are not my concern. I am only pleased that you aren't going to rake me over the coals for my past peccadillos. And since you clearly are not going to oblige me by adding to their number tonight, I bid you good evening."

When he had left her with a courtly bow, Amanda felt very much like striking something. But since all the objects in the room were alarmingly solid, she took up her pen instead, and commenced to add to her latest message to Giles. She had not written more than an uninspired line or two, so preoccupied was she with continuing the unfinished discussion with the viscount in her own mind, this time with witty answers and clarity of expression, when Gilbert popped his head in through the doorway.

"Oh, how marvelous!" he said happily, strolling into the room still chewing upon the remnants of an iced cake he held in his hand. "I hadn't hoped to find you alone and awake. It's so hard," he complained as he settled himself in a chair, "to get to bed after a party, don't you think? I think," he volunteered, ignoring her silence, "that parties should go on till everyone drops from exhaustion, because it's clear that no one goes right off to sleep after attending one anyway. Why should we all sit in separate rooms and rehash things alone, when we could still be together?"

He frowned as he pondered what he had said and then went on, "Christian used to sit up with me in the old days but the gudgeon's off to his rooms without a word tonight. Looked in a foul temper, too. Did you two have a lovers' spat? Well, I shouldn't worry about it, for I expect that's the way of it. Not that I've ever been in love myself, you understand, but I'm quite looking forward to the experience. Except that there aren't any interesting young females in the neighborhood, save for Becky Hobson, and she's walking out with John Saunders, anyway. Do you have any sisters by the by, Amanda?"

Amanda had gotten used to Gilbert's manner of expressing himself in nonstop fashion. He often spoke thus, as though the simple piling up of each idea as it occurred to him could be construed as conversation. But he was always amiable, and she always welcomed his company. The fact of his physical presence at Windham House had made her visit far more enjoyable. His constant attendance upon her and his brother blunted the viscount's seductive-

ness. Perhaps it was only that even that gentleman could
not bring himself to attempt a young woman while his
brother was looking over his shoulder, but Amanda felt
that there was more to it than that. Lord North might be a
careless fellow in many ways, but he seemed to be very
careful of Gilbert's good opinion. When the three were
together, the viscount treated Amanda more as a unique
person and paradoxically, in many ways, she had grown to
know him better with Gilbert at their side than she had
when they had been alone. So she lay down her pen and
smiled at Gilbert. She looked at his hopeful, square, and
honest face and said hesitantly,

"Yes, Gil, I do. Two, in fact. And Mary's rising eighteen now, too. She's a dear, clever girl and very lovely as
well. But Gil," she said softly, not wishing to dim the
eager look in his eyes, "she is like me, an Amberly. I don't
know how much gossip you have heard, I've never mentioned it to you but now that you bring it up, my family
has a rather—ah, widespread reputation."

She had never discussed anything personal with Gilbert,
nor had he ever offered up any but the most inconsequential conversation to her. In either case, he seldom waited
for anyone's reply to his discourse. But tonight she was
weary and unsettled, and curiously, having been dampened by the viscount, she felt brave and forthcoming with
his brother.

"Oh, you mean the fact that half of your lot is illegitimate?" Gilbert said cheerfully, as though he'd just said
"freckled" or "musical." "Why, we don't live in the
antipodes, 'Manda, only the countryside. But that don't
make any difference to me. A chap's got enough to do to
account for his own actions, never mind apologizing for his
ancestors'. She's pretty, you say, and bright as well? How
tall is she? Wouldn't do for a chap my size to court a
beanpole, we'd look foolish. But if she's of a height, that
wouldn't be so bad. Becky Hobson's only a few inches my
better and she made much of it," he brooded.

"You speak so easily of it?" Amanda said in shock.

"Of what?" demanded Gilbert, thinking darkly that her
sister must be a giantess, from the horrified look upon

Amanda's face. But recalling the conversation he relaxed. "Oh, about your family? Certainly I do. Why are you so astonished? You said yourself that your reputation was widespread. Lord, I haven't said anything amiss, have I? Chris would have my head. He's the best of fellows, but I wouldn't wish to stir him up."

He looked so anxious that Amanda assured him she did not take any of his comments wrongly, but she added, with a note of wonder, "But Gilbert, if you have heard of the Amberly Assortment, why should you wish to align yourself with us further than we are already linked? I should think one disreputable blot on the family's escutcheon would be enough for you."

She was astonished at his reaction to her bemused comment. He rose from his seat ponderously. He loomed over her with his hands clenched, and she was both startled and suddenly afraid of his totally uncharacteristic anger.

"I know you're promised to Chris," he said coldly, no longer the playful young man she knew, "and indeed I like you very well, 'Manda, and was exceeding happy Chris had found you. But I'll not countenance your holding his birth against him, no matter what the cause. You may have had a tiff with him, I cannot say, that's between you two, but he is my brother, no matter what idiot gossip may hold. Indeed, no bond of blood could make him more my brother than he is, and as I love him, I'll not heed a syllable about a thing in which he had no fault. I'm not saying he's led a blameless life, but in his birth, at least, he had no part. I'm surprised at you, 'Manda," he said in the manner of a disapproving elder.

"But Gil," Amanda defended herself, "I was referring to my own family, and the fact that I was surprised you'd even countenance having another such as me beneath your roof. I never spoke of Christian."

The swift change that came over Gilbert was almost pitiful. Within moments he was abject, begging her forgiveness, pacing the room, knocking a fist against his head, and damning himself for a fool. In her attempts to calm him, Amanda said, "Gilbert, I did not know you even knew the truth about my family, much less about Christian. Why, I myself did not know about him until I arrived here," she explained.

He stopped his pacing and looked at her.

"I don't wish to hurt your feelings, 'Manda," he said gruffly, "but a blind man could see it. It's common enough gossip, and I've never questioned it myself. I've known it since I was a tyke, and then I had at the baker's boy for telling me about it. But it don't make any difference, don't you know? He's been all the brother a fellow could want. Too much of one, sometimes," he said, thinking aloud, "worrying for my schooling, taking care of the estates, and seeing to our welfare. I've no wit for that sort of nonsense. And well my father knew it. Why, when he was breathing his last, he told me he was glad that Chris was to have the ordering of things when he was gone. They were two of a kind, companion spirits. He called him 'son' when Chris came in to bid him farewell. Even at the last, I heard what Chris whispered to him. He offered to give all over to me, but father summoned up enough strength to declare that he was the rightful heir. And so he is."

Gilbert subsided for a moment and then added morosely, "I cannot say why Mama dislikes it so, but then, I've never understood women at all, 'Manda, I'll confess that to you even though you are one of their number. No offense intended," he put in quickly.

Amanda assured him that none had been taken, and she passed the next few hours placating him by discussing those subjects dearest to his heart: the party, Amanda's sisters, and Lord North's nobility of character.

When the candles had guttered low, Gilbert rose and stretched. "Now, let's keep our meeting to ourselves," he said thickly, "for I don't want Christian to rate me for keeping you up till all hours. I just dropped in to see if I could mend fences. When I saw his face and then yours, I sank, 'Manda, I truly did. But I can see that it was just one of those lovers' misunderstandings that you'll doubtless clear up by morning. It wouldn't do for you two to part," he went on as he led her to the door, "for you're perfect for him, you know. I'm happy for it, for if ever a fellow needed someone to call his own, it's Chris. I feared he'd never wed, you know," he added on a huge yawn. "I think he had some maggot in his head about not wanting to marry for fear of cutting me out of succession. Ain't that just like him though?" he laughed wonderingly. "Giving up his whole future for my sake? But I wouldn't have it. I planned never to wed until he did. Can't you just see the two of us? Two stubborn old bachelors sitting here in cobwebs until we shriveled?"

As he bowed over her hand at the top of the stairs, he chuckled richly.

"But you've solved the problem, 'Manda, and I'll dance at your wedding till my shoes wear out. With Mary, I think," he mused, "the little one with the freckles you was telling me about. Thank you, 'Manda," he said feelingly, and went off down the corridor to his rooms, whistling softly, vastly content with himself.

Amanda lay awake in her great bed fretting till the turning of the night about how many people would be wounded by the successful conclusion of her schemes. And she fell to sleep at last after wandering in that netherland between consciousness and repose wondering at how many scars she herself would bear no matter how it turned out.

XI

Even in midwinter, the forest was alive with light. The trees were powdered in snow, the bracken underfoot was hidden beneath white mounds, and wherever there had been moisture some unseen hand had transmuted it to glittering ice. The landscape lay spangled and translucent under a sharp winter's sun. The riders' voices rang clear in the cold air; they did not hurry down the paths as they might have in some more clement season. They knew that the most sure-footed mount might have a misstep since even innocent hillocks could conceal the sheerest stretches of treacherous ice.

Amanda was enjoying herself very much, even though she might have preferred it if the excursion had been taken on foot. For though she was a good rider and had known some amiable horses in her time, she preferred to think of the beasts as either transport or pets, and did not think much of them as recreation. She confided this to the viscount, who rode at her side, along with the notion that she had always thought it a pity that one couldn't ride dogs. They, she affirmed, might be the best sort of creatures to take excursions upon, being entirely less haughty and willful companions.

Lord North agreed, and only commented upon how diverting such sport might be if one's mount spotted a cat while riding. Gilbert, who rode on ahead of the pair, tossed back a reprimand over his shoulder to his brother, for he allowed as how Amanda had the right of it and only think of the sort of hunt one could have if one's steed could not only pursue but also tree one's prey. When the viscount agreed and then speculated upon the result of patting the noble beast in appreciation and then having it fall to the ground in delight, waving its feet in the air so that its stomach might be scratched, the three laughed so heartily that the vibrations of their merriment dislodged bits of snow from the overhanging branches. The resultant miniature storm created by their mirth only caused more of it, and the forest echoed to their boisterous laughter.

Amanda wore a habit of rich red-brown, with a hat that sported a jaunty partridge feather. Since a dollop of snow had fallen on that brave feather and now was melting down in a trickle upon her head, Amanda swept off her hat and upended it to dislodge the snow. Her spice curls shone in the sunlight and her gray eyes reflected all the dazzling winter white. All three of them were enhanced by the clean light, the viscount of course, with his brilliant hair and jeweled eyes, was an acknowledged creature of the element, but even dark Gilbert's hair and form stood out in bold relief against the purity of the scene.

So Amanda would always think of this place, from the viscount's house to its surround, as some magical prism endlessly casting sharp and gemlike images. When Gilbert cried a great haloo, and pointed ahead, she saw the lake before them, broad and blue and white, seeming like some great diamond- and sapphire-filled bowl. She left off attending to her ruined hat and cried, "Ah, this must surely be the most beautiful place on earth!"

Lord North said nothing, but only looked at her and not at the lake at all. Gilbert, however, ever one to take things literally, said only that it was very nice to be sure, but in his opinion not a patch upon Hollyhedge, their estate in the gentle Cotswalds. Their piece of the Avon there, he allowed, while not so mighty a spectacle as the lake, was a more manageable bit of scenery and more to his liking. Amanda was surprised when his brother replied in a cautionary tone that this riding excursion was not a proper place for Gilbert to go off riding on his favorite hobbyhorse again. When Gilbert subsided into glum silence, the viscount added that they had been all through that particular subject and would not discuss it again, no matter how deftly a fellow might think he had brought it up.

Never one to remain in the sullens long, Gilbert, obviously dying from inactivity as they had been sitting still upon their mounts for the space of two minutes, spied Amanda's devastated feather.

"Ho, 'Manda," he cried, "that bit of plumage is done for. Tell you what, I'll go scout the edges of the lake for some partridge. See if I don't find a covy. We can come back later and flush a dozen of them and have your hat back in fine fettle again."

Before Amanda could protest that she did not fancy adorning her head with fresh-plucked feathers from some still warm carcass, Gilbert was off down the trail happily hunting down the traces of a bird fine enough to embellish a fair lady's hat.

"Let him go," the viscount said benignly, "for he's fretting for some exercise. We two elderly parties set far too slow a pace for him. He'd hunt raspberries in the snow if he thought it would give him an excuse for activity. I doubt there's a partridge in the land dim enough not to elude the racket he's making, so you'll not have to worry about having to sport gory feathers upon your hat."

Amanda chuckled, and they rode on slowly, pacing their mounts easily along the path around the lake. They chatted absently on a variety of unimportant trivia, but so pleasantly that Amanda felt all her constraints slipping away. Here in the sun and the air the viscount did not dwell conversationally upon her charms, or upon his motives pertaining to them, and this lack of threat freed her tongue.

"Why," she said at last, "do you not stay here more? For I can see how very much you love this place and all that is upon it. If I had such a love for my home, I should not leave it so easily. You have been gone for two years and yet it seems as though you have recalled each tree and rock as though you've held them in your mind's eye constantly."

But at those innocent words, his face changed and he assumed the bored, laconic drawl of the salon again. "So I have," he said, "and so, I imagine, I always shall. But it is not mine, and never was. I am only a cuckoo in this palatial nest. My true home is in some barnyard, I expect. Even now, if it were not for fate's intervention, I should be mucking out a stable, or winnowing winter wheat, or ministering to a pig. This is Gilbert's legacy, and I only tend it for him. His father entreated me to keep the title and the land. I do, for I promised, but I feel a usurper doing so. Though Mama resents my very presence, Gilbert loves me well. But I cannot say why, for if I were he, I should not. So every now and again," he went on more lightly, as though recalling how very nearly he had begun to speak his true mind to another being, "I take a little jaunt to the continent and disport myself as a fellow of my caliber should."

They rode on in silence, Amanda realizing that there were as many deceptively innocent patches in their conversation to avoid as there were under their mounts' hooves. But the viscount seemed reluctant to let the subject go, and soon he said, in a constricted voice as though he had been trying to shape the words into an entertaining fashion but could not quite do so,

"He keeps harping on the subject of Hollyhedge, for now he thinks that I'm to marry, he wants to take himself off there and set up his own household. It's a well enough site, a particularly choice holding in fact. But this is his home, and I cannot understand why he does not love it as I do."

He fell silent again and in an effort to change his mood, Amanda said brightly, "He thinks the world of you. He's forever singing your praises to me."

"Ah, yes," Lord North smiled, "was that what you and he were doing till late in the night? I wonder that you did not drop off to sleep immediately he began. That's the only way to discourage him, you know."

Again, Amanda was surprised at how much that transpired about him the viscount noticed even when he seemed to be the most oblivious. The thought that came to her mind came to her tongue instantly.

"That must be why you were such an excellent spy!" she exclaimed.

The viscount let out such a peal of true laughter that his mount's ears flattened back.

"Oh lord," he laughed, "what mare's nests has Gil been exhibiting to you? What I told him was no more than the truth, 'Manda. I did try to be of service to my country, to be sure. And I did carry a few messages from Elba to Sicily and thence to Vienna. At first, you see, it was most effective double-thinking, for the powers-that-were thought it supremely amusing to use a fellow everyone would think too conspicuous to be a spy, as a spy. But once our foes twigged to the scheme, my role was done. No, my dear, I passed most of my time in Vienna just as you would think, in wenching and gaming and sport and wenching."

He gave Amanda a glittering smile.

"It really is a great pity, Amanda, that you are not tempted to try what I am best known for. I feel rather like a master chef forced to keep company with someone who dines only on vinegar and water. For what I most enjoy you seem to appreciate the least. But," he continued, with a sidewise look that caused Amanda's hands to tighten involuntarily upon her reins, "I am eternally optimistic. And there may yet come a day when you are willing to try my wares."

Amanda made such a brave show of trying to change the subject that her very efforts had him merry once again. She was enormously relieved when a crestfallen Gilbert rode back to report that all the deuced partridges seemed to have flown south for the winter, or had been poached out of existence from the very planet.

They rode back to the counterpoint of Gilbert's incessant plans for luncheon, as the ride seemed to have whetted his appetite beyond merely mortal limits. He was still musing aloud about his expectations of game pie, and brooding as to whether his chief competitor in the larder at Windham House, Cousin Emily, had snabbled up all that excellent Stilton, when they arrived in the courtyard. They gave their mounts to grooms and entered the main hall again.

The viscountess surprised them all by coming to greet them. In the natural order of things, she kept to her rooms or her own occupations most of the time, meeting them only at table or occasionally sitting with them in the long evenings. But now she came to them readily, almost blithely.

"We have another guest," she announced in sprightlier tones than usual for her. "A friend of Lady Amanda's, I understand. A friend from home. I made him welcome in your absence."

Amanda stared at the figure who emerged from the salon behind her hostess. The gentleman was tall, neat of person, and wore a bland expression of politeness.

"Giles!" Amanda breathed. "Oh, Giles!" she cried.

Amanda had the sudden wild impulse to race forward to embrace Giles, but fortunately she recalled herself before she could so disgrace herself. Even had she been alone with him and not engaged to wed another, such a rash show of emotion would have been incorrect. It was the sight of his quiet, watchful face which checked her before she could commit such folly.

Constant association with both the viscount and his brother had made her careless. For Gilbert was forever patting her absently, as though she were a favorite spaniel, as he did to all those he considered his familiars. The viscount, she now realized, also somehow always managed to contrive to touch her, even if it were only the slightest brush of his hand against her cheek.

Giles had always reserved any show of physical affection toward her for times late in the evening when they were quite alone, and then, only after a lengthy prelude of quiet talk.

Amanda put out her hand and smiled as Giles took it.

"Giles. How delightful to see you. What brings you to Windham House? Nothing is the matter at home, I hope?" she asked with some trepidation, not daring to believe her letters had been successful, and now envisioning disaster.

"No, nothing is amiss," he answered in his cool, even voice. "It was only that I had some business to attend to locally and decided upon the spur of the moment to have a look in at you, so that I might report upon your condition to your papa."

Since Amanda knew that her papa, in all likelihood, had

not even yet realized she was gone, and in any case was not in the habit of inquiring about her or chatting with Giles about anything but the merits of a particular vintage or fox run, she flushed with pleasure. Giles's pointed stare recalled her to her surroundings once again.

"Giles, where are my manners? Please let me make you known to Viscount North," she said. "Christian, this is a near neighbor and a dear friend of mine, Sir Giles Boothe. And this is his brother, Gilbert Jarrow. Gilbert, Sir Giles Boothe. And the viscountess, I am sure you have already met."

"But we've not yet been properly introduced," Giles corrected her quietly, as he took the lady's hand in turn.

The viscount had been standing at Amanda's side, and now he placed his hand upon her shoulder in proprietory fashion as he said sweetly, "How very pleasant for us that you have come to pay Amanda a call. Since you have come this far, it seems wasteful for you to hurry off. I hope you will be able to stay for some time. Please give us the pleasure of your company for several days, Sir Boothe."

Amanda held her breath until she heard Giles say in reply, "So kind of you, your lordship. I should be delighted to, if it is no bother."

As the viscount reassured Giles, Amanda let out her breath. As she looked about her, she could not escape noticing that though they all wore polite smiles, it was only the two ladies present, herself and the viscountess, who seemed to be genuinely pleased at the turn of events.

If the object of her series of painstakingly devised letters had been to lure Giles to Windham House, then she had succeeded. But if, Amanda thought morosely as she sat to dinner a few nights later, her object had been to spur him to attempt to dissuade her from her forthcoming marriage, she could be counted a dismal failure. For she had not even been able to get him alone for private speech above the space of a few moments. And those few words he had spoken, which she had gone over in her mind a dozen times since, could only be construed as mildly hopeful to her cause at best.

The very first evening he had come, he had met her in the hallway as they were going in to dinner.

"Amanda," he had said carefully, "your letters prompted this visit. As your friend, I felt that I could not rest easy until I had assured myself of your well-being in person."

Then they had gone into dinner, whereupon he had been swallowed up in conversation with Miss Emily and the viscountess. Since that night, he had gone riding with Gilbert, strolling with Lord North, shooting with Gilbert, and touring the countryside with herself and Lord North. The rest of his time had been filled with playing at cards with the entire company or discoursing with them.

Now, looking over the centerpiece of hothouse flowers at him, she felt frustration at how she was hemmed in by the very proprieties he represented. As an engaged female, she could not very well seek him out and draw him to her side alone. Giles was not the sort of fellow one could be that easy with. Such an action would have startled him as much as it might have persuaded him of her unhappiness, for Lord North played the doting cavalier as though he had rehearsed the role since childhood.

Amanda bit at her lip and ignored her fruit compote. To be sure, Christian could not suddenly turn upon her and treat her vilely here in the midst of his family. But his portrayal of a smitten swain did nothing to advance her purposes. Although Giles remained expressionless whenever Christian ran his hand absently across her arm, traced a wayward curl, or held her about the waist before assisting her to mount, she knew Giles must think she had run mad to compose such doubting letters to him when her new fiancé showed such fond courtesies to her. She could only hope that he understood that her infinitesimal leap of shock each time Christian touched her was caused by her dismay, not her pleasure.

She let her dish be removed untouched as she observed Giles and the viscount as they chatted together. Any other eye, she decided glumly, would have found Giles overshadowed by his host. Though both men were slim and straight and wore sober, correct evening dress this night, there was that in the viscount's bold coloring and aspect that made him seem theatrical. Giles's steady dark gray gaze might look, she conceded, ordinary when compared to the viscount's changeable varicolored eyes. Neatly brushed brown hair might pale compared with that glistening golden crop. And Giles's precise, toneless speech might strike the ear as commonplace when compared to the viscount's amused and dulcet tones. Giles was a few years older, admittedly, and nothing in either his aspect or his countenance denied that fact. But there was, she thought loyally, certainly nothing in that reserved countenance to dislike. He even had, she remembered, as she sought to find advantage for him, a few inches of height over the viscount.

But, Amanda thought, stabbing into her cream cake, Giles had not honed his humor against the diamond wits of the land and continent for decades. He had not danced attention upon a score of light ladies, nor had he tutored himself to be as universally pleasing as a fellow whose confessed avocation it was to play upon the sensibilities of weak-willed fellow creatures had done. It was because of Giles's very plainness, his unexceptional steadfastness and respectability that she had originally been drawn to him. She sighed and laid aside her cake fork as the viscount threw back his head to laugh and Giles permitted himself a smile at the same jest. If Giles had cultivated the same aspect as the viscount, she should not care for him in the least, she reminded herself.

When dinner had done and they were all assembled in the salon again, Gilbert suggested a hand of cards. Amanda looked forlorn even as all the others readily agreed. As Gilbert rummaged through a drawer to fetch the cards, Amanda wondered if she would not have to resort to slipping through the corridors in the depths of night to seek out her erstwhile suitor for a private talk.

"I suggest," Lord North said easily, watching Amanda's reaction to his words with an expression of vast amusement, "that we four family members play the first hand and let Amanda and Giles catch up on old times together. We've been such good hosts that I fear they've not had a chance to exchange a bit of gossip."

Giles said properly that he would be pleased to play

immediately, but there was no question that the viscount
alone constituted a majority in his family. Soon the four
relatives were playing at a table set near the fire while
Giles and Amanda were seated near the window together.
They were far enough from the others for private converse,
but still, for the first moments they had nothing to say to
each other at all.

Amanda could have wept from sheer frustration. She
wanted to have Giles's ear privately, but the manner in
which the viscount had provided her with that which she
had most desired had made the moment even more difficult.
It was hard not to feel as though she were betraying him
by what she most wanted to say, and she could not shake
the feeling that she was committing some sort of verbal
adultery, when her unsuspecting fiancé had made such a
magnanimous gesture.

"You seem pleasantly situated here, Amanda," Giles
said at last. Amanda had then to leave off her ruminations
and think out her next words with painful concentration.

"So it would seem," she replied inconclusively, to buy
time to frame her utterances concisely.

"I only came here," he went on, picking up a round
paperweight and turning it in his long fingers, "because
your letters implied some doubt as to your circumstances.
We have been friends for so long that I felt it would be
remiss of me not to play the part of elder brother—that is,
if you needed counsel."

Amanda stifled her mental protest of "Not elder brother!"
and instead said quietly, "I have been treated very well
here, to be sure. But Giles, I do need counsel. I could
scarcely ask Mama's advice—Christian is a pet in her set.
Nor, as you know, could I broach the subject to Papa. I'm
very glad you have come."

"As I thought," he said, nodding his head sagely. "But
then, Amanda, you can scarcely expect me to speak against
my host while I remain under his roof."

Amanda sat back and fell still. He was quite right as
usual. All the things she was about to say died on her lips.

"But I can say," he stated softly, "that I think it unwise
for any female to make a decision that will shape her whole

life so precipitously. Or for any gentleman to do so either," he added.

"But especially in your case, Amanda, with your background," he continued blandly, "it seems unfortunate that you raced to such a decision. Still, I find myself wondering how much of the matter was due to your calm thinking, and how much was because you found yourself dealing with a type of person you had little experience of. I do think my trip was not in vain. We shall talk more later. Only know that I have your best interests at heart, and shall attempt to guide you honorably," he concluded.

Amanda had to be content with that utterance about her future. For Giles soon turned the conversation to precisely that which the viscount had mentioned, gossip. She learned of all the doings of her neighborhood, from dogs littering to barns burning, but nothing of the workings of Giles's heart. Soon she was able to rise and rejoin the card players when they summoned her, knowing all that she had no interest in, and nothing of what was her paramount concern.

Throughout the rest of the evening Amanda noted how Lord North observed her with heightened consciousness. When he let his fingers linger against hers, or touched her shoulder, or bent his brilliant smile upon her, it was the fact that she knew Giles was watching as well that made her breathing quicken and her eyes widen. The game that went forward around the gaming table was far more exciting than any of the cards dealt. But that game had only three players, and each concealed his hand from the others well.

When the others had gone off to their beds and Lord North had disappeared into the shadows of the hallway, once again Amanda had a second of privacy with Giles. He took her hand and said softly, "Perhaps we can go for a ride early tomorrow morning, Amanda. Before the others have arisen. Even with a groom attending us, yet we can talk."

"Oh yes, Giles," Amanda concurred.

"At seven then," he said before he made his bows and left her.

She stood at the bottom of the stair, gazing into the direction he had gone.

"How romantic," a drawling voice intruded upon her thoughts. "How greatly daring. What ardent fellows you become entangled with, Amanda."

She wheeled about to face the viscount, who was standing with a decanter and a glass in his hands.

"He can scarcely do more while he is your own guest, my lord," she said heatedly, feeling oddly embarrassed by Giles's proper demeanor and curiously finding herself defending that which needed no defense.

"Oh, I have no complaints," he said happily. "I am a very willing cuckold, remember? It is only that it intrigues me to observe the mating rituals of the respectable. Perhaps I can learn something. Only think, never an impassioned word, not one delicious, hurried, clandestine kiss. It is just that one has to take great care not to stand in the direct line of sight between the two of you, or else risk being blistered by the heat of your stolen glances. And sighs! Lord, one could steer a boat across the lake on the collective strength of those unbottled sighs."

Aware that she was being mocked, and somehow now, with Giles beneath his roof, acutely aware that she and her purported fiancé were alone in the darkened hallway, Amanda felt anxious. She sought words to dispel the nervousness his nearness and his powers of observation brought to her.

"Abominable," she declared vehemently. "Why should you make sport of that which you helped to bring about? I cannot understand you," she complained.

She gave him one last furious look and then marched up the stairs, leaving him alone in the dim light.

"No, how should you," he said to the empty air, "when I expressly wish that you should not?"

XII

It was such an early hour that the horses left fresh track marks upon the skein of hoarfrost the sun had not yet had a chance to melt. The groom who trailed behind the two riders shook his head at the foolishness of the gentry, who would ride so early when they might sleep so late. But Giles had been right, Amanda thought; there could be nothing clandestine about a couple going for a gallop before breakfast.

Neither Amanda nor Giles could know that this was the viscount's customary favorite hour for riding, and as the groom had been specifically requested not to bring the matter up, they could not know that Lord North watched them from his bedroom window as they left the graveled front drive. They rode in companionable silence for a while, for the quiet was so immense that any sound they made might travel easily to the groom's ear. Thus, the first part of their ride was filled only with equestrian sounds: the snorting exhalations of the horses, their hoofbeats, and the creaking sway of the saddles. Even the birds, who were generally subdued of a winter's morning, were as yet completely mute.

When they reached a prospect that looked out over the lake, Giles at last requested Amanda to dismount so that they might stroll the narrow path's perimeters. They gave their mounts to the groom to walk and went on together alone.

Giles was a study in flint tones this morning, Amanda noticed, from his riding jacket to his breeches. The color suited him and she thought he looked distinguished, clear-eyed, and handsome. He appeared every inch to be precisely what he was: nobleman, local magistrate, and authority, at least in her small corner of the kingdom, on all that was just and seemly. She had always considered it a great honor that such an admired gentleman paid court, however tentatively, to her, and now as always she deferred to him and kept silent to await his invitation to speak.

She was glad that she had worn her cherry-colored habit, for he had said when he had first seen her that she looked very nicely. That was a great compliment from him, as he was a man of few, always well-considered words. But he spent no further time with idle chat and said at once when he felt the groom was out of earshot,

"Do you plan to marry North, Amanda? Are you deep in love with him?"

She did not reply straightaway, for if she said a bald "no," he would think her a fool to have gotten involved to the extent that she had. Neither, of course, could she possibly say "yes." So she said, at length,

"I do not know, Giles. Indeed, that is why I wrote to you so often. It wasn't only to get your thinking on the matter, it was also done in the hopes that seeing the thing set out in bold letters might give me a clearer idea of how I was to go on. But I do not know."

"Then you should not wed him," Giles said sternly. "For matrimony is an estate that should only be entered into wholeheartedly. There are enough mistakes made by those who feel sure of success; there is little chance for happiness when there is doubt from the onset."

Although these were the very words she had been hoping to hear, Amanda felt she ought to offer protest.

"But Giles," she said, looking down at her toe tips as she paced, "it seemed the right arrangement at the time we decided." And so, she thought wryly, it had been.

"You have not," Giles began, then hesitated before he plunged on, "you have not committed yourself to an irremedial extent, have you?"

Amanda paused and looked at him. She could not quite

understand his words, so he went on, his usually composed face looking rather strained. "That is to say, Amanda, if I am going to advise you, I think I have the right to know, you have not . . . given yourself irrevocably to him, have you?"

It was his acute embarrassment, evinced by the fact that he looked supremely uncomfortable and did not meet her eyes, that made her realize what he was getting at.

"Oh no!" she cried, so loudly that he swung his head around to see if the groom, who was a distant figure behind them, had heard. "No, of course not. Why, whatever do you think of me?" she went on, now growing a little heated.

"I think you are an unworldly female," he said, his expression composed again, "and I think North uncommonly adept at seduction. I thought so from his reputation, I thought so from the tone of your letters, and now I have met him, I am sure of it. Oh, he is intelligent, and charming to a fault—indeed, he could not be otherwise to have earned such a name for himself. But you are no match for his wiles, Amanda."

She began to speak, but he cut her off with an uplifted hand.

"You asked me to tell you my mind, and so I shall. You cannot blame me if you do not care for what you hear. I will speak my piece, and then be done. But obligation to one's host or not, I did not ride all this way just to return with my thoughts kept to myself."

They halted in their steps and he faced her as he spoke. He seemed almost to be lecturing, and she did not breathe a word lest she misconstrue one word of his discourse.

"When I first heard of your engagement, Amanda, I tell you truthfully I was wounded. Not only that you had promised yourself to a stranger, but that you had not thought to speak to me about it first. We have known each other for several years now, and I thought at least you owed me that courtesy. It was hard, Amanda, to read of it in the papers. Your letter made it no easier," he scolded.

She bowed her head. He nodded and then continued, "At first I was very angry. I thought that I had been entirely wrong in my assessment of you and wondered at how I could have been so blind to your true nature. I confess, I wrote you off and considered my judgment sadly deficient. But then, as I began to receive your letters, I saw that all was not what it seemed at first stare. Clearly, you were confused, and already beginning to regret your rash decision."

Amanda kept her head low and so could not see the triumph briefly flare in his eyes. Nor could she see his face soften as he observed her contrite expression.

He took Amanda's arm and began to walk forward with her again.

"I do not think you should wed him," Giles repeated while Amanda kept her face averted so that he might not see the eager hope with which she received his judgment. But he was too involved with picking out his words to note her reaction this time.

"I have thought about it at length. North is entirely too jaded a creature for you, my dear. It would not be long before he would be off about his philandering once again. He is sadly unsteady in nature. It is true," Giles said expansively, taking note of the fact that she had not raised a protest to his assessment of her fiancé, which he felt she must have if her heart were truly involved, "that the fellow cannot help himself. It is the way he was born, it is the way he will go on."

"What do you mean?" Amanda asked, raising her head.

"You are unworldly, Amanda," Giles said comfortably, "but by now even you must know of his condition."

"You mean," she said, stopping short and causing him to do so as well, "because he has the reputation of a rake?"

"I mean," Giles said, shaking his head because of the unfortunate words he must next utter, "because of his very birth. The fellow is base-born. Not all the accouterments of gentility can alter that."

Amanda's eyes widened. Giles had never mentioned that matter as pertained to her own family, and she was amazed that he would bring up the viscount's circumstances.

As though he realized that, he went on, "Surely you

have suffered enough because of your own mama's actions that you need not seek out such another for husband?"

There was both everything and nothing wrong in what he said, so Amanda could not reply at once.

"Do you think that I have not witnessed your own struggle to surmount the infamy in which your name is mired?" Giles asked with a wintry smile. He stood to face her and took both her hands in his and raised them as though they were children about to play at London Bridge. Then he said earnestly,

"I believe that with time and care you will succeed. But never if you align yourself with North, for he has never attempted to deny his birthright by word or action."

Amanda could only ask bluntly, "But Giles, there are far more base-born members in my own family. Are we not two of a kind?"

Although he dropped one of her hands, he still held one securely as he replied, "You should not equate yourselves. You're legitimate, Amanda. You can still surmount the obstacles that your family has erected about you. North cannot. The world knows what he is. I wonder if you completely realize that. Did you know that aside from being jested at as the 'Vice-Count North,' he is known in some circles as 'Fitz-North'? Even if he improves his behavior, yet he can never escape that particular epithet. It's common knowledge that his parentage is more anonymous than that of the cattle in the field, for at least the well-bred among them have documented pedigrees. Perhaps if he wed some female of good family, he might come to have his children's children accepted. But if you two married, it would be disaster for both of you. It would only illustrate to the general run of society that the apple does not fall far from the tree."

As Amanda stood and gaped at him, speechless by virtue of all the speech which vied for predominance in her thoughts, he went on, "Similarly, if you should wed a gently born fellow, in time your past might be forgotten. But it is not a thing which you, or he, if he has any wit, ought to rush into in any case."

"Giles," Amanda said, disengaging her hand from his

with a note in her voice quite different from her usual tone, "surely you do not believe that one must suffer for the sins of one's parents? For if so, I wonder that you bear me company. For some of my best friends," she laughed shakily, "and kinfolk, too, are bastards, you know."

His expression did not change, though Amanda felt that she had let a monstrous thing fly from her lips, and had split the world in two with her plain speaking. He only nodded as though satisfied in some strange fashion, and said, "I understand only that the company you have kept of late has influenced your mode of expression. And to its detriment, I might add. This is not you speaking, Amanda; this is the overlaid veneer of sophistication you have adopted to please North. But since you have chosen to be so free of speech, I shall be as well. The world is well aware of love children, it has been so since the dawn of time. But the world has rejected them since then, and with good cause. We remember William the Conqueror and Leonardo, but recollect that we recall them as much for their state of grace at birth as we do for their genius. Rightly or wrongly, bastards are outcasts, Amanda; they are mongrels in a world that values good breeding."

"I should like to go back now," Amanda stated flatly, afraid of hearing more. She had wanted him to discourage the idea of her marrying the viscount, but she had never wanted the reasons he put forth to be given to her.

"But, Amanda," Giles said quickly, staying her by holding her arm firmly, so insistent on what he had to say that he forgot the presence of the groom in the distance.

"I must say further. Not only do I think you ought to break off with North, I think you should return home as soon as possible. We, the two of us, can go on just as we were. I will forget this episode. I do not believe you are irrevocably fated to become like your mama. But I believe that if you remain with North, then you are lost."

"I understand," Amanda said tightly as she wrenched her sleeve from his grasp and walked forward to her mount.

But in truth she did not, she complained to herself as they rode sedately back to Windham House. She did not understand her reactions at all. Giles had said no more than what she might have expected. It was precisely what she herself might have thought a scant month before, so she could not be angry at him. But she was enraged, though she could not fathom why, or at whom the fury was directed. All had gone exactly as hoped for.

Her scheme with the viscount had come to fruition. There was no further need for dissembling. Mama's foolish meddling had been undone, as Giles had said; all could be forgiven and forgotten. But it was not a happy end to her misadventures, for something had changed in the interim and whatever it was, it was certainly not Giles.

It was at three in the afternoon, while the other ladies were napping and Gilbert had cornered Giles for a game of chess, that the viscount finally ran Amanda to earth in the study. She was seated at the desk writing furiously when he entered the room, shut the door behind him, and paused before her.

"Behold me ill with anticipation," he cried. "I have been in a fever of anxiety. How did it go this morning? You and Giles were sublimely indifferent to each other at breakfast and at lunch. But Hodges said you were holding hands during your excursion at dawn. Judging from your pattern in the past, I assume that was your version of ecstatic lovemaking. Has he offered? Am I to gnash my teeth and rattle sabers when he confronts me with the news of your defection?"

"It was as you had thought," Amanda said impassively, ignoring his histrionics.

"Then he has offered? Then I am lost?" Lord North said merrily enough, though he turned to face the windows.

"He only offered his advice," Amanda said, "and that was that I leave you and this place and go home again. He added that we could go on as we were before Mama slipped you into my bedcovers."

"Now that," Lord North said, turning to grin at her, "he did not say. But no offer? That does surprise me. We shall have to cook up something quickly, so that you do not leave here ringless. Gilbert's been nasty enough about the fact that I never gave you a precious token of my devotion; we ought to see what we can do to make Giles come across with something faceted for you."

"You needn't cook up anything," Amanda said, putting a finishing flourish on the letter she was writing and standing. "I shall be leaving here as I came—ringless."

"Ah, that rankles, does it?" he said, walking to the desk. "But I could hardly offer you one for fear you'd fling it back into my face. What's that you've been penning, then? Since you've already gotten Giles here, I assume it's a suicide note to commemorate your failure in netting him. No," he said holding the letter to the light, "I see it's only an excruciatingly polite thank you to my dear mama for all her kindnesses. You needn't have bothered. Your exit will be thanks enough for her. She's been wretchedly unhappy since you set foot in Windham House. The thought of you thwarting me in my attempt to spawn legal brats will far exceed any gratification she could receive from a mere note."

He put the letter down and watched as she scrubbed ink from her hands with a penwiper.

"Why leave before anything is resolved?" he asked idly.

"Nothing will be resolved for some time," Amanda said, avoiding his eye, "so there's no sense in my remaining here. It is enough that we have been able to mend matters; the rest will take time."

"I see," the viscount said thoughtfully, "he plans a wait of five years so that he may be sure you don't err again, perhaps two more to ensure your penance, then a three- or four-year engagement to be absolutely sure of your steadiness of character. You will wed from an invalid chair if you're not careful, Amanda. You'll have to listen to the vicar through a hearing trumpet as well. I can just envision a decrepitated Giles attempting to wedge a ring over your arthritic knuckles as you quaver, 'I do.' Don't do it, Amanda," he said, his face suddenly still.

"What?" she asked stupidly, unsure of what he had said.

He took her by the shoulders with hard hands.

"Don't marry him," he said, his bright face strangely solemn. "It wouldn't be right. Not for you. Oh, you'll get him to the altar in due course of time, but it isn't worth it. He's not for you."

"He said the same of you," she replied, gazing into his distinctive eyes.

"He's right there. But so am I," Lord North said. "It would be hellish, you with him."

"I know you think him stolid and stodgy," she began, but he shook her gently to silence and went on abruptly, as though the words were driven from his lips.

"No, no he's not. I thought you had painted a picture of a suitor who was fair, true, and solidly worthwhile, and so he is. You are not a fool, your judgment was sound. But it's his respectability you're after, my girl, and never mind his wide shoulders and his big gray eyes. And that very respectability will be what drives you to despair. For if ever you happen to sigh over an actor upon a stage, or laugh at a butcher boy's cheekiness, or comment on any fellow's fine figure, he'll impale you with his stare. He'll never trust you, Amanda, not in his heart. In time, you'll stop trusting yourself. You'll either diminish to a Cousin Emily or outdo your dear mama for spite. It won't do, love. It would never do."

As he shook his head and smiled at her, Amanda gazed blankly ahead. There was so much truth in his words that she felt her heart constrict.

"Perhaps," she murmured, "perhaps you are right. But I'm free of my predicament. I'll go home now, Christian. My way is clear to that, at least."

"Home?" He laughed scornfully. "What sort of refuge is that? If you had had a proper home, my sweet, you would not have yearned for Giles so passionately. Do you intend to go home and collect cats or dwindle to a housekeeper for your papa when he tires of the slattern he's keeping? Don't wrench away from the truth, 'Manda, and that is that you would be better off repairing to a nunnery straightaway than traveling home again."

Having given up her brief struggle to be free of his hands upon her shoulders, she now attempted to turn her head aside so that he could not see her face. But this he did not permit. His mood seemed to turn to cruelty, so he held her fast as he went on angrily,

"You are three and twenty, 'Manda, too old for childish illusions. Shall you let your entire life pass by while you air-dream of what could be, if only, perhaps?" he mocked.

"Without illusions I should become like my mama," she cried, heedless of her angry tears. "Is that what you wish for me?"

"No, 'Manda," he said more quietly now, as though her tears had dampened his rage, "it is only *with* illusions that you could emulate your mama."

"And what is your advice, then," she asked, lifting her chin, "if I am not to marry Giles, and not to return home, and not to take up where my mother has left off? Shall I indeed hang myself from some convenient rafter?" she said bitterly.

"No," he said calmly, "but something very much like. Marry me, 'Manda, and be damned to the lot of them."

She gaped at him as though he had run mad.

"It makes perfect sense," he said, releasing her as she wiped savagely at her face with her hand. "I am responsible for your distress, or at least as much so as your mama. I proposed this scheme, and now I see it is unworkable. I offer recompense. Come, 'Manda, think on it. I, of all souls on this planet, will never throw your family history in your face. It would not bother me in the least if you had a legion of illegitimate relatives."

"I thought you never wished to wed," Amanda said, forgetting the import of his offer in the very strangeness of it.

"Why, so I didn't," he smiled. "I see you have been speaking deeply with Gil. But as I cannot give up the title unless it is over Gil's lifeless body, for so he has told me, I cannot ensure that he and his inherit the succession in any case. I can sign Windham House over to him, though, and have always intended to do so anyway the moment he himself weds. We can be very snug at Hollyhedge, 'Manda, or in my town house, or even upon the continent. I'm very warm in the pocket. Do not fear we will have to dwell in a hovel. I offer a fair exchange. I took your reputation, I offer you mine. It isn't much, lord knows, but I think it is far better than any other alternative open to you."

Amanda stood and studied him. Her arrested expression was so altered, so unlike her, that for a moment he felt as though she were a stranger coolly weighing him up in a balance. Then she spoke slowly.

"And all this for my sake? Come, my lord. Wherever is the advantage for you? You are not such a selfless fellow as this, I think."

Her words were so at variance with her appearance, for at the moment she looked so small and so young, her gray eyes misted with tears, her little pointed chin still trembling, that the harsh truth she spoke seemed to have come from another's lips. He gave a crow of delight.

"Very good! You have some defenses left after all. Well, I shall tell you, sweet. Wherever in all this world shall I find a female who is at once gently bred, literate, comely, and pure, who will not forever hold my birth against me? You have grown up considering my state commonplace. You are quite unique on this island England. I should have to go to Arabia, at least, to find another such. For there, gently bred females are accustomed to seeing their fathers sire multiple offspring from diverse females. Only then, I should have the trouble of teaching my bride not to eat with her fingers, to say nothing of the language barrier. And I refuse to harbor camels," he laughed.

He looked so merry, so alive and enthusiastic, his face lit with such mischievous joy that it seemed he was proposing some schoolboy lark, rather than marriage.

"And I am of an age to wed, past it, actually. Unlike Giles, I cannot see the advantage of waiting until my dotage to exchange vows. I cannot fancy myself being as toothless as my own firstborn when that happy event occurs. You have told me that you don't wish to follow your mama's lead, and I readily believe you. I don't have to let a decade crawl by as I closely observe your honesty. Come, 'Manda, don't you wish to kick dust in all their faces?"

He gazed down at her and went on, as though he wished to carry her along by the sheer exuberance of his reasoning.

"You cannot be so noble that in some secret part of you you don't wish to see Giles confounded by your marital happiness, left to cursing himself for a fool for not snatching you up when he had the chance. And I confess, I have the most base desire to see my mama wail at my wedding. Let's do it, 'Manda," he urged her with a grin.

"You would wed me," she said carefully, "because you owe me recompense, because we share a shameful heritage, and because we can confound everyone by our union?"

"You want more than that?" he asked, cocking his head to one side. "We have more than that. We get on very well together, you know. We make each other laugh. Not enough?" he asked curiously as he saw that her face was grave.

"Greedy thing," he laughed low. "You shall have even more then."

He pulled her into his arms. "We have this as well," he whispered in a low voice as he kissed her. His kiss was long and deep and thorough, and she never for a moment sought to escape him. By the time that he drew back from her with a wondering exclamation, he realized that for once he had gotten back in full all that he had given.

After he had waited quietly without receiving a word of her reaction, he asked softly, "You see?" He looked at her expectantly, this time without using the many words he could usually call up so easily. Instead, he only touched her cheek gently and asked again, "You see, 'Manda? It is an excellent idea."

Amanda stood stone-still, wavering slightly, her eyes half closed. She looked lost until at last his words and touch called her back to him again.

"Oh I see," she answered finally on a shuddering sigh. "I see clearly now, thank you."

Then she straightened her shoulders and gave him such a blazing look of fury that he blinked. "I see that you and Giles are kindred spirits, for all your outward differences," she said vehemently. "You are opposite sides of the coin, but you are both cast from the same metal. He has not offered for me because I am my mother's daughter and you have offered for me only because I am my mother's daughter. There is your commonality. There is the one most important thing about me for both of you. For if Giles would have wed me years ago if it were not for Mama, I doubt you would even consider me for your wife if it were not for her."

"Well, it won't do," she cried as she stepped away from him. "It will never do," she said furiously as she stalked to the door.

"I am Amanda Amberly, and I am myself. And if neither of you can forget for a moment that I am one of the Amberly Assortment, then I say the devil fly away with the pair of you. You do kiss very well, my lord," she added fairly as she opened the door. "But there's more to marriage than that, I think. I am leaving Windham House, and you are free, and Giles is free, but most of all, I am free."

"But where shall you go?" he asked in honest perplexity.

"Why to the very place for me," she said, her head held high, "to the only one whose presence accounts for all my desirability to you and lack of desirability for Giles. To the one neither of you seems to be able to get out of your minds for a moment when you think of me. I'm going home to my mama, of course."

After curtsying very deeply and respectfully, she left the room hurriedly with all the calm dignity she could muster—except she did slam the door behind her till it rattled on its hinges.

XIII

Amanda paced the morning room as she waited for Miss Emily to be done with her breakfast so that they could be on their way at last. It had been three days since she had made her decision, and now all that remained to be done was to make her last good-byes to Windham House and its occupants. That it was only she and the viscount who knew that these were to be quite final farewells only made her task more difficult.

She had already had her last words with him. Although she had passed the previous days attempting to avoid all the inmates of Windham House by pleading so much physical infirmity that they could have been forgiven for imagining her on her death bed nightly, she had suffered through one further private interview with her host.

Lord North's demeanor had been cool and detached and he had only asked if she might reconsider her decision. When she hotly denied any such possibility, he had merely shrugged. He had listened to her plan of action quietly, his face so composed throughout her recitation that she had difficulty recalling the warmth and brightness with which he had previously attended to her.

When he at last suggested reasonably enough that she be the one to place the notice of their "disengagement," as he termed it, in the papers so that he would not appear to be a complete bounder, he had seemed so distant that Amanda could scarcely believe that she had ever seen that vulnerable, hungry look upon his face when he had done kissing her.

As he calmly informed her that he thought it only fair

that she take Cousin Emily back with her, if not for propriety's sake, then at least as an act of charity toward the poor inhabitants of Windham House, Amanda could detect nothing but ironic amusement in his light voice. She marveled at his attitude. For if she could not as yet forget the extravagant sweetness of his lips upon hers, as much as she attempted to, then it seemed that he did not even recall there had ever been such intimacy between them. She had to conclude, when he left off the interview by casually wishing her well, that practiced rakes such as he had conveniently dim memories or at least never looked backward upon pleasure, only forward toward the acquiring of more. She found the possibility that he had not derived as much from that embrace as she had too lowering to contemplate.

Now, as Amanda fretted and wondered at how many more cups of tea and racks of toast Miss Emily would consume before she deemed herself equipped for travel, she thought that at least she had acquitted herself well at that last hurried meeting with her former affianced. For she had not let her eyes dwell upon his face when she promised that her public announcement of their engagement's dissolution should be made only after she had left Windham House forever. And she had never once let her voice falter as she had agreed that keeping the news from Gilbert until she was far away enough in person and memory from him to blunt the blow was the kindest course.

Last night Gilbert's eyes had grown wide as saucers and she glimpsed the child behind the man when she had announced at dinner that she wished to return to her mother's house for a space. When Lord North had followed up that pronouncement by pleasantly agreeing that he thought a young woman ought to be alone with her mother for a time, Gilbert had actually laid down his fork in the midst of attacking his favorite meat pie.

Those simple twin announcements had in fact created a vast stir about the table. Giles had stiffened and stared hard at her before he regained his composure. The viscountess had enough years of control and breeding to allow no more than a flash of wild eagerness to come into her eyes before she had quickly lowered her gaze over her pleasure. Miss Emily had gone on eating, only pausing to announce that she would be delighted to see the dear countess again, but Gilbert had neglected his meal entirely and had passed the dinner hour looking accusingly at both his brother and Amanda in turn.

After dinner, Amanda successfully eluded the entire company by again fleeing to her rooms, but not before she heard Giles's disclosure. For he flatly stated that as Kettering Manor was on his route home—only off it, he conceded to Gilbert's outraged stare, by some mere fifty miles or so—he would be pleased to accompany the two ladies to their destination. As the viscount raised no protest and Miss Emily immediately expressed her delight, Amanda remained mute about the acquisition of an escort.

Amanda mentally unpacked her traveling cases now to be sure that she had left nothing behind. She had just located her paisley shawl in her mental luggage when a triumphant exclamation shattered the silence of the morning room.

"Aha!" Gilbert cried as he stormed into the room. He stood gazing at her, his fists on his hips, his legs apart, glowering as though she were a prisoner in the dock and he, the king's prosecutor.

"I've run you down, 'Manda, and I shall have my say," he threatened. "Chris is mute as a stone on the subject, and what with your headaches and toothaches and brainstorms and lord knows what else, you've been playing least in sight with me. But I've steered Cousin Emily to the ginger preserves and bought myself some time with you at last. Now what's this all about, my lady?"

Without giving her a heartbeat of time to answer, he walked up to her and continued, all anger gone and only a petulant expression upon his face, "It's clear as ice to me that you're giving Chris the final push, and for the life of me, I can't say why. Why, you two suit, 'Manda, you suit right down to the ground. I know the fellow's got a shocking reputation, but you knew that when you promised yourself to him. You were wise enough then to know that it's not all his fault. The chap's got such a pretty phiz, he can't help it if the ladies fling themselves at him. He's not made of granite, you know, but I'll wager he hasn't cast a glance at any but you since you've met. No, and neither will he in future, for I know the chap, and he's as solid as a rock beneath that damnable care-for-nothing air of his."

Gilbert went on in his usual fashion, attempting to put all his arguments before her in one breath.

"And I've eyes in my head and I never saw nor heard any insult given to you, and he could cut glass with that tongue of his if he'd a mind to. Why, he's leagues in love with you, 'Manda. And if he's overstepped his bounds in his ardor—" and here Gilbert had the grace to flush before he said hurriedly—"not that it's my place to know or speak of it, but it would only be because he's an affectionate sort of fellow. But the moment you tie the knot, he'd be yours forever. He won't take up with another female, if that's what's concerning you. For he's not a sneak, nor unfaithful in any of his dealings. Why are you running out on him, 'Manda?" he concluded unhappily.

"I'm only going home to Mama for a visit, Gilbert," Amanda said, but her voice was so weak and insincere that it sounded hatefully cozening, even to her own ears.

Gilbert's lips set in an angry pout as he declared, "And going back with that stick Sir Boothe to hold your hand. The Friday-faced fellow hasn't an ounce of life to him, 'Manda. Ah, I cannot understand this. Mama's in alt at your leaving, but then she's never been fair to Chris. I'll say it and be glad. She's aces high on me, and I'm not a patch on him. It ain't only that he's no blood of hers, I'll venture. It must go deeper than that. Perhaps it's because Papa doted on him. The two were like peas in a pod. Always jabbering together on what was catnip to them both, their books and travels and politics and what not. Yes, and I'd stake my life that Papa wouldn't have let you just sail out of here and out of Chris's life. No, he wouldn't, and I wouldn't either if I had an idea of how to stop you short of crippling the horses."

Gilbert subsided into brooding, looking so woebegone that Amanda could easily believe that he had cast himself headfirst into the briars in his infancy when in high emotion. All she could do to attempt to cheer him was to offer up further paltry excuses about a daughter's devotion to her mama. She did not have to go on very long in this embarrassingly insincere fashion. Within moments, Giles came into the room, already clad in his greatcoat, and Miss Emily, sated at last, came to tell Amanda to ready herself for their journey.

Gilbert stood at the top of the stairs as the two coaches awaited their passengers. He gave Amanda a gruff goodbye, but would not meet her eyes. She felt heartsick as she turned to the viscountess's genuinely gratified and warm farewell. Then Lord North bent to Amanda to say his last. Although the day was shockingly cold, he had put on no coat, and for a moment Amanda was tempted to caution him to return to get one. As he had been working in his study, he had left off his jacket as well.

He stood before her, his white shirt cuffs fluttering in the brisk wind, his golden hair whipped across his forehead, and he smiled such warmth at her that he dispelled all thoughts of winter.

"Fare thee well, 'Manda," he said softly, "and return even more swiftly," he added more audibly for benefit of the company that awaited her departure. But then he bent his head to brush his cool lips against her cheek and whispered for her ear alone, "You can change your mind, 'Manda. You can change your mind at any time. I shall be here."

Then he assisted her into the coach, although Giles stood waiting to do so. Even to the last, as the lead coach pulled down the drive, Amanda stayed turned to watch him. In his white shirt and buff breeches, his light hair so vivid against the dim day, he appeared to be one lost beam of sunlight illuminating the stair. She gazed back at him till she could see no more, since it seemed the cold breezes had made her eyes water so profusely.

It ought to be mandatory, Amanda thought crossly as she sought a comfortable position in her corner of the lurching coach, for a couple contemplating matrimony to be locked together into a traveling coach and forced to occupy themselves with nothing but conversation for a day. If someone like Cousin Emily was included in the bargain, she was sure that a substantial portion of church income would be lost forever. She had a great deal of time to spare for such disgruntled musings, as she sat and observed her traveling companions, for she had not spoken a word for over an hour.

Giles and Miss Emily had been carrying on a most mutually satisfactory conversation steadily since they had stopped for luncheon. If, Amanda corrected herself, one could call that which was issuing from the pair conversation at all. For the discourse consisted of Giles airing his viewpoints on a variety of subjects, with Miss Emily interjecting appropriate sounds of agreement and delight throughout. Amanda's own response was not solicited, since, she realized with a sudden jolt that made her sit up straight, she seldom was asked to contribute more than Miss Emily was now providing.

As she watched the pair through narrowed eyes, Giles smiled at her, thinking her abrupt reaction caused by her enthusiasm for a point he had just made. She smiled back tentatively, guilt spurring her as much as politeness. For it could not be Giles's fault that her recent sojourn had so altered her perceptions.

They seemed to have been traveling forever and that was odd as well, for Amanda's experience had taught her that some unwritten physical law of nature always made a return trip shorter than the way forth. But on the first journey, she remembered, she had scarcely marked the hours, having been first occupied by her trepidation and then with the attentions of the viscount. She had originally marked all these same weary miles with wit, with laughter, and with lively interest. For the viscount never said a thing without expecting her response. If she had merely nodded or exclaimed about his wisdom, he would have roasted her alive. She nodded at Giles again and pushed away all inappropriate thoughts of another gentleman's intent, alert reactions.

She bore another day's travel in much the same fashion.

But when they at last achieved the inn where they were to stay the second night, she could no longer escape the lingering presence of her former fiancé. For they rested at the Fox and Grapes again. Though Amanda had a secret moment of amusement imagining the landlord's private thoughts about a female who came to his lodgings so often with a variety of gentlemen escorts, that was the only present enjoyment she had. All the rest was in remembrance of times past in his establishment.

There was no strange, intimate conversation after dinner in the private parlor, since Giles so rightly heeded convention. There was no half-frightened, half-anticipatory reaction to Giles's good night to her, for she knew he meant only to bid her good night. But there was little sleep for her in any case, since Lord North's presence was as palpable as though he were sitting in her room, helping her to keep watch through the long night.

So it was that when at last the carriage stopped in the drive of Kettering Manor, Amanda sprang forth from the coach like a jack-in-the-box loosed from its confines. She greeted her mother with outsize pleasure as that lady hastened from the hall to admit her unexpected visitors. But one look at her mama's shocked face drained all of Amanda's enthusiasm.

"Amanda!" the countess gasped, "whatever on earth are you doing here? Where is North? Whatever have you done?"

"I've come back," was all that Amanda could manage to say.

"Oh lud," the countess sighed, ignoring Amanda's companions in her distress, "you've gone and mucked it all up."

"Out with it," the countess cried, bustling into Amanda's room and flinging back the draperies to admit the morning light. "I've waited half the morning for you to show your face, and cannot bear to wait a moment longer. I understand that you could not speak last night; it's a hard journey down from North's establishment. And so I let you go to sleep with all my questions unanswered. Lud, child, you look hagged," she said as she peered at Amanda rising from her coverlets. "Did you get no rest at all in all these hours?"

She had not, but Amanda passed a hand through her curls and said, "I always look so in the morning."

The countess looked doubtful, but only said, as Amanda stretched, "I've spoken with Emily Atkinson, and though she is the most convivial soul, the dear clearly does not know the day of the week. I refuse to pass another word with Sir Boothe. Not that I've come to cuffs with him, for I know better than that, but he's so politely disapproving of me that I long to turn him from my door. All he will say is that you wished to bear me company for a while and that he accompanies you since he is returning home. But as Kettering Manor is not on the west road, I take leave to doubt that. What is going forth, Amanda? I demand to know."

As Amanda's face was now immersed in suds in the wash basin, there was no reply. The countess contented herself with rummaging through her daughter's luggage while Amanda vanished into a side chamber to attend to her morning's ablutions. When she emerged tying a sash about her robe, the countess seated herself in a chair by the window and motioned Amanda toward its twin facing her.

"Now," she said curtly, "not a bite shall you eat nor shall you leave this room till you have told me what has transpired."

Amanda toyed with a tassel at the end of her sash and observed her mama. The countess sought to maintain a stern expression, but a look of concern kept crossing her delicate features. Amanda tried to temper her next words.

"I have left North. It was a sham, Mama. I could not keep it up any longer."

"He offered you insult?" the countess asked fearfully.

"Oh no," Amanda sighed, "never, not really, no never in words." She paused as she realized that he had never truly insulted her in actions either. He had passed so much time in warning her of his base intentions and she had spent so much time imagining what he might do, that it had not occurred to her until now, as she sought to explain it, that he had actually never wholeheartedly begun the seduction he was forever warning her about.

"No," she said at last, wonderingly, "no never in actions, either. He was a gentleman. Or at least as much of a gentleman as he could be," she temporized, wondering if a true gentleman would kiss and cuddle a lady who was a guest beneath his roof. But then, she wondered if a fiancée, mock or not, was considered quite a lady guest.

Her mama watched the puzzlement chase the astonishment across Amanda's face and then asked again, "He asked you to leave, then?"

"Oh no," Amanda corrected her immediately. "In fact, he asked me to stay on. He asked me to marry him, in fact."

"And you would not?" the countess asked in confusion. "I cannot understand. I thought you two so well matched, that is why I brought you together. In a manner of speaking, of course," the countess added hastily, her face becoming rather red. "For it was my silly mistake about the gray and the blue rooms which accomplished the thing prematurely. I had every intention of introducing you properly at the first possible moment. For I know North of old. He has a dreadful reputation, but I swear he is one of the best fellows I've ever met. He's very honorable in all his dealings, and witty," she continued, hastily sliding over certain aspects of the viscount's reputation. "Wise enough for your most exacting standards, young enough to be flexible, but old enough to know his mind. Wealthy, and handsome as sin. What is there to dislike in him?"

Amanda sat without replying and tangled the tassel upon her sash as her mother awaited her answer. Finally she said in a very low voice, "He does not love me."

"Ah," said her mama with a world of comprehension in the syllable. Presently she asked slowly, "But my child, North was never a one for conventions. He would not have proposed marriage for respectability's sake. Now why else should he have offered for you if his heart was not involved?"

Amanda stood and turned from her mother. What she

had to say now was a thing she had never mentioned to that lady.

"He told me he offered because we had so much in common," she said in a low voice. "You see, because of my history, he felt that I could never fling his dishonor in his face. Oh, Mama," Amanda said desperately, wheeling about to face the countess, "he is base-born, I'm sure you know of that. And it is a thing which eats at his soul, as well it might. Because of my experience with his kind, he feels that I would not mind marrying him. Similarly, he thinks that flaw in himself, which might prevent marriage with a gently bred female, would make no difference to me. And for that reason, and that alone, he asks for my hand. With no word of love," she said as though to herself, "or devotion or caring. Simply because we share a shame."

"You have a care for him, then?" her mother asked thoughtfully.

Amanda only made a bleak gesture with her hands, and sat again. He had been right, she thought; she was not a fool. She did have good judgment. And she had known almost from the moment she had left Windham House— although she had not admitted it to herself then—that she had left some integral part of herself behind there with him. She felt the lack of him acutely and had done so during the interminable coach ride as Giles had prosed on with Miss Emily. She had missed him constantly at the Fox and Grapes. Last night, while her aching body had demanded sleep, her active mind had pictured his bright face, her ears had retained the echoes of his soft voice.

Almost she regretted having left him now, though every reasonable thought applauded her action. Had she stayed on she might never have left. Had she wed him, she knew, it would have meant disaster for her. To enter marriage with no expectations of anything but light affection would have been to sow the whirlwind. She could not have endured the indignity of knowing she alone brought love to the union. And what if he discovered love only after he had wed her, but with someone else? She could not have borne the years of watching him disport with other females, in any case. For she would be impelled to pay him back.

How long then, until the Countess of Clovelly's daughter became even more infamous than her mama?

All this she thought, but all she said to her mama was, "It makes no matter. I came back to you to tell you I have ended it."

"And you intend, instead, I take it, to wed Sir Boothe?" her mother asked heavily.

"Oh no." Amanda laughed. "No longer. Though I expect I shall never have the chance to refuse him. Giles likes me very well, but he does not care for my name. I'm sorry, Mama, but there it is. There it always is," she said, unable to speak further, having already spoken more from her heart than she ever had done with her mama.

"I'm sorry for it," the countess answered, "though not if it prevents your taking up with Sir Boothe. For I cannot like him, and never have been able to."

"But you've only just met him." Amanda smiled sadly, feeling quite alone, realizing the impossibility of having a serious conversation with her lightheaded mama.

"No, there you are out, Amanda," the countess said calmly, "for I do know him. I've met him times without number in London. Don't look so amazed, child. I know most souls in the land even if they chose not to noise it about. Your dear Sir Boothe amuses himself handsomely when he is on the town. He may set himself up as a saint when he is at home, as so many of his kind do, but I've seen some of the birds of paradise he flies with when he is on the strut. Don't goggle, Amanda," she chided, "it ill becomes you. You may be very educated, but you've a great deal to learn. There are a good many respectable folk who point a finger at North or me and my set while they themselves have a great deal to hide."

"I've never spoken to you about myself, Amanda," the countess continued, plucking at her skirts, "because it never seemed the right time. First you were too young, and then when I turned around, you were too old. But I believe it is time now. For if you must live with my name, at the very least you deserve to know how I got it. Oh dear," she sighed, looking so prettily confused for a moment, so much like the mama that Amanda knew, that she could scarcely believe the sensible words she began to speak.

"I'm sorry for the difficulties you've had being my daughter," the countess said. "And indeed I never thought on it, being quite a selfish creature, I'm afraid. But I did not set out to scandalize myself. I wed your father as he wed me, with and upon the instructions of our families. There was no vow of love, nor was any expected, but I attempted to be a good and faithful wife.

"When you were rising four," the countess said restlessly, as though she did not enjoy her remembrances, "your father informed me that he required no further heirs. You understand," she interrupted herself to gaze at Amanda, "that meant he allowed me my freedom and did not plan to frequent my bedchambers any longer. I did not believe him, even when he took up with another female, for I was far more strictly raised than you, my dear."

The countess allowed herself to laugh at her own utterance. Then she sobered and said carefully, "I went to London and took up with a fast set. I expected that word of my behavior would reach your father and that he in turn would come to bring me home. I was," she sighed, "extremely youthful for my age. To be brief, I met up with a rake, the Marquess of Carrick, fancied myself in love for the first time, and soon had to return home to bear Mary, for he would have no part of me when I told him of my situation.

"When I returned to town, I vowed to be more clever. But then I met a gentle, good, and compassionate man, Sir Harley Kilcane. I do not apologize for my liaison with him, my dear, and never shall. If he were not already tied to an invalid wife, we should have wed. He was beside himself with both despair and delight when Alicia was born, and determined to risk his name and his reputation in divorce when James was on the way. But he was even less robust than his wife, and succumbed to consumption before it was possible. The more fool I," the countess sighed, brushing at her eye, "for I had thought his pallor interesting and the bright spots in his cheeks due to his ever high spirits.

"After that I met my own dear Bobby, and after Cecil

came, we decided to flaunt convention and dwell together. The duchess will never give him his freedom; she is content to live with his name and without him. And, to be sure, there is no longer any reason for us to wed; we rub on together well enough the way we are. Divorce is no easy thing, my dear; there are only a handful obtained every year, and those only after so much scandal and name-blackening that it is hardly worth the effort.

"So you see," the countess said simply, "I am not such a wicked lady as you may have thought. Or perhaps I am, at that. But I am not light in my affections, Amanda, no matter what you have heard, nor have I ever been for sale. Mind, I do not ask you to excuse me, only to understand me."

Amanda sat very still. The countess, construing her amazement as disapproval, said, as though defending herself, "And at that, I believe I am villified the most for my honesty. For I could never give my children up. Many of the same grand dames who pretend to be aghast at me have gone for their own little repairing leases in the country in midseason. Oh yes," the countess said sagely to Amanda. "They begin to grow a little stout and then claim an overwhelming fondness for rustication. When they return, they are slim as wands, and some farmer's family has another child donated to help with work in the fields.

"And of course, the light sisterhood does the same," the countess reflected, "for there is little help for it. The gentlemen may like to forget it, but certain doings result in offspring, without fail. I am not saying it is common practice, but it is common knowledge, at least. All are not so fortunate as I," the countess grimaced, "to have such a free-thinking husband. But still I cannot understand how any could lightly give away a child as though it were a frock one had outgrown."

"What becomes of them?" Amanda asked suddenly, her mind returning from her mother's story to her own problem, "the cast-off children, I mean."

"They are taken in for a sum by farmers and the like, I imagine," the countess replied, "for they always need an extra hand to turn to work. And I have always thought that they are kinder to their children than we who purport to be above them, for they welcome each new addition to their house, or so it seems."

"Have you ever heard of the reverse?" Amanda asked quickly. "A farm-woman giving away her child?" She would have liked to clarify her question when her mother gazed at her uncomprehendingly, but dared not say further on a subject she felt was not hers to ask about.

"Why no," her mama replied. "As I have said, they treasure their offspring, there is always some relative to take them in. And who would seek them out, anyway? Children are cheap commodities as they are so easily gotten, Amanda," the countess sighed. "I know many who would pay a king's ransom if they could purchase a good way not to have them. But that's not the point. I have told you my tale because I believe that though one's life is one's own, parents owe their children explanation at least, for any stigma that might attach to them as consequence of their actions. Have you any questions you have hesitated to ask?" she ventured.

Amanda had a great many questions about a different set of parents and their actions, but none that her mother could answer. Still, she thought she owed her mama some query in reply to show that she understood and appreciated her candor, so she put her own thoughts away to frame one.

"Mama," she said slowly, as that lady steeled herself for whatever she might choose to ask, "I do have one question that I have been told I ought to ask. As we are speaking so frankly, do you remember a stack of slim green leather volumes that you secreted in the library years ago?"

Her mother started and glanced at Amanda nervously, wondering if her daughter's mind was wandering due to all the shocks she had been subjected to. But seeing Amanda's serious expression, she cudgeled her wits to recall the volumes as Amanda, choosing her words with great care, described them and their contents.

"Lud!" the countess cried, holding one dainty hand to her breast, "I thought we had burned them all. Never say you discovered them? And if you left them there, so they remain there to this hour, for Bobby and I are not great readers," she said regretfully. "I must have them destroyed before anyone else discovers them. They are rude, and crude as well, and there is nothing but malice in them."

The countess rose and hastened toward the door, but Amanda stopped her by saying gently, "But Mama, before you burn them, there is a question I must ask about them."

The countess stopped and looked very ill at ease as her daughter attempted to frame her request.

"My child," the Countess of Clovelly began, "the verse about me was untrue, you know, and as to the others, I can hardly vouch for their authenticity . . ." Her voice trailed off in uncertainty.

"No, no, Mama," Amanda said kindly, "I care nothing for the verses. It is only that I have always wished to ask you . . . it has been suggested that I ask you . . ." She hesitated and then plunged on, a look of fierce embarrassment upon her face, ". . . about the illustrations."

"Ah," the countess replied, nodding her head sagely. She glanced at her daughter's averted eyes and then pulled herself together in a very businesslike fashion. "An excellent idea, Amanda," she said briskly, "a meritorious idea. I shall just nip down to the library and fetch a copy now. As you are three and twenty and unwed, I believe it is past time we discussed them. And then," she added slyly, with a hint of the look that had brought the gentlemen of London to their knees decades before, "then we shall warm ourselves about a comfortably burning book while we decide what to do with your future."

XIV

The gentleman packed his portmanteau rapidly. His valet, he decided, as he paused for a moment to assess the number of neckcloths he needed and then cast several in without counting them, could do a far superior job of it. But that fellow would have taken hours with the task that he was accomplishing in minutes, and now he valued time above precision. He would let Atkins pack the necessary at leisure, for he had given him his direction so they could meet up later. Now he was in a fever to be off and would not let merely fashionable considerations forestall him.

As the viscount went to his wardrobe to get some shirts, he thought with a grim smile that he had done this so often that the actions came to him without thinking. It seemed that he had been constantly traveling since the moment he had decided to return to England. But as he reached for his shirts, he realized that he had been in transit for many years before then, as well. Whenever the company had palled, whenever he had found himself in a situation that had become tedious, whenever he wished to escape something or some thought, he had pulled out his portmanteau as though he could pack all his doubts in it with all his clothes, and had gone off without ever a look behind him.

This time was no different, although it was altogether unique. This time it was not the presence of someone that he was fleeing, it was the absence of someone. Since she had left, the viscount thought, packing his shirts deep within his traveling bag, Windham House had become intolerable to him. He had walked, he had ridden, he had paced the long halls until he had realized that he must be quit of this place. Now his mind was made up, and no thing on earth could divert him; it had always been so.

It was not that he missed her, it would have been impossible to miss someone whose unseen presence was felt in every corner of his house. It was instead that he could not rid himself of her. Lord North flung an extra pair of boots into his bag with a careless vehemence that would have made his valet wince, and thought of how many manifestations of her he had encountered in the long days since she had left. That was odd too, for he was used to more static ghosts of the past haunting him.

He paused for a moment at his dressing table, his hands arrested in midair above his brush, as he mused about the phenomenon. Most persons he had locked in his mind's eye seemed to be forever fixed in one aspect, as firmly and unchangeably imprinted upon his memory as each of his family was posed and frozen in their portraits in the bright, long gallery. When a name was recalled to him, he would recall that face as it had appeared in one distinctive expression.

Gilbert would always be that beet-red furious infant, lower lip jutted out, face swollen with outrage, eternally poised as he was about to fling himself into the nettles. His mama would always come to his mind as she had been in that one moment of frantic spite. Not one of the warm, compassionate smiles she wore in his childhood could be recalled without effort. Although they customarily slid by each other carefully since he had attained adulthood, and when he surprised an emotion in her eyes as she covertly observed him it was generally one of embarrassed regret, yet he could never forget the malignant look she had borne that one day. His adoptive father would always come to his mind as he had been on a distant winter's night, as a gently smiling adversary in a chess game that he replayed frequently in his memories, with that same anticipatory look of glee upon his gentle face that had caused him to betray his move and lose the game.

Some persons he had never bothered even to frame in his memory. It would shock most of the females he had ever known, from those partners in affairs that had lasted for months to those chance-met bedmates he had taken through boredom, if they could know that he could recall them only in fragmentary fashion. Here a smile, there a dimple, now a flash of breast, or then a moment of repletion, he remembered them as spasmodically as he had entangled himself with them. For as he had taken them only for pleasure's sake, they had returned nothing but delight to his senses and thus he bore no trace of them upon his heart or mind.

It was not that he was an uncommonly cold fellow, but he would have had to be wanting in wits to take any one of the light ladies from his set seriously. He had deliberately never sought the company of well-bred eligible young females, knowing that he could never provide them with the one thing they sought—a respectable name. He was not fool enough to court mockery. But now, he had been well paid for his one lapse.

For Lady Amanda Amberly, he thought, shaking his head as he placed his hand about his hairbrush, could not be contained in merely one image, nor could she be dismissed as a vagrant, fragmented memory. No, she broke the mold, for she appeared to him both complete and in endless guise.

He seized up the brush and hastened to cram it into his bag. He could not fix the damned chit in his mind in one completed final portrait and be done with her. She appeared to him in as many pictures as there were occupations in his day. He had only to enter the study and she would be there, her face filled with concentration as she penned one of her damned letters to another man, her lip caught up in her small white teeth as she struggled with invention. If he walked by the lakeside, she would pace with him, her face turned to his, a study in attentiveness, her long gray eyes lit with coming laughter.

He saw her bemused as he spun out his tales to her, he envisioned her wary as he drew near her, he pictured her valiant as she sought to conceal her distress at her situation in life. In the night, he saw her as he had first encountered her, deep in slumber. And then, due to his wide experience, he was easily able to envision her as he had never seen her, without her pristine white nightshift. And then, he would rise from his bed and damn his fertile imagination.

It was not just that he desired her, he was no stranger to that emotion. It was that he desired her conversation and good opinion as well, and that was a novelty to him. He had told her about himself and it had not fazed her. Although there was a good deal more that he could have told, he had the distinct notion that though he might disappoint her, she could never fail to understand him. Perhaps it was as he had said, because she had grown to adulthood in the shadow of inherited disgrace as well, that she was able to accept him as a being apart from the label of his birth. Perhaps that did not really matter at all and by insisting that it did, he was only perpetuating the same prejudice that he deplored in others. The cause no longer mattered. The matter was that he could not forget her.

She had spurned the only offer of marriage he had ever made, and yet he was not surprised. He was too clever at cards not to know that even the best bluff might be called. Thinking on it now, as he placed the last of his toilet articles in his bag, he acknowledged that he would have been more shocked had she accepted him. For he knew even better than she had just what he had left out of his offer, having been so careful to do so. Had she whispered a shy "yes" when he had done, he would have in some corner of his mind been disappointed in her and in his reading of her character. For he had not mentioned love, nor fidelity. It had been his deliberate intention not to.

Love, Lord North thought angrily, closing up his portmanteau and looking about the room absently for any item he might have missed, *love* was not a word he had ever used, or needed to either. She had noted it; she had wisely declined his offer. He congratulated her now on a savage underbreath as he picked up his bag.

Lord North reached to open his door and found himself clutching air as it swung wide. Gilbert stood there, his expression so very nearly like the infant his brother had been imagining that it was laughable. But there was no laughter in the viscount's eyes as he looked the younger man up and down.

"Here to assist me in carting my luggage?" Lord North asked coolly. "I am not so up in years that I cannot manage by myself."

"No, and you know it, too," Gilbert said gruffly, his lower lip so extended that his speech became blurred.

"Ah," Lord North sighed, putting his traveling bag down, "so be it. Come in, brother, and open your budget to me before I leave, for I see that I shan't step a foot out today until you've unburdened yourself. But do try to hurry, won't you, for I've a horse waiting and many miles to go."

"That's just it," Gilbert said unhappily, stomping into the room and lowering himself to the edge of the viscount's bed dejectedly. "Don't want you to go, Chris, don't know how I can get you to stay, neither. But I never felt so worthless in my life, and there's the truth of it."

"I'm touched by your devotion, Gil," Lord North said sweetly, as he closed the door and turned to the forlorn youth, "but as you've mentioned your reluctance to see me depart only a few hundred times in the last days, I don't see why we should go over it again."

"Yes," Gilbert cried angrily, "and you've remained mum as a mouse to whatever I say. But I'll say it again at any rate. If I had a fiancée like Amanda, I shouldn't take myself off to the continent and forget her forever, no I should not. For that's what it would mean. You may say that it is all right for her to remain with her mama, but I say never! For Amanda's nothing like her mama, that I do know though I've never set eyes on the countess, nor do I need to. And Sir Boothe may be a stick, and no denying it, but a fellow would have to be addled to leave his promised bride alone with a chap that's got eyes for no one else but her. And finally," Gilbert said in vexation, "since Mama's so pleased with what's transpiring, I should think you'd know it was the wrong thing for you to do. She's made for you, Chris," Gilbert concluded, mixing up his mama and his brother's fiancée in one last mighty attempt to make his brother see the light.

But all that slender, expressionless, flaxen-haired fellow did was to smile and then say, softly, "Yes of course," in response to his brother's impassioned plea.

"Oh, yes, I knew you'd say that . . ." Gilbert began, but then broke off and gaped at the viscount.

"Yes, Gil," Lord North said reasonably, "you are quite right. And that is why I am leaving now."

The look upon his brother's face was so turbulent that the viscount relented. He put a hand upon Gilbert's shoulder and said kindly, "I'm going to get her, Gil. I'm leaving to go to Kettering Manor now to put an end to all this charade."

But as he put spur to horse, and waved farewell to Gilbert, the viscount wished that he had some of his brother's eternal optimism. For he did not know if he would succeed. He knew that he had his lady's interest, he knew that he could ignite her physical desire. But he did not know if that was enough for her. Plainly, it had never been enough for him.

He could only hope to persuade her by offering her that which he had never tendered to any other female, and that was a meager enough gift, he thought wryly, for it was only himself, entirely.

If he won her, he thought, as he galloped forward, it would mean that he must give up his wanderings, his constant conquests of alien flesh, his solitary life, and his devotion to only his own interests and entertainments. And as though he could not bear to wait to be free of these, his former pleasures, he leaned forward to push his mount to greater speed.

The day was clear and bright, but the journey was bumpy as the road was filled with so many frozen furrows left by other vehicles' passages. The brief winter afternoon was dimming and the occupant of the lurching coach sighed as she realized that the journey, which might have been accomplished within a day, would take yet another due to the ruts and hollows that impeded the coach's swift progress. It was as well, Amanda admitted, that her mama had insisted upon her packing for an overnight stay. For as much as she disliked the idea of it, there was no longer any doubt that her mission would take longer than she had planned or hoped.

It was only the cruelty of fate, she decided, as she snuggled down within her cape to elude the chill winds that stole within the joinings of the carriage, that prolonged her journey. For as it was a trip that was conceived in desperation, executed on a moment's notice, and embarked upon with trepidation, each hour that it wore on, wore down the weak reasons for its very being. It had been one thing to decide upon a course of action in the depths of the night in one's snug bed, and quite another to be forced to examine that decision minutely once one was already involved with it.

She glanced over toward the sleeping maid in the other corner of the coach and envied the girl from the bottom of her heart. If she could only lose herself in sleep so easily, she would be free of the thousand doubts and regrets she now suffered. Free of them, Amanda groaned as she pulled her hood over her face, as well as the biting cold that now filled the vehicle. She had only herself to blame for that as well, for she had insisted that no time could be spared and had refused to stop for a luncheon, or even for so long as to have the bricks at her feet reheated.

This very morning she had woken from the broken sleep which had plagued her since she had arrived at Kettering Manor, and had been suddenly full of resolve and determination. This journey had seemed then the only sensible, indeed the only feasible, course that she could follow. Mama, who had projected a dozen different solutions to her problems, only to have them each and every one met with firm denial, had agreed with her at once. But that, Amanda now thought, was only because the usually astute lady was anxious to see any plan go forward, any action taken, no matter how nonsensical.

Mama could not have truly approved of the scheme, Amanda knew, if only because she had not known the half of it. There were some things that her daughter could not divulge to any other being, and the real reason for this impetuous jaunt was one of them. Indeed, Amanda thought as she gazed upon the patterns of hoarfrost on the coach window, if she had been completely honest and clear-thinking this morning she might never be sitting where she was right now. But, like her mama, she too had only felt the pressing need to do something, to take some action, however foolish.

She wanted to see Lord North again, no, she corrected herself, she had to see him again. But if she wrote to him or sent for him, she would be signaling that she accepted his terms. They would both know that, no matter how witty or subtle her summons. And to accept him on his given terms would be to accept a second-rate life.

But she could not be free of him. Just the thought of him even now in the cold coach, was to make her feel as though she had been sitting beneath a summer sun for hours. As she burned in the cold from the memory of him, she mused sadly that so it always was when one gazed too long at any bright, unobtainable shining object. For just as the sun will sear its image into one's aftervision long beyond the time that one has looked upon it, so doubtless she would always bear his imprint upon her consciousness. But memory was not enough for her.

He was never the pillar of respectability she had thought she would wish to wed. There was no evading the truth that he had been a thorough reprobate, as free with his morals as any from her mama's wild set. But still, she knew as surely as she accepted the rising of tomorrow's dawn that he had caught her life up in his.

She could not send for him, she could not go to him. As she neither wished for nor could wait for some natural disaster or death in the family, she knew she must invent some subterfuge so that she might at least look upon him once again. There was only one last avenue of possibility: If she could discover something to his interest, she could then summon him to hear of it without committing herself to him.

It was in the bleakest hour of the night that she hit upon her mad scheme; indeed, it was then that she could not escape it. For the whispers and random comments she had heard echoed in her head and dismissed sleep. She heard

Gilbert saying that the viscount and his father "were like as two peas in a pod," she heard her mama's sighs over farmwomen's devotion to their offspring, she listened again to the viscount's voice telling the brief tale of his birth. There were too many contradictions in the phantom voices that banished slumber.

She could not believe that his mother had been so low as to sell him for "a crust of bread." No, not when nobility was written into every fine lineament of his person. Nor could she believe that a gentleman such as his adoptive father would have taken in any chance-gotten by-blow and raised him as a son. Not when, as Mama had said, children of all stripes were such easily gotten goods.

The notion had come to her with such force that she had sat straight up in bed, that the late viscount had known the waif's parentage, that he had been well aware of the pedigree of the child he had adopted. Amanda's desire that the idea be true had given it more credence. Though in that one tense interview the woman had said she was the mother, it might not be true. He might have been left to her fostering by some titled lady, through shame. If she had borne him, the woman herself might not have been without honor. It may have been that his father was gently bred. A thousand possibilities sprang to mind, and Christian himself, out of shock, anger, and disappointment, had explored none of them. Due to her own pressing need, Amanda had decided that she would investigate.

It had seemed so possible in the morning, she had found herself buoyed up by courage then. She had packed quickly and told her mother no more than the fact that she must be gone to Ashbourne for a day, to discover something that might aid in her decision as to her fiancé. Mama had asked no further, but had only insisted that she prepare for a possible overnight stay. But she had been adamant above all else that a reliable coachman be taken for protection, as well as a reliable maid for protection against gossip.

Giles had been livid at her departure without his escort and without his knowledge of either her destination or reason for leaving, however briefly. Remembering his fury, Amanda wondered if she would see him when she returned,

and felt colder still when she realized that she hardly
cared. But worst of all was the realization that her enthusiasm for her scheme had grown cold as the day and her
chances for success with it as dim as the light that was now
fading from the sky.

When the coach pulled into the courtyard of the only
inn at Ashbourne, the Gilded Plum, Amanda found herself very glad that it was too late in the day for her to try
her luck with her wild scheme. She put it out of her mind,
and instead occupied herself with the delicate matter of
booking accommodations. Though the landlord's eyebrows
went up as she insisted on separate rooms for herself and
her maid, she remained calm as she insisted on the extraordinary arrangements. Beth was Mama's personal maid, and
though the countess had sworn that she had picked her for
the journey because the girl was known to never let a word
of tattle escape her lips to reach another servant's ear,
Amanda had the shrewd idea that no word of gossip Beth
heard ever failed to reach her mama's ear either. But no
matter what the landlord's reactions, the undertaking
Amanda was embarked upon was private. If even she was
unsure she had the right to pursue her inquiries, she was
determined that Mama should never know of it.

After a meal eaten more from necessity than from desire,
Amanda took to her room. Though she wanted to sit up
and plan and consider her ambitions, she soon found sleep.
Thus, she awakened early in a strange bed, in an unfamiliar room. Her first coherent thought was that she had made
a dreadful mistake and was on the verge of making another.

She had no right, she thought as she took two sips of
chocolate, to pry into the viscount's secret affairs. She had
not a shred of a claim to unearth facts about his past, she
told herself as she broke her toast into interesting fragments.
But so long as she had come so far, she decided as she sent
for her coachman, she might as well just have a look
around her.

Amanda left her mama's maid behind to carry on a
lively flirtation with an ostler. She told the girl that she
was only going for a little ride about the town and did not
require escort. But for all of her supposed interest in the

bold looks and wicked suggestions of the hearty ostler, the
girl did not miss hearing her mistress's daughter tell the
coachman to find the direction of a farm holding known as
Land's End. Now what, the girl wondered as she fended
off a bluff familiarity from her new suitor, was Lady
Amanda doing decked out for a visit with the queen if she
was only going to a farmyard? For the lady was wearing a
smashing pink frock, with a deep rose woolen cape with
ermine trim that all the maidservants coveted, and her hair
had been brushed until it shone.

Still, the countess's maid thought as she called the ostler
a "naughty fellow" even as she batted her lashes to encourage him further, she could not be expected to hike up her
skirts and dash after the carriage. She had told the countess that she would keep her eyes and ears open, and that
she would. For the moment, she was content to keep them
opened very wide indeed, as the ostler embarked upon
relating a string of compliments whose recollection would
keep her as warm as Lady Amanda's dashing cloak might
through the rest of the long winter.

It was, Amanda thought, just as he had said it had been.
It took just a little imagination to flesh out the details of
the winter-stark surroundings so that she could envision
them as he had seen them in the full bloom of summer.
There where the lane ended the cottage stood neat and
contained within a copse of trees. There were the skeletons
of rose bushes trailing about the front wall of the house
and standing rigid about the doorways. There was no
young man with extraordinary eyes working about the
place to be seen, but Amanda could scent and see the curls
of wood smoke rising from the chimneys. The coach paused
in the lane in front of the cottage for so long that Amanda
thought that if she waited much longer, the bushes might
indeed begin to put forth flowers.

At last, she opened the door and stepped down from the
vehicle. She stood in the cold, one foot poised in front of
the other, preparing to go down the winding gravel walk
to the front door, and then she stopped. She had come all
this way to the very doorstep of her future, and found she
could go no further. What could she say? "I am the Lady

Amanda Amberly, here to discuss your bastard child that you gave away decades ago"? Or perhaps, "How do you do. I am engaged to the Viscount North and as he is a well-known by-blow, I thought I might have a word with you about why you sold him when he was an infant"? Or would it be more suitable if she simply said, "I am one of the notorious Amberly Assortment, and as I am to wed a bastard as well, I felt I ought to find out something more about him"?

Amanda's shoulders slumped and she gave the little cottage one last, longing look before she turned to enter the coach again. The past was done; she could not enter it again any more than any other being could. And as it was the past that had brought her together with the viscount, it would be the past that remained to keep them apart. She had placed one hand upon the coach, preparing to enter it again, when she was halted by an earnest young voice.

"Excuse me, m'am . . . miss," it said, "but my mum asks if you would care to step in for a cup of tea."

Amanda turned and looked down to see a pair of worried eyes considering her. The boy was fourteen or so, and for a second Amanda blinked, wondering if some fancy had caused her to actually see the same youth the viscount had seen all those years ago. But as the eyes that looked beseechingly at her were both blue, she was relieved to find that, however odd, at least this encounter was real.

"Please, miss," he said earnestly, "she said as to how I should bring you in for a visit."

Amanda could only nod. She cast a glance at the coachman, but he had heard as well and only touched his hat before he leaped down to cover the horses while they waited for her. She followed the youth up to the door of the cottage as though in a daze.

The front door was drawn open by a woman of her own mama's years. Though she wore country homespun and her fair hair was pulled back neatly rather than artfully arranged, she, in her own fashion, was easily as lovely and youthful as the countess.

Amanda paused at the doorstep, seeing a neat parlor behind the woman, a fire crackling on the hearth, and a lazy old dog rising stiffly to its feet to greet her as well. She suddenly found herself an interloper and could not think of a word to say. Her training came to her rescue and she licked her dry lips, put out her hand, and said nervously,

"Good morning. I am Lady Amanda Amberly."

"How do you do," the woman said very hesitantly in a soft voice. "I am Annie Holcroft. I was Annie Withers. I've been expecting you, my lady."

XV

Amanda sat at the edge of her chair and bit the end of her pen as she tried to think of the words she must use in her brief message. She had rushed back to her room at the inn, flung her cape over a chair, and poised herself at the desk to compose a compelling summons. But she had been unable to phrase it in suitably oblique but meaningful terms, and now the afternoon sun illuminated the best guest bedroom at the Gilded Plum and she had only set down three lines.

When the first sharp knock came to her door, she rose. But she had no time to answer before the door flew inward with such force that it trembled on its hinges. The gentleman had not bothered to knock twice. He burst into the room even as the door had, but he did not venture far into the chamber. Rather, he took only a few steps forward and then stood, arms akimbo, and glowered at Amanda.

She gazed at him as though she had run mad. For it was as though her very concentration upon him had produced him in a vision for her. But she had never imagined him as he now appeared. The viscount's usually immaculate clothes were travel-stained. His cravat was slightly askew, his boots badly mud-covered. His bright hair was in disarray, there were hollows beneath his eyes, and a faint tracing of golden beard showed on his lean cheeks. His eyes glittered dangerously and his whole being seemed taut with scarcely concealed anger.

"Writing again?" the viscount asked. "My dear, your wrists must ache with your interminable scribblings. Penel-

ope stitched, Arachne spun, but Lady Amanda, she is
endlessly writing. Ah, but you must have something worthy to put to paper. What is it? Not another letter filled
with entreaty for Giles? Or just some delicious bits of
gossip you have discovered about the sensational history of
a blackguard sprung from the fields to take on the name
and airs of a gentleman? Or perhaps you are dangling for
an invitation so that you may acquire some more? Come,
Amanda, you have not undertaken a journey like this and
procured pen and paper just so that you might dash off a
bread and butter note. Do tell me about it, I might find it
amusing as well."

"I was writing to you," Amanda said dazedly, as she held
the note up for him to see, though she never took her eyes
from him for a moment as she did so.

He strode into the room and snatched the letter from
her fingers. He quickly scanned the lines.

"Yes," he muttered, and then "Yes" he spoke wearily as
he dropped the paper. Then he looked at her again with
sorrow and puzzlement.

"Why?" he asked softly, all anger gone and only deep
disappointment in his voice, "why have you come here?"

Before she could answer, he went on, "I rode the best
part of two days to Kettering Manor to surprise you, to
. . . it makes no matter now. But I rode down one horse
and hired another so that I might reach you more quickly.
Imagine then, how delighted I was to discover you had
gone. Not to your father, nor even with Giles. Rather,
your mother informed me, with a merry twinkle in her
eye, to Ashbourne. Ashbourne, of all places! It was not
difficult to get your direction as this is the only inn at
Ashbourne. For there are no spas here, no gay assemblies,
no touring points of interest for you, save one. And that
only the existence of a wretched slut who bartered her
infant for pennies. I told you of her, Amanda, so that you
might understand me better, not so that you might dredge
up muck that is best left undisturbed. Whey did you come
here?" he asked again.

"Because you ought to have," Amanda answered quickly.
"Oh Christian, you should have come back long since.

Nothing is as you had thought. I was writing to tell you to come at once, for there is somethng you must hear with your own ears."

"So you have already spoken with her," he said with resignation. "What did you do? Offer her a goodly sum for the tale, and a bonus for a happy ending to it? Amanda, my meddling fool, a drab who would peddle her own babe will tell any sort of tale you would wish for a handsome enough price. I can understand why you came," he said, gazing at her ruefully, "for I always liked that tale about the frog prince myself when I was a child. But I am precisely what I am, my dear. And if you thought to make the best of my offer by offering up a fiction to embellish my name, it won't do. Neither your kiss nor your hand will transform me, princess, nor will some expensively gotten fairy tale."

"It isn't like that," Amanda insisted. "I came to Land's End because there was so much you had not told me, indeed, so much that you could not have done and more that I guessed at. But when I came to the cottage, my courage deserted me and I was about to turn and go. But she had seen me from the window. And she was expecting me, she said, and had been for years. Oh, not me, but someone like me, some fine lady, she said, as she knew that someday you would wed and that your lady, at least, would want to know certain facts."

Amanda reached down for her cloak and flung it about her shoulders as she said eagerly, "Only come with me now. That is what I was writing to ask of you, and now we can do it at once. Come back with me now and hear it all from her own lips. It is not a fairy tale. There are documented proofs, only I doubt you will need to see them once you have heard the facts yourself."

The viscount stood fixed where he had paused and fingered the edge of the writing desk Amanda had been seated at.

"I think not," he said slowly. "Or at any rate, not at this moment. Tell me the tale, and I shall decide whether it is worthy of facing that woman again. At any rate," he said more lightly, "I am in all my dirt. I rode to Kettering

Manor without pause, and when I heard of your destination, I rode on again as though demented. I believe I need some rest, perhaps time to change my attire, time to——"

"No," Amanda cried so vehemently that she surprised both herself and Lord North. "No, that won't do. For then you'll find another reason not to go. It's best done at once, before you can change your mind. How can you bear not knowing a thing that I know?" she asked then, with such a poor attempt at cunning that he laughed.

He shrugged his shoulders, as though he had just lost some inner debate, and then straightened.

"Very well," he smiled, as he ran his hand against his jaw. "Although I do believe that I ought to have shaved first. Yet, perhaps this is best. It may comfort the lady to see that she has spawned true, and that I suit a barnyard better than a ballroom."

Amanda grimaced at his light words. But she went unhesitatingly with him to the door, and then to her coach for the short ride to Land's End. Lord North sat back in the carriage, his bright head resting against the cushions, his facile tongue stilled for once.

Amanda tried to break him from his reverie by saying conversationally, as they drove off,

"She has married again, and her husband knows all. Indeed, he welcomes your visit, for he knows that will ease her mind as well."

But the viscount wore an abstracted air and she could not tell if he attended to her words at all. He might be weary with his travels, she thought as she fell silent, but no amount of riding could have diminished him so, or could account for the drawn look upon his pale face. She knew she was forcing him to journey toward the last place on earth that he wished to go, and wished that she could spare him this pain even as she inflicted it.

When the carriage stopped at last, she glanced at him fearfully. But he only took in one deep breath and then turned to her as though to admit her existence at last.

"Come, my dear," he said coolly, "this promises to be an interesting performance."

This time it was Annie Holcroft herself, still wiping her

hands on a dishcloth, who came to their summons to admit them to her little house.

Amanda caught in her breath as the slender, fair nobleman encountered the small fair woman on the doorstep. She thought, on a wild interior giggle, that their mutual moment of hesitation might be caused by their inability to put such a bizarre meeting into proper social terms. But Lord North was equal to any occasion, and after a pause, he bowed and said calmly, "Good morning. I am Christian Jarrow. I believe we met before. I understand that my fiancée, Lady Amanda Amberly, has been speaking with you and that you wish to have further discussion with me."

"I called after you that day," Annie Holcroft said immediately, her eyes searching his for some human reaction to her, "but you were gone so quickly. I wrote once, too, or at least, had someone write for me, as I cannot. But you never answered my letter."

"I was off at school," Lord North said. "And no letter was ever forwarded to me."

"I could not write again," the fair woman said quietly, "for I promised not to."

Amanda stood looking at the pair, one whose eyes showed nothing but concern and anxiety, and the other whose eyes seemed glazed over as if by the frost. It was Amanda's shifting from foot to foot that recalled the older woman to her senses and she stepped aside and said hurriedly, "Come in, please. Please be seated. My boys are out helping their father with chores, so we can speak privately."

When they were seated in the snug parlor, with the old dog settled back on the hearth rug, Annie Holcroft began to speak.

"I thought you knew," she said at once, without preamble, as soon as the viscount had seated himself. "But when Lady Amanda told me you did not, I knew that I must explain. Your parents should have. I'm not the person to cast stones, but I would not have done as I did if I thought you were never to be told the truth some day. It may be no honor to be my son, but there was no dishonor in the begetting of you."

She spoke softly and Amanda, having heard it all before, could sit and watch Lord North's face as he listened. His mother's words were well chosen, for she had once, in her youth, been a lady's maid and still bore the markings of gentility in her voice even as she yet bore the traces of the beauty she had once possessed.

"I was married when I was very young," she said at once, "to a farmer on your father's estates. But he was killed in an accident, when our baby was only a few months old. It was not easy for me then, for I had no family and I feared that I would be thrown out of our house. I could never have found work with a babe at the breast. It was your father who saw to it that I could stay on at Windham, and keep our cottage. He was a good, kind, generous landlord.

"I was very grateful to him," she said carefully. "He would come to see if I were in need, he would visit to see how the baby was growing. All of his tenants knew what sort of a man he was and we all thought it a great shame that he had no children of his own, for he would make such a fuss over our little ones. He would bring my little fellow trinkets and toys and sometimes he would stay and let the baby play with his fobs, or when he grew older, give him rides in front of him on his great horse. As time went by, he would spend hours sometimes with me and my boy. For my baby was a stout little toddler, with no end of daring, and your father said he was the most taking little chap he had ever seen."

The viscount stirred. An expression of distaste was clear upon his fine features.

"Please spare yourself further effort, madam," he drawled. "I quite understand now. You are telling me that my father came to love dear little Billy or Tim so much that he straightaway offered to adopt him. And you were so overjoyed at the tyke's good fortune that you accepted. It was only that evil gossip erupted when I appeared at Windham House. I quite understand. A delightful, heartwarming tale to be sure. So then, I am to infer that I am legitimate and legitimately gotten?"

"Oh no," the fair-haired woman demurred at once, quite

missing the sarcasm as she said earnestly, "for Georgie is my oldest son. You saw him when you were last here. He's grown now with babes of his own. I should never have given him up, not even to a fine gentleman like your father, for he was the last I had of my own husband. You are your father's son," she said seriously.

The viscount sat back abruptly, all evidence of the sneer he had worn quite vanished, as she went on more slowly, "Your father kept paying me longer visits, and I could see in time, that he had something on his mind. At last, one snowy morning I remember, he came when he knew that Georgie was having his nap. He said that he wished to speak with me upon a grave matter. He came into the parlor and paced for a long time before he spoke. Then he said that he had an offer to put to me, and that if it did not meet with my approval, I should speak my mind straightaway and that he would never hold it against me, no, nor never even mention it again. He said that I should have no fear of refusing him.

"He and the viscountess could have no children, they had waited for nine years without issue. So he asked if I would have a child with him, so that he could have an heir to carry on his name that was of his own blood, at least. The problem lay with his dear lady wife, the doctors said. He made it clear that it was a business matter," she said hurriedly, as the viscount stared at her, "and he promised me that he would see to it that I never suffered shame nor want. But as he admired me and my Georgie, he thought I might give him a fine child. The viscountess had agreed to the scheme," she added quickly, "for neither of them wanted to see Windham House go to his brother, who was a wastrel. And they both wanted a baby.

"I thought about it for a week," she said, now with her eyes to the carpet, "and I thought on what a good, kind man the viscount was. Then it came to me that I could do no better in this life than to oblige him. I liked him very well," she said softly, "and I knew that there would be nothing between a tenant's widow and a great gentleman, so much as I liked him. But this, I could do for him. And

it was clearly a business matter, so I did not feel like a
. . ." Her words trailed off.

Amanda, seeing the far-off look upon the woman's face,
again took leave to wonder just how much of a business
arrangement the young widow had thought it, and how
much of it had been more, at least upon her own part.

"I agreed," Annie Holcroft said, holding her head high.
"And your father visited me often. But then, once I was
sure you were on the way, there was no more . . . He only
visited me then to see how I was faring," she said sadly.
"Although I often wondered if he should like to . . . but he
was an honorable man," she concluded proudly.

"When you were born, you were given over to him
immediately, Georgie and I came to Land's End, and we
were well off for I was given an independence. He sent me
notice of how you were growing, how very happy they
were with you. And I was never sorry for what I did until
that day you came to see me and I knew somehow it had
all gone wrong."

The viscount was quiet after his mother had done
speaking. Both women watched him carefully as he sat in
deep thought. Then he laughed abruptly. It was a chilling
sound. He rose and looked down at his mother, a sort of
exultant despair upon his face.

"So I am my father's son. Since you cannot make me
legitimate, I expect that's the next best thing. I congratulate you. It is an excellent story. I am to believe that I am
not some random object acquired after a few fevered moments in a haystack, a chance-gotten brat of a chance
encounter, but rather the carefully conceived son of a
gentleman and a good woman paid to bear me. You are,
then, I take it, only a little more than a wet nurse, or some
sort of surrogate for my own poor barren adoptive mama.
What a clever invention! I should be very happy with that
tale if it were not for one thing."

He looked down at her scornfully and then said with
bitter triumph, "How comes it, then, my dear clever mama,
that neither you nor my papa have these strange varicolored eyes you see before you? The very same ones I recall
my half-brother Georgie appears to have had? I have

searched this land and over again to find one male gentleman, or vagrant, of the right age who possesses such odd eyes, and have not yet found him. Come, be plain with me. It no longer matters. I need no bedtime stories, I am a grown man. Who was my father?"

His mother stood so that she faced him squarely. She smiled and said, "Those eyes are common in my family, your lordship. And have been for generations. They crop up where they will. But you could not have looked too closely that time you were here, and you have never looked me in the eye since you have set foot over my doorstep. Do so now," she said proudly, turning her head to the light, "for your papa was used to say that my eyes reminded him of a warm August afternoon when there was thunder in the air. For my left eye, he said, was as bright and blue as a summer's sky, while the right clearly showed that dark storm clouds were brewing."

As the viscount leaned close in amazement to study the small gray motes which obscured the purity of blue in his mother's eye, Amanda wondered how businesslike his father had found that odd arrangement all those years ago, if he could quote such tender poetry to a woman who would merely bear his son for convenience's sake.

Although the dinner served at the Gilded Plum was the same for each of its patrons, one would not have guessed it from observing the couple in the small inn's private dining room. For one of the guests, a handsome blond gentleman, laughed frequently and poured wine as generously as he poured out his thoughts. His companion sat and ate sparingly, and only listened to the gentleman quietly.

They had declined his mother's invitation to dine. They had left her after they had spoken a while longer, and after they had shaken hands with the tall, soft-voiced man who was now master of the little farm. It had been a subdued farewell, for though there were no longer any recriminations, each of them had known that the relationship established that afternoon could and would never go further. The son had learned details of his birth and family history. The mother had learned that he bore her no ill will and respected her decision. That had been enough, and more, for a lifetime for the two of them.

Lord North had stayed silent, as though stunned, all the way back to the inn. But after washing and changing his garb, he had lived with his history long enough to emerge at dinner as a relaxed, merry companion. Now, as he filled Amanda's glass again, he shook his head in wonder and said, as he had just done moments before, as though he needed to reassure himself,

"Just imagine. The crafty old fox. Two sets of papers. One for the baptismal record for all the village to see, saying that I was the viscount's legitimate son, before God. And the other, for less supreme and forgiving beings, locked in his man-at-law's safe against the day that his brother should challenge my inheritance, saying that I was his son by Annie Withers, legally adopted. A superior ruse, but," he said ruefully, "he could not know that both he and his brother would be gone before I came of age. And he could not guess that his dear wife would withhold knowledge from me, out of spite. Nor could she have foreseen," he sighed, "that bearing her own child at last would engender such regret and hatred for her earlier bargain and its result."

He downed his wine and his face cleared again.

"But it makes no matter," he said. "For I do know now. And I thank you, my little meddler. You can have no idea of how pleasant it is to know who you are at last. It's not only a wise child that knows his own father, it is a very lucky one. You are quiet tonight," he said, gazing at her curiously before he laughed again and said, "but what else can I expect, poor lady? When I have spent the night babbling on about my good fortune. Now it's your turn. Tell me about Giles and your mama."

Amanda told him listlessly of her decision to come to Land's End, and of Giles's annoyance at her journey. She seemed so distracted that the viscount's own expression lost some of its vivacity and he bent himself to entertaining her so completely that soon she found herself smiling despite her lowered spirits.

But the hour grew late and Amanda knew that the

evening which she wished would spin out forever, was done. The fire in the hearth had burned down until it only spat fitfully, and the landlord had appeared several times to clear his throat in the doorway, but still she had delayed the hour of parting from the viscount. Because, she thought somberly, as the viscount related an amusing story about Gilbert, this time it would be a final parting.

She had brought about his present happiness. She had lifted the burden of his unknown ancestry from his spirit, but by that very act, she now knew that she had brought about the end to their relationship and ended any air dreams she might have had about a future with him. For as his father had truly been the viscount, now he must know that both his title and his beloved Windham House were his by rights older than any society might impose. Now he could, without guilt, stroll the bright gallery at Windham House and see his heritage and his past clearly affirmed.

With the mystery of his dark origins erased, he could change his life. He no longer needed to racket about with the careless persons of her mother's set. He no longer needed to punish himself by an alliance with a lady of infamous name, a wife whose very presence would be a constant reminder to himself of his unjustly ignoble state.

And as he had not brought up the subject of his previous offer since he had made his discovery, although they had passed many hours together in privacy since, she realized with sinking heart that he must no longer wish to remember it. So be it, she thought, but for her own pride's sake, she must be the one to end it, not he.

Although doubtless he was relieved that she had not accepted his spontaneous offer, yet even so, she could not regret what she had brought about for him. He need not stoop so low now, Amanda thought, to get himself a suitable wife. He could, she sighed, gazing with longing at the vivid face which had become so necessary to her, he should do better. She had wanted to linger so that she might have her fill of looking at him and listening to his voice. But now she saw that the shadows beneath his eyes were pronounced, and that no matter how ebullient his spirits, his changeable eyes were heavy with fatigue.

Amanda had not wanted the night to end, for she saw the course of tomorrow, but she rose and said, "If we don't leave now, Christian, the servants will fall asleep stacked in the doorway. And I have a long journey that begins at dawn."

He arose at once, berating himself for his thoughtlessness. As they mounted the stairs, he told her that he ought to have noticed the hour, for he was sure he would fade away as soon as his head touched the pillow, having been kept awake so long only through sheer excitement, like a boy in the night before his birthday morning.

When they reached the door to her room, he smiled down at her tenderly and said with a hint of a wicked leer, "Now then, Lady Amanda, is this the blue or the gray room?"

"It is my room, Lord North," she said carelessly as she opened her door and stepped in, "as you can plainly see."

He paused at the door and then wandered in after her. He looked about him with a frown.

"But where is your maid?" he demanded. "I did not see her before and thought she was off on some errand, but surely she should be here at this hour?"

"She is in her own room down the hall," Amanda replied as she closed the door, surprised at his annoyance. "Pray do not wake her with your shouting. I did not want her to note my comings and goings," she explained, "for I did not know what I might discover at Land's End and felt it was not her business in any event."

"There's wisdom in that," he conceded. "But nonetheless, 'Manda, you ought not to be here with me unattended."

She stared at him in amazement and then began to laugh.

"Good heavens, Christian," she said when she was able, "never say that you are concerned with the proprieties?"

She still wore a smile, but he replied without a trace of mirth, "You think me such a complete rakeshame that I don't care if my betrothed acts with propriety then?"

Amanda turned quickly so that she would not have to

look into that still, stern face, and answered lightly as she flung down her shawl upon the bed, "Lud, Christian, I swear you know better than that. I am not precisely your 'betrothed,' you know."

He placed two hands upon her shoulders and swung her around toward himself, but still she would not meet his eyes.

"What the devil is going on here, 'Manda?" he asked. Her behavior puzzled him, it was uncharacteristic, at once artificial and coquettish. He had thought to declare himself to her once he had recovered from his surprise at the discovery of his origins, but now her attitude discomforted him.

"Whatever do you mean?" she answered, knowing precisely what he meant but being evasive since she did not know how to go on. For she had lost her courage and could not end it all between them here and now, this night.

" 'Manda," he said dangerously, "do not play with me. If you would not let me within yards of your room when you were beneath your mama's roof, nor within leagues of it at my house, how comes it that you stroll into an empty bedroom with me at midnight now?"

Amanda found anger simpler than explanation.

"I cannot help it if you think of only one thing," she snapped, unfairly even to her own ears. "I only wished to say good night."

"And what might that one thing be?" he asked as he stared down at her with his odd, glittering eyes. "Might it be this do you think?"

He bent his head and kissed her very lightly. He had come to reason with her, but forgot all else now but the challenge he heard in her words, and the promise he tasted upon her lips. When she did not pull away, his hands tightened on her shoulders and he drew her toward himself for a long, sweet embrace. When he lifted his head, he could see that she stood waiting, only breathing lightly, her eyes half closed. He studied her face for a moment and then, wrapping one arm about her shoulders he walked her

the few paces to the huge bed and sat with her at the edge
of it. Then he pulled her back into his arms again.

After a few moments, his caresses, which had been light
and gentle, began to change with the rapidity that his
conversations always had. His lips left hers and strayed to
the side of her neck. One of his clever hands traced the
outlines of her breast, while the other surely and swiftly
undid the tiny buttons at the back of her frock.

She had not wished to begin this, Amanda thought, she
had not known that she could begin this. She knew that
she should stop him or herself, and had known that from
the moment he had begun. But she had kept promising
herself only one more moment of intimacy. Even now, as
she experienced both delight and a muddled sense of panic,
she could not bring herself to form the phrase to begin her
final good-bye.

She kept her eyes tightly closed as though by that means
she would deny all that was happening. She felt her woolen
frock slip slowly down and away from her shoulders and
her breasts. The chill of the night air made her gasp, but it
was swiftly replaced by the warmth of his hands and his
lips, which made her gasp again. She seemed to be ablaze
in the cold room beneath his skillful touch as he murmured
her name over and over.

No word of denial came to her command as he presented her with new sensations. But helpless tears sprang
to her eyes and coursed down her cheeks at her foolish
inability to frame the words she knew she must, the words
that would return her world to normalcy. Then she felt
suddenly chilled again, as all the splendid heat was withdrawn from her abruptly. She sat cold and confused and
she heard his breath go out in an explosive sigh and then
heard a loudly muttered curse that made her open her eyes
wide. He sat next to her and ran a hand through his bright
hair distractedly.

He glowered at her with such force that she shrank
back. His gaze dropped to her breasts, which she was
shamed to see startlingly naked and white in the dim light.
As she attempted to hide herself with her hands, he reached
out and dragged her bodice up.

"Cover yourself," he said harshly.

She fumbled at the back of her dress with numbed fingers, and he sighed again.

"Here," he said gruffly, turning her, "let me do it. Bother," he muttered in a more natural tone, "I can't do these things up it seems, although they are little enough trouble to undo. You're always presenting me with new experiences, 'Manda," he said now as conversationally as if he were in a drawing room with her, "for I have never had to button up a female before. Hold still, please.

"No doubt I could get these things done up more quickly if I worked from the front as I am accustomed to usually undoing them. But then we'd be in the same predicament again straightaway. There, that will have to do. Now," he continued, as he stood quickly and looked down at her, "wipe your eyes and kindly tell me what the purpose of that little episode was."

She dashed a hand across her cheek and said unhappily, "I was just saying good night."

"And how much longer would you have continued to permit me to bid you good night in my thorough fashion?" he demanded.

"I was going to stop you soon," she protested.

"Oh, soon," he said knowledgeably, as he paced before her. "And had it never occurred to you that soon it might become too late for soon? I pride myself on remarkable control, 'Manda, but there is a point, and we might have speedily reached it, where even a flood of tears would have been to little avail. And why?" he asked angrily as he wheeled to confront her. Seeing her downcast eyes, he asked more softly, "Was it because it was 'good-bye' rather than 'good night'?"

"Yes," she said very quietly. "How did you know?"

"Oh," he said savagely, "I must be remarkably acute. For all my lovers usually sit stock-still as statues and commonly drop scalding tears upon my face as I make love to them. I rather like spice, and salt adds a little something to my performance."

As Amanda hung her head in guilty silence, he paced a few more steps. Then he commented bitterly, "Your sud-

den warmth was charity, then. But did you not know that
such benevolence extended to a libertine like me might
have resulted in your presenting Giles with just the sort of
squalling wedding present you vowed never to give to any
man? Damn you, 'Manda," he said coldly, "I do not accept
charity."

"It was not charity," she cried. "I am not going to Giles.
I'm not marrying anyone." Amanda wept now. "It was
only that it was hard to say good-bye to you."

"Then why the devil should you?" he asked, bewildered.

"Because," she said on a sniff as she drew herself up, "I
won't marry you, Christian. I could not when you said
you wished to because we would suit due to our back-
grounds. And now that you know who your father was,
even that poor reason is forfeit. Now that you know you
have moral entitlement to your name, you can court some
lady who is of better repute than one of the Amberly
Assortment could ever be. Can't you see?" she asked
fervently, "that now, with clear conscience, you may seek
a wife from whatever rank you please?"

He stood arrested. Then he drew her to a stand and
held both her hands tightly in his own.

"I can only see that there could be no one of higher rank
than you, 'Manda," he said gently. "I am well served for
my cowardly offer to you before. Yes, cowardly, 'Manda,
for I didn't dare admit to you how much I wanted you for
my wife. I made a joke of it, I made a game of it, for it is
easier to take a blow in jest than in earnest. But now I
earnestly tell you that I love you. I would have told you so
when I first discovered you here, but the tale you greeted
me with scattered my wits.

"Why do you think I chased you halfway around the
kingdom these last days? For all my jests at being a seducer,
I have never really exerted myself so before. It was always
enough to merely offer. But I have never offered wedlock
until I met you, and if you refuse me, I never shall again.

" 'Manda," the viscount said, taking care to hold only
her hands though his eyes signaled all his desire to do
more, "I promise to be a very constant husband to you,
and I shall never doubt you, either, for I think we both

have seen enough of the results of inconstancy to last us forever. I love you entirely, and will always hold your happiness above all else. But that's only selfishness, for your happiness will always ensure mine. Marry me, 'Manda," he said as he held her close again at last. "You must."

As she could not answer, he whispered, "One other little thing. I don't know exactly what you've been thinking of, but I assure you that I am still quite illegitimate, my sweet. Knowing my father's name is delightful, but I was nevertheless born out of wedlock. Yet even if I were conceived with a vicar at each bedpost and a bishop on the pillow, I would want no other wife but you."

She raised a radiant face to his, but he put a finger across her lips and said, "Say 'yes' first."

"Yes," she whispered happily. "Oh, yes," she sighed.

After a moment, he stepped away from her.

"Oh no," he said, dropping his hands as though she had singed them. "I won't go through all that buttoning and unbuttoning again tonight. I won't tarry one second longer here with you. For 'Manda," he said as he backed to the door, "we shall be married soon, and if I stay, we won't be able to confound all the famed mathematicians your mama and mine will invite for the occasion."

As Amanda gazed after him with puzzlement, he laughed and added, "Though some of them cannot decipher a grocer's bill, and others may not be able to calculate above a hundred, still all the dear lady guests, I assure you, are experts at adding up to nine. And when we are at the altar, they shall all nod and commence to count to themselves."

He gave her a longing look, and then said, "Our heir, my love, oh most especially *our* heir, should not make his appearance in this world one second before a full nine moons have safely risen past the moment that the vicar unites us. 'Manda, only here from the safety of the doorway can I tell you that I cannot allow you to seduce me, if only for our son's sake."

He gave her one last regretful smile. "But bolt your door, please," he sighed before he left, "for the combination of my morals and your face as it looks to me now, may yet cause a miscount."

XVI

Fanny Juliana Octavia Amberly, Countess of Clovelly, sighed happily to herself. Her cup ran over at last. The wedding had been a smashing social success and the ball following it would be talked about for ages. Those guests that were staying elsewhere had departed and those remaining beneath her roof had toddled off to their own beds or discreetly tiptoed into others. Now the great house was quiet at last.

Dawn would come within the hour and the countess looked at her own bed longingly, for as soon as she had completed just one more task she could enjoy her own well deserved rest. She sat at her delicate inlaid writing table to set down a few lines upon paper, so that she would not forget them when she awoke.

When Robert, Duke of Laxey, came through the connecting door between their rooms a few moments later, he looked unhappily at the great empty bed. He maintained his own bedroom, as it was considered very unfashionable to share one's own chamber, but he never actually slept in any bed but the countess's. It was no longer done solely for the sake of carnal pleasure but rather, as he always told his lady, because he couldn't get a wink of sleep without her soft, plushy form cuddled up to him.

Now as he absently scratched at the deep grooves the whalebone of his corset had left upon his stomach beneath his nightshirt, he said with only a trace of petulance, "Dash it all, Fanny, I thought you'd be abed by now."

"I would be, Bobby," the countess answered absently as

she wrote, "but I had just one more thing to take care of."

"Can't think of what it could be," the duke grumbled as he shambled to the bed. "Thought everything was done. And done very well, too," he conceded handsomely, as he climbed beneath the coverlet. "It was a bang-up affair. Ought to be proud of yourself. Everything went smooth as silk. Thought we'd have a spot of trouble between our little family and his lot, but everyone could not have been merrier."

The countess paused as she thought of the groom's mama's doleful face throughout the wedding service, but then she said reasonably, "Quite so, Bobby, but then I expect it was because they were all on their best behavior. Even my husband minded his manners. Our friends exerted themselves to be as stiffly correct as possible, and North's family attempted to unbend so that they wouldn't appear priggish, and somehow everyone seemed to meet in the middle and have a fine time."

"Just so," the duke grunted happily as he arranged his hands over his stomach and found just the right position on his back. "Why by evening, everyone had unbent so much that you couldn't tell the two groups apart. None of this bride's side, groom's side nonsense."

The countess smiled to herself as she thought of the results of that intermingling, some of whom were even now continuing their new associations in her house and at inns nearby.

"Lovely fellow, that Gilbert Jarrow," the duke continued, now giving up the idea of sleep for the equal comforts of a nice gossipy rehash of the events of the day. "Danced his feet off all night with your Mary. Think they'll be a match from this day's work, Fanny?"

"I doubt it," she answered calmly. "He's very young yet, as is our Mary. And I'm not sure I'd encourage it either. Now that North is setting up a household, his brother's gone to live at their estate in the Cotswolds as he said he's always wanted to, but the viscountess is going with him. I'm not sure our Mary is equal to putting up with a dragon like that."

"Brrr, quite right," the duke agreed. "Face like a Monday morning. I wish young Gilbert joy of her. But," he said brightening, "she and that Sir Boothe were the only wet fish. Surprised at him, I really am. Fellow oughtn't to drink if he can't hold it. Took three footmen to pour him into bed, don't you know."

"Ah well," the countess smiled, "he had his reasons, I'm sure."

"Can't see them," the duke commented drowsily. "Splendid affair, everyone merry as grigs. And why shouldn't they be? Beautiful bride, charming groom."

The countess thought of the couple, and felt a lovely prickling of tears in her eyes. She had wept at the ceremony, of course, it was expected of her, after all. But the real moment of joy had been when she had come upon the pair unaware, as they were preparing to leave on their wedding trip. She had stolen into the corridor to bid them goodbye, for they had told her they wanted no great fuss made over their leaving the festivities. She had surprised them alone, as they were preparing to steal away.

The elegant Lord North had been standing locked in an embrace with his graceful new wife. The countess had sighed at the completeness of their embrace, much impressed by what she could see of the groom's expertise, and the bride's response. She had been about to make her presence known, when the viscount had lifted his head and said tenderly to his lady, "One. My love, at last we can start counting."

"Oh, you'll have to do better than that," Amanda had whispered tenderly, as her hand caressed his shining golden hair, "for three is the number I had in mind."

"Three?" he asked quizzically.

"Yes," she had replied, ducking her head a little, "for I had this frock made especially for our wedding trip."

At his amused look of incomprehension, she had gone on, "I'm surprised you haven't noticed, Christian, since I put it on most especially with you in mind. It only has three buttons," she said shyly.

He had thrown his head back in a shout of laughter, and before the countess could reveal herself, he had swept

Amanda up into his arms and carried her out to their waiting coach.

Now the countess nodded in satisfaction as she bent to her note again.

"Aren't you coming to bed?" the duke asked piteously.

"In just one moment," the countess answered.

"What are you writing, anyway?" he complained.

"Only a note to the housekeeper, about some redecorating that North suggested to me today."

"What?" the duke asked, sitting up in bed, "suggested redecorating on his wedding day? If that don't beat all. I knew the fellow was up to all the rigs, but I didn't know he gave a hang for furnishings. What's amiss with Kettering Manor anyway?" he asked suspiciously, for the house was his pride and he complimented himself that it lacked nothing.

"It was only that he noticed something amiss with one of the rooms and took me aside to ask that I see to it," the countess said calmly. "He said that Amanda had not noticed as yet, as she had been too excited each time she stayed with us, but that he had been aware of it from the first day he rested here. He suggested I have it taken care of before she visited again, and he is quite right."

"Which room?" the duke demanded, so upset that there was a failing discovered in his beloved manor that he knocked his nightcap askew in his distress.

"The gray bedroom," the countess replied as she finished up the note.

The duke thought for a moment and then a sly smile spread over his face. There were a great many things he did not know, and he was the first to admit it, but he was an expert on the subject of his home.

"North's got windmills in his head. Ain't no gray bedroom," he said triumphantly.

"Precisely," his lady said as she rose and blew out the candles, "but there shall be."

"Very good," the duke said with relief as he lay back in the darkened bed. "Wouldn't like the manor to lack anything. Excellent idea. Should have had one long ago if we lacked one," he mumbled sleepily.

"No, my dear," the countess said gently as she got into bed beside him, "as it turns out, it was very fortunate that we did not. At least," she mused as she curled up against him to sleep, "North said it was."

Coming next month

AN UNCOMMON COURTSHIP
by Martha Kirkland

Miss Eloise Kendall could never forget that Gregory Ward was a rascal. But in the heat of the moment, who remembers the past?

"One of Regency's brightest new stars."
—*Romantic Times*

0-451-20132-9/$4.99

THE WARY WIDOW
by Barbara Hazard

A widowed countess encounters a devious man from her past—and the only one who could save her is the one man she thought she couldn't trust....

"Barbara Hazard always delivers the best!"
—Joan Wolf

0-451-20131-0/$4.99

MISS CHADWICK'S CHAMPION
by Melinda McRae

Lord Gareth knew that the only way to restore his family's fortune was to marry for money. But what were the odds that the beautiful woman with whom he was falling in love was an heiress?

"Melinda McRae is a stellar talent."
—*Romantic Times*

0-451-19857-3/$4.99

To order call: 1-800-788-6262